Nicholas Carter lives near Bristol and has been a journalist in the West Country for seventeen years. He is a member of The Sealed Knot. His first three novels in this series, *Turncoat's Drum*, *Storming Party* and *King's Men Crow*, are available in paperback from Pan Books.

Also by Nicholas Carter

TURNCOAT'S DRUM

STORMING PARTY

KING'S MEN CROW

NICHOLAS CARTER

HARVEST
OF SWORDS

THE
SHADOW
ON THE
CROWN

Book 4

PAN BOOKS

First published 1998 by Macmillan

This edition published 1999 by Pan Books
an imprint of Macmillan Publishers Ltd
25 Eccleston Place, London SW1W 9NF
and Basingstoke

Associated companies throughout the world

ISBN 0 330 35039 0

1 3 5 7 9 8 6 4 2

A CIP catalogue record for this book is available from
the British Library.

Typeset by SetSystems Ltd, Saffron Walden, Essex
Printed and bound in Great Britain by
Mackays of Chatham plc, Chatham, Kent

DRAMATIS PERSONAE

MENTIONED IN HISTORY

King Charles I.
Prince Rupert of the Rhine, his nephew.
Prince Maurice, Rupert's younger brother.
Charles, Prince of Wales; James, Duke of York: His Majesty's sons.
The Duke of Richmond, a friend of Prince Rupert's.
Mary Villiers, Duchess of Richmond, a very good friend of Prince Rupert's.
Lord Falkland, His Majesty's Secretary of State.
Patrick Ruthven, Earl of Brentford, commander of His Majesty's forces before Gloucester.
Sir Jacob Astley, commander of Royalist foot.
Sir John Byron, commander Royalist cavalry.

Sir Edward Massey, Governor of Gloucester for the Parliament.
Robert Devereux, Earl of Essex, principal Parliamentarian warlord.
Oliver Cromwell, MP and rising Parliamentarian warlord.

UNMENTIONED IN HISTORY

Parliamentarian:

William Sparrow, former officer of militia and cavalry
cornet, now captain, Mercer's regiment of foot.
Colonel Archibald McNabb, Scots professional soldier
serving with Waller.
Colonel Tobias Fulke, a gallant but rather elderly
gentleman, acting commander of Mercer's regiment of
foot.
Henry Mercer, cheesemonger and colonel.
Colston Muffet, sergeant, serving with Mercer's regiment
of foot.
Hereward Gillingfeather, an agitator, William Butcher,
sharpshooter, Caleb Cruickshank, orphan and pikeman,
presently serving with Mercer's regiment of foot.
Shem Bentham, John Ruell, Bob Riley, London riff-raff.
Gallen Fey, captain of Parliament's ship *Conqueror.*
Nathaniel Hawker, captain of Parliament's ship the
Honest John.
John Grey, his mate.

Royalist:

Sir Gilbert Morrison, disgraced MP, former colonel of
militia, wool merchant and turncoat, Governor in waiting
of the Royal Westward Society of Oceanic Venturers,
presently awaiting assignment.
Maynard Morrison, a West Country miller, Sir Gilbert's
brother.
Captain Jamie Morrison, Sir Gilbert's son, recuperating
from battle vapours.
Bella Margueritte Morrison, Sir Gilbert's daughter.

The Earl of Dartland, known as 'Black Bob' Dyle, Royalist magnate and justice.

John St John Dyle, Lord Clavincale, his son.

Mary Keziah Pitt, Bella's maid and confidante, William Sparrow's sweetheart.

Master Algernon Starling, clerk to Sir Gilbert.

Captain Hugo Telling, Prince Rupert's regiment of horse.

Colonel Michael Slaughter, an officer recently returned from service in Ireland.

Valentine Cruikshank, captain of the King's privateer the *Messalina's Purse.*

Edward Callow, his mate.

Terrence Gable, captain of the King's privateer the *Blue Doubloon.*

Colonel Scipio Porthcurn, Cornish officer of foot.

Major Brinks, Captain Took, in command of the Royalist garrison of Penmethock.

Compton Speedwell, captain of dragoons.

Henry Graves, Auld Guppy, Martin Pike, Royalist dragoons.

Margaret, Lady Ramsay, widow of the Royalist squire Sir Marmaduke Ramsay.

Anneliese Ramsay, her daughter.

HARVEST
OF SWORDS

PROLOGUE

*'It is impossible to avoid the doing of very
unhandsome things in war.'*

John Evelyn, diarist

The pox-sorry tub was wallowing like a harpooned whale in the rip, laden to the gunwales with God knew what, a cargo of bloody lead, by the look of it.

Terrence Gable, master of the *Blue Doubloon*, lowered the perspective glass from his right eye, grinned at the bullfrog-throated mate waiting patiently beside him. 'The bastard might just as well plough with dogs as try and escape us in that pickle barrel,' the swarthy captain chuckled. Matthias Ghent, his vastly experienced mate, nodded his broad, shaven head in agreement with the chief's assessment.

The *Blue Doubloon* was coming in on the starboard tack with the merchantman one point off the bow – an easily plotted interception course. A child could have worked out that their lumbering quarry was doomed. The over-laden vessel was already taking a risk, hugging a leeward shore like that. The captain must have been in a mighty hurry, to attempt the dash down the Channel in broad daylight – at the mercy of the Dunkirk pirates who roamed the North Sea.

They were King Charles' unofficial navy – but no less effective for that.

The smaller, swifter privateers took a grievous toll of

Parliamentarian merchant shipping passing up and down the long, exposed coastline of Norfolk and Suffolk, fat prizes with jammed hulls hurrying to feed and furnish the rebel masses in London.

Gable had chosen his hunting ground well. He knew the tides and currents, carried a map of the complex offshore sandbars in his head. The long headland of Orford Ness was a favourite ambush point. An endless sweep of almost featureless coastline, mile upon mile of reeds and sedge reclaimed from the sea, stretching away in a tedious grey belt towards Felixstowe. If he was spotted, the merchantman might try and duck into the narrow network of channels and creeks behind the exposed spit of Hollesley Bay, but the *Doubloon* drew less water, and the dog would run aground before he had gone a mile.

'We'll put a shot across the bows and put a crew aboard. You can sail her back to Dunkirk for me, how's that?' Gable asked, slapping the mate across the broad, salt-stained back of his sea-coat. Ghent grunted approval, peered over his shoulder as the crew hurried to their posts. They had put on every scrap of sail they could in the wind, and the gunners were already busy about their cannon. A dozen demi-culverins on the top deck, four sakers on the quarterdeck, ten culverins on the lower deck, and a pair of sakers on the poop. More than enough to play pat-a-cake with a wallowing pisspot like this one.

Gable raised his glass, noting with satisfaction they had already closed in on the panic-stricken merchant ship. He could see the crew scrambling over the deck, wrestling with what looked like . . . crates of chickens! The captain's dark lips pulled away from his tallow-coloured teeth in a rictus of delight. Chickens! He swung the glass around, and saw a couple of their men trying to manoeuvre a small swivel gun in the bows. One little pea-shooter against a fourteen-gun broadside? They'd strike their colours before they dared open fire!

'Hold her steady, Mr Ghent!'

'Aye, sir!'

The *Blue Doubloon* seemed to skim the waves, the wind blowing strongly in her massed sails – in clear contrast to the badly laden merchant vessel which pitched and rolled alarmingly in the lively swell. The damned amateurs must have misloaded the cargo, spoiling any natural balance the old tub might have possessed.

Gable grinned, watched the crew throwing baskets of flapping chickens overboard. What difference were a few fowls going to make? The bastards must have been pissing their breeches in fright, showing about as much sense as their unfortunate cargo. More and more baskets were thrown overboard or tossed aside in a squall of white feathers. The men on the swivel gun had dashed back amidships, clearly abandoning any idea of opening an artillery duel they were in no position to win.

Gable swung the glass back to the chaos on her deck.

And his smile slipped away from his skull in disbelief.

He was staring down the grim black barrels of a pair of vast guns – demi-cannon at the least – being hauled around by dozens of what looked horribly like highly experienced gunners. Where the devil had they come from? Even as he watched, the merchantman's hull winked and blinked as half a dozen gunports, previously hidden by carelessly hung rigging, were thrown open. No bloody wonder the bastard had been wallowing, it was carrying as much iron as a first-rate!

'All hands to go about!' he croaked. 'Go about! That's no bastard merchantman!'

Ghent turned and barked the order to the helmsman, but Gable knew full well there was no hope of avoiding the treacherous beast. They were too close now, and he was outgunned.

'Give them everything or they'll blow us out of the water!'

The bucking merchantman was enveloped in a cloud of boiling white smoke. In another moment they heard the thunderous crash of the guns, and in another the appalling shriek of roundshot ploughing through the air at the horrified pirates. Three balls tore vast holes in the gunwale, knocking a brace of cannon aside and mincing the crews trapped between them. The *Doubloon* was smothered in smoke, punctuated by the shrill screams of the wounded.

'Open fire!' Gable yelled. His smaller calibre guns crashed in response, a ragged broadside with little hope of hitting the wallowing merchantman. It seemed to be dead in the water now, the gun captains busy registering their swiftly moving target. The merchantman had pulled about a couple of points to starboard, bringing the enormous weight of cannon to bear while the *Doubloon* could only register four of her smaller pieces.

Gable winced as the enemy vessel opened fire again. A chance shot hit the *Doubloon*'s rudder as she began her turn, the vulnerable stern exposed to the bastard-whelp of a Roundhead. He felt the privateer shudder like a bitch in heat as the swell pulled her back once more. He staggered to the gunwale and peered through the smoke, squinting against the acrid fogs boiling over the deck to try and estimate the damage the rebel dog had inflicted.

God damn the cheating rogue to pits of Purgatory!

Then he heard the bowel-loosening banshee rattle of

chainshot – iron balls linked by hissing chains, rammed home on a double-charged bed of spikes, nails, slugs, and stones. Gable ducked down instinctively as the hideous squall tore through the air and lashed his decks. Dumbstruck sailors were sliced in two. Heads and arms and pieces of steaming flesh were scattered in all directions as the point-blank barrage swept the *Doubloon*'s damaged decks. The gun crews caught the worst, hideously exposed to the terrible storm of shot and scorching iron. Gable grabbed a spurting wound in his arm, cursing in five languages as the crippled privateer cruised towards the merrily bobbing hulk. He waved the nauseating smoke away, tried to think his way out of the appalling catastrophe.

He knew in his bones it was too late for anything.

The *Doubloon* was damn near dead in the water, the damaged rudder swinging uselessly in the fierce swell. Shattered rigging was blowing free, jagged rents appearing all over the shot-blasted canvas. Wounded sailors caught aloft crashed down into the splintered, blood-splattered deck. Ghent had sat down with a sigh, his broad fingers locked over his vitals, vivid blue and red entrails pulsing between the buttons of his coat with every ragged breath.

Gable turned and dashed to the far side of his stricken ship, waving the wide-eyed survivors towards the longboat swinging drunkenly on its cat's-cradle of rope.

'Abandon ship! They'll string us all up if they catch us!' he yelled. His men were cursing and shouting as they pulled themselves up the steps, fleeing the smoky gangways below deck. Another almost surgical broadside had lashed the gun deck, vicious fragments killing and maiming the panicking sailors crouched beside the ports. Some of their colleagues had already fled the carnage and were already diving into the water in terror.

Roundshot cracked through the scorched air, disabling the last gun on the top deck. Deliberately aimed shots to destroy his fighting capability. The bastard might just as well have been using a scalpel on a dead rat, Gable thought grudgingly, as what was left of his crew lowered the longboat over the side with feverish haste.

'They're lowering the boat, Captain. We'll have to come about,' the mate bawled, his teeth showing up brilliantly against his powder-smothered features.

Nathaniel Hawker grimaced as another acrid cloud of smoke and soot boiled up over the quarterdeck, stinging his already running eyes.

'Come about, Mr Grey, and cease firing!'

'Cease fire!' The order was bawled along the deck from one deafened crewman to another. The chickens which had survived the brutal engagement and the massive concussive blasts from the hidden guns seemed stunned, shivering inside their baskets at the monstrous man-made storm.

Hawker had concealed the cannon beneath stacked crates and great knotted nets of rigging, giving every impression his ship was as slovenly officered and sea-worthy as some native canoe trading up the infested swamp-rivers of West Africa. Placing such heavy guns on the top deck was always a gamble – the ruse had played havoc with the ship's centre of gravity – but Hawker lived on his luck, and his dangerous expedient had paid off handsomely despite the misgivings of his crew. He had employed the stratagem twice before, and looked set on using it again – certainly this damned barge wasn't going to carry any tales of his trickery back to its bloody base on the Continent. The crew, however, were another matter.

'I want a boarding party made ready, Mr Grey, we're bound to catch some of the dogs aboard!'

'Aye, sir.'

Hawker was a Plymouth man by birth, and like so many of his kinsmen had spent all his life at sea. He had fought the Spanish, Dutch, and Portuguese, feeding like a vampire bat on the bountiful, desperately stretched arteries of their trade routes. Now he was home, in colder waters, but his appetite for a fight was every inch as acute. What better man to fight the Dunkirk privateers than a Plymouth privateer who had learned his trade from the writings and journals of the old masters – the long-dead generation which had made Queen Elizabeth's navy the terror of the seven seas?

These days his quarry was rather more difficult to catch than the galleons of his youth. Sleeker, faster, well armed, the privateer fleet was a menace to the Parliamentarian cause, threatening to ruin the merchants who bankrolled the crusade against the tyrannical king. Charles, this weak-willed toy of the Catholic empires Hawker had fought so valiantly for twenty years. Now, according to the news-sheets, the stubborn monarch was about to bring whole fleets and legions of his sworn enemies over to England, to crush the revolt with true Continental cruelty.

Hawker had been an enthusiastic supporter of the rebellion from the beginning, taking his small but effective squadron over to join the Earl of Warwick's revolted fleet. But his new assignment, cruising the coasts as part of the Parliamentarian blockade of the Royalist-controlled north, had not fitted his feisty, ocean-going temperament, and he had fallen out with his superiors over what he saw as their hopelessly flawed tactics. The enemy vessels were faster and more manoeuvrable than their own, and nine times out of ten their furious pursuits ended all too predictably with the enemy ships disappearing over the horizon. Hawker had argued that trying to play the privateers at their own game would embroil the fleet in a wasteful game of fat cat and greased mouse. Instead, he had called for daring new tactics – the use of trickery and deception rather than brute force. His superiors, stung by criticism of their marked lack of success, had grudgingly relented. They had approved his plan to fit out specially selected merchantmen with powerful defensive armament and use them as decoys – fooling the lighter-armed privateers into risking an all-out attack.

Six months on, and his brilliant stratagem was paying handsome dividends.

The *Blue Doubloon* was dead in the water now, pulled about by the powerful current, dragged from its original course by the smashed rudder.

'Pass the word to Mr Stutt, superb shooting,' Hawker ordered. The captain frowned. Superb shooting, all right, but if she wasn't righted soon the abandoned privateer would be in great danger of foundering before the hectic winds.

'Where's that damned longboat?' Hawker growled, scanning the green sea for the fugitives who had leapt from the bow of the stricken vessel, away on his larboard side.

What were they hoping to do, row back to Dunkirk? They certainly wouldn't be able to give chase, that was for sure.

The fierce wind which had carried the *Blue Doubloon* across the sea on its irresistible interception course was blowing straight at his ship, the *Honest John*. The alarming pitch was becoming more and more acute the longer he stayed broadside-on to it.

'Blow them out of the water, Mr Grey, I don't want the scum carrying tales to their friends back home,' he called.

The *Doubloon* had come about now, racked and pummelled by the winds which raked her splintered decks and tore through what was left of the rigging. The privateer was being tossed this way and that, a pistol shot away from the larger, violently pitching merchant ship which had ensnared her like a wasp in a spider's web. They would either have to get aboard or they would lose her, Hawker thought with a snarl of anger.

'Bring her alongside, prepare to board!'

Three hundred yards further east the *Doubloon*'s longboat was enveloped in another boisterous wave, the survivors clinging to the benches as the oarsmen bent their backs against the tide, frantically attempting to open the distance between their frail boat and the cannon-heavy enemy. Gable crouched in the stern, soaked through and shivering, watching his pride and joy wallow in the swell, swallowed up by the pot-bellied bulk of the merchantman. The waves were capped with flotsman and jetsam and the bobbing heads of his unfortunate crew. They waved and bawled as the greedy sea sucked them under. Gable tore his eyes away from their panicked thrashings. 'Row, damn your black hearts, if they catch you it'll be the gallows for you same as me,' he roared. The fearful crew redoubled their efforts, peering over their shoulders at the two vastly opposed ships, clinging together like lovers in the rising swell.

Ten more back-breaking minutes and the two ships were somewhat smaller, black-backed beetles on the green sea, the grey arc of the monotonous coastline receding in the distance. They just about made out the tiny cross of St George as the *Doubloon*'s black colours were torn down and replaced with the despised Parliamentarian battle flag.

'A cunning bastard, lads,' Gable called, encouraging the exhausted, pale-faced survivors with a careless, swaggering gesture. 'But we won't get caught a second time, eh?'

PART ONE

DUTCH RECKONING

'A soldier must have something for his toil and trouble.'

Count Tilly, Imperial general, justifying the sack of Magdeburg, May 1631

CHIPPING MARLEWARD,

SOMERSET, LATE AUTUMN 1643

He'd seen villages burn before. Dirty twists of smoke smudging unfamiliar horizons. Grubby villagers with pinched faces hurrying down the lanes away from the crackling shadows, anxious to save their skins if they couldn't hang on to their carefully hidden property. Pots of gold? They would be lucky to have a pot to piss in, once the soldiers had done.

The pale Cavalier peered down into the gorge, a steep-sided valley hollowed and hacked by the neolithic might of a retreating waterfall – nothing more than a chattering brook to cool the horses' hoofs now. He squinted into the sooty cloud rolling up over the deserted fields. The pungent smoke set his sore eye running all over again. The infection he'd picked up lying up in the cold fields around Newbury the fortnight before had stubbornly refused to give up its well-caked hold – despite all the potions and poultices the camp quacks could come up with. He rubbed the salty crust away on the back of his gauntlet and blinked the tearful film away, clicking his tongue with irritation. The tired bay he had ridden down from Bristol hoofed the turf, threw its sweat-roped head as if in sympathy with its anxious master.

'Mess a smoke down there, sir,' his new groom commented in an unconvincing bid to sound as nonchalant as possible. The poor boy was terrified by the smoke and smells, uncomfortably aware that his mother's recent prediction that he would come to a bad end joining the King's army looked all too likely, and all too quickly, to have come true.

Hugo Telling hadn't heard him, wasn't even aware of his existence. He wrung his greasy reins through his gloves, completely at a loss. Smoke? Twenty miles from Bristol, in the heart of the King's own loyal West Country? A chimney fire, perhaps. A smoky oven, even.

He knew in another moment it was no such thing. Houses were burning, frosted glass shattering, tiles cracking with the blistering heat. He recognized as well the pungent, strangely herbal aroma of blazing thatch. And something else, sharper, meatier. He recognized that too; from Landsdown and Roundway and Gloucester's filthy trenches. The cloying stench of roast flesh. A witch fire to boil a cauldron full of mischief.

Telling imagined the scurrying rodents and birds as their fiery bower collapsed, stripping the eaves from the frightened people – dead or alive – trapped within.

Enemy cavalry, then, probing this far west? A rogue troop fleeing the killing fields around Newbury? The bitterly contested acres and corpse-choked lanes between Kennet and Enborne. What a fight that had been.

But surely the Earl of Essex's battered and bruised army had drawn off towards London, taking its injured and its grumbling, crop-haired apprentices with it? Lightly wounded and sick with the fevers himself, he had been detailed to help escort one of the many caravans of wounded away to the Royalist depots in the rear. The officers had been left at Bath to take the waters and recuperate. He had been looking forward to tonics of a rather more animal intensity – his own true sweetheart

Bella Morrison. She would put him right, and in return he would marry and make a real lady of her. Whatever her damned father had to say about it.

'Should we go back, sir? Fetch 'elp?' Joseph Thackray asked, tugging his ragged nag's head around so the spitty bit clanged against its bared teeth.

'Help? Where from?' Telling asked, irritated by his groom's all too obvious terror.

Hugo felt no such fright, merely a vague anxiety that his wedding plans would be somehow compromised by this unlooked-for interference. Eighteen months of skirmish and battle had hardened him to foul smokes and choking stenches: it would take more than a blazing hovel or two to shake his resolve now.

'We'll go slowly, circle round the far end of the village, keeping the stream between us and them.'

'Them!' Thackray squealed. Telling glanced sourly at the youngster, his plain features wooden with fear, like some carefully whittled native totem. He had recruited the boy in Bristol, one of the few city strays whom Sir Ralph Hopton had apparently overlooked as he furnished regiment after regiment of West Country men for the King's hungry armies. Thackray could ride better than he could march, as his left foot had been twisted up on itself since his birth, seventeen summers before. In sharp contrast to his scowling master, Thackray wore a plain brown coat, a shapeless felt hat, and a pair of heavily patched breeches. His only weapon was a straight tuck, a mass-produced infantry sword he had been issued at Bristol Castle. The frightened youngster seemed to have been wedged into his cheap dragoon saddle, propped up by Hugo Telling's miscellaneous belongings, weapons, and wardrobe. A ragged-arsed Sancho Panza, trotting dismally along behind his arrogantly attired knight. Telling had picked out his best clothing to go courting, a shimmering suit of Venetian red velvet with slashed sleeves and elaborate frogging around the collar and cuffs. His creamy shirt, somewhat tarnished by his long ride down from the city, was nevertheless loaded down with lawn and lace. He had tied his kingfisher-blue sash around his narrow shoulders, and thrust a brace of peacock feathers into his wide-brimmed hat. A dashing chevalier, fit to grace the sumptuous court of King Louis himself.

But hardly the sort of costume to wear into a street fight with a gang of ruffians, Telling thought crossly. He frowned, scratched his cleanly shaven chin. He could hardly turn tail and ride away now, could he, with Bella waiting somewhere in the valley for him? He felt a sudden twinge of concern. Bella Morrison was not the kind of girl to cower indoors while intruders played havoc in her home village. Her father, that damn blasted turncoat of a merchant, was equally unlikely to stand by and watch some deserter set his precious wares ablaze. Without a further thought, Telling drew his sword and kicked the bay down the slope. Thackray spurred up behind him, eyeing the bushes as if they concealed a multitude of whispering apprentice boys, crowing for his blood. Up ahead, they could see pale tongues of flame licking through the boiling smokes and hear the greedy crackle of the flames. They skirted a low drystone wall and pulled up behind a stand of withies by the bridge. The mossy milestone told them they were but half a mile from Chipping Marleward.

But who was at home?

*

They reckoned themselves a troop, but Speedwell's dragoons were nothing but a band of gypsy horse thieves, armed to the teeth with the pick of a dozen bloody fields. Their own mounts would have had a horse butcher shaking his head in disgust. Broken-winded nosebags who snuffled the dust at every stop and left steaming lagoons of muddy green manure behind them. Variously skewbald, piebald, grey, or yellow, the carelessly picketed beasts resembled nothing more than a washing line pegged with a dozen sets of patched trousers. Nobody in their wits would have given the sorry animals a second look.

Which would have been their first mistake, if not their last.

Speedwell's dusty coated Vandals covered three times the ground of a typical cavalry troop, six times that of the average infantry company. Their shaggy little mounts carried them at the same rollocking, ungainly gait, transporting the leering soldiery from one frightened hamlet to another.

Compton Speedwell, their cruelly smiling captain, looked as if he had spent the previous ten years learning his trade on the Continent, one of the ragged bands of marauders who had turned Germany into a blood-soaked ash-heap, a land of human fat for the fantastically gorged crows. He was tall but stooped, his shoulders drooping from long hours spent in his well-padded saddle. He had acquired a long and ugly blue scar beneath his bottom lip, which some men would have had the decency to conceal behind a beard. But not Speedwell. To most folk the vicious wound was proof enough of his courage – and his durability. Where had he picked up such a hideous wound? How was it he had lived to tell the tale?

In actual fact Compton Speedwell was an all too typical product of his times – a gifted beginner, by now all too proficient in the deadly art of war by rampage. He had been in arms less than six months. A wheelwright by trade, he had set aside the chisel and plane for a looted sword and a pair of pistols, and hadn't looked back since. Cropping heads was much more fun than balancing a set of oak spokes, after all.

The chaotic aftermath of the storm of Bristol had flushed more than rats from the burning city stews. The ambitious and aggressive youngster had found his way into one of Sir Ralph Hopton's newly formed cavalry regiments. Strong, quick-witted, and possessed of an unusual degree of careless ferocity, he had been quickly picked out to lead the leftovers of the new command – the deserters, thieves, and whoremongers whom the ever-frowning Hopton had weeded out of his new units. The malingering, sickly screws couldn't be trusted with a length of soaking-wet match, let alone a musket, and would in all probability slink away into the night at the first opportunity. But the hard-pressed Hopton needed every man, trustworthy or not, and he preferred all his bad eggs in one basket.

Let the dregs become dragoons. Speedwell's dragoons.

Their task was to patrol the recently captured rear areas, the great rolling hill country of northern Somerset, the broad chalk plains of Wiltshire. Rascals and crooks every one of them, they would be even more terrifying to the surly villagers whose taxes and assessments they were charged with collecting. Woe betide the hamlet which could not find its monthly contribution to Hopton's sparse war chest.

With most of the more formidable Parliamentarian sympathizers away to London, the villages had been left in the charge of frail elders or beardless boys. Just the sort of men to quail before Speedwell's hideous double smile. He had gotten the wound falling on a bottle during one of his increasingly frequent drunken binges at the Tap and Bilboe near Bristol Bridge, a riotous pigpen where lesser men slept in his slops. Speedwell had taken over the inn as his unofficial headquarters, the bleary-eyed nerve centre from which he ran his own racketeering empire in the name of an unknowing King Charles. Hopton got his precious taxes, but Speedwell took a saucy share of the farmers' hard-earned pennies.

They called him the Curse, because like their lifeblood he drank he came round once a month. Nobody had dared gainsay him or his lecherous lieutenants riding far out into the hills to do his dirty work – until, that was, the day one of his patrols had been ambushed by the furious villagers of Chipping Marleward. Until his tax-collecting troops had been set upon by brazen trollops and dizzy girls, routed by a meat-armed matron with a laundry paddle.

His crooked sergeant, the cross-eyed veteran Joshua Lawton, had been bludgeoned to death in the main street by the suddenly ferocious villagers: lambs turned to wolves by the constant demands of their parasitical hosts. Other dragoons had been brained with buckets or impaled on pitchforks. The astonished survivors had leapt onto their multicoloured nags and spurred off at an equally astonishing gallop, to tell tales to their disbelieving commander as he attempted to sleep it off beneath a vomit-smeared bench. Of course it had taken time to call in his men from their widespread raiding, to gather the force necessary to teach the impudent rebels a lesson. A bloody lesson they would never forget.

And all in the name of the King.

Sir Ralph Hopton, the King's general and mouthpiece in the west, had scrawled his signature beneath the order, too busy to do much more than wonder what the ugly incident had been about. Too caught up in the convoluted coils of this hated war to enquire why the normally docile and well-affected villagers of northern Somerset had turned on his assessment officers like so many bloodthirsty bandits. If he could have spared the time he would have investigated the matter himself, or at least sent one of his trusted lieutenants down to sort out the trouble. But his master the King had been in desperate straits, and it was to Charles that Hopton owed his first responsibility. Burdened with hundreds of wounded after the disastrous pummelling match at Newbury, the King was even now manoeuvring back towards Oxford with a rapidly disintegrating and ill-equipped army. He had left Hopton to secure the rear and collect muchneeded money and reinforcements. Petty fallouts like this peculiar incident at Chipping Marleward would have to wait.

In the meantime, Captain Speedwell would nip the trouble in the bud, sort out the ringleaders, and bring the guilty rebels back to Bristol to face their well-deserved punishment.

The warrant he signed listed five of the principal offenders. Hopton had wondered what had made the womenfolk join their husbands in such a desperate venture, so far from the rapidly retreating forces of their Parliamentarian friends.

He never did get to the bottom of it.

'He sez they'm buggered off. Taken off down the Foss or summat,' the straw-headed giant called, giving the old man another teeth-rattling shake. The wild-eyed elder was swinging like a trussed chicken, his patched working coat caught up tight in the overgrown brute's careless grip, his shirt tugged up about his scrawny neck.

Compton Speedwell let the man hang a while longer, until the purpling tongue began to peep between the old pot-walloper's blistered lips.

'Let him down,' he sighed. The slow-witted dragoon in the flapping pea-green coat opened his fist, dropping the choking elder to the cobbles where he curled up in a ball, pulling at his throat.

The dragoons had sealed the village like a sack of wine, plugging the exits and watching the bridge. Speedwell had sent half a dozen scouts up the main street, a mad steeplechase of clashing hoofs and blasting pistols. Nobody had dared peep out of doors – let alone fire back. Satisfied the distempered villagers had shut themselves up from trouble, he had led the main body up the slope and dismounted outside the Blue Boar. Henry Graves had hauled the quaking landlord down the steps, holding him up in one hamlike fist while he clutched a bright red hat in the other. Graves had handed the terrified landlord's headgear up to his commander. A jaunty red Montero with a fine blue beading around the dented rim.

'Here's John Chetworth's hat, Captain. John Chetworth as rode with Sergeant Lawton!'

'I found it in the street! I never thought it had come off a dead dragoon, sir!'

'You rock-bollocked strunts usually cock your beaver in kit like this, eh?'

'I found it, sir, after all the mess was cleared . . . buried . . . properly buried, mind you, sir, with proper words and all!'

Speedwell had let the man fret while he swallowed his share of the stone jar of urine-coloured cider being passed along the troop. He smacked his scarred lips and passed the jar back on down the stalled column of restless men. Thirty riders, including the five who had been chased out of the place with their tails between their legs the month before. Michael Rivers brave enough now, with an old man at his mercy. The captain turned his irritated gaze from the dragoon to the coughing grandfather.

'Where down the Foss?' Speedwell enquired. Graves booted the groaning elder in the back. He writhed like a trapped eel in the dusty road, bony hands raised in supplication.

'Gaw bless you, zur, down Wey'muf way, zur,' the terrified landlord called, scrambling to his knees and tugging at his greasy forelock.

'Weymouth? This bloody laundress runs a fleet of sail, does she?'

The restless riders chuckled unpleasantly. Gwen Pitt, the burly matron who had led the recent rebellion, had apparently had enough of their filthy shirts and stinking breeches. They'd need a damn good noose to string up her twenty stone.

'Aiming to sail off into the sunset or something?'

'Mazur Morrison's folk down them parts, so Oi've 'eard

tell,' the landlord chattered. 'It bein' his daughter as was one o' them 'urt.'

Hurt? She'd been a sight more than hurt, according to Michael Rivers. Shot in the head during the improvised firefight, the merchant's daughter had been lying among his slaughtered dragoons when their brave comrades had ridden out on them. A pity really, as the girl was supposed to have the best set of tabs this side of the Mendips – and wasn't shy of showing 'em either, by all accounts.

A Morrison, eh? The turncoat merchant had already raised a regiment of villagers for the Parliament, only to desert them for the Royal cause the moment Ralph Hopton was within pissing distance of his damned lair. Speedwell had heard the oily merchant had since raised another regiment of men for service with the King, only to have had them all shot to pieces outside Gloucester. He might have known the old trickster would have had something to do with this.

'Where did they take the bodies? Did they bury them here?'

'With all the words and suchlike, back of the church-yard with the Trained Band men,' the landlord nodded miserably.

'All together?'

'All together what, zur?'

'You're saying they buried my men with Miss Morrison?'

The landlord frowned. 'They never buried 'er, beggin' your pardon. Took 'er off to the big house white as a windin' sheet, we've none of us 'eard more.'

Speedwell pondered this new intelligence for a moment. So his suspect had been shot, but not necessarily to death?

'They took her up to the big house and all. The Ramsay place on the hill, zur.' He pointed over the rooftops toward the wooded slopes rearing above the town. Somewhere beyond those carefully nurtured plantations was Kilmersden Hall, until recently the seat of Sir Marmaduke Ramsay, the noted Somerset Royalist who had met his end on Lansdown at the beginning of that fateful summer.

Speedwell picked the creased warrant from his saddle case and unrolled it with a dramatic flourish. He read the names aloud, a sardonic grin unpicking the creased flesh beneath his narrow mouth.

'Gwen Pitt, Mary Keziah Pitt, Bella Morrison, Mordecai Pitt, and James Morrison.'

The landlord nodded eagerly, a beaten cur dribbling with fright beneath his nag's hoofs.

'Tha's right, zur. Gone, the lor of 'em. Daft Jamie with 'em. It was 'im as started it, zur,' the old man called spitefully. 'Stalkin' about without his breeches. It was 'im that started the trouble, zur!' He peered down the column of resentful faces, picking out the dragoons he recognized. 'Ain't it right, boys?' he called pityingly.

Speedwell had heard the details a dozen times from their miserable mouths. Lawton and his cronies had been taking their ease in the village when the idiot boy – the turncoat's feeble-minded son – had wandered into the village buck naked. They had been baiting him in the street when the boy's fiery sister had appeared leading a posse of irate villagers to his rescue. There had been an argument and shots had been fired. Rivers had sworn he'd seen the Morrison girl shot through the temple, yet this idiot landlord reckoned her no more than hurt. Maybe she'd been killed or died of her wounds up at the hall. Then again, maybe she'd been lucky, struck by a spent ball or a chance ricochet. Maybe she was already boasting to her friends how she'd routed his warriors.

His lip curled in agitated disgust. The waiting riders licked their lips and held their breath. Speedwell had a bloody temper on him the best of times, no telling what he would let loose now.

The captain eyed them with undisguised malice. His dragoons, he remembered with a twinge of anger. The dragoons who had been bettered by a bunch of hairies from the hills.

'And they've fled you say, to Weymouth?'

'That way, zur, certain.'

'Apart from Morrison himself.'

'Holed up at the hall, that's right, zur.'

'You've been a wonderful help,' Speedwell allowed. He drew his pistol and fired into the old man's wrinkled features, obliterating his nodding nose in a sudden splatter of blood and splintered bone. Henry Graves jumped back, idiot face speckled and gaping. The riders glanced over their shoulders, studying the stubbornly closed shutters and one another's pinched faces. The reverberating shot put up a flock of rooks from the oaks over the slope. They cawed off over the river and hid in the tall, wind-blown elms.

'That's what happens to buggers who make sport with my men,' the captain growled for the benefit of the cowering folk behind the shivering shutters. Speedwell twisted around in his saddle and nodded at the shocked troopers. Before they could move he had drawn the second pistol and fired. Michael Rivers, one of the five who had galloped out of Chipping Marleward the previous month, sat back in his saddle, grinning stupidly. He coughed once, pointed, and toppled over the rump of his startled piebald. 'And that's what happens to buggers who can't get the better of a bunch of frightened farmers. When I shoot you, you're fucking well dead. Any other swine want to say something?'

He had fired both pistols, but his threatening presence seemed to lift the tiles from the silent houses along the street. Twenty-nine riders twitched nervously before his murderous stare, running their reins through frightened fingers.

'Right. Fetch some faggots and burn the laundry – that's where she got the better of you, wasn't it? The mighty fortress which resisted your brave assaults?' he crowed, mocking them. He stared down at the bodies, pools of glistening blood running away between the cobbles, grey islands in a red sea. 'And throw these lousy cunts in with 'em while you're at it. They were shot resisting arrest, isn't that right, now?'

'Ah, right enough, sir,' Henry Graves mumbled, as Speedwell's hated stare snagged on his oafish features. 'We all saw it, I'd swear it.'

He tried on the battered red Montero, but found it far too small for his enormous straw head. He passed it up to one of the young recruits instead. Eager to cut a dash in the dangerous unit, the delighted boy fixed it over his greasy locks.

All of a sudden, he felt like a proper soldier.

Hugo Telling rode through the grim curtain of soot and sparks, face averted from the boiling stench of roast flesh belching from the blazing laundry. He pulled the nervous horse up in the familiar main street, sat still and watched half a dozen laughing dragoons going in and out of old

Morrison's abandoned house further down the street. His father-in-law's house, he thought with another prickle of pride. The drunken looters were clearly taking whatever they could move with them. A splintered chest, long since emptied. A scorched brown head – by God they had . . . no. The dragoons had torn the ornamental post from the merchant's splintered stairway and were tossing it between them like a football.

'Butter-fingers!'

The heavy oak sphere cracked on the paving stones and rolled to a halt beneath Telling's horse. The looters looked up, startled by the apparition in red, framed by the flames dancing in and out of the laundry house windows.

'What the devil's going on here?' Telling demanded, backing up his enquiry with a cocked pistol. The dragoons glanced at one another, caught like schoolboys in an orchard by this fiendish maverick.

'On whose authority are you firing this village?' he snorted. 'There's no Roundhead here!'

The dragoons seemed to relax, cramped shoulders flexing, eyes alert and mobile. Henry Graves straightened up, smiled woodenly.

'Cap'n Speedwell's, sir. He's a warrant and all.'

'From whom?'

'Sir Ralph Hopton!'

Hugo Telling peered around at the hovel opposite. A spindly, bow-legged ape in a battered buff coat was lounging in the doorway, the wormholed planks hanging on their rust-gutted hinges. He was holding a stone jar by the index finger of his left hand, a carbine in his right. The smoky barrel was aimed at Telling's head.

Hugo swallowed, studying the intruder's cruelly minted

features. He hadn't gotten that scar in an alehouse, Hugo thought idly. The massive dragoon in the pea-green coat stepped over Morrison's chest and grabbed Hugo's bridle. Telling glared at the oaf's cornflower blue – and completely lifeless – eyes.

'And who might you be, creeping up on folks and giving your orders?' Speedwell asked, amused by the youngster's arrogant anxiety.

'Captain Telling, Prince Rupert's lifeguard,' Hugo snapped, yanking his reins back from the stupidly grinning dragoon.

'Ooh, Rupert's lifeguard. *The* Rupert?'

'I wasn't aware there was more than one.'

Speedwell grinned, tickled by the youngster's pluck. Typical cavalry material, a little too used to seeing his social inferiors grovelling in the dirt, maybe. Speedwell's blue scar wrinkled, doubling his repulsive smile.

'Well, I've a warrant, matey, and I suggest you show me yours before I drill you an extra earhole,' the dragoon chief leered, raising the barrel a notch higher.

'My troops are waiting over the bridge, I warn you,' Telling breathed with all the authority he could muster. He was beginning to wish he had followed Thackray's advice and skirted the trouble. Damn the boy, where had he got to?

'If I'd ridden up on a burning village I wouldn't have left my men behind the stream,' Speedwell countered craftily. Telling coloured slightly.

'I have orders,' he croaked. He wiped his eye.

'Smoke botherin' you, Captain?'

'It's nothing,' Telling replied, cursing his rapidly filming eye. Speedwell seemed to have had enough chatter.

He stepped down into the road and strode toward the reluctant Cavalier. Telling raised his own pistol.

'One step more and you're dead, I warn you.'

Compton Speedwell paused, glanced around the street. His dragoons had appeared from windows and doors, peered around the side of the refuse-filled alleys.

'It would appear you are at a disadvantage, Captain,' Speedwell said quietly. 'Now you'd better show us these orders of yours before we get you off that bloater the hard way!'

'This village comes under the jurisdiction of the Governor of Bristol,' Telling called, cold with fear now. His horse's ears were twitching with terror as the leering men closed in on them.

'Quite right. And we've to collect the assessment.' Speedwell tugged the rolled parchment from his opened coat, held it out to the nervous rider. 'There was trouble here last month, some of my men were killed. We caught two of them in the laundry there, looters. You might have picked up the smell as you rode in. The rest . . .'

Telling snatched the order from the captain's dirty fingers, unpeeled the sticky sheet. His sea-green eyes widened in alarm as he scanned the warrant. Even Speedwell was taken aback for a moment by the youth's astonishment.

'Bella? Bella Morrison?'

'You've heard tell of her too, eh?' he asked with a wink. 'They've fled the nest, the little buggers. Wounded or dead, we don't know which. Still, they can't have got far, not a few women and a couple of cripples, eh? Turned vicious on my boys, if you'd credit it.'

Telling frowned as he digested the horrific indictment.

Speedwell wondered why the Cavalier was so interested in the mealy-mouthed merchant's daughter. Maybe the young blood wasn't such a jobberknol after all. Maybe he had only come looking after the saucy little polecat same as the rest of them. Maybe . . .

Telling fired the pistol straight at him, kicking out at the dozy dragoon beside him in the same moment. Henry Graves recoiled in surprise, his thick fingers groping for the bridle and closing instead on the dog-eared warrant. Off guard, the giant dragoon stumbled on his heels taking the incriminating document with him. Telling made one despairing lunge for the torn paper but his horse shied, leaving him clinging to the saddle and groping air.

His ill-aimed pistol shot had parted Speedwell's hair and splintered the partially demolished door behind his head. There was a scream from the top storey of the ransacked hovel as the frightened inhabitants imagined new slaughters.

'Grab him!' Speedwell yelled, blinking in the acrid smoke.

Telling ducked down over the bay's ears and dug his spurs into its flanks. One of the dragoons in a bright red hat groped for him but he was caught in the shin by a flying hoof and leapt back with an oath. Telling leaned to his left, backhanding another startled looter with the barrel of the smoking pistol. The big bay slipped on the cobbles, thrashed wildly, and regained its feet. A pistol shot cracked a spider-webbed window inches above his head as he yanked the charger into an alley. The disturbed looters groped for their weapons, realizing most of their firearms were tied up with their horses.

'Well, don't just stand there, get after him!' Speedwell

yelled, standing in the smoky street as the young intruder made his getaway.

Telling was hurled sideways in the slipping saddle, crashing into the crumbling stonework as the frantic horse charged down the alley. His suit tore, his hat was knocked off as he ducked under the arch into an untidy garden. Telling spurred the horse through a tangle of bean canes and put the bay to the tumbledown fencing which prevented the neighbour's pigs from getting at the vegetables. The bay splashed into the filthy sty, the squealing pigs dashing this way and that as the lurching Cavalier held on for grim life. A flurry of ill-aimed musket shots splattered into the filth as Telling gathered the horse up and spurred at the second rail. The big bay, terrified by the squealing pigs and the crackling musketry, would have cleared a small river, let alone the weather-beaten fencing. It sailed over the obstacle and careered down a nettle-lined lane toward the carelessly picketed dragoon nags, who tossed their heads in irritation as they munched their oats.

Telling hauled back on the reins, drew his sword, and slashed at the filthy rope which had been knotted to a fence post.

'Yah! Yah! Run, you cankerous old shitbags!' he yelled, waving his sword above his head. The panicked herd of piebald ponies tugged away from the slack rope, kicking and bucking in the narrow alleyway at the rear of the gardens. Telling forced the larger bay through the snorting beasts, kicking and slashing at the stampeding mass of reeking horses. In another moment he had cleared the lane, driving half of the dragoon mounts before him. They cantered into a stubble field and scattered in all directions. Telling ducked down low, aimed the bay at the high hedge towards the stream. He could hear the dragoons shouting behind him, trying to catch their frantic nags.

There was only one place to go now, he thought breathlessly, one man to turn to.

His doting father-in-law to be, Sir Gilbert.

KILMERSDEN HALL,

BITTERWELL HILL, SOMERSET

There had been no gentle introduction, no gradual acclimatization to the reality of war. One moment he had been listening to the throaty warble of a wren, hidden somewhere in the overgrown hedge beside the lane, and the next he had been gripping his reins in terror, shaken to the core by a series of rasping ricochets which tore through the shrubbery – silencing the twittering animal life as surely as a poacher's whistle. A dozen shots rattled the tiles on the red-brick cottages beyond the deserted gardens, putting up the rooks from the trees to his left. The storm birds flapped away toward the stream, taking his for ever fractured peace of mind with them.

Joseph Thackray had been thrown in the deep end from the word go. Less than two days had passed since he had offered his services to this hateful catalyst Telling, and he was already up to his protruding ears in a mess of trouble. 'Told you so,' his old mother would have said. He pictured her, sucking in her toothless gums as if she was harbouring a mouthful of wasps. 'You leave this bliddy war to them that started it, boy. Tain't anything to do with the likes of thee or I.' By God, he wished he'd followed her sourly delivered advice now.

Captain Telling had left the boy at the foot of the slope, his listless grey mare concealed in a spectacular bower of bramble and burdock. The scowling Cavalier had eyed his new squire with undisguised contempt, but he would be damned if he was going to stick his neck out at the very first opportunity. It was all right for the captain, with his swordplay and paired pistols and peculiar ideas about honour and glory. Wasn't much glory to be had poking your nose into other buggers' business in some pukepot of a village twenty miles from home. And what had honour ever done for anybody? Got 'em bliddy well killed, that's what. His talent for violence had only ever extended to strangling a few pullets on his uncle's smallholding, yet here was Captain High and Mighty Telling expecting him to charge into a whole regiment of bliddy strangers, for all he knew. His old mother had been right all along. It was nothing to do with him. And he'd tell 'em so too, if they came looking.

The quaking youth had crouched over his saddle while Telling continued his ill-advised reconnaissance, listening to the careless creatures rattle and tap the bare stems about his twitching head.

The sudden flurry of shots had turned his bowels to beef jelly.

After the shots, a stomach-churning and largely unintelligible outburst of shouting completely undermined his wavering resolve. Had his master walked into some native feast? Had he been stripped and trussed for the pot, sitting up in his own stew with his thin nose in the air?

The grey tossed its head, ears pricking at the series of terrified whinnies from over the slope.

That's it. That's enough, Thackray thought, yanking the mare's head about in one panic-stricken contraction. Telling could fight his own damned battles. The youth squinted down the alley between the overgrown hedges, cocking his head as the terrifying tumult built in an irresistible crescendo. Run, run! Where, where?

Hoofs drummed hollowly through the very bones of the hill, setting up an infernal vibration which might have knocked the teeth from his head. Loose tack jingled with malicious glee, a bejewelled witch ducking down over her cauldron. He couldn't move, paralysed like a young cony caught in the open by a hungry fox.

And then all of a sudden a black and red demon burst through his pitiful barricade, scattering what little was left of the poor boy's wits.

'Aggh, dear God save us!' Thackray spluttered, mortified by the rearing beast, a fiery centaur from hell's sulphurous stables sent to reap his quivering soul. He closed his eyes tight shut as a finger of steel sliced through the greasy rim of his antique hat.

Telling's sword caught the sun, flashing like a lantern as the Cavalier checked his panic-stricken thrust.

'You bitch-spawned bastard,' Telling croaked, lowering his sword and hauling the bay's head about before it careered into the brambles opposite. 'Jumping out on me like that!'

Thackray opened an eye, focused on the red-coated youth panting like a dog as he hung on grimly to the skittish charger.

'Another blink and I'd have cloven you in two,' the breathless adventurer snapped, bending over his crupper to peer back through the bushes, scanning the untidily kept gardens bordering the smoking village. Thackray could barely speak, his heart seemed to have leapt up out of his constricted chest and filled his mouth with sour-tasting dough.

Telling pointed the blade on down the arched alley-way, twirling his reins in his left hand.

'God's wounds, don't sit there shitting yourself, after me!' he said thickly, urging the bay past the bewildered mare. Thackray took one look through the sun-dappled hedge, swallowed the bile which had coated his tongue, and dug his heels into the reluctant beast.

So this was war, Joseph thought bleakly. Well, you were bliddy welcome to it.

Hugo reckoned he might have earned himself a ten-minute reprieve – if he was lucky. It wouldn't take those bastard dragoons long to catch their broken-winded beasts and set off after him, and he wasn't likely to make good time with his idiot groom trotting along behind, gawping about him like a hedgehog on a spit. He turned sharp right at the boggy bottom of the lane, urging the panting bay up an earth bank and through a barricade of nettles and creepers into a narrow, sun-glad meadow. He had to wait precious seconds as Thackray put his mare to the steep obstacle, cursing under his breath as he recovered what was left of his nerve.

'Boot the bugger on or I'll leave you to them,' Telling hissed through the branches. Thackray peered up at his agitated master, transferred all his brittle spirit into his heels. The grey whinnied, tossed its head, and took the slope in a series of frantic bounds.

'There's a couple of dozen dragoons on our heels. If you can't keep up you'd best hide yourself away. They don't know you were with me,' Telling gasped, running his sleeve across his sweat-stained features.

'What did you do?' Thackray asked wonderingly, urging the grey on after the longer-legged bay.

'Spoiled their fun, for one thing,' Telling called over his shoulder. Interrupted their ill-disciplined search but whetted their appetite for mischief, set himself up as their day's sport. Arrest Bella? For God's sake, why? Was she wounded, dead? Had that damned dragoon meant Bella or Jamie, Mary Keziah or her corpulent, sharp-tongued mother?

He cursed under his breath as he led the way over the meadow, peering back at the silver trail they had left in the grass. By God, a blind donkey could have picked up their tracks! Hugo spurred on across the field, pulled up beneath the carelessly spread skirts of an ancient oak. The luxuriant green canopy had long thinned the lush turf beneath and its grey-knuckled roots had sucked the moisture from the cracked soil, leaving a ring of hard-baked earth.

'What are you doing?' Thackray squealed, watching with horror as Telling folded himself out of the saddle and grabbed the bay's dripping bridle.

'Dismount and follow me, we'll have to lead them into the nearest bushes.' His petrified groom needed no further urging, cocking his leg over the bulky baggage strapped to the grey's saddle. Hugo frowned, drew his dagger, and advanced on the drooping beast. Thackray sighed with relief as Telling cut the strapping holding the various bundles together, letting his precious wardrobe fall to the floor. His entire worldly household, dumped for those thieving magpies hurrying after him. A fine way to come courting, sweating in a torn suit without so much as a handkerchief to your name. What would Sir Gilbert have to say about it? Bella's formidable father had had a good deal to say the last time they had met, if he remembered rightly. Something about never seeing his harlot of a daughter again, 'as long as he had breath in his body'.

'We must move quickly,' Telling explained to the twitching groom, shoving the dagger back into his belt and waving the bewildered boy on after him.

Telling studied the ground carefully, choosing the bare earth between the massive oak and the hedge as his causeway out of the treacherous meadow. He couldn't hope to conceal their tracks completely, but there was no point in leaving finger-posts to mark their way. Hugo looked up over the bay's shoulder, peered back down the grassy slope. No signs of pursuit just yet.

They pushed and shoved their way through the thick autumn hedgerow and recrossed the brook, pausing to arrange the trampled brambles behind them. The hill reared up in front of them now, skirted by another broader meadow and a tumbledown drystone wall. Beyond the wall, a hundred yards of steep rabbit-cropped turf and then the trees, a welcoming crown of cover stretching along the summit. If they could get to the plantation they might just shake the damned dragoons off.

Telling handed Thackray his reins while he feverishly reloaded his pistols, his pale scholar's hands trembling slightly as he primed and wound the beautifully matched weapons. He had lifted them from a dead Roundhead major he had come across beside the River Enborne barely a fortnight before. A corpulent fellow who had been practically decapitated by one of Prince Rupert's irresistible horsemen. But the crowd of noisy apprentices the unknown officer had commanded hadn't scattered like a flock of closely cropped sheep, they'd bunched together closer than ever, shouting and screaming and gripping their pikes, forcing the caterwauling Royalist horsemen to wheel away once more. The London Trained Bands had stood like so many rocks, a patchwork breakwater which had defied a dozen charges. By the time night had fallen, the Earl of Essex's battered army of which they formed the core had barely held on to its original position, but the King's forces had been exhausted – shorn of a quarter of its effectives and in chronic want of powder.

The lumbering Parliamentarian army had resumed its advance the following day, forcing the impotent Royalists from the London road and bolting back to the capital before Rupert could rearm his tattered squadrons and come after it. Essex had marched home in triumph, a red-cheeked Caesar acknowledging the rapturous cheers of the fickle London mobs – he had more than earned it. He had relieved Gloucester and brought his army back to the capital through hell and high water. Shrewd observers knew full well he could hardly claim an outright victory, but at least he had staved off the catastrophic defeat which had appeared all too likely earlier that summer.

Hugo frowned, replaced the pistols in the long leather holsters each side of the crupper, and hauled himself back into the saddle.

'Ride for the trees. Don't stop for anything or anyone,' Hugo told Thackray, who bit his bloodless lips, nodded dumbly. If they catch up with us, I don't know you, he thought maliciously, staring at his master's hunched back as he took off over the fields once more.

'Geddup, geddup, you old lardguts,' he hissed into the grey's ear.

Don't stop for anyone – that was what he had told his wild-eyed groom. But Hugo would have stopped for Bella. Stopped dead for one moment with his fickle faery queen. Great God above, that damned girl would be the death of him yet, Hugo fumed as he spurred the bay over the drystone wall. He prayed – more fervently than he had ever prayed before – that the girl was safe. Wounded at worse. Dead? How could she be dead? How could he even contemplate life without his life, without his wife?

Hugo's heart and lungs and stomach seemed to have swollen with some hateful distemper, risen like bloody baked dough and crammed into his throat.

He'd known from the beginning she was a wild one, a man-eating tempest all strapped and buckled into a delightfully narrow bodice, but it seemed he couldn't leave the wretched minx for more than five minutes without another life-threatening catastrophe.

Bella Marguerite Morrison.

Her name alone was like some devilish talisman, an all-powerful spell to steal the wits of men. God knew she'd stolen his wits often enough, led him by the nose into one scrape after another. He hoped that when they finally married the little strumpet might put an end to his troubles, or at the very least put a check on them. Thought perhaps things would settle down a little, once they had set up home together. He concentrated hard, banishing any idea she might be dead, any gnawing doubt she might never share his dream of domestic bliss.

Home? His greatest expectation at that moment would

have been to provide his true love with a mouldy tent in the middle of a shit-splattered field. The best he could ever hope would be to share some gloomy garret in an overcrowded Oxford hovel. And besides, nothing could ever be properly settled until this damned war was over and done, Hugo thought feverishly.

And he would never settle if Bella, the light at the end of his gunsmoke-crowded tunnel, had been extinguished by some lousy bogtrotter of a dragoon.

Bella, Bella! His brain ached as her name rebounded around his reeling mind.

She was as wildly unpredictable as battle, as reliable as a one-legged German mercenary with a purse of looted gold stuck down his breeches, and about as trustworthy as her own bloody father. What a merry dance she'd led him these past months, fluttering her auburn lashes one moment and kicking him in the stones the next!

That time she'd trampled his hat into the dirt, for instance! Or the time she'd paraded her new beau in front of him, as if she had craved to see them fight over her, despised rivals for her transparent heart.

They had fought all right, aye, and his rival Anthony St John Dyle – Lord Clavincale, no less – was dead because of it. She could count that bloated oaf out of her kiss-and-run games. Telling had won her fair and square, saved her from her own senseless ambition in the nick of time. Would she have really gone through with it? Married the obnoxious bloat? Probably, he thought darkly. It was a good job fate had thrown them back together again, together under Gloucester's wool-packed walls. Bella had been tiring of her new amour, bored to distraction as the Royalists attempted to force themselves into the stubbornly held town. Telling had had a sight more luck

43

breaking down her defences, he thought with a secret leer. Fighting all day and slipping away by night for a secret tryst in the woods. They might have been happily married by now if it hadn't ended in disaster – the pair of them caught buck naked in the middle of a rainstorm by her red-faced father and equally apoplectic fiancé.

Telling had defended himself as best he could against the furious Clavincale, and he and Bella had finally gotten the better of the overweight nobleman – only to be caught in the act by Prince Rupert himself!

But then again, Hugo remembered with some satisfaction, Rupert had had no business being in the wood either. Midnight liaisons with a mysterious woman, strongly rumoured to be Rupert's best friend's wife – well, he could hardly point the finger at Telling when his own activities were open to question. If it hadn't been for the furious but grateful Prince, Telling might have found himself on trial for Clavincale's squalid murder. But Rupert, mortified at the prospect of having the details of his not-so-secret affair revealed to a shocked court, had preferred to let sleeping dogs lie, and ordered the charges against the bewildered boy dropped.

Hugo, instead of being clapped in irons for braining his lordship, had been promoted to Rupert's elite lifeguard, his precious captaincy the price of his continued silence. At least if he was riding in his bodyguard Rupert could keep an eye on the damned fellow. Telling, delighted at his unexpected good fortune, had determined to take full advantage of his powerful patron, make his name and fortune and marry Bella while the going was good. But Sir Gilbert Bastard Turncoat Bloody Morrison had put paid to that little plan, dragging his true heart off home before he could make his move. By the time Hugo had been released from custody and installed in his coveted new command his sweetheart and partner in crime had been halfway back to Chipping Marleward! And now, a month later, here she was in trouble again. She might even be dead. Dead? His imagination paled and trembled at the appalling possibility. Wounded perhaps. Blinded, deafened, crippled, anything but dead. What in God's name had she done this time, to have been caught up in a fight in the village, to have a warrant issued for her arrest? Could it have something to do with the business with Clavincale?

Hugo shook his head, urging the bay up a steeply terraced slope. He narrowed his eyes, remembered the other names on the dragoons' list. James Morrison – Bella's dim-witted brother. Mary Keziah, her sharp-tongued maid, Gwen Pitt, the laundress, and Mordecai, her crippled son. What on earth had Bella been thinking of, mixing with rubbish like them? What in God's name had she done to so upset those damned dragoons? Hugo knew full well there was only one man nearby who might know the answer to that terrible question. The only difficulty lay in the fact that Hugo would probably be the last person on earth Sir Gilbert would be inclined to confide in. He hadn't exactly showered his would-be son-in-law with praises, had he?

Hugo spurred the tired bay along the ridge, following a leaf-strewn track he had walked with Bella on several happier occasions in the summer. Was it really just a few months ago? He ducked down over the bay's sweat-caked neck, pulling up beneath a chestnut tree. Hugo tugged the branches aside and peered over the shrubbery towards the rambling mansion house, half swallowed by creeping dragons of crimson-and-gold ivy. With the menfolk dead and buried and most of the servants long since departed, the once proud home looked as if it was being reclaimed by nature, reduced by degrees to a half-forgotten cabin in a half-remembered glade.

'Watch out behind, we're not far now.' The bedraggled Cavalier spurred his panting charger down the crumbling bank and led the way across the weed-choked courtyard of Kilmersden Hall.

'Starling? Starling!' Damn the fellow, he'd told him to collect a few handfuls of straw, not gather the harvest! His undernourished clerk would have him in Knave's Acre yet. Sir Gilbert Morrison dropped the sack of candlesticks he had been cradling into the cluttered belly of the wagon, gripped the oak frame and tried to get his breath back. 'Starling?' he called, slapping his handkerchief over his plump red face and peering around the corner of the house after the absent servant. Where had he gone for the damned straw, the Americas? He glanced down into the loaded hull of the great wain, frowned at the tinker's assortment of junk he had salvaged from the old house. Lady Ramsay had followed him around the rambling ruin as he made his feverish inventory, glaring at him with even more ferocity than usual.

'You know as well as I do, ma'am,' he had growled, 'the house and all its contents belong to me in default of your late husband's debt.'

'So you mean to strip the last few relics we have left? Have the weeds from my back, if you've a mind.' Sir Gilbert had no mind to have the widow's weeds off her back, although her fetching daughter was quite another matter. The pair of them had watched with horror as the thoughtless boor tore the frames from a selection of Dutch miniatures, folding the delicate silhouettes into his already stuffed pockets.

'If it'll raise more than a penny, I mean to sell it, aye. You know damn fine I can't stand by and watch her die!' They hadn't dared gainsay that, had they?

He had taken everything that hadn't been nailed down and thrown it into the massive cart. What remained of his own perilously stretched fortune had been hidden in a leather sheath and stapled to the underside of the wagon's running-board, safe from prying eyes.

'STARLING!'

'Here I am, there's no need to shout,' Algernon Starling said waspishly, peering though a halo of loose stalks. Sir Gilbert straightened up as his cadaverous clerk staggered around the corner of the house, an immense bundle of straw clamped in his arms.

'Spread it over this lot and hurry up about it,' the merchant called, cocking his leg over the oaken flank of the wagon, 'or we'll have every beef-witted bastard from miles around poking his nose in.'

He stood back as the grumbling scarecrow staggered forward to complete his sweaty assignment, glanced up at the drawing-room window. Lady Ramsay was scowling behind the dirty panes, her cheerless features framed by the chequerboard lead piping. Let the old bitch rave, it was his house, he'd dispose of its contents how he liked. He smiled winningly, watched the widow turn her back and disappear into the gloomy interior of the house. Her mausoleum, Kilmersden Hall. The grand, if rather faded, country seat of the recently deceased Royalist Sir Marmaduke Ramsay.

The scatterbrained squire had been blown to smithereens

on Lansdown earlier that frightful summer, but not before he had mortgaged virtually his entire estate to raise money to pay his small garrison. Ramsay had obtained the lifeblood loan from the only man left in Somerset with the wherewithal to do so: his once bitter enemy and rival turned *firm* friend Sir Gilbert Morrison. The canny merchant had taken the squire's markers for a grand total of £1,245, putting the landowner – and subsequently his formidable widow Lady Ramsay – completely in his debt.

Morrison, gleefully making the most of his hold over the blue-blooded Ramsays, had practically moved in with the mortified widow, and had set about brokering the marriage of his temporarily unhinged son Jamie to Ramsay's surviving heir, the dark-haired, infinitely thoughtful Anneliese. There had been little the energetic widow could do to oppose the match – without selling the hall to the highest bidder and taking to the road with the rest of the war's waifs and strays. And she could not – or had not yet been able – to bring herself to leave what had after all been the site of her family's home for six centuries.

With the menfolk dead, the garrison gone, and Findlay, its loyal guardian and gamekeeper, away with the King's army, the isolated house had closed up on itself like an old clam. The trees and shrubs had invaded the once proud lawns. Rats and vermin swarmed in the cottages and outbuildings. The very glass in the windows seemed to have misted over like a drowned man's eyes. Sir Gilbert Morrison couldn't give a fig for the sorry old structure. It was just so much bricks and mortar to him. What mattered was the name. *Ramsay.* He'd grasped and wangled his way up from the gutter, but he would be a common or garden Morrison till the day he died. A sharp trader with an eye for a deal. His children, though, well, that was another matter. He had hoped to marry young Bella off to Ramsay's hideously scarred son Thomas. But Thomas had been killed on Lansdown along with his equally unlucky father. That had left young Jamie and Anneliese. But Jamie had come back from the wars with his head up his arse, talking nonsense to anyone fool enough to listen. Strangely, Anneliese seemed to have taken a shine to the drooling oaf, nursing him back to something like health with infinite, almost angelic patience – much to the disgust of her mother. That was until Jamie's catastrophic relapse, that is. Sir Gilbert closed his eyes and pinched his fleshy nose between his fingers at the painful memory.

Daft Jamie had wandered down to the village without his clothes, and walked straight into a pack of hysterical dragoons. Young Mordecai Pitt – who ought to have known better with his crippled leg and all – had gone to his aid, but the scurvy troopers had turned on him. Then Bella had . . . damn damn damn it all! Why hadn't she run back to the house and forgotten all about it? Oh, no. Not Bella. She had gone sailing in giving her orders, and sparked the riot which had left half a dozen of them dead! Dear sweet Jesus, what had he ever done to deserve such an irresponsible Amazon?

Bella had been shot in the head by a pistol ball, practically before his own eyes. They had carried the deathly pale girl into the tavern, where they had laid her out on a table and stood back trembling with shock, expecting to watch her gasp her last. Sir Gilbert would never forget her white features, the ghastly mask of blood they had mopped and daubed away, leaving her shift stained pink. Or the tray of torture tools the village quack had picked from his canvas sack, arranged in needle-sharp ranks over the stained oak table. The callipers and scalpels and hooks and bores glimmering in the dismal light shed by the candles Bella's fearful friends had placed beside her torn skull.

Thank the Lord the ball had not penetrated the bone. When the sweating sawbones had finally prised the flayed skin and sopping flesh from the terrible wound, they had realized the slug had merely cut a deep grove from the fleshy corner of her right eye toward the top of her pink, blood-splattered ear. Dr Conroy had wiped his brow on his dirty sleeve, picked tiny specks of lead from the furrowed flesh as if he was prospecting for gold.

'She'll live, won't she, tell me she'll live,' the merchant had hissed.

'Aye, she'll live,' the doctor had confirmed, lifting the girl's alabaster wrist to check her flickering pulse. 'Though she'll have the devil of a headache when she wakes up.' He leaned over the seeping wound, prodded the torn skin with his scalpel with professional curiosity. 'And she'll scar. You don't stop an ounce of lead without collecting a lump or two.'

The merchant's heartfelt sigh had sent the shutters banging at the windows. 'Thank the Lord for that.' A scar? It would do her good, remind her every time she looked in the mirror how close she had come to death.

Just like the dragoons lying sprawled and forgotten in the street.

They would be back, aye, and more of them. Country folk didn't get away with doing in dragoons, whether they were in Somerset or Saxony. Sir Gilbert knew that well enough, and had laid his plans accordingly. His first thought had been to deceive the inevitable pursuit. He would have turned Lady Ramsay's dwindling household out around a freshly dug grave if necessary, invited the entire village to witness the burial of his beloved, if wayward, daughter. If the whining old baggage had still possessed the wherewithal to afford a serving girl, he would have thrown her into it as well! The bastards were bound to find their way up to the hall, and they wouldn't have been satisfied poking around a pile of earth. They would have had to have their pound of mouldering flesh.

Sir Gilbert had discarded the scheme as grossly unreliable. For one thing, the widow did not employ any female staff who would pass muster in any post-mortem comparison with Bella. Lady Ramsay wore her heart on her sleeve and would therefore have made a piss-poor liar. Any story he concocted – no matter how elaborate – would have been blown out of the water the moment he entertained it. Besides that, some blabbermouth from the estate or the village he'd abandoned at the beginning of that desperate summer would be bound to work things out for himself, go scuttling to the authorities. No, deception wasn't going to work. Habeas Corpus and all that lawyer stuff.

If he couldn't bury her, Sir Gilbert had decided, he would hide her. Get her safe away from the furious dragoons. But to complete a successful escape he would need coin. And good coin was a rare commodity in the Ramsay household that damned autumn. Well, the Ramsays owed him, and now he intended to collect. What did Lady Ramsay think he was planning to do, run out on his own flesh and blood? Of course not. He'd sell these damn trinkets and buy the convalescent Bella a passage to France, hire a ship and spirit her away until the whole damned business had died down. When it was safe enough to do so he'd think about a lawyer, let them argue the rights and wrongs of the matter in a properly convened court of law. There might be a war on but they weren't savages, by God! A good doctor wouldn't come amiss either, what with the headaches, the double vision, the nightmares and shivering fits, he thought ruefully. Why hadn't she stayed put?

Sir Gilbert paused on the cracked steps of the shabby old house, temporarily overwhelmed by the appalling turn of events. If it wasn't one thing it was another! He mopped his brow, shaking his white whiskers in agitation. He paused, cocked his head. He could have sworn he'd heard . . . he had! Horses!

The red-faced merchant trotted back down the steps and hurried over to the wagon. Starling stood like some crooked raven in the back of the treasure-laden wain, and then set about attempting to cover the hoard with the straw. Sir Gilbert shielded his eyes and peered down the white gravel path, watched two indistinct grey blobs detach themselves from the trees. They'd be after their horses, if nothing else! No less than six scrawny cobs were swishing their tails between the traces, the only beasts he'd managed to lay his hands on for miles around. Every decent scrap of horseflesh between Cornwall and Gloucester had been driven off long since by one army or the other.

The wily merchant pulled an antique duck gun from the running-board and turned on his heel with surprising agility as the approaching riders slowed up, their horses' hoofs kicking up a tattoo on the untidily heaped gravel.

'Telling, you candle-wasting young clod, I might have known it would be you.' The merchant lowered the brass-bound weapon a notch, squinting along the gaping barrel as the leading rider pulled up in a flurry of white dust. The panting Cavalier pushed his hair back from his sweat-caked features, nodded sourly at his would-be relation.

'Sir Gilbert,' Telling gasped, coughing on the thick white cloud they had kicked up coming down the un-kempt path. 'I came as soon as I could. Is she all right?'

Sir Gilbert eyed the miserable whelp with suspicion, raised the cumbersome trumpet as the captain tugged at his coat.

'Have a care, Telling, or I'll blast you over half of Somerset!' Sir Gilbert called stoutly, glancing to his right as Lady Ramsay, her daughter Anneliese, and ancient Bates sallied out onto the steps of their long-suffering fortress to see what the commotion was about. Telling gave them the briefest of acknowledgements, returned his attention to the blustering merchant.

'She's not dead? Please God she's not dead!' Telling cried. Anneliese, overcome by his obvious distress, burst into tears. Sir Gilbert waved his paw in irritation.

'She's alive, no thanks to clods like you.'

Telling almost swooned, adrift on his saddle as if it was a reed raft in the middle of the ocean.

'She's been hit in the head,' Anneliese called. 'She's badly scarred but she'll recover.'

The merchant turned on his heel, glowered at the

loose-tongued girl. Thank Christ he wasn't trying to convince those pox-powdered dragoons!

'They've issued a warrant for her arrest!' Telling wailed. 'Where is she? What's she done? Is she within?'

Sir Gilbert struggled to hold the heavy blunderbuss steady, his generous lips parting over his teeth. 'Aye, we heard they were after her,' he growled. 'But I can't imagine what business it is of yours!'

'You know damned well what business it is to me, we're to be wed!' Telling shouted back, taking a quick glance over his dusty shoulder.

'Joining giblets with my Bella? Don't hold your breath, my lad!'

'Where is she? What has she done now?' Telling repeated, almost weeping with frustration. Sir Gilbert chuckled, lowered the blunderbuss as if he couldn't be bothered even to shoot such a worthless upstart. Anneliese Ramsay glared at the merchant, shocked by his gloating smile.

'On your way, Telling, can't you see we're busy? She wouldn't want to waste her time on you, spoiling her recovery with your bustling and fussing! Even if she was here!'

Telling yanked the bay around, glared down at the crafty merchant. 'So she's away? Thank God! There has to be some mistake! Why are they trying to have her arrested?' He looked imploringly at Lady Ramsay, standing resolutely before her invaded hall.

'We haven't time for you and your university pranks!' Sir Gilbert warned. 'She's safely away for now, we don't need you muddying the waters, not a scrofulous whippersnapper like you!'

Telling pointed down the path. 'There's a troop of

dragoons on their way for her! They're sure to know to look here,' the Cavalier warned, walking his horse alongside the wagon and peering over its weather-beaten oak ribcage. The wagon had been loaded with diverse sacks and chests, rolled paintings, and skeletal candlesticks. Barrels, boxes, bundles, and books had been stacked haphazardly in the deep hold. All that remained of the Ramsays' fortune, the captain guessed. So they were running out, were they? Telling glanced up at the burly, black-robed widow, who was watching him like some vast osprey from her perch on the step. She seemed to deflate slightly, pierced by his pinched features, moved by the miserable Cavalier's all too evident distress.

'Lady Ramsay, in the name of God, why is she to be arrested?'

'There's been a mistake,' Sir Gilbert grumbled, 'there was some trouble in the village. Some of the dragoons were hurt. They think my Bella had something to do with it.'

'Hurt? Brained, more like it,' Lady Ramsay snapped. 'If it hadn't been for that idiot boy of yours none of this would have happened!' she exclaimed.

Anneliese opened her mouth to say something but thought better of it, closing her small fists in white-faced frustration. The merchant glowered at them, fingering the cumbersome blunderbuss as if he meant to shoot the whole pack of them. Telling returned his attention to the merchant, lurking at bay beside the loaded wagon.

'Then you know where she is, she's safe?'

'As if I'm about to tell you!' Sir Gilbert crowed.

'By the bowels of Christ, those dragoons will have it out of you soon enough!'

'I'll send them on their way,' the merchant roared,

pointing a stubby forefinger at the exasperated Cavalier. 'Clear off, you vaporous scoundrel!'

'They've fired half the village, do you think they'll leave this place alone now?'

'That's why we're taking a few precautions with our valuables,' Morrison grated.

'*Our* valuables?' Lady Ramsay enquired archly.

'He's going to use what's left of the plate to get poor Bella aboard ship!' Anneliese piped up at last, shivering like a leaf between her ferocious mother and the elderly manservant Bates. The merchant swivelled around and glared at the girl, who glared back defiantly, tears stinging her eyes. 'She was only trying to protect Jamie, your own son!' she sobbed.

'We haven't time to go over that again,' Sir Gilbert snapped. 'Once they're safely away we'll sort the whole thing out. Get a good lawyer to argue her case. Dreadful mistake. That's all.'

'Tell me where she is,' Telling demanded.

'Not on your life.'

'Take us, then, we'll escort you. You won't outrun a troop of dragoons towing this lot.'

Sir Gilbert paused, moustache twitching. Beads of sweat had jewelled his creased forehead, wetting his copiously oiled grey hair. He looked for a moment as if he might melt away altogether. He nodded.

'I was going to send Starling here to a man I know,' he frowned, a worried old man all over again. 'You can buy us some time, give us a chance to get out on the Fosseway.' He peered up at his sardonic servant for confirmation. The ghoulish secretary picked stalks from his sober black suit, nodded.

'Starling and Thackray can drive the team, you can

come with me,' Telling countered, waving his bewildered groom up from the rear. 'We wouldn't want to lose one another, would we now?'

The merchant bared his teeth, nodded: 'All right, have it your way.'

Thackray climbed down from the panting grey, handed the reins to the red-faced merchant. Sir Gilbert presented the limping youth with the enormous blunderbuss in return. 'Anybody tries to follow you, give 'em a gutful of this,' he instructed with a piratical leer. Sir Gilbert bowed toward the astonished widow, turned, and heaved himself up into the mare's sweaty saddle. 'Madam, take care of the house for me, I'll be back as soon as everything is settled.' Lady Ramsay raised her chin, snorted something under her breath.

Telling clapped his spurs into the bay's streaked flanks and led the way back down the path. Sir Gilbert heaved up and down on the panting grey, urging the reluctant beast on after the impetuous youth. Starling and Thackray had taken up station on the running-board of the treasure wagon, the wide-eyed groom clutching the brass blunderbuss as if it had been dropped from heaven slap bang into his lap.

In the sudden clatter of hoofs and harness none of the men heard Lady Ramsay's warning shout or noticed her daughter's sudden dash across the courtyard. 'Anneliese! Come back!' The determined girl ignored her mother's protest, hoicked her skirts, and darted in behind the lumbering wagon. She sprinted after the creaking carriage, gagging on the thick dust thrown up by its wheels. In another moment she had reached out and hauled herself aboard the vast galleon, clinging on for dear life as it rumbled down the track. All that was left was a cloud of dismal grit sinking slowly through the slanting autumn light.

Lady Margaret Ramsay, widow and mother, was quite alone now. Well, not quite alone.

'Best get indoors, ma'am,' Bates said quietly, anxious not to disturb her sullen, tear-misted study of the parkland trees.

CHIPPING MARLEWARD,

C ompton Speedwell seethed on the steps of the looted hovel, teeth clamped together as he strode back and forth striving to overcome the furious currents boiling through his vitals. Stop your damned cursing and think, he told himself for the umpteenth time, his notorious temper cooling by the second.

Slowly his vision stabilized as the red mist he was squinting through dissipated. The cross-eyed pack of damp-powdered pricks he had the misfortune to command were still running about as if the undernourished Cavalier had set their breeches afire, in the apparent belief the more they screamed the less he'd mind. Henry Graves, the hulking dragoon who had loosed the boy in the first place, had stalked back into the garden leading a brace of recaptured ponies while his companions busied themselves trying to corner the rest. The patchwork beasts hadn't gone far – they knew better than to stray too far from their grub – but were only dragged away from the villagers' vegetable patches with prolonged and noisy encouragement from their ragged-arsed masters.

Henry Graves glanced at his unpredictable captain, noting the livid white patches beneath his shifty eyes had dimmed somewhat. He decided it might be prudent to wait another moment before he offered any opinion. The unusually thoughtful dragoon held out the torn warrant like a peace token, and pretended to study the barred shutters above the captain's bent head.

Speedwell took the mildewed scrap with a subdued snort, lifted his grey eyes from the familiar warrant to corner Graves' carefully vacant stare. 'You wait for the rest of them to catch their mounts,' the captain breathed, a bobbing boat on an ebbing tide. 'Take the back markers towards Bath. Send a couple up to the top of the hill to keep a lookout.'

'I will, sir!' Graves cried eagerly. 'He won't slip us a second time.'

Speedwell licked his lips. 'There's only two quick ways out of this gorge, the Bath road or the Wells road. Either that or he's gone wildside, which means he'll still be near.' He leaned forward, studied the jackdaw-grey cliffs which reared over the steeply wooded hillsides to either flank. Beyond the jagged peaks, high downs and summer gallops stretched away to either horizon, their green hems nipped and tucked by the contortions of the ancient bedrock. Blind alleys and steep-sided dales a rider might have taken a horse – if he'd been after concealment rather than flight. 'I don't want him harmed unless you've got to, is that clear?'

'Clear as daylight, sir.'

A sweaty dragoon in his shirtsleeves hurried up the lane leading a truculent herd of captured ponies, their footsore owners trotting along behind with their firearms thrown over their shoulders. Griffin, one of the survivors of the previous debacle in the village, thrust his thumb back the way they had come.

'He's over the stream b'now, sir. We lost him in the meadows yonder. Found his coat, mind.' Griffin held up a smart green doublet, studded with silver tassels. Speed-well gave the man a withering smile.

'Then I suggest you mount up and get after him. And Griffin . . .'

'Yes, sir?'

'Don't bother coming back, if you don't catch him that is.'

The gap-toothed dragoon grinned nervously. 'Oh, I shan't, sir. I truly shan't.'

Thirty men split three ways in a three-mile gorge steeper than a spread whore – it was like trying to plug holes in a colander, Graves thought bleakly, urging the farting pony on up the hill. The fading afternoon sun was barely strong enough now to dapple the boughs of the trees pressed in on either flank, filtered by the interlocked canopies which formed a golden-brown bower over the steep slope. A nice bit of shade or a welcome screen from the elements, while travellers tackled the switchback ridges of Bitterwell Hill.

'Christ Jesus, though, Harry, did you see that cocking beaver pop Mikey?' Griffin enquired, bringing his own panting piebald alongside the corporal's heavily laden slate-grey cob.

''E must have parted me nose 'airs with that shot. Never think it of a town boy like that, would yer?'

'Ah, he's a bad 'un if you ask me. That ole feller from the Blue Boar, f'r instance. Tweren't nuthin' a do wi' 'im at all. What's pickin' up a 'at got to do wi' anything, eh? I tell yer, I cassn't 'elp thinkin' there might be some stroppy bastard makin' sport like that wi' me kin back 'ome.'

Graves glanced at the toothless tomcat alongside,

frowned. 'Aye. We'll catch it all back one day, mark my words.'

The depleted patrol completed its lazy reconnaissance, glaring into the crowding vegetation as if they would spot the red-suited devil pissing against one of the trunks.

'That bugger was well mounted, he'll be long gone by now.'

The damned wagon seemed to have been built with the specific intention of alerting passers-by to its creaking progress. An immensely vain oaken galleon, desperate to attract the glances of admiring country folk as it rumbled and clanked around the lanes. The immense wheels, fully six feet across, howled and squeaked like a tortured cat, every popping and grinding timber striking a loud chord along the youngster's agonizingly taut spine. Joseph Thackray was staring back down the way they had come, noting with dismay the deep ruts they had left in the dusty track. Any moment now and the echoing glade would be stuffed full of enemies, riding them down with contemptuous ease. If he risked popping one of them with the blunderbuss they would only catch it worse.

He was crouching on the running-board, fretting like an old hen, when he caught the flash of movement in the foreground. He glanced down and spied a pale hand groping blindly over the rear running-board of the noisy wain. Thackray yelped with astonishment, pointing and gibbering like some broken-brained village halfwit. He couldn't have been any more frightened if he had seen the slim fingers pushing the slab from a mossy tomb.

'Look out behind!' Thackray croaked, half rising to his

feet but thinking better of it, crouching in mid-air so he appeared to be moving his bowels over the toiling horses. Algernon Starling twisted around in his seat beside him, shackled as he was to the bunched reins wound tightly about his skeletal fists. The ghastly retainer raised one eyebrow in surprise, watched the thin fingers lock about the oak frame as if they meant to tear the back from the wagon and spill all Sir Gilbert's hard-won spoils into the road.

'What in God's name . . .' Thackray raised his ludicrous weapon but checked his twitching finger in the nick of time as Anneliese Ramsay hauled herself over the running-board and flopped down in an untidy heap in the carefully strewn straw. She sat up with a yelp, pulling an iron candlestick from beneath her rather threadbare gown.

'What are you thinking of, startling folk with your mummery?' Starling snapped, completely oblivious to the girl's flushed charms. 'And you can put that down and all. Sir Gilbert's got it all fair and square and has your father's chits to prove it!' he called, fanatically loyal to his slippery superior. Anneliese smiled nervously, straightened her bodice with belated modesty.

'I don't give a cuss for the candlesticks, nor anything else for that matter,' she cried petulantly. 'I couldn't stay there, not a moment longer. There was nothing left to eat or do or sew or talk to, except Mother and Bates. And besides,' she said, smarting under their drop-jawed gaze, 'I want to see Jamie. He'll be cracking up by now, wondering what's going on.'

He wouldn't be the only one, Starling brooded, returning his attention to the sweating cobs. The ideas these uppity girls were getting, just because their menfolk were away busy with the war. Thank the Lord he had no such tricksy trifles to bother himself about.

'And it's no use going on,' Anneliese went on stoutly, smoothing the creases from her dusty dress, 'I'm in no more danger with you and Sir Gilbert than I was back there.'

Starling ground his streaked teeth in irritation, while the boy sat down heavily, the unwieldy gun resting in his overheating lap. 'He'll not want passengers, not where we're going,' the scowling clerk snapped over his black broadcloth shoulder. 'You might just as well climb down now. This is war, not some damned summer outing for bored schoolgirls.'

'Ah, don't be hard on her, uncle,' Thackray said, grinning broadly. 'She's right and all. It's not safe for a lady anywheres, these days.'

Starling's ill-natured retort dried up before it had got anywhere near his rat-trap mouth.

Five riders had appeared around the next bend, dappled by the flickering rays of sunlight spearing through the closely packed trees. Starling didn't need to see them any clearer to know they were trouble, pistols and muskets cocked and ready.

'Chuck that damned cannon over the back before you shoot someone by mistake and get us all butchered,' Starling said without moving his lips. Thackray swivelled around, the slow grin fading from his face. He yelped in alarm as he saw the riders spread out across the road. Starling hauled back on the reins, bringing the six shaggy cobs to a grateful halt. Thackray sat still as a statue, the brass blunderbuss still clamped in his frozen paws. Starling cursed. Too late now, the riders were approaching, spotted and starred with golden motes which fractured their outlines, turned them into a menacing, multicoloured cascade.

Sir Gilbert's trusted clerk watched the two leading riders pull up directly in front of the paired cobs, the rest breaking to either flank, muskets held ready across their saddles.

'Afternoon, Father,' the hulking brute in the pea-green coat called, his oafish, farm boy features split into a broad grin.

'Afternoon.'

'Wrong day for market, Father,' the leader called.

'We're not off to market. We're off to collect Mr Mason's bits and pieces, him as moved up to Wells and all.' Starling's narrow features were as bleak and expressionless as a raven's, his amber eyes everywhere and nowhere as he lied through his teeth. He'd been in Morrison's service long enough to have learned the art of spinning tales at the drop of a hat. The dragoon spurred his pony closer, pulling up on the passenger side of the huge cart, a yard from Thackray's trembling shoulders. The rider raised himself in his stirrups and reached out, turned the trembling mouth of the blunderbuss away from him with a gentle flex of his sausage fingers.

'Bit off-putting for folk, to have to talk to a body glarin' down that bliddy trumpet,' he said easily, glancing up at the terrified boy. His eyes narrowed. 'Christ Jesus, your lad here's lathered up like a Turk. He ain't got the sweating fever now, has he?' Neither of the men on the wagon spoke. 'What you been up to, boy, latherin' up like that, eh?'

'What d'you think he's been doing, you great cloth-eared Swede?'

The dragoon flinched at the disembodied voice, his cornflower blue eyes widening and then closing slightly as his broad face rearranged itself into a grin. He clicked his tongue, walked the pony alongside the cart, and hauled himself up to peer over the side.

Anneliese reclined on the straw, her gown stuck with stalks, her bodice strings hanging haphazardly from her provocatively adjusted bosom.

'Hello there, missy. Didn't realize these fellers had company. Friends of yours, are they?'

'Me father's hired men,' Anneliese improvised, reddening beneath the dragoon's gaze – the flat-eyed stare of a hungry leopard. 'I'm Anna Mason, d'you know my father, the corn-factor?'

'Ah,' the dragoon breathed at last. 'I don't recall I do. Moving on, you say?'

'Well, the soldiers have taken so much of his . . . ah, but here's me telling you our problems.'

The dragoon in the pea-green coat nodded understandingly. 'Where you off to, then? You'll never make Wells by nightfall.'

'Oh, we shall stop presently. Maybe you'll show us the way? Suggest a place where we can rest and, you know, have a bite.'

The dragoon grinned.

'Ah, I'm partial to a bite myself,' he said delightedly, licking his lips as he regarded the black-haired beauty making herself comfortable in the back of the wagon. He clicked his tongue again, remembering his mission with a lustful twinge of resentment. Captain Speedwell would flog him at the tumbler if he caught him dallying about with some honey blob in a cart. Not with that bliddy scarlet devil of a horseman on the loose. He sat back in his saddle with a sigh, glanced back at the miserable statues on the running-board.

'You ain't see a young whippersnapper on a big bay, have you? In a hurry, he was,' the dragoon asked.

'That rude bugger in red? The one as wanted a ride in our cart?' Starling enquired.

The dragoon nodded eagerly. 'Saucy student type in a red suit, funny little moustache like a bit o' down blown off a duck!'

Starling nodded sourly. 'That's him. I told him he could pay for his ride same as other folk, if you see what I mean.' He winked broadly at his interrogator, inclining his head toward the invisible girl in the bower behind him. The dragoon caught his drift, leered up at the pair of them. Butter wouldn't melt, eh?

'And I bet he wasn't keen on meetin' yer price, am I right?' he slapped his greasy breeches, brayed with laughter. The tension evaporated in a moment, blown away by his gusting sniggers. 'Ah, well, good on you, Father. Which way did the bugger go, then?'

'Well, he followed us for a while, if you want the truth, then he sloped off into the trees a mile or so back, I think he had to pluck a rose.'

'I bet he did, the slippery sod, he was shitting himself good and proper back in the village yonder.'

'What has he done, this man of yours?'

'Oh, he's not one of ours – leastways, he's no Roundhead, I'll grant yer.'

'One of the King's men, like yourself?'

'Said he was with Rupert's lifeguard. Rupert's guard, all the way down here? They'm never more than a day's march from the fightin', every bugger knows that.'

'A deserter, I imagine.'

'Ah, mayhap. Anyway, he'll not get far.'

'Not with your men on the road,' Starling called ingratiatingly, giving the brute an encouraging nod.

The dragoon sighed heavily, waved his drowsy patrol on up the hill.

'Come on, you lot. You 'eard the man. He ain't gone far.'

Only he had gone far, further than the bewildered, sweaty dragoons would have guessed. Hugo had left the hill the hard way, twisting and turning the stumbling bay through the tangled pine plantation which skirted the steep northeastern slopes, leaning back until he was lying practically flat out along the charger's caked rump. Sir Gilbert had given up, sliding out of the uncomfortably pinching saddle to lead the grey down the treacherously crumbling hillside. He had followed behind as best he could, half slipping, half striding through the boggy mulch, glaring up at the surrounding trees as if their interlocking canopies concealed a host of enemies.

The merchant gasped as they paused to rest on a bramble-clogged terrace, halfway down the hillside.

'The bastard dragoons must have exaggerated the fight, lied through their teeth about the villagers. There's not a shred of truth in any of it.' Sir Gilbert coughed raggedly, spat something into the bushes.

'Resisting assessment collectors, they wouldn't have needed much elaboration,' Telling admitted, patting the trembling bay. He had noted with alarm the horse was already favouring its right foreleg, standing with the mulch-packed hoof tilted forward on its leading edge to ease the painful burden.

'That old onion of a widow was right, mind, it was my Jamie's fault. He's never been right since he got back.' He tapped his flushed temple significantly.

'But they're all away, away safe?'

Sir Gilbert glanced at the exhausted scarecrow, shook his head. 'I told you. She'll carry a scar to her deathbed, and mayhap it'll stir up what little sense she has.' He grunted under his breath, squinted up at the hollow Cavalier. 'Ah, you come along and watch my back, but I'm not telling you where they are.'

'What have I to do to convince you?' he exclaimed. 'Haven't I already risked enough on her behalf?'

Sir Gilbert frowned. 'There's nothing new about young bucks performing tricks in front of my Bella,' he barked. 'She'd be married a dozen times over if she'd fallen for every daft stunt.'

'You'll please yourself, no doubt,' Telling snarled, sucking in his pale cheeks. 'It's time we were moving. We'll follow that stream bed off the hill, and work our way back to the road at the bottom of the gorge.'

Sir Gilbert shielded his eyes, peered toward the impenetrable jungle of scrub and pinewoods. He'd walked these hills many a time, speculating on various business deals, usually involving the deceased squire Sir Marmaduke.

'There's no path, and there's not much go left in that bay,' he said dubiously.

'What do you suggest? We walk back to Bristol?'

'Bristol? Who mentioned Bristol? Ah . . . you sly whelp, still trying to catch me out, eh?'

'Well, there are surgeons in Bristol! And more in Bath besides, with all the wounded down from Newbury! I saw Corelli, the Italian fellow, and he doesn't come cheap!'

Telling scowled, pulled the bay on down through the

treacherously tumbled scree. Leaves and twigs and loose stones formed a shifting carpet over the rocky fissures, becoming steeper and steeper as they went on. Telling was forced to adjust his course, setting off across the face of the cliff, the stumbling bay dragging and bucking behind him.

They reached the gully they had spotted from the terrace, and dragged the sweating animals down into the desiccated gash through flailing ropes of bramble and beds of slashing stinging nettles.

'We might just as well have jumped off the peak,' Sir Gilbert grumbled, ducking his head to negotiate the thorny tunnel. 'By God, Telling, we would have been safely on our way if you hadn't turned up, poking your nose in.' Telling ignored his sour commentary, used his sword to clear the worst of the brambles from their path. The bay was trembling like a leaf now, its apple eyes bulging in pain, fear, and exhaustion.

'You're right about one thing. I'm not going to get far on this one now,' he sighed, pausing in a pebble-lined hollow to catch his breath. Sir Gilbert closed one eye, glared at him.

'Well, the grey's mine, so you'd best start walking,' he snarled.

Telling raised his scuffed chin defiantly. 'Do you think you'd get the beast past me, eh?'

The merchant shrugged, running his sleeve over his sweaty face. 'Harm me and you'll never see Bella again,' he leered.

Telling sucked his teeth, nodded sourly. 'It looks as if we might have to stay together after all,' he said peevishly.

*

'Well, he's gone to ground somewhere,' Compton Speed-well grated, squeezing his greasy reins through his fist as if the strip of leather had been tugged from Telling's twitching neck. 'We would have heard from Mitchell and the others by now if he'd gone towards Bath.'

Henry. Graves shrugged his enormous pea-green shoulders. 'I left two men on the hill, came straight back to you,' he explained.

'We can't search the whole hill, not two dozen of us,' Griffin called, arms crossed as he leaned over his ragged piebald's neck. Speedwell squinted up at him. The dragoon straightened with a sickly grin. 'Leastways, not with it getting dark and all,' he added limply. Speedwell's features bloomed with angry colours, his grey eyes fixed on the deep blue sky.

'We've missed him. He's gone over the hill or something.'

'Through that lot? You'd need 'Annibal's 'effalumps, cliffs like that.'

They hadn't dared light the lantern for fear of alerting the pursuing dragoons, but by some miracle of sight or sound the five of them had bumped into one another six miles south, not far from the junction with the Fosseway. The old Roman way led south, cutting across the lush farmland of northern Somerset. The right fork was little more than a cart track, leading lost travellers into the low-lying expanse of bog and sedge known as the Somerset Levels. Centuries before, Alfred had hidden there from the Vikings, using the levels as a base for an effective guerrilla war. The track had to be constantly maintained, built up with bundled withies and baskets of stones, or it would sink once more beneath the dreary platforms of sedge and the all-encompassing bog waters. Nobody in their right mind would have risked a heavily laden wain over such a fragile causeway – and so Sir Gilbert hadn't hesitated to choose it for their midnight rendezvous. The misty wilderness was alive with sudden shrieking cries, guttural grumblings, and flickering, faery light fireflies. The damned place had given Thackray the shivers, and he was mightily relieved when his master had finally put in an appearance.

'I thought twas a dragon or sichlike, coming out of the wild wood after me,' Thackray called, recognizing his errant knight propped up straight behind the scowling merchant. Neither of them looked happy with the arrangement, and the poor broken-winded old grey didn't look particularly delighted either.

'We had to set the bay loose, lame,' Telling explained, slipping to the ground clutching his pistols. Sir Gilbert crouched over the exhausted grey, nodded up at his ever loyal clerk.

'Good man, Starling, I shan't forget this,' he said.

Starling accepted the praise with a shrug, his thin lips twitching in bleak imitation of a smile. He had heard it all before, of course. He had been in Morrison's thankless service for years, and yet remained miserably content with their symbiotic arrangement. It was a wild, wicked world out there, no place for a little man like Starling to go it alone. The calculating clerk did not resent his dependence – making do with the crusts and crumbs from the merchant's table. It was by far the best-laid table he'd ever share.

'Did you see them dragoons?' Thackray asked, watching his master climb up on the back of the wagon. Telling paused, startled by the rustle in the straw as Anneliese made room for him.

'What are you doing here?'

'I'm coming with you. To see Jamie,' she explained, attempting to impersonate Bella's usually effective glad-eyed simper. Sir Gilbert squinted in at her, shook his head. The only Ramsay with a bit of spirit and not a bollock to call her own, he thought coarsely.

'I don't know what your mother will think, taking up with the likes of us,' he said, curiously tickled by her determination. Just like his Bella. Must be his daughter's influence rubbing off on her.

'I couldn't stay at home for ever,' Anneliese said quietly. 'Besides, Bella might need me, when she sees her face,' she added under her breath.

'And we can't sit here for ever either,' Starling reminded the whispering coven behind his back. 'Set her down and let's get on.'

'We can't leave her out here, man, prey to those blasted bandits!' Sir Gilbert breathed a cloud of vapour, clambered down from the panting grey and hung its reins around the rear crossbar. He strode around toward the front of the wagon, nodding up at the gloomy Cavalier. 'Telling, you'd best sit in the back with your man there. We've got Ramsay's old duck gun and you'll find a musket or two under the straw. Miss Ramsay, as it appears you'll have to come with us at least as far as Wells, I suggest you keep your head down as far as possible. We're not out of this yet, you know.'

Telling nodded, presented Thackray with his pistols while he went in search of the muskets.

'I can shoot. Mother taught me how when we held the house for the King,' Anneliese announced eagerly. Sir

Gilbert smiled weakly, grunting with the effort as he pulled himself up beside Starling and nodded him on. The clerk clicked the reins over the horses' backs, urging the tired team out onto the road. The cold gravel glimmered in the pale starlight, illuminating their creaking path out over the croaking swamp.

Mitchell and his scouts had gotten themselves lost. Three others had taken themselves off somewhere, and the rest were grumbling like monks as they followed their irate commander back down the damned gorge, through the still fuming village, and out the other side. Kilmersden Hall, the draughty pile merchant Morrison had pressed into service as his unofficial headquarters when the war had gotten too hot for him down in the village, had proved to be deserted. Apart from the broken-down old widder-woman and her scrawny servant the hall had been emptier than a looted tomb.

But the glistening tracks in the overgrown path leading up to the old place had told their own story.

'You bloody fool, Graves, hoodwinked by some flirt-gill with her tabs hanging out!' Speedwell had growled when they had eventually pieced together the mystery of Telling's escape. 'He must have been hiding under the straw, you damned fool!'

'Ah, Captain, if he was that damned gal ought to be on the stage up Lunnun. Cool as you like, the saucy cat.'

Speedwell hadn't had time for further explanations. He had taken the dwindling troop back down the hill and off towards Wells, following the tracks in the rutted road.

'Come ahead, you bastards, keep up,' he cried, twisting in his saddle as the stragglers fell further and further behind. He couldn't believe his own eyes when he realized the damned fools had fled down the wrong road, out over the marshes!

Cold night. Brittle stars. A fresh breeze getting up from the east, carrying the pungent flavours of the Somerset swamps. By God, he'd follow that bastard Telling into the sea if necessary.

'Can you hear that? Captain, hang on, I can hear it!' Griffin called, urging his piebald up with his own mount.

'Hear what?'

'The wagon, it was creaking like a whore's floorboards!'

Speedwell tilted his head, strained his ears as he listened. Unmistakable! The rhythmic clank and clatter of a heavily laden wain! He kicked his pony on, filled with fierce determination.

'With me, you bastards, with me!' Speedwell leaned over and drew his pistol, spurring his labouring beast on into the black night. 'Close up, they'll never shake us in that damned tub!'

Griffin, several stones lighter than his captain, pulled ahead, cackling like a banshee. Graves, several stones heavier, fell behind with the rest. Speedwell was furious, wrenching his neck as he peered behind him. An indistinct mob of knackered nosebags, drifting further and further back, the white road empty. The trees had fallen away from the road as they left the gorge behind them, crossed the narrow network of meadows bordering the levels. Only one way to go now, only one path across the sliding meres.

The creaking wagon shrieked and whistled, heralding its own progress down the bumpy causeway. He could see it now, a massive grey ship on a silver sea, gloriously visible against the carelessly marshalled rushes and reeds. The grass banks fell away steeply to either side, duckweed ditches filled with scuttling voles and flapping waterfowl.

'Telling!' Speedwell shouted a challenge, overtaking Griffin once again, leading the mad steeplechase over the narrow causeway between the fragrant shifting bogs. The dragoons were strung out in a ragged mob, sixty yards from Speedwell to the cursing back marker.

The blast, when it came, lit the night like a bonfire. A spectral glare to terrify the marsh sprites and scatter the fuming fireflies. Griffin caught the worst, the hail of pellets tearing strips from his stolen coat and clawing scraps of flesh from his scrawny shoulders. The wounded man was torn from his saddle and hurled into the road, his blinded pony whinnying in pain and bounding to the left, collapsing in a tangle of blood-flecked legs down the steeply angled bank. Speedwell's pony took a handful of shot across its streaked chest, buckled up in agony and collided with the rutted track, spilling Speedwell out of his saddle and over its impossibly twisted neck. The captain held his hands over his face as he hit the ground with appalling force, knocking out several teeth as well as what was left of his wind. Speedwell slid over the stony causeway, his clothing tattered by the fearsome impact. Graves automatically hunched his enormous shoulders, his powerful thighs gripping his unfortunate slate-grey cob as the maddened pony veered to the right. He yanked back on the reins, checking its panic-stricken stride before it followed its friend into the shifting bogs. The rest of the band halted in a cloud of dust, staring down at the bloody wreckage of man and beast, completely unnerved by the terrifyingly unexpected blast.

'Griff's down!'

'Where's the cap'n?'

'What they got in the back o' that cart, a bliddy culverin?'

Graves swallowed hard, walked his trembling pony in a tight circle as he peered up the silver arrow of the causeway. In the supernatural silence following the blast, he could hear the wagon slowing down, safe in the enveloping darkness. Slowing down?

'We'll go round 'em!'

'Into that bog? You can go first, Martin Pike!'

'Stay where you are,' Graves barked, resentfully gripped by shivers of fright. 'There's not more than one or two of 'em armed, we'll catch 'em up quick enough across the causeway,' he shouted, imposing his authority over the wavering troop in the absence of its mad captain.

'Ah, sod 'im, and you, Harry. They've plenny of time to reload that cannon and we can't 'zactly outflank 'em!'

Henry peered into the darkness, searching the pale faces for the coward who had spoken. 'Martin, was that you?'

'No, twern't I, twere Auld Guppy there!' Martin Pike called from the back.

'Guppy, you bell-wether turd, keep your spook talk to yourself!'

Graves raised his pistol, aimed it at the frantic mob of riders packed into the darkness behind him. He could sense rather than see them, sense their muttering resentment. 'Are you going to charge or not?' he drawled, daring them.

The determined crunch of heavy boots brought him around in a second. He bent his head, peered into the impenetrable gloom.

'Captain Speedwell, sir?' he enquired, transferring the pistol into his right hand. By God, he'd be for it if the scar-faced bastard thought he was trying to take over his troop!

The fearsome footsteps crashed closer. Crunch crunch crunch through the closely packed gravel. Graves felt the blond hackles on the back of his neck prickle in agitation.

'Is that you, Captain?' he repeated.

His answer was wrapped up in a shower of sparks, cocooned in a blossoming white cloud. A teeth-rattling bang as the pistol sent a lead ball flying through the night, a deadly breath across Graves' face. A split second later the dragoon reacted, throwing his arm across his blinded features, accidentally squeezing his trigger. His startled horse bounded sideways, crashing into the terrified herd packed in behind.

The second shot came from the left; angled upwards, it struck one of the ponies in the forehead, the startled beast collapsing with a throaty grunt and shudder. The rider leapt out of the saddle and bolted into his companions, grabbing for their stirrup leathers and shrieking like a goose-girl.

Hugo Telling doubled along the steep bank, his riding boots dislodging great slabs of soil which slid into the swamp with a resounding slap. He had fired both his pistols, but had also lifted Griffin's from his brittle fingers. The stampeding herd had backed away from the flashes, the dismounted dragoon waving his arms in their terrified faces. Telling was close enough to see the terror in their eyes, pinched features staring into the night, not even looking for him down there, down on the bank. He raised the pistol and fired. The pistol fizzed in his fist, and the scowling Cavalier threw the useless weapon into the swamp.

The dragoons had had enough though, unnerved by the relentless supernaturally delivered barrage. 'It's a trap! Save yourselves!'

The men at the rear turned their ponies and spurred off back the way they had come. The fragmented formation snapped like ice on a pond, the terrified individuals ducking down over their ponies' flanks and escaping into the welcoming embrace of the night. Graves had no choice but to go with them, Martin Pike – his pony lying dead in the road – clinging to his huge leg with his pale grey eyes standing out on stalks. Graves glowered down at him, flailing at the youngster's groping hands, cracking the butt of his smoking pistol over the boy's forearm and elbow. Still Pike clung on, sprinting alongside Graves' lopsided pony. The overloaded beast, already way beyond its endurance, gave a hollow cough and ploughed into the track chest first, spilling Graves out of the saddle. Pike screamed, his leg snapping beneath the beast's punctured bulk. He tried to haul himself clear, tugging at his hidden boot despite the sudden flare of agony from his shattered kneecap.

Hugo Telling strode out of the night, his sword gleaming wickedly in the feeble starlight. Pike froze, clutching the road as the red-suited demon stalked forwards. Graves, panting like a broken-winded gun dog, scuttled towards the bank on his hands and knees. There was a scatter of stones and a splash as he disappeared into the bog.

'Telling, come away, for God's sake,' a hoarse voice

called from the darkness. 'Bloody idiot'll get us all killed, mark my words!'

Telling looked down at the trapped youngster, propped up on his torn elbows beneath the whimpering pony.

'Don't ever make sport with me again, boy, or I swear I won't rest till I've butchered the lot of you,' he hissed, his cold breath fogging his narrow features. 'And don't ever, ever come after my fiancée either.'

'No, sir!' Martin Pike squealed, nodding his head eagerly over a maddening crescendo of creaks and groans. He glanced to one side as the great grey hull of the wagon rolled into view, misty figures peering over the running-board. He thought for one horrible moment they were going to run it right over him.

'Telling, I won't tell you again, get back in the cart!'

The Cavalier straightened up, backed away from the frightful carnage.

'The boy's been at the rye bread again, he's quite cracked up, I tell you! Charging through the rogues single-handed, who does he think he is?'

Telling sighed. 'I've seen true-hearted men charge ten times their number of rebels and scatter all before them,' the captain called back. 'You wouldn't understand, Morrison, it's a question of *belief*.'

Morrison snorted, shook his head as the young monkey clambered into the wagon using the enormous wheel as a climbing frame.

Oh-ho, *belief*, was it? Belief his hare-brained antics might win his daughter's hand?

Telling dropped back down into the cart, breathing heavily. His heart was pounding erratically inside his chest and his hands were shaking like an old pot-walloper's gin-gnarled paws. He clamped them together around his knees, smiled thinly at Anneliese, crouching with her dark head ducked down safely behind the running-board. She stared at him, her pretty mouth forming a perfect red O.

'We thought you'd fallen off,' she croaked, eyes brimming with tears of relief.

'They would have caught up with us eventually,' he said woodenly.

By God, he'd hardly thought what he was doing as he had boosted himself over the side and doubled off into the darkness. The dragoons might have been lined up ready for him, muskets aimed at his heart.

How had he ever convinced himself they wouldn't be ready for him, that they wouldn't stand and fight? By imagining it had been Bella in the wagon, looking on approvingly while he saved their bacon, that's how.

'The next time you feel the urge to show off in front of a young lady, give me a little warning first, eh?' Sir Gilbert called sulkily, breaking Telling's aching reverie. The merchant smoothed his well-ruffled feathers. 'Good skin don't grow from seed, and I want to stay attached to mine a while yet, boy,' he growled.

Telling peered up at the bulky merchant, squatting beside his superbly indifferent clerk. Starling had barely moved a muscle as the night erupted around them. He didn't have skin at all, just so much pink frost over his wasted frame. A leather bellows for a heart, a leaky faucet for a mouth, and a couple of rusty washers for eyes.

'I knew what I was doing,' Telling repeated, mastering the slight tremor in his tone. 'Now perhaps you will do me the honour of informing me where we are going.'

Sir Gilbert deflated a little, running his thick palm over his sprightly white curls.

'We'd never have escaped without him, and besides, Bella would want him with her, a time like this.'

Anneliese's indignant observation must have hit home.

'Yes, well. I suppose you have redeemed your reputation a little, seeing as how you led the buggers up to the hall in the first place.'

Telling ran his tongue over his lips, rolled his eyes at the prickly merchant. Sir Gilbert breathed a trident of vapour into the chill air.

'My brother's place, if you must know. Down south aways. Blind Man's Moor.'

'On the coast?'

'That was the general idea,' Sir Gilbert agreed. 'I reckoned they might smell a rat if we'd hauled a boat a hundred miles inland for her, besides, the air might do her some good,' he growled, looking away.

Telling relapsed into a brooding silence as the wagon resumed its rolling, creaking voyage over the levels. His own sweetheart, hiding out on the lonely moors? He pictured their joyous reunion, her fractured face still beautiful despite its terrible wounds and weals, their . . .

'And don't think for a moment you've got my blessing for my Bella's hand, boy, because mad buggers who charge troops of horse by their lonesomes aren't top of my list of prospective sons-in-law,' Morrison barked, reasserting his authority over the cartload of fugitives.

Twenty feet to his right, halfway down the bank of the silvery causeway, Compton Speedwell let his torn head rest gently on the blood-splattered sleeve of his riding coat.

He'd heard all he needed now.

PENMETHOCK HARBOUR,

DORSET

The village of Penmethock had grown up like a colony of red-tiled limpets, a huddle of windswept hovels crouching in a glaciated basin between the cliffs. A tumbling brook whispered lists of secrets as it scurried and sorted its boulder-strewn bed between vast walls of rock which seemed about to engulf it, winding and falling, stooping and sliding around the long-abandoned cataracts. The ancient glacier had turned belly-up when it had finally gouged a path to the sea, shifting towards the west to tear a vast bay in the otherwise formidable coastline. Sheltered by the outflung arm of the cliff, the shallow bay made a perfect anchorage. Over the years the toiling fisherfolk had hauled boulders and slabs from the nearby quarries and put the finishing touches to nature's grand design. A stubby grey mole, encrusted with the ancient detritus of the ocean, rode out from the western bay towards a similar, stubbier structure beneath the Hare Rock – the massive headland which had turned the mighty glacier aside. The massive stacks of rock had broken and shifted over the ages, forming a towering shoulder crowned with two jagged peaks – the hare's ears which had given the headland its unusual name.

Sheltered by the cliffs from the sea and a range of

sturdy, sheep-cropped hills from the downs of western Dorset, the village had grown up and in on itself. Marriage between the village girls and boys was as strictly overseen as horse-breeding, and liaisons outside the village were frowned upon. Penmethock took care of its own, a granite guardian to a brood of lichen-nibbled houses. The headland along with the vast tract of moorland surrounding it belonged to the Earl of Dartland, a fabulously rich West Country magnate who had managed to oversee his scattered empire despite the pressures exerted by his variously belligerent neighbours. The earl had managed to retain his political independence while the rival parties fell out, maintaining his allegiance to the Crown despite an ever-closing ring of hostile garrisons.

Now, in the late autumn of the first year of war, those enemy outposts were being swallowed up one by one by the all-powerful Royalists. The western counties of Dorset, Devon, and Somerset had been Parliamentary strongholds last October, but the triumphant advance of Sir Ralph Hopton from Cornwall, and the subsequent mopping-up campaign undertaken by Prince Maurice, had completely transformed the situation. Vast tracts of land had been cleared of Roundhead forces, and the shattered merchants and their Puritan-minded supporters had either escaped to the east or had knuckled under to the new regime. Parliamentarian forces which had earlier that summer been threatening strongholds like Corfe Castle – with a singular lack of success – had hurried back to their bases, convinced the end was nigh. The tables had been turned, the Parliamentarian forces which had wandered at will becoming besieged in their turn. Hundreds had been cut off in Plymouth, more rebels had been shut up in Lyme, and a hard core of Dorset Roundheads had been blockaded in the windy peninsulas around Poole, where they were only maintained by the fanatical zeal of their leaders and ever-present warships belonging to the Earl of Warwick's Parliamentary fleet. The King might not have been able to claim a garrison in every town, but his generals' skilful progress had for all intents and purposes emasculated the opposition.

Exeter had fallen in September, even as King Charles' own armies failed before Gloucester's wool-packed walls. Dartmouth had followed, along with a string of smaller castles and towns.

The King's triumph had not, however, come cheap. His loyal West Country retainers had been bled white by both sides, and many great families had lost sons as well as their best plate to the voracious demands of His Majesty's war.

The Earl of Dartland's eldest son, Anthony Dyle, third Baron Clavincale, had determined on taking a rather more active role in the war than his canny father. He had supervised the confiscation of various rebels' goods and chattels, combing their mills and farms and manor houses for war *matériel* and plate that he could turn into hard cash for the King's strained war chest. He had of course diverted some of the cash he had raised into the family estates, small recompense for all his good work on His Majesty's behalf.

But acting as agent and bailiff to the Crown had not suited Anthony's ambitious temperament. It was soldiers, not salesmen, who were claiming the King's ear now.

Anthony had decided to raise and equip a regiment of men, and had set off for Gloucester in high spirits, confident he could conquer all before him. It was here he had apparently fallen for a bewitching trollop with a mane of auburn hair who had reportedly stolen his mind and addled his wits.

The full details of the sorry case would never be known.

The letter the earl had received from Lord Falkland (shortly before his own death at Newbury) had been somewhat vague as to the precise sequence of events which had resulted in Anthony's brutal murder. As far as the provost had been able to make out, poor Anthony had been lured into the woods by this slavish minx, and then set upon by a gang of ruffians. He had been slaughtered in the struggle, apparently defending the slut's questionable virtues from the footpads. King Charles had added his own sympathetic note to Falkland's letter, thanking him profusely for the ultimate sacrifice he had made, and assuring the earl that his own troubled family was at his service.

But fine words wouldn't bring Anthony back, and the gouty old earl was too old and ill to go chasing about the country pursuing his son's neglected business interests, much less seek his revenge against the authors of his son's death.

They went unpunished, but the bitter bile they had poured into his guts soured and twisted him by the hour, allowing him no rest. He simmered and ranted, his wasted flesh drying up like seaweed on a beach while pressing hatreds bred gall in the snapping oyster of his heart. He bawled at the servants and berated his cowering family for any minor misdemeanour. He set the citizens the same exacting standards, punishing any crime or failure with draconian ruthlessness. But although he hammered out his hatreds upon his own fiercely loyal flock, he had bile besides for the unfortunate wretches who came into his clutches from the opposing party. Soldiers, sailors, and sympathizers had all suffered beneath his bloody henchmen's whips and clubs. Beaten, tortured, and beaten again, his rebel prisoners soon learned there was more than one devil at work on God's earth.

The glowering earl had set himself up as judge and jury, merciless master of the local assizes. There was only one way to deal with scum of that stamp: hurling them bodily from the jagged cliffs to their much-deserved deaths. Such a course would have quickly made him new enemies at court, however. The weak-willed King and the watery reptiles who advised him had adopted more conciliatory methods, encouraging his satraps to show mercy to the mutinous dogs who roamed his realm. Instead of a one-way walk to the windswept cliffs, he set the rogues to work in the quarries along the coast, chipping boulders to rocks, rocks to pebbles, pebbles to sand. Great blocks of crudely dressed stone were then transported along the coast to help prop up Royalist strongholds – to repair the puny holes Roundhead culverins had knocked in the graceful curtain walls of Corfe Castle, forty miles down the road. The labour was unrelentingly brutal – the earl had been gratified to hear at least a dozen had broken down and died over their mallets and hammers. But the King's armies were flourishing and there was no shortage of barefoot pikemen, bewildered musketeers, or bow-legged sailors to take their place.

Let them toil in the quarry until the world ended or turned upside-down. The old earl would never slake his thirst for their vile, treacherous blood. Let it fill the quarry and flood the brook, let it stain the harbours black.

Penmethock would swallow the slicks and shambles,

lick its chops after each and every sacrifice, a dragon of brick and tile and granite cliff, hungry for their traitor souls.

Parliament controlled most of the navy, but its admirals and captains had been unable to stem the rising tide of Royalist fortune in the west. Contrary tides, bad luck, and faulty intelligence had pulled the fleet in all directions, and piecemeal actions, however brave and bloody, had achieved nothing against the powerful, though largely landlocked, King's armies.

No man felt that failure more sharply than Gallen Fey, Captain of Parliament's ship *Conqueror*. The formidable warship had already survived a dozen desperate fights before Fey had ordered his crew to run the gauntlet of the River Exe, in a suicidal bid to assist the closely besieged garrison of Exeter. But their sacrifice had been doomed from the start. The Royalists had set up their artillery along either bank, and had slowly blasted the brave battleship to matchwood, sinking the massive first-rate on a sandbank. Gallen Fey and his crew had been taken prisoner, and marched off shortly afterwards with the survivors from Exeter, which had been forced to surrender on 4 September. The intervening weeks had not improved the fiery little captain's notorious temper.

He was built like a boat-hook, a shaft of a man with bow legs and thin arms, the legacy of a childhood fever. His head was large, his shoulders crooked. His arid features had been burnt and blasted by sun and sprays into the consistency of well-rubbed pumice, his broad hands as rough as the bottom of a boat. They were tied now, or as good as, locked up twenty-four hours a day in the filthy cells beneath Penmethock Assizes, the ghastly red-brick lair of the earl himself – Black Bob. But although Gallen fumed and fretted at his disgusting and clearly illegal treatment, he was in considerably better shape than the survivors of his crew, most of whom had been marched off to the quarries. The senior officers had been separated from the men, locked up in the jail while their charges were put to work alongside thieves and tinkers, deserters and whores – prisoners of war no longer. The furious captain had paced his cell, forever amending the case he would present to his unjust accusers.

He could hear them coming for him now, heavy foot-falls in the passage.

He paused at the studded door, scratched and pitted by previous inhabitants so that the old oak appeared to have been half eaten by worms and insects. That was all they were to this damned tyrant, Fey thought with another savage twist of rage. The turnkey clashed his iron-bound bundle against the lock, heaved the door back over the obstructing bed of soiled straw.

'Stand back, you bastard,' Humphrey Gale growled, holding the door in his enormously meaty fist. The jailer's arms were like vast pink hams, swirled with pale brown hairs. The brute stuck his hideous snout into the cell, stood aside to admit his master.

Abraham Bacon was a short, rotund man with a sardonic eye and a mean mouth. His hair was long but combed back severely from his heavily creased forehead. He wore an old blue suit, the threadbare material concealed behind a carefully adjusted red silk sash.

Black Bob's repulsive messenger and mouthpiece.

Fey opened fire while the clerk was still blinking rapidly, adjusting his eyes to the gloomy dungeon.

'I presume you have carried my message to the earl, informing him of the scandalous state of these quarters? You will be aware, sir, of the strict international rules governing the treatment of prisoners of—'

Abraham Bacon held up his hand, smiling indulgently at the bustling seaman.

'I have informed the earl of your opinions, be assured he is not unmindful of his duties to the King and to the country,' Bacon said smoothly.

'And to Parliament, sir.'

'Indeed. Now would you kindly come with me? The earl has received certain intelligences concerning your immediate future.'

'And that of my men, I trust.'

Bacon pursed his lips. 'Your superiors in Whitehall have not seen fit to arrange an exchange for the common men.'

So that was it, they were to be exchanged, just as Captain Truscott had predicted?

'I will not be leaving this damned crab pot without my men,' Fey said stoutly.

Bacon ignored his familiar outburst, watched the captain jam his leather hat over his greasy brown locks and stride out of the door. Truscott, a one-eyed veteran who had slipped out of Dartmouth shortly before its fall only to be intercepted by a Royalist patrol on the outskirts of Plymouth, was already waiting in the dimly lit hall, along with half a dozen other officers. The party was closely guarded by an equal number of heavily armed jailers, under the bull's-eye stare of Humphrey Gale. As well as keys and leather knout, the broad-shouldered pirate had stuffed a pair of pistols under his belt and wore what looked like a Muslim scimitar, the jewelled hilt curving down beside his baggy blue breeches.

It was clear to Fey he and his men had fallen into the hands of savages, Barbary pirates holed up on the Dorset coast, as out of place and alien as sharks in a village pond.

He fumed and stared as he followed the shuffling men down the hall and up the steep, slimy stairs toward the blinding white light of the courtroom.

A crude ivory crucifix had been fixed to the wall beside the doorway, a ghastly totem of their savagery.

God would give him the strength to clear their vile nests, wash them out of their fouled caverns like a tempest, a scouring fire of burning waves. The images popped and crackled behind his eyes, his narrow mouth contorting as he uttered a brittle prayer. He swore under his breath that he would never rest until every trace of their repulsive empire had been erased from the coast, wiped from the rock like the salt splatter of a seagull.

He ducked his head beneath the smooth stone rafter and stepped out into the courtroom, blinking at the barbed sunlight which streamed in freely from the tall, barred windows. He was shoved along with the others, herded into the dock like a common criminal. The guards pushed and prodded them into line before the sober stare of the judge. Fey wiped his eye on the shoulder of his coat, focused slowly on Black Bob himself.

The wizened old man in the bulky robes reminded him sharply of a shrunken head he had picked up for a shilling on the Gambia River during one of the endless passages of his youth, years before the war. The earl's skin was shrivelled to his staring skull, the bright eyes dark as raisins in their sunken sockets. His mouth was a rat trap of sawn-off shapes, his lips colourless, his large tongue appearing too big for its bankrupt cavern.

He wore a discoloured wig, tawny with age, kippered with resinous smokes, the curled mats hanging limply over his shoulders.

Fey watched Bacon stride beneath the dock and take up his position in the large chair beneath the judge's altar.

Black Bob peered across the empty courtroom at the prisoners, his lip curling from his equally discoloured teeth.

'Answer your names,' Bacon called, lifting a sheaf of papers from his desk. 'Fey?'

'Aye. And I should like to—'

Humphrey Gale shoved him in the back, crushing him against the iron rail which ran along the front of the dock. 'Shut your trap, Roundhead, or I'll break your back, so 'elp me!' Gale murmured in his ear. The furious captain knew it was no idle boast.

'Answer your names and no more,' Bacon called. 'Trembucket.'

'Aye!'

'Porter.'

'Here.'

'Truscott.'

'Aye.'

'All prisoners present and correct, your honour,' Bacon said, nodding up at the desiccated tyrant crouched above him.

The earl appeared to shiver with revulsion, horrified by the ignominious duty he was about to perform. Black Bob glanced down, straightening the springy scroll he had laid out before him. He picked the brittle red seal in distraction, his fingers curling in anger as he reread the curt instruction. His Majesty had agreed to exchange *certain rebells* in the earl's keeping with some noted *gentlemen*, of worthy and loyal service to the Crown, who had been lately captured by the forces of the Parliament. Major Brinks, of Porthcurn's foot, bearer, to oversee the exchange outside *Plimouth*, with a certain Colonel Roland Bean, at a convenient date to be fixed.

The earl scowled with bitter frustration, mortified these scoundrels who had encouraged the unruly mobs of England to such hideous disorders should be returned to perform the same function all over again.

'It has been decreed,' he said scathingly, 'that you are to be exchanged with certain gentlemen of quality who have fallen into the hands of your treacherous chiefs. You will go with this gentleman,' he nodded down at the stocky officer waiting beside Bacon, 'under guard, to Plymouth, where you will be reunited with your people.' He spat. 'And may God teach you cooler counsels, because I give notice to each and every one of you that I will not be as lenient to any who come before me again – no matter how I am instructed,' he added darkly.

Fey bristled, shrugging himself free of Gale's hamlike presence. 'There are clear codes of conduct regarding the treatment of—'

'Silence!' the judge roared.

Fey closed his eyes, went defiantly on. 'You have put my men to work like slaves in the Indies. I will not permit such a—'

The quickly delivered rabbit punch doubled him up in agony. His kidneys shrieked as if he had been caught in the belly with a roundshot.

'Guards . . . take the rogues out of my sight,' Black Bob

rasped, his shrunken features mottled with rage. 'Major Brinks, you will escort these bastard traitors to Plymouth forthwith, before I deal with them as they deserve, and not as His Majesty, in his wisdom, has decreed!'

'You have no right!' Fey bellowed.

'I have every right, sir! Away with you, before I have you ground down and fed to the sharks! Take them down, sir!'

Chained, cuffed, kicked, and ridiculed, the prisoners were dragged through the narrow streets of the enemy village, every red-eyed native howling for their blood. Goodwives and children, old men and awkward boys had turned out into the streets to greet the captives with hoots and jeers, a face full of tobacco-stained spittle. 'Drown the rebels! Throw 'em in the sea!'

The jailers marched on either side of the shuffling column, encouraging the prisoners with blows from their knouts and kicks in the back of their bare knees. Fey crashed to the cobbles, his arms almost pulled out of their sockets as Truscott stumbled behind him, inadvertently tightening the rusty chain which bound them together like an iron umbilicus. 'That's right, string the buggers up!' They endured the fusillade of shouts and insults, marching down the middle of the main street toward the crowded quays.

Old nets and conical crab pots, baskets of oysters and coils of heavy rope had been stacked along the harbour-side. The fishermen had left off their work, scrambling up the steps as the noisy party swung around the corner. At least a dozen brightly painted boats were moored along the Crossbone Quay, barefoot boys leaping from prow to prow like Neptune's own children. They waved their fists and threw scraps at the prisoners as the gulls wheeled and screamed overhead.

Major Brinks marched ahead, scowling at the wild faces of the villagers, and thanking God for the hundredth time they had chosen the King's side. He would have hated to have been with the shackled captives, at the mercy of such a barbarian horde. He was a Plymouth man himself, and many of his friends had made different choices when push had come to shove the year before.

'Keep back, there,' he growled, pushing some of the reeking fishermen away with the blunt end of his halberd. 'Let these men through!'

'Drown 'em!'

'Where's your King Jesus now, boys?' a toothless crone leered, shaking her gnarled fist.

Major Brinks wiped his gauntlet across his mouth. A stray sprat had hit his hat, and the oily sop was dripping down his face.

'Get back out of it, I say! Sergeant, get those men away from the steps!'

Gale, the grinning jailer, nudged his pirate mates. 'Hear that, boys? Away from the steps as the major says!'

One of the guards yanked on a length of loose chain, spilling three of the Roundheads into the filthy cobbles. Brinks peered over his shoulder, his own men closing in around him, nervously surveying their brutal allies.

Gallen Fey forced himself to his feet, the angry crowd forgotten. He was staring through the press of furious faces, the knotted clutter of the fishing boats' masts, the swooping white shapes of the gulls. Shouts and screams and barked commands faded like a bad dream in the morning. Disgusting odours, sweat and ale and fish and blood, evaporated under his twitching nose. There, across the emerald-green harbour, lay a blood-red ship.

The sleek hull was built for speed, bobbing lightly on the swell like a greyhound in the slips. The sails had been neatly furled, the deck scrubbed, and narrow hold emptied. Barrels of powder and brandy had been swung over the side and stacked on the quay, along with various baskets and flasks and tightly bound chests. The handsome cutter had delivered a rich cargo of supplies for Prince Maurice's all-conquering army, having run the gauntlet of the Parliamentarian blockade. She had been part of a small flotilla which had been set upon off Swanage by a brace of Roundhead warships. The armed merchantmen had been fortunate – capturing two of her slower sister ships – and had made off with them in triumph to their base in Poole. But they had not stood a cat in hell's chance of catching up with the insolent privateer.

The weather-beaten shore gang who had been unloading the ship had dropped everything and rushed around the quay to swell the mob. The crew, too exhausted or idle to join the fun, were taking their ease along the deck, watching the events ashore with evident interest.

Fey knew that ship.

Three months previously he had taken his own beloved *Conqueror* in furious pursuit of the blockade-runner, a lumbering ox behind a graceful antelope, flying across the waves like a bloody blur. Fey remembered the day, the God-given day when he had come up blindside of the brilliant privateer, with all the advantages of storm and sea and tide and current. He had borne down on his prey with murder in his eyes, his spewing crew clinging to the rigging as he closed the gap between them.

How was it he had managed to escape, the master of that red-painted privateer? How had he managed to prise a breathing distance between them?

By throwing his cargo overboard. A human cargo. Broken-winded old men and raw-boned boys, captured on Roundway Down and sold, unknowingly, into virtual slavery, for service with the hard-pressed Spanish Tercios away on the Continent.

Fey had sworn to avenge their shameful deaths, sworn to revenge the few poor souls they had whisked from the crushing sea.

The *Messalina's Purse* curtsied daintily across the water, the sleek bows nodding toward him in an almost ironic salute as she picked up some unseen current beneath the jewelled water.

'What are you staring at, Father? You're not going in 'er!'

'Wish to God they were!'

'In the boat with 'em!'

'In the sea with 'em!'

Major Brinks shoved his men into a rough cordon and waved the prisoners toward the steps. A pinnace had been tied up at the far end of the quay, ready to transport the party along the coast.

'Get back, damn you, those men are under the protection of the Crown! Get back, I say!'

The mood of the crowd had shifted once more. The fact the enemy were to be carried along the coast rather than being forced to march barefoot down the main road along the cliffs seemed to inflame them even further – if that were possible. Fishermen, villagers, shopkeepers, and their wives and children surged forward over the obstacle course of nets and pots and ropes and chests.

The pistol shot froze them in their tracks, the retort bouncing supernaturally around the vast bowl between the cliffs. Even the *Messalina*, bobbing insolently over the water, seemed stilled by the deafening crack.

A young man in an expensive if rather careworn grey suit urged his thoroughbred down Crossbone Quay, the murmuring crowd parting reluctantly before his ferocious stare. He waved them away with the smoking pistol, clicking his tongue as the skittish horse tossed its head.

Fey peered down the crowded harbourside, watched their mysterious saviour guide the handsome chestnut through the bitter press, ordering them to get home with a barrage of hair-raising oaths.

The youth drew up alongside the prisoners, putting the nervous horse between the crowd and their quarry.

'These men are to be exchanged for senior officers captured by the Parliament,' he bawled. 'If you harm one hair on their heads, our own lords and generals will suffer for it.' The youth's impassioned plea seemed to sober the volatile mob in a moment. 'I don't like it any more than you, to see rebels released from the jail they deserve, but the King has given his word they will not be hurt. He has given his word they will be exchanged. If we break the King's word, then we are no better than they!' the boy cried.

Fey admired his spirit even if he did not care for his argument. The young gentleman had clearly demonstrated some degree of rapport with the heathens, but had not allowed his obvious authority to be compromised by their communal madness. It was perhaps fortunate the boy was at home and not commanding troops in the field, Fey thought.

The boy looked down at the bloody sprat-splattered

prisoners. His features were flushed, frowning. 'Major Brinks, get the men aboard ship,' he called.

The Royalist officer waved the shackled prisoners on down the slimy step, the water lapping over the weed-bedded rocks. Fey watched his footing as he followed Truscott down the wet steps and took his place on the pinnace.

The crowd evaporated, muttering sourly as they trudged back to their homes. The grumbling shore gang resumed their work, transferring the valuable supplies the *Messalina* had delivered into the vast grey warehouse which dominated the quay. The fishermen returned to their bobbing boats, weaving their nets, bloody murder forgotten like a puff of wind in their slack sails. Major Brinks stepped uneasily into the pinnace, his highly relieved guards taking their places on the sea-speckled thwarts. Fey knew by the way they stared at the wavelets they were not seagoing men. Brinks took off his hat and wiped his jewelled forehead.

'Who was that, on the horse?' Fey asked, nodding at the youth who sat still in the saddle, watching the pinnace put out across the harbour. Brinks sighed.

'That's young John, or Lord Clavincale, I should say now. I'm glad for your sakes he was there,' Brinks said with some feeling. 'You wouldn't believe he'd sprung out of the old man, would you?'

'What old man?'

'Black Bob . . . the earl,' Brinks chuckled. 'It was the elder boy's death as set old Bob off, you see? He's never really recovered, if you know what I mean. Pickled him all up inside, so to speak. Now the elder boy's gone, John there's the next in line. A fine lad and all, not a bit like his pudding of a brother, God rest him,' Brinks went on easily.

The old hands manning the pinnace found their stroke, oars dipping into the slow water, carrying the boat away from the dwindling quay.

Fey stared at the *Messalina*, the pale faces of the crew peering down from the blood-red decks as they passed under the helm.

Brinks lapsed into silence. Fey listened to the thrum of the tide under the keel, glad to be back on the sea he loved best, the sea he knew like his own mind. They slipped out of the harbour, between the outflung arms of the man-made mole.

The cliffs reared above all, dwarfing mole and ship and quay and man. He looked down, his eye attracted by a sudden dull flash of light. Just above the jagged, seaweed-strewn rocks there was a broad platform of granite, a handy spot from which to fish for the young pollack which swarmed over the tide-racked reef. The little cove could only be reached by a narrow rabbit track beneath the overhanging towers. A perfect site for the star fort they had built beneath the sheer walls. Fey could see a couple of men in their bright coats, standing on the improvised battlement as they watched them go. He looked lower and saw the black eye of a medium-sized cannon protruding over the wall. Fey twisted about in his seat, squinted at the more distant coastline across the bay. The cliffs were not quite as steep, and the scouring tides had left a small tongue of sand and pebbles beneath the tottering, tumbling heights. Fey made out the dim outlines of a second fort.

Penmethock had been protected from the sea all right, and not just by nature.

'What's wrong, Captain? I would have thought you would be glad to see the back of that particular stretch of shore,' the jocular Major Brinks enquired. Fey gave him a short smile.

'I will be back, sir,' he said simply, with sublime self-assurance.

Brinks pursed his lips. Damn these bloody Round-heads. They were as bad as old Black Bob, when you got right down to it. He couldn't be doing with fanatics, no matter what colour sash they favoured.

The wind got up, and the crew hauled the small sail.

Penmethock winked like a far-off candle, and was presently lost to sight.

BY

FLAXPITS MILL,

BLIND MAN'S MOOR, DORSET

Sir Gilbert had urged caution, loudly insisting they should hole up off the beaten track during the day and complete their eventful journey by night.

'We don't want every slack-jawed monkey for miles around knowing our business,' he had ranted. 'It won't take the buggers long to work out there's something up at me brother's place if we all turn up in broad daylight!'

Hugo Telling, his nerves long since rubbed raw, took a long look around the blank features of the wild moor. 'I don't see any slack-jawed monkeys,' he said, letting his red-rimmed eyes rest on the merchant sitting up front on the wagon. The merchant sighed with exasperation. 'I don't see anything more threatening than a few lost sheep,' Telling went on, bringing the tired grey mount to a halt alongside the stalled cart. Anneliese sat up in the back, shielding her eyes as she scanned the gorse-speckled horizon.

'Not so much as a sparrow,' she added unnecessarily. Sir Gilbert simmered, shot her a ferocious look.

'Well, that's as mebbe,' he breathed. 'But just because we can't see them, it doesn't mean to say there's no one there!' Sir Gilbert exclaimed, knowing he had been over-ruled by this young buck Telling all over again.

Ever since his remarkable charge back on the causeway, the entire party seemed to look to him for orders rather than the garrulous old merchant. Anneliese wouldn't stop smiling at him, and even the normally sour Starling seemed to favour the lad with the occasional sickly grin. The terrifying ordeal in the valley had also transformed Telling's lacklustre groom into a boastful, crowing braggart, forever remembering some detail of their fabulous adventure and taking great delight in recalling his own part.

'All I am saying, is we don't want to get folk gossiping about goings-on at the mill. You never know who might get to hear of it,' Sir Gilbert warned.

Telling sucked his teeth for a moment, his bleary eyes blazing.

'I've been parted from her long enough. If you won't come I'll ride ahead,' he vowed.

'You don't know where to find it!'

'I'll find it,' Telling vowed.

Aye, and he probably would at that, the merchant thought furiously. He'd be after Bella's scent like a dog after a bitch.

'Well, don't get any ideas you two are going to pick up where you left off, I'm not having my Bella taking a stone up the ear for you!' Sir Gilbert cried.

Telling bristled. 'I'd never allow her to play the whore for any man,' he breathed dramatically. Anneliese sniffled in the wagon. Thackray nodded thoughtfully, admiring his knight's true-hearted stance all over again. 'I mean to marry her, not put her on the streets,' Telling went on.

Sir Gilbert grimaced. By God, the dog had spirit, he'd give him that. It was beginning to look as if he was going to have to give the bastard a whole lot more besides. The benefit of the doubt, for one thing. Best let nature take

its damned course, now affairs had progressed this far.
Trying to keep Bella from this burr would be the least of
his problems now.

'We'll see what my Bella has to say about it,' he
decided. 'She's been known to change her mind before
now,' he crowed.

That was true enough, Anneliese thought ruefully.

Maynard Morrison was a tall, spare man with knotty hands
and a slack, fleshy mouth. His bald dome was ringed with
a brittle thatch of floury hair and his clothes appeared to
have been pressed in the mill gears themselves, they were
so thoroughly weighed down with the all-conquering
white dust which lay everywhere about. The well-seasoned
miller stood on his step as the cart rolled up in the
courtyard, attracting a flurry of excited squawks from the
pantry. He stepped aside with a grunt of annoyance as the
girl in the blue gown kicked up a fresh tornado, left him
coughing in the fallout.

'She'll 'ave them stitches out, chasin' about like a
damned flirt-gill!'

Bella Morrison careered out of the kitchen door like
a valkyrie, with one pale hand clamped to her heavily
bandaged head. She staggered towards her bewildered
beau uttering a peculiarly shrill wail, her skirts hoicked
up around her bare knees. Telling just had time to swing
his legs over the tired grey's back, opening his arms to
catch her, as Bella weaved across the courtyard, wrapped
her bare leg around his middle with a shriek of agonized
delight.

'God's nails, the girl's lost her reason, I tell 'ee,' her

exasperated nurse called, following the reluctant patient into the yard with a fresh dressing thrown over her formidable forearm. 'She'll not mend flingin' 'erself about like a conger! Tell 'er, Mr Maynard, sir!'

The miller glanced at the red-faced cook and shook his head, releasing a tiny fall of flour. The cranky old bachelor had already gleaned all he needed to know about his vivacious niece, and realized the headstrong wench would take as much notice of him as she did of his blustering brother. He had opened his door to the wounded girl, of course, but had stayed out of the way while her battalion of nurses had fussed and fiddled, dressing, cleaning, and sewing the nasty gash above her eye.

The journey down from Chipping Marleward – across the levels in the back on the merchant's well-sprung dog cart – would have knocked the bristles from a wild boar, and yet young Bella had climbed down from the running-board as if they had been out on a picnic. By Christ, if brother Gilbert had seeded his boy with the same stamina Jamie would be a sight more use than he appeared to be now.

Mary Keziah and her formidable mother had tended the girl during their terrible journey down south, holding her hands and packing poultices to the wound. Carefully examined the following morning, it seemed the gash had looked a deal worse than it actually was. Miss Bella had been lucky.

Mrs Pride had taken over from the exhausted Mary, but had quickly locked horns with her reckless mother over the best course of treatment for the wayward girl.

'She wants rest above everything,' the miller's scowling

cook had exclaimed. Gwen Pitt had rolled up her sleeves as if in a direct challenge, elbowed the equally formidable woman aside.

'There's no rest for us, with them whoresons after us,' she had replied. 'They won't rest till they've levelled with us, that's for sure. Miss Bella'll 'ave to be up and about if she's to get away from 'em!'

'She's in no state to go trolling off about the county! It'll be the death of her if she goes one ell!'

'Beg pardon, Mrs Pride,' the obese washerwoman had snarled, 'but 'ee don't know the girl's mind like I do. I've nursed four boys and three girls and not one of 'em had her spunk for fighting off ills and chills!'

'Ills and chills is one thing, Mrs Pitt, lumps o' lead is quite another!'

'Well, it missed 'er eye, look, she'll not thank 'ee for treatin' 'er like a babe in swaddlin'!'

The miller was astonished by the girl's rapid recovery. Perhaps it was the invigorating winds which blew this way and that over the moor. Perhaps it was Mrs Pride's beef-broth possets which had done the trick, or Mrs Pitt's wonderfully aromatic poultices (concocted from the greater portion of Mrs Pride's store of roots and herbs, much to the latter goodwife's disgust). Whatever the cause, Bella had been up and about in a day, shuffling about the orchard in two, and enquiring after pony rides in three.

The miller had always known his niece to be a feisty, high-tempered little honey blob, now he found himself awed by her endless energies, her truly remarkable reserves of grit.

*

Hugo didn't know whether to laugh or cry. He staggered back against the frightened pony, his trembling knees buckling under her furious assault.

'God's bud, girl, where's your decorum?' Sir Gilbert wailed, clapping his palm to his forehead at the appalling display. Her poor mother would be turning, if she could see how her bright-eyed darling had turned out, slinging herself about like a polecat in an alley, a great calico bandage tied around her head like a Turkish pirate!

'Hugo! Hugo!' she whooped, alternately crying his name and smothering his astonished face with kisses. She tugged her hands through his knotted hair so that his slack mouth collided with hers.

The object of her fearsome assault was swooning in his boots, swaying drunkenly as his pulverized senses tried to make some sense from a gut-cramping kaleidoscope of fevered impressions. She smelled of warm bread and sticky summer honey – he could have chewed off her pink ears as he bent forward, bent his face into her neck. Her hair, released from the confines of the dressing, was finer and more fragrant, her eyes brighter and lips redder than anything his fevered imagination had conjured up.

'I thought you dead,' he croaked. 'When that oaf said . . .'

'I'm pounds better, it's a graze, is all.'

'A graze?'

He clamped her to him once again, making her squeal with pleasure and pain.

'Don't get throttling her, boy! She's come this close to a ball in the brain and you're trying to squeeze the hairs from her head!'

Hugo relented, hanging on to her like a sticky shadow. He had made do with groin-buckling, palm-wetting half-truths these last weeks, pale forgeries of her. Here she was returned to him, as vivid and vital and scorching to touch as the night they had parted beneath the trees back at Gloucester – the night she had come to him wrapped in her cloak, her stockings rolled down around her riding boots.

'Bella!' he croaked, mortified to find he was crying – or drooling – as freely as she was.

'Telling, I shan't tell you again! Put my daughter down, sir!'

'I'll fetch a pail of water, sir, if you've a mind,' Starling chuckled.

The merchant's furious rantings must have finally penetrated some forgotten core of the youth's head. He set the girl down, clutched her by the forearms as he stood back and admired his battered prize.

'She's not a damned saddle-horse! Get your hands off her,' Sir Gilbert roared, tumbling down from the wagon and trying to prise the girl out of his bewildered grip.

Thackray helped Anneliese climb down from the wagon, grinning sympathetically at the tearful girl. Anneliese had never seen Bella so pale and yet radiant, so bewitchingly beautiful as she seemed now, clinging on to the blushing Cavalier with no more thought than a goose-girl. She had always been so restrained, so reserved, so calculating in the distribution of her affections, and here she was flinging herself completely at the frail rider. Bella's stunning transformation brought a hard lump to her throat. She looked around the flour-damp yard, but there was no sign of her own love. Poor Jamie had probably forgotten all about her by now.

'Steady on, girl, what your poor mother would have

said,' Sir Gilbert appealed, detaching the blissful couple one limb at a time, as if he were separating an octopus from a colony of particularly stubborn barnacles.

His daughter ignored him completely, working her hand free and pulling the feeble-minded Cavalier back and forth as if she was trying to plant a scarecrow in a row of beans.

'Bella,' Telling managed, peering over her outraged father's hunched shoulder. 'Marry me,' he croaked. 'Marry me this morning, before anything else goes wrong!'

'Something'll go wrong with you all right, my lad, if you don't let that girl go!'

Maynard Morrison had survived his coughing fit on the mill steps, and staggered down into the yard to take a closer look at his new guests. He moved with surprising energy, striding across the yard to take his niece by the left arm while Sir Gilbert took the right. Between them they finally managed to lift the swooning girl away from the blushing captain.

'Marry her? By God, somebody'll have to, the way you've been carrying on! You'll remember, sir, she has a reputation to think of even if you don't!' the merchant barked. Maynard winked craftily at his agitated brother. Always had ideas above his station, old Gilbert. Telling stood crookedly beside his horse, his carefully calculated air of arrogant indifference as shamefully exposed as his desperately peaked breeches. He covered himself as best he could, hopping behind the tired grey cob to conceal his painful dilemma.

'You'd best get that wain in the barn, and get your-selves inside,' Maynard warned, as if it was possible the eventful arrival hadn't already alerted every other creature on the entire moor to their presence. 'No point in lightin' beacons, now, is there?'

'You'd think he—'

'AAGGHHHH!'

The brothers jumped in alarm, Bella pulled between them like a foul-hooked fish as Anneliese pointed up at the hay loft.

The emotional reunion was forgotten in a moment as they stared up at the angel on the ledge.

A ghostly spectre, summoned from the pits of hell by their lewd couplings? Maynard wondered, squinting up at the terrifying vision.

'Jamie!' Anneliese cried, hands flying to her face. 'Jamie?'

Sir Gilbert groaned inwardly, watched the idiot youth reach out and grab the rope dangling from the rusty pulley and lower himself to the ground in a puff of dust.

His eldest son had stripped off all his clothes and covered himself from head to foot in flour. Scrofulous handfuls of it had turned his thick brown locks to frost. His genitals looked like partly rolled pancakes. The youth hit the yard, the counterweight rising behind him as if he was some godforsaken conjuror from the Indies, performing tricks at an Arab bazaar.

'Behold, the Angel of the Lord!' Jamie cried blasphemously, opening his arms theatrically. The counterweight plummeted down, hit the yard with a sickly thud which seemed to stagger the daft boy for a moment. Anneliese moved first. She ran toward him in short bursts, as if she couldn't make up her mind whether to brain or embrace him.

She stepped closer, realized his flour-daubed, finger-patterned throat was jumping up and down as if he had swallowed a live toad, grey tears rolling like diamond dumplings down his gaunt white cheeks.

'I didn't think to see you againing,' he mumbled. 'When they came to take me awaying.'

Anneliese turned, frozen with horror and sick to her stomach with despair. Sir Gilbert shambled across the yard, his bristling red bulk deflated in a second. An empty gourd, a holed pot.

'Jamie,' he said, sucking his breath in asthmatic gulps. 'Jamie, lad, whatever have you gone and done now?'

'He was doing nicely thank you, considering,' Maynard allowed, taking his pipe from his mouth and pointing the chewed stem at the daft youth, wrapped in a blanket beside the hastily banked-up fire. Anneliese was crouched on a stool beside him, unable to think what she should do to comfort the boy. Unable to make up her mind whether she wanted to comfort him at all. Every single time he had looked like recovering from his brainstorm he had relapsed once more, retreated into the shadows. The pitiful shadow creature they had brought back from the wars.

'Didn't seem to know rightly where he was,' the miller went on, shaking his head and releasing another tiny flurry of flour. 'Takes you funny ways, I reckon. There's your girl there with her skull laid open as right as rain, and yer boy as daft as a brush with no mark on him! Still, they were always a pretty pair!'

Sir Gilbert had taken up the bench opposite, where he could converse with his brother and keep a wary eye on those two bed faggots sitting demurely in the parlour.

Bella and Telling were sitting a little apart from the others, leaning over as far as they were able without actually falling off their stools to exchange breathless whispers you could have overheard out in the yard.

Mrs Pride, the overlooked cook, was plucking a goose for their supper, muttering under her breath as she released rich handfuls of white feathers which seemed to float around the couple like a halo of clouds descending from heaven.

The merchant tugged at his twitching lower lip, glanced back at his brother.

'Ah, he's never been the same since he came back from Roundway. War don't agree with him, seemingly. I thought the lad was over the worse, though,' he admitted.

'He was,' Anneliese scolded, 'until we had to pack him off all over again.'

'Because he'd started a bloody riot in the village!' Sir Gilbert snapped back, stung beyond endurance by the viciously vindictive turn of events. By Heaven, he'd upset somebody up there to be punished like this. His own flesh and blood a frail bone-white crucifix standing above the yawning barn. Why me? he wondered, unable to rid himself of the terrifying, insinuating vision. He'd make amends, he thought furiously. He'd change his ways. Before it was too late.

'If I had a moment's peace from me other worries,' he growled, 'I'd get them both a decent doctor. That Italian fellow, Corelli, he's up at Bath, they say.'

Maynard puffed his pipe. Doctor? A doctor wouldn't do that jobberknol any good. He was as mad as a March hare and beyond any of 'em, if you asked him. He nodded loyally, however, realizing his belligerent brother was dithering about on the verge of tears once again. Not like old Gilbert to blubber like that, always been a hard-headed sort of fellow. Cry 'em out and have done, he thought. He wouldn't be the first father to do so, this damn war and all. 'Ah, mebbe, you know your lad, Gilbert,' he replied thoughtfully.

Anneliese looked up once more, her dark hair puffed and patted with floury handprints. She had lent a hand as Mrs Pride had been called in to dust the poor youth off, looking away demurely as the raw-boned cook had man-handled the boy back into his breeches. Defeated and defied on the trying issue of Miss Bella's convalescence, Mrs Pride had redoubled her assault on the girl's brother, taking him securely under her wing, determined not be gainsayed by city folk from up the Fosseway.

Thank the Lord the interfering old bag with the frizzy red hair had taken herself off with her remaining sons, hoping to make it across the county to a friendly garrison.

'Where there's soldiers, there'll be dirty shirts. We can start again back up Lunnun way,' the irrepressible laun-dress had vowed as they packed what little they had left into the well-travelled dog cart. She had been forced to leave poor Mary Keziah behind; going on five months pregnant she was in no condition for any further journeys across the wintry countryside.

'I was right bleary to see 'er go,' Maynard admitted, nodding his domed head. 'Time we had a decent wash-house down here.' Mrs Pride looked up from her partially stripped goose, her plump features creased with pro-fessional pique. 'But she's not a woman a man can conveniently corner, if you're with me. Gave me a piece of 'er mind when I said as she shouldn't.' Sir Gilbert nodded. Old Gwen had run her old man ragged for years. Until the Royalists had run the poor old bugger ragged back at Claverton, that is.

Somewhat mollified by the miller's confession, Mrs Pride had gone on stripping the goose. She wouldn't miss the loud-mouthed laundress, that was for sure. Young Anneliese was no match for Gwen when it came to suggesting sensible courses of treatment, but she had been allowed to lend a hand where she could. She was stirring Jamie's broth, blowing on the steaming spoon as she poured the rich liquor between his flour-caked lips.

'He'd be fine if folk left him alone,' Anneliese said stiffly, tears rolling down her damp cheeks. She lowered the bowl and dabbed her eyes. 'All he wants is some peace and quiet.'

The miller raised his bristling eyebrows. 'All any of us wants, Miss Ramsay,' he replied.

Sir Gilbert slapped his thighs, bringing their dreary reflections to a full stop. 'Well, peace and quiet don't grow from seed, as well you know. We've got to take a grip on matters if we aren't all going to end up ... regretting everything,' he said lamely.

'Thinking of moving on, then, Gilbert?' the miller enquired.

'Not unless you want to see us left fugitives in enemy territory with barely a copper penny to our name.'

The miller, all too familiar with his brother's melo-dramatic outbursts, sucked his pipe reflectively. 'Well, mebbe it's as well the laundress has taken herself off with her boys. Fewer of you there are here, the less conspicu-ous ye'll be. They don't take kind to strangers, round these yere parts.'

Sir Gilbert grunted agreement. They had originally

intended to rendezvous at the lonely mill and lie low while the hue and cry had died down. Hidden out on the wild moor Sir Gilbert would have time to address the thorny question of how they were going to escape from Hopton's blasted clutches. Taking ship from one of the lobster-pot ports along the coast seemed favourite. Finding berths for the whole pack would cost him a pretty penny, but he would still have preferred to know where old Gwen and her boys had got to.

'They were aiming to go south-east, get to London through Ham'shire and whatnot,' the old miller elaborated, waving his broad paws to represent the uncertain geography of their likely route. 'Those lads of hers seemed sensible enough,' he said with another puff on his pipe. Sir Gilbert frowned.

'Aye, but if they get caught they'll make 'em talk. I was hoping to lay 'em a false trail, so they'd reckon on my Bella being shot dead. That would put 'em off the track a whiles.'

Hugo Telling looked up from his stool, horrified by this reminder of his sweetheart's miraculous escape. He patted Bella's knee and got up to join the men for a moment.

The two brothers sat back in their seats, watched him stride over with all the new-found dignity he could muster.

'I intend to go straight to Rupert,' he informed them. 'Once Miss Bella is safely recovered, of course. His Highness will get to the bottom of the whole sorry business. From what Be— she says, the whole incident was the fault of those damned dragoons.'

The brothers regarded the youngster with scornful amusement.

'He'll spare the time to get to the bottom of it, you reckon?'

'Of course he will,' Telling sniffed. 'Once I've explained Bella's side of things. His Highness and I ... share an understanding,' he said delicately. Sir Gilbert snorted into his beer. Telling ignored him and sat down next to the miller, leaning closer as if Mrs Pride was some fiendishly clever spy. 'But in the meantime, we need to get Bella out of their clutches. Those dragoons will be distributing details to all the garrisons round about.'

Maynard ran his broad thumb along his nose, leaving a dusty trail along the pock-marked bridge.

'I've put out a few feelers,' he said guardedly. 'Course, the fact that young madam is wanted by the *King's* side complicates things more than somewhat. They've got the coast sewn up now, apart from Poole and Lyme, and Plymouth of course. Prince Maurice is bottling them up as best he can, so we'd better not risk putting her through that way.' The visitors stared gloomily as the conspirator blew another dithering ring toward the eaves.

'I reckon our best move will be through one of the smaller ports, where a little Oil of Angels might go a long way, if you're with me.' He tapped his nose again.

'Oil of Angels?' Telling exclaimed.

'A bribe,' Sir Gilbert sighed. 'We slip the harbour master a few shillings to look the other way while we get her aboard. Anything in mind, Maynard?'

The miller sat back, nodded slowly. 'Mebbe. I've heard tell of a ship that puts in down the coast aways, brings a little bit of this, takes off a little bit of that. D'ye know Penmethock at all?'

Sir Gilbert frowned. 'I'm not a seafaring man myself,

brother, as well you know.' He squeezed his fleshy nose between his fingers. 'But it rings a bell somewhere. Penmethock, you say?'

'A smuggler's cove?' Telling theorized. Maynard and Gilbert exchanged glances.

'Aye. If you like. Though they'd call themselves something else, I'd wager. Wouldn't be the first time I've had dealings with her, either.' The miller took a thoughtful puff on his pipe. 'Ye've heard of her, the *Messalina's Purse* out of Dunkirk? The fastest ship in the Channel, they reckon, and worth her weight in the gold she's taken, if you listen to the sea folk round abouts. They say for every penny that reaches the King the captain takes a score for himself!'

Sir Gilbert hadn't heard of her. He was more interested in the pecuniary implications of the transaction than some corsair of a captain's hollow boasting.

'How much?' Sir Gilbert breathed. His brother shrugged.

'Who can say? Depends what he's got in the hold going out. If he's not got a decent cargo, fifty would do it.'

'Fifty?'

'Don't start any of your Dutch reckoning on her passage, brother, if they find out the King's men are after her she'll find her weight in gold!'

Telling turned around, beamed at his sweetheart waiting patiently across the room, her hands clasped in her lap as if she was sitting for her portrait, the calico turban barely diminishing her beauty.

'We'll find it, every penny, if it's a question of her safety,' he vowed. The merchant rolled his twinkling eyes.

'Ah, we will, will we, Simon Soon Gone?'

'What d'you mean by that? You can have my fortune, sir, every penny of it,' Telling declared.

'Your fortune wouldn't get her a seat on Teignmouth ferry, let alone passage to France!'

BY

FLAXPITS MILL,

BLIND MAN'S MOOR, DORSET

Supper proved to be an unusually subdued affair, the large number of variously troubled guests on edge and frequently at odds with one another. It was as if the tensions and anxieties they had determined to suppress during their nerve-racking escapes to the south had found an outlet at last – pouring a sour sauce over an otherwise welcome meal.

Sir Gilbert presided over the fractured feast, a hastily assembled selection of barrels, chests, and other household items pressed into service to accommodate the sullen company. Maynard Morrison hadn't minded making room at the head of his table, allowing his bustling and rather more socially advanced brother to steer the broken conversation this way and that – in much the same way as he pursued pieces of roast goose around his brimful dish.

The merchant – fresher than any of his overtired guests – had placed the troublesome Bella to Maynard's right, where he could keep a wary eye on her, and his daft son Jamie to his left. Anneliese had resumed her nursing duties, making sure the grinning oaf didn't make too much of a mess with his wooden spoon. Telling fumed quietly to himself, his bent back burnt raw from the well-banked fire. Starling and Thackray were sitting at a wobbling barrel at the colder end of the pantry, with Mrs

Pride and the millhands similarly cramped in around a woodworm-racked dresser.

Mary Keziah had made an appearance at last, hands folded over her gently rounded – and rather visible – abdomen, and sighed into a seat beside her mistress. The expectant maid seemed unusually overawed by her surroundings, and picked uninterestedly at her rapidly cooling goose. The pool of grease into which she dipped her spoon was already making her feel quite sick. The news her absent sweetheart William was alive and well failed to lift her gloom, demoralizing rather than delighting her, his continuing existence somewhere in the country sharpening her sense of acute loneliness. Hugo had expected her to react to his news as had Bella to his arrival, dashing about with childish abandon.

'He was well enough at Newbury, at any rate,' Telling continued, picking at the fat-soaked gristle Sir Gilbert had served him with a moment earlier. Mary had glanced around the improvised tables, studying each chewing face in turn as if she feared she might be cast out as a whore and wanton.

'You saw him, then?'

'Aye, close as we are now. He'd just been chased off a hill by our horse,' Telling went on breezily. 'They were milling about like a flock of sheep. One good charge would have scattered them.'

'A thousand pities you weren't able to oblige,' Sir Gilbert interjected, hoping to undermine the boastful youth's arrogant commentary.

'My horse came down by some bushes and I was trapped by the leg,' Telling countered. 'William came back up the bank at me with that meat cleaver he carries ready to finish me off once and for all.'

'God be praised he spared you,' Sir Gilbert muttered around a mouthful of succulent goose. He wiped his chin on the back of his sleeve. 'By Heaven, Maynard, but your cook's worth her weight, this bird's a treat after the raw squirrel gizzards they served up back at Kilmersden Hall,' he went on, forgetting for a moment his late hostess's daughter had joined their little expedition.

Anneliese paused, frowned, and resumed feeding the selfish merchant's vacantly staring son. Telling took a deep breath.

'I was telling Mary here,' he said, 'William thought better of whatever it was he intended and had to run off with his cronies. But not before I'd told him you were . . . well,' he added foolishly.

Mary coloured up instantly, glancing at Mrs Pride as if the cook hadn't already divined her distressing condition.

Five months before, she had lain with William in a draughty stable in Chippenham – the night before the disastrous battle on Roundway in which William had been knocked off, captured, and whisked away from her. She hadn't seen her sweetheart – the busy baby's father – ever since.

Bella touched her hand for a moment, smiling encouragingly. 'There, didn't I tell you he'd be all right?'

'He may be all right, miss, but he's up London way somewheres, and I'm down here and don't know for how long,' Mary replied, holding her apron up to her mouth as if she was about to be sick. 'As fast as I know what he's up to, I'm off the other end of the country,' she sobbed.

'Can't be helped, Mary,' Sir Gilbert boomed. 'Come now, this isn't like you! What cannot be helped must be endured, you'll see your William again, aye, one day.'

Telling peered down the laden table at the merchant,

his shirt opened and his neckerchief askew. His busy eyes were watering with the brutal fireside heat. 'She's in enough trouble without setting her cap at rebels,' Telling declared thoughtlessly. Mary's fork clattered into her dish. Bella flashed her lover a warning look. He squirmed but held her gaze defiantly, determined to overawe the girl once and for all. 'If his damned chiefs back in London had left well enough alone none of us would be in our present straits,' he added waspishly.

'And you would be stuck up at home in Wainbridge, being bullied by your brothers and ignored by your father,' Sir Gilbert remarked. The shaft went home. Telling glared at Bella, the merchant's only possible source for such a horribly accurate slur.

'Well, it's only a matter of time before the rebels are brought to heel,' Telling went on, deflecting their stares by opening the debate up to military hearsay rather than his personal motives for going to war. 'The King is clearing the north and west, only London and the south-eastern counties remain.'

'Our present difficulties are with His Majesty's over-zealous servants, not his justly chastened enemies,' Sir Gilbert reminded him.

'And the only way Bella can be protected is if you agree to our immediate marriage,' Telling retorted, thrusting his plate away in a huff. Bella glared at her father, an oily lord in his threadbare throne surrounded by his distressed nobility.

Exiles. That's what they would be now. Bella sucked her cheeks in agitation. So Hugo would be forced to marry her to save her from prison or worse? Doing his duty by her as he was his king?

Sir Gilbert daubed his forehead with his neckerchief,

dried his eyes to glare down the table at the absorbed guests. 'I'll not be blackmailed in me brother's house by a candle-wasting mongrel like you, Telling!'

Hugo thrust himself away from the table, tipping his stool over the pantry floor.

'And who'll marry Mary? Who'll marry me?' Anneliese asked, reaching out to hold the Cavalier by his coat sleeve.

Telling frowned down at the ardent girl, his gaunt features chewed up with agitation. 'Prince Rupert's patronage will protect Miss Bella from these unfounded allegations.'

'Half a dozen of their dragoons done in, it'll take more than your precious Prince to get her off the hook!' Sir Gilbert accused. 'I would have thought he'd had enough of your damned antics after that horrid little business outside Gloucester!'

Bella simmered, staring from Hugo to her father, furious she had been sidelined by their acrimonious debate. 'I'm not a child,' she screeched, 'I will not be passed around like a bag of bullets!'

Telling thrust his narrow chin out, leaned across the forgotten supper at his gentle-hearted love. 'I don't think I need remind you of the scrapes you've gotten us into,' he said imperiously.

Bella bristled at his supercilious manner, grasping the table in fury. 'That I've got you into?' she spluttered.

Sir Gilbert climbed to his feet, waving his paws at the glowering combatants. 'There's no gain in raking over the past, what's done is done,' he cried. 'She's not the only one who's left dragoons lying dead in the road either.'

'What d'you mean? He hasn't shot someone?' Bella asked.

'Getting away from the hall,' Anneliese said quietly,

wiping James' mouth on a cloth with serene indifference. 'The dragoons came after us and Hugo drove them off.'

'Hugo drove them off? He was showing off to try and impress me,' Sir Gilbert brayed. 'But I've told him before I'm not going to wet my breeches like some goose-girl every time he sets spark to powder!'

Telling seemed to swell up with fury, and then deflate a little before he responded. 'Whatever I did I did for Bella,' he declared. 'And I'll do it again!'

'That's fine, that is, you'd put her in widow's weeds before you'd been married a week! At least that clown William's had time to put Mary there up the duffer before he gets himself killed.'

'Father!' Mary Keziah lowered her head, surrendering to the tears that had been brimming up in her sorrowful brown eyes since she had come down. Her condition had played havoc with her usual level-headed nature, whittling her emotions to brittle kindling.

'Now look what you've done,' Bella scolded, throwing a protective arm around the weeping maid.

Mrs Pride leaned over the cluttered dresser to Sebby Boyce, the heavily bearded mill foreman who had remained rapt by the fascinating arguments, helping himself to Mary's untouched goose. 'Excitable folk, Miller Morrison's kin,' she said with masterful understatement.

The women had drawn off upstairs to whisper and whinge, leaving the three wise men to decide their futures. Thackray and Starling and the millhands had been deployed to the stables, where they had been warned to keep a watch on the courtyard. The dumbfounded

Dorset men had listened mesmerized as Thackray filled his listeners in on the astonishing turn of events which had sent the party fleeing to the south.

'Course, we had to cut our way through a troop of horse to get here,' Thackray told them as Starling rolled out his well-travelled horse blanket on a bed of straw. 'Master Telling, he's one of Rupert's own horsemen, see,' he went on.

'Don't look to Oi as if he could blow 'ead from a danny-lion,' Sebby Boyce said, shaking his head.

'Ah, that's where you're wrong, boy. He's the heart of a lion, that one.'

The young groom's scowling hero was pacing the pantry, tortured with doubts as he listened to the miller's dubious plans to ship Bella out of harm's way.

'France? Who do you know in France?' Telling barked. 'She's better coming with me, straight back to Prince Rupert. He'll sort this business out quick enough.'

'And I keep telling you, Rupert's at the other end of the country at the moment. You'd have to escort her through a hundred and fifty miles of Royalist territory. It's the Royalists as put out the warrant for her, not those dogs at Whitehall!'

'She'll stand a better chance married to a captain in Rupert's lifeguard than she will as the daughter of a damned turncoat!' Telling bawled back. The merchant closed his eyes, stung by the barb. His brother looked between the two of them, smiled uneasily.

'It seems to me you two can't see the wood for the trees. You both want her safe, above everything, that right?' His belligerent guests bit their lips, nodding. 'Well, then. She'll be safest if she's married to the captain here, and out of harm's way offshore. If you want my mind on it, Gilbert, you'd best let the plovers join giblets before it's too late.'

The merchant closed one eye, stared at his sibling in silent condemnation.

'It's no good eyeing me like that, Gilbert. If you can't see your girl's made her mind up, you're dafter than you look.'

'She'll get over him,' Sir Gilbert snarled.

'When hens make holy water, p'raps,' the miller responded.

Telling straightened up, peering at the demoralized merchant in expectant triumph. The bristling merchant flicked his wrist in annoyance.

'He's stood by her so far,' he said grudgingly.

'Is that a yes? You're agreeing we can marry?'

'Aye. Where d'you think you're off to?'

'I'm going to go and tell her!' Telling exclaimed.

'There's plenty of time for that. And you needn't think you're going to peep in on 'em later, either! I've given Mrs Pride precise instructions in case you try greasing through the keyhole! Telling!' he called to the Cavalier's fleeing back.

From the inadequate reconnaissance he'd been allowed of their room, Bella had chosen the side of the bed nearer the window, furthest from the guest-room door. He had been peering on tiptoes over Mrs Pride's bonnet as she shoved him back out of the room, a guttering candle held warningly in her fist.

'Lord above, where's your manners? Just 'cus there's a war on you don't go marchin' into a lady's chamber like the town bull!' she said scornfully.

Anneliese had already taken off her overripe gown, and was trying to persuade Mary Keziah to leave her be and get into the bed. Bella had stretched out full length in her shift, her arms folded carefully under her bandaged head. She had grinned up at him, turning his insides to ham jelly. Mrs Pride cuffed him again, propelling him away from the threshold and into the hall.

'Go on with you, you're down the hall, unless you want to squeeze between the master and his brother! Leastways, you won't go cold,' she chuckled, closing the wretched door on his thin face. Telling stared at the studded oak, and then retraced his steps downstairs.

The brothers looked up from their silent contemplation by the dying embers.

'You two should drink to the match, at least,' Maynard called, holding up the half-emptied brandy flask. 'You'll be kin soon enough!'

Neither man appeared delighted at the prospect.

'I'll drop in to see old Moulton at Horn's Cross on my way to see about this ship of yours,' Maynard offered.

'There's no rush,' Gilbert growled.

'No rush, Gilbert? Bugger me down dead, it looks a mite bit late, if you ask me!'

PART TWO

PLAYING
MUTINY

*'Sir, the State, in choosing men to serve them,
takes no notice of their opinions: if they be willing
faithfully to serve them, that satisfies.'*

Oliver Cromwell, writing to Laurence Crawford
regarding the appointment of Henry Warner,
a Baptist, spring 1644

CAVAYE COURT,

OWL'S END, NEAR HEMEL HEMPSTEAD

T he hastily abandoned pantry was crowded with soldiers now, the old maid and her superannuated household having moved out of the main hall and taken up temporary quarters in the gatehouse cottages. Mrs Ensor, widow of the well-known tobacco merchant and MP, had felt it her duty to throw her house open to the Earl of Essex's famished and frozen troops, but had soon wished she had let the troopers stay cold in the picked-clean park. She had been expecting an army of godly, sober Christians, not a pack of ravenous, foul-mouthed hounds who consumed her larder like a plague of locusts and emptied her storehouse besides as if they hadn't eaten since Edgehill.

Full to farting, they had nothing better to do now than sit about in their shirtsleeves, chewing bones and blowing smoke rings as they whiled away the afternoon. They wouldn't have admitted it if they'd been stretched on a rack, but most were already bored to distraction with their long autumn lay-off. Winter quarters, the greybeards called it. A chance to lie up and lick wounds while General Weather gripped the world in his snowy strangle-hold. The draughty old mansion in which Henry Mercer's cruelly reduced regiment had been billeted might just as well have been a prison hulk moored in the Thames, so near and yet so far from the simple pleasures of the capital. Hoary, sawdust-speckled apples, ancient bacon, and a blanket bed on a cold stone floor, well, it was hardly the holiday Mercer's veterans had had in mind.

The old sweats moaned, the new recruits pined for their own fields, the wounded caught chills, and the weaker-willed sloped off into the frosty nights, leaving fragile tracks over the frozen landscape. Every morning a different set heading off in a different direction. Bold, determined footprints, as if the war-weary deserter had nevertheless marched off in full kit, or less distinct abstract shapes, uncertainty written large in every shuffling step.

Even the most ardent Parliamentarian was heartily sick of this enforced inactivity. If the fighting was done let the soldiers go home, sign a truce till the spring, they grumbled. Home, however humble, drew men like gold lust, tugged their minds from the grim reality of the endless war and denied them the respite their equally weary officers had promised them throughout the abominable summer campaigns.

Most of the locally recruited men had already managed to wangle a precious pass, hurrying back to the capital and their wives, sweethearts, loved ones. The London regiments were pale skeletons of the units which had fought so stoutly at Newbury, while the units dispatched to replace them complained they had been marched out of the city for nothing, if all they were to do was sit around and smoke.

The rest, lean and bitter orphans of the war, were too far from home to have much sympathy for their belligerent cockney colleagues. Many of them had found themselves stuck on the wrong side of the lines, their towns and villages occupied by the enemy party. Others had already lost homes and loved ones besides, their families caught up in the lottery of despair the armies had apparently tired, for the present, of playing.

The heavily armoured cavalrymen making their way through the tangled undergrowth of unwashed feet and discarded equipment killed their various conversations quicker than a firepike in a powder mill. The lounging Roundheads stared suspiciously, avoided the intruders' eyes as they looked up and down the littered barracks. Their buff coats had been bleached almost white by alternate seasons of wet and wind, sleet and sun. Their heavily lacquered lobster-pot helmets had been thrust down low on their heads, nasal bars lowered like thin black tusks as if they were expecting trouble.

Veterans. Hard men. The restless company could tell that by the intruders' spurs, clanking mechanically as they strode through the pantry, giving each man a scornful inspection. They hardly noticed their own commander, hobbling along in his velvet slippers behind them, twittering like a bullfinch in a wire cage. The newcomers seemed to know who they were looking for, closing in on a ragamuffin squad of soldiers by the window. The loungers had pulled the benches away from the walls and set them up around a wax-encrusted barrel, on which they had set bottles and plates, beakers and caked cutlery. The racked ribs of a chicken lay in a pool of spilled wine, a mouldering shipwreck in a red lagoon. The diners had clearly enjoyed their meal, and had set themselves up as comfortably as possible to sleep off their repast.

'William Sparrow, Mercer's?' the shorter of the two horsemen asked, taking off his gauntlets.

A burly, thick-limbed fellow in a stained shirt opened one green eye, regarded the intruders for a moment. 'Who's askin'?'

'That's Sparrow,' Colonel Tobias Fulke called, peering around the cavalryman's buff-coated shoulder. 'Captain Sparrow, one of my best,' he added, nodding his tangled white head in confirmation.

The captain in question glanced from one intruder to the other, noting the square, stubbled jaws behind the businesslike bars of their helmets. It was as stuffy as a crypt in the pantry, and only a damned Ironside would bother keeping his lid on this far from the fluctuating frontlines. He looked up enquiringly at his commander, rather more casually attired in nightshirt and slippers, his frosty thatch of hair set to resist the stoutest brush. The old man seemed a mite preoccupied this evening, Sparrow mused.

'You're Sparrow, then?' the larger of the two intruders enquired, checking the scrap of paper he had taken from his satchel.

'That's right. And if you're wondering where the rest of 'em have gone, they're all off to London. With the colonel's permission,' Sparrow added. No less than thirty members of his company had homes in the capital, and been allowed passes to visit their families.

The cavalryman seemed unimpressed with his explanation. 'You're under arrest.'

William, five months with the colours and more than accustomed by now to the organized anarchy of army life, hid his surprise with well-practised skill.

'Oh, yes,' he replied nonchalantly. 'What for?'

The big man leaned over and picked the jug from the barrel, topped his tankard up with frothing ale. Tobias Fulke gave him an encouraging grin.

'They want a word with me too, William,' he assured his slovenly officer. 'It's about Newbury.'

Newbury? What had he done, trodden on some old turd's vegetables? Sparrow had commanded one of Fulke's companies of foot that day, thrashing about with a broad-bladed halberd as he led his motley assortment of men into push of pike with a succession of hard-bitten Royalist regiments. They could hardly claim to have won a resounding victory, but it had been the King's army which had given up the ground that night, not the Earl of Essex's Roundheads.

The crop-haired crusaders had taken all the King could throw at them, and fought his bastard nephew Rupert off when he had tried to interfere with the rearguard outside Aldermaston. Once again the fiery Prince had scattered the Parliamentarian cavalry, but Skippon's brave boys had held on, firing volleys of shot at the milling Cavaliers and driving the hotheads off with their pikes. The Earl of Essex had led his laurel-wreathed legions back into the capital to howls of delight, roars of adulation.

The London mob had actually resigned itself to greeting the King.

The earl's brave regiments had been in quarters ever since, spread out in a vast arc around the western approaches to London in case Charles felt strong enough to risk another stab at the heart of the great rebellion. The cavalry and dragoons had been given the most dangerous billets, out in the bitterly contested buffer zones between the wintering forces. Beating up enemy quarters one night, the careless cavalry would be beaten up themselves the next. Neither side was gaining any particular ground or advantage, but Prince Rupert's presence – as always – was worth a fortune in gold to the Royalist pamphleteers, who bombarded the fickle Londoners with desperate tales of imminent invasion. Nearer the capital, the pitifully reduced foot regiments tried to resurrect their strength for the campaigns ahead, more concerned with stockpiling supplies in their commandeered winter larders than interfering with the enemy.

William, a tall, raw-boned printer's apprentice, had made the most of the opportunity to stuff himself silly, and had quickly replaced some of the weight he had shed, filling out the worrying fissures in his previously rather gaunt face. He had been in arms since the beginning of the summer, learning his new trade the hard way on Lansdown and at Roundway – up on Bristol's walls and down Newbury's corpse-choked lanes. He had been tempted away from a promising career as a Parliamentarian pamphleteer, and had unexpectedly found himself taking a rather more physical role in his country's vicious life-or-death struggle. William hadn't been back to his home city for four months now, five if you didn't count the siege of Bristol. He'd hardly been paying a social call then, what with Prince Rupert's screaming legions swarming around the narrow streets. He'd been lucky to come out of those battles alive, and could hardly resume his interrupted career with most of his right index finger missing and a livid scar across his forearm into the bargain. By some horrible mischance, the injuries he had picked up during the summer's fighting had progressively robbed him of his civilian livelihood, virtually ensuring he remained with the colours. He could grip a halberd right enough, but pens were trickier, fiddlier.

Even worse than the loss of his career, home, family, and friends, William had been parted from his sweetheart, Mary Keziah. Poor Mary, stuck back at Chipping Marleward in the heart of the Royalist-controlled West Country. And if that obnoxious candle-waster of a Cavalier Telling had been telling the truth, she was pregnant. Pregnant by Sparrow.

He couldn't even write home to find out one way or the other – Mary Keziah had never been quick with her letters. He had nevertheless sent a whole ream of urgent correspondence, but it was anybody's guess where it had ended up. Hanging on a rope beside a Royalist latrine, he wouldn't be surprised. William had lain awake at night summoning up imprecise portraits of his achingly pretty sweetheart. He often wondered how it was she had become so captivating now she was nigh on two hundred miles away from him. It was strange what you started to think about when you were away soldiering. By God, he had spent half his life in her company before he had joined up. But instead of settling down with Mary while he had the chance he had chosen to ignore her, preferring to waste his spare time pursuing her flighty mistress, Bella Morrison. Beautiful Bella, he thought with another pang of lust, envy, and guilt – not necessarily in that order.

No no no, Mary was the one for him now. So long as she had remained true to him, of course. He wasn't going to bring up some Royalist's damned whelp, that was for sure.

William pictured the dark-haired maid in her mother's laundry, sitting on a stool amongst a heap of soiled sheets as she struggled to decipher his meaningless messages.

Ah, sweet Jesus. Mary seemed another lifetime away

now, as if the vast oceans of time and space had spirited him away to another planet. The last time he had seen her had been that night before Roundway. Sparrow remembered with a twinge of irritation that he had bumped into his old rival Telling on half a dozen occasions since then but fate seemed to have conspired to keep him from his sweetheart, stretching the distance between them into eternities of emptiness.

Even more galling, Telling had been much more than fortunate in pursuing Bella Morrison than *he* ever had.

Sparrow had had plenty of time to reflect upon the gut-souring aggravations of his dislocated existence, stuck at Cavaye Court with what was left of his company. Most of his true friends – Long Col Muffet, Hereward Gilling-feather, and Billy Butcher – had taken themselves off home with the new man, Stephen Talbot, who had broken his leg at Newbury. William had been left with the waifs and strays – Samuel Jackson, the morose Gloucestershire farm overseer turned pikeman, forever finding fault with the layout of Cavaye Court's 'foreign' barn and outlandish outbuildings. Sam had brought another youngster with him to the wars, a gangly teenager called Gar Maynard. The boy looked too awkward to risk stealing apples with any degree of confidence, but looks could be deceptive. The spotty youngster had already seen his father and best friend killed by the Royalists.

War was no respecter of age.

Nicodemus Burke, the company runner, was even younger than poor Gar. Their little lost boy-soldier in the outsized red coat, still crying for his mother every night. And then poor old Caleb, the simple-minded giant they had adopted out of sheer pity. The daft lad had been cast adrift by his own piratical father – thrown into the sea with a dozen even more easily expendable Roundheads. Caleb couldn't remember a mother, so he had nobody left to cry for.

Damn all this waiting around, it was making him morbid.

Maybe one day fate would bring them together with Caleb's savage bastard of a sire, the cruel captain who had tossed them all overboard as if he had been clearing his filthy hold of so much rubbish. William wondered where the lunatic master of the *Messalina's Purse* was hiding now, which sea he was polluting with his demonic presence. It was no surprise William fought for Parliament, if the King had turned to scum like Cruickshank to win his war for him.

Hereward Gillingfeather, who was by far the most profoundly religious man in the regiment, assured them it was only a matter of time before they caught up with the piratical Antichrist himself. Fate had already set their sweet revenge in motion, and the damned captain's days were surely numbered – according to the wild-eyed zealot of a musketeer.

William wasn't so sure. He never paid much attention when Gillingfeather was in full flow, preferring to keep his own dealings with God rather more private. If only the vast majority of his countrymen had kept equally cautious counsels the world might not have found itself in such a frightful pass. He could have done with his more experienced mates with him now, though, answering this pike-eyed horseman's questions.

William shook himself inside the stained shirt, eyed the grey-eyed cavalrymen, standing at their ease before him. They had fought, aye, and they had suffered, just the same as these two buff-coated Hannibals, he thought vindictively. Different fights and different fields maybe, but the dangers, the hurts were just the same.

'What are you going on about, arrest? What am I supposed to have done?' Sparrow enquired at last.

'I don't write the orders, me baab, I just deliver the goods,' the horse soldier snarled, nodding his bullet head towards the pantry door. Sparrow could see another couple of cavalrymen waiting in the yard, straddling a couple of brutal-looking chargers which were hoofing the dust in agitation.

'Best go along with them, son,' Tobias Fulke advised. 'It'll all sort itself out. Some mistake with the paperwork, seemingly.'

'I haven't done anything,' William protested, rather more alarmed now. He swung his boots off the barrel and stood up, a head taller than either of the veteran riders.

'We've heard that before and all,' the dour stranger brayed in his thick country accent. Sparrow couldn't place it, much too broad to be a local man.

'Orders is orders,' the other one said woodenly. 'At least, they are to us.'

'What's that supposed to mean?'

The gloomy ante-room was fully panelled with weary old walnut, barely lit by the dust-smothered window high in the left-hand wall. A thin beam of sunlight illuminated a row of sombre portraits, boss-eyed Elizabethan noblemen with enormous ruffs and goatee beards. They seemed to scowl in at the crowded chamber, as if they were passing judgement on the miserable rebels on behalf of their own long-dead queen.

To Sparrow, deeply alarmed by the dangerous turn

of events, the various officers assembled there might as well have been chained to their seats, so many hostages to Parliament's fluctuating fortunes. The big captain slouched in his chair, his heavily stubbled chin cupped in his fist, while they waited for the agitated clerks who bustled in and out to collect them. Three days, they had been waiting now. Three whole days!

Not exactly prisoners, but as good as. Their inscrutable guardians, Baab Renwick and Thomas Hurst, refused to elaborate on what he and the colonel were supposed to have done. They would have had the greatest difficulty in picking up the gist of the charges even if they had proved more forthcoming, as the two Norfolk men spent most of their time babbling in their own incomprehensible dialect. The bewildered officers had been given a room in a busy inn, the Paradise in Lambeth, just across the river from Westminster. They were marched down to breakfast and escorted over the bustling bridge every morning, to take their place with the rest of the unfortunate soldiers presently being taken to task by their political masters.

'Three days? That's nothing,' a grubby captain who seemed to drift in and out of a deep, dreamless sleep told them, adjusting the bandage wrapped about his wiry ginger hair. 'I've been here since Newbury. You were there too, eh?'

'We were there,' Sparrow agreed, watching closely as the stranger blinked to clear his suddenly fogged vision. He held his index finger up to his troubled eye, focused slowly as he pulled the grubby digit away from his pale face.

'That's better. Took a bit of a tumble when we bumped into a troop of Rupert's in the farmyard there. Half my lot buggered off, but the rest did well enough.'

'I would have thought a dressing station might have been your first port of call,' Tobias Fulke offered, leaning around William's slouched carcass to smile encouragingly at the cheerful dragoon.

'This? It's not too bad, just a bit of a headache is all. Besides, Major Gerrity got his arm blown off, so I'm rather hoping for a promotion. Are you two looking for a leg up, or have they got you chalked down for the chop?' the blandly smiling captain enquired. Baab Renwick, standing at attention just to their left, said something to his companion in his broad Norfolk twang.

'We don't know the full details as yet,' Fulke admitted, sitting back in his chair with a sigh as Thomas Hurst sniggered nastily.

'Ah, I shouldn't worry too much. If Essex doesn't want you I hear old Waller is at it again. New army for the south, they say.'

The two generals – certainly the most senior and well-respected Parliamentarian commanders this side of the Trent – were known to be great rivals, each of them ever more scathing of the other's abilities. Sir William Waller had been making all the running earlier that year, but a string of disastrous decisions in the West Country had brought his promising career to an abrupt halt.

However, much to the Earl of Essex's disgust, Waller hadn't been stripped of his command and thrown in the Tower. He had been awarded with the responsibility for a whole clutch of southern counties, and recruiting had been stepped up to find him a new army to replace the one he had mislaid on Roundway.

'We've fought with Waller before,' Sparrow grated. 'And damn near drowned for the privilege.'

'Drowned?'

'It's a long story. We were captured on Roundway, and then marched off west . . .'

'Goar me, thee muz reckon t'have done mos' the fittin' yarsulves! We min fittin on orf since las' 'Tober, 'm I reet, Tam?' the cavalryman enquired of his nodding neighbour.

'Thee's reet, bay. These Taffs, do'n 'em ever go ann?'

'Taffs? Taffs? We're not bloody Welsh!' Sparrow cried indignantly.

The cavalrymen exchanged a quizzical look.

'What'd 'e zay, Baab?'

'Blowed if I know,' Baab said, shaking his bullet head. Further discussion was curtailed by the arrival of a breathless, overweight clerk in a bright purple suit, who carried a sheaf of papers clutched under each arm.

'Colonel Fulke, Captain Sparrow, Major Slaughter, in that order, please,' he called out, glancing up and down the expectant queue.

'Here!' Tobias Fulke lifted his arm in greeting, propelled himself to his feet with a grunt. The formidably equipped officer who had been sitting opposite the little group shook his head in silent contempt, and climbed to his feet. Sparrow noticed the officer's supercilious look, but thought better of challenging him. The lean, black-haired brute looked as if he would have taken on the lot of them with his hands tied behind his back. If that was Slaughter, he'd certainly live up to his name.

Tobias Fulke slapped William on the back.

'Let's get it over with, sort it all out once and for all,' he said, as optimistic as ever. The bungling beginner and tired old man tramped down the dimly lit corridor after the clerk, bending down to retrieve the papers and scrolls he had not been able to retain. The clerk paused at a formidably studded door, stuffing the escaped documents back under his doublet for safety. He knocked loudly, bent his ear to the oak to catch the muffled reply.

'There we are, then. Colonel Fulke first. Captain Sparrow, you'd better take a seat.' The clerk nodded toward the straight-backed chair which had been placed to one side of the door, horribly isolated in the gloomy chamber.

The clerk pushed the door open and stood aside.

'Colonel Fulke, come in,' said a disembodied voice from within.

THE PALACE OF WESTMINSTER,

LONDON

S parrow had no idea how long he had been waiting. The formidable oak panelling and vaulted ceiling of the hall in which he fumed and fretted seemed to defy the passage of something as pitifully insignificant as time. He imagined the war might have come to an end outside, and that nobody caught up in the hive in which he found himself would ever know, nor care.

The door opened with a resonant, self-centred click. Tobias Fulke stepped out of the room and paused in the corridor, a white-haired ghost come to taunt the living. He stared straight ahead, without even acknowledging William's existence.

'What have they done?' William croaked.

'Captain Sparrow!'

Fulke hobbled to one side, a string of frail humanity in his armoured carapace, his minutely engraved Flemish helmet clutched in his trembling white hand.

Sparrow swallowed, strode past his bewildered commander into the pitiless chamber Fulke had escaped. Another vaulted ceiling, criss-crossed with an impregnable resin of smoke, dust, and age. Bare panelling polished to a dull shine so that one's face stared back like the phantom features of some long-forgotten inhabitant. A long table had been set up at the end up of the room, a broad brown moat between him and the three men ordained to cast judgement on William's questionable career. Various reports, scrolls, and curled maps were deployed like paper armies at their elbows. A large pot of ink and a bundle of quills, heavy ledgers marked with pieces of red ribbon stood ready for action.

William looked up at the men behind the desk, a ghost of a smile playing about his mouth.

If you had stacked the scowling tribunal one on top of the other, they would barely have reached the ceiling, but their air of sombre, self-assured authority dwarfed the captain, sent his fragile store of courage scuttling for the mouseholes in the scuffed wainscoting. They looked like rock men, boulder-headed demigods chiselled from Whitehall's grey-faced motherlodes. Primitive faces like the totems the woad folk had worshipped before Caesar came.

None of them appeared to be armed with anything but will-powers bordering on the supernatural, but their basilisk stares would surely have unnerved a regiment of Rupert's horse.

William felt absurdly and absolutely naked, his usual cynical good humour evaporating in a moment, as he waited for one of them to say something. The grim trio regarded him as if he had just emerged from the crack between the floorboards. The burly soldier to his left had his head bowed, sparse sandy-coloured hair plastered over his rocky skull. He had spread his broad farmer's paws on the table, and sat still as if he was divining the faults in William's character through the grain of the old wood.

The civilian in the centre was older, greyer, fleshier, and flabbier, in a tired lemon-hued shirt and exhausted black suit turned practically grey through long wear and little air. The third man was younger but equally care-worn, a blindworm whose life sentence in the chamber must have begun the moment he had been born, deliv-ered into his uncompromisingly uncomfortable chair. He wore his dark hair long over his collar and sat regarding Sparrow, tapping his cruelly cut quill against his nose as if he was conducting the movements of his meagre, arctic-blue lips.

The man made an immediate note on the report before him.

'Captain Sparrow, is it, Mercer's foot? I am Jedediah Lloyd, Clerk to the Commissioners, the gentleman in the chair is Parliamentary Commissioner Frederick Buck, and the gentleman to your left is Colonel Cromwell, who joins us this day from his recent duties with the Eastern Associ-ation of Parliament's forces.'

Buck! William blinked in bewilderment. Whatever on earth had he done to be called before the notorious finan-cier, deft administrator, and terror of Whitehall? One of the most formidable figures in Parliament's all-powerful hierarchy, according to the worshipping news-sheets dis-tributed to its humble troops. The fellow next to him, a rigorous and aggressive MP and Parliamentarian hardliner, was also beginning to build a name for himself at the head of his remarkably successful regiment of horse, somewhere up in the wild north.

'We've just finished with Colonel Fulke.' Literally, Spar-row guessed. 'He informs us you were under his command at the late engagement outside Newbury?'

William smiled weakly, trying to catch one of their eyes. They seemed intent on overseeing the inquiry without actually looking directly at him, now they had taken the measure of his unkempt soldier's garb. He had to concentrate hard to follow, to imagine what the wretched pen-pusher was nattering about.

'At Newbury, yes,' he mumbled, bewildered and more alarmed than ever. Surely he'd done all right, hadn't he? He'd not run away like so many of them had.

'At Newbury,' the chairman agreed, contributing to the debate for the first time. 'We are here to discover how it was your company, sir, ended up on the other side of the river.'

'That, in a nutshell, is why you are here,' Cromwell snapped, as if irritated Sparrow had not worked this out for himself. The soldier looked up for the first time, giving Sparrow a long, hard look. William had never seen a face like it. Boiled and beaten from a ball of resin, it was a battleground of lumps and carbuncles, warts and moles sprouting thick black hairs. His eyes were large and brownish, cowlike if it wasn't for their demonic intensity. The nose was broad and pugnacious, and allied with the rest of his formidable features he looked as if he might think the bricks out of the walls and pound poor William into those floorboards all over again. His mouth was an ugly scar, large and mobile, shaping each word with peculiar care as if it was some rough nugget to be smoothed and polished. Sparrow realized his accent was akin to the guards' outlandish Norfolk patter, but he had clearly taken care to master his pronunciation, clipping their endlessly extended vowels into more manageable English.

'This preliminary inquiry, you understand, has been appointed to discover why it was at least half of your regiment deserted their posts on the right flank.'

William recoiled, stung by the appalling clarity of the accusation. Deserted?

'Were you or were you not in command of the flank company of Mercer's regiment on Biggs Hill, overlooking the River Enborne?'

William paled, desperately trying to rearrange the kaleidoscopic sequence of events in his mind's eye. The barnacled officer eyed him dubiously as William recalled a series of jumbled, blood-splattered images. A butcher's ballet devoid of any order or sense, completely beyond his convenient reckoning. They might just as well have asked him for an inventory of the grass, a list of the stars and their positions over the stricken field.

'We came down behind the London men, and marched up on their right,' William recalled. 'There was nothing in front of us.'

'According to all the reports we have read you must have been facing half the King's army,' the young clerk observed waspishly.

'No, sir, at first the road was clear towards London, we could see straight across the common, apart from all the smoke, that is.'

'The London Trained Bands were at that time under heavy attack from a brace of cavalry and at least two foot regiments. Major General Skippon gave the order to break out in four directions,' the clerk read from the report before him. It was news to William.

'The officers were down the other end of the hill,' he snapped, a brittle ball of anger crystallizing in his gut. 'I looked around and saw the Trained Bands break up. Somebody said, "Charge your pikes," but the men panicked and all hell broke loose.'

'The Trained Bands did not break up, they broke out,' the chairman growled. 'Kindly refrain from tarring Major General Skippon's men with any dishonourable intent!'

'We were being attacked from all sides by then,' William cried, the floorboards turning to quicksand beneath his boots. 'It looked like they had been broken up by the enemy attacks. My men panicked and ran off in all directions. We never heard any orders where we were!' he exclaimed. 'We were being hammered by a culverin from the left-hand side, and there was a regiment of foot in blue coats coming up the hill at us. Some of my men were running straight at them, I had to grab them back!' He paused, caught his uneven breath, highly aware of his own increasingly shrill voice. 'The next thing, the musketeers retired into the pikeblock, the whole lot caved in, and they legged it, down the hill towards the river. Loads of wounded, down in the bulrushes.'

The tribunal was silent for a moment, allowing the soldier time to gather his thoughts.

'I tried to hold them together,' he croaked.

'On the far side of the Enborne,' the young clerk cried triumphantly.

'No! Well – yes. The majority of my men ran down the hill, like I said. They got mixed up with the wounded, ours and theirs. Then we saw a couple of troops of their horse coming down the side of the hill at us. We would have been cut to pieces if we'd stayed put.'

'So you admit you ordered your men across the Enborne?'

'They were jumping into the river already, trying to get away. I told Nico— I told the ensign to save the colour, re-form the men on the other bank,' William agreed. 'I thought they might stand, if we could have a breather. We grabbed stragglers from other units, then marched down the bank and recrossed behind our lines,' William went on, his indignation overcoming his anxiety. 'Nobody deserted their post, we would have been slaughtered if we had stayed where we were, slaughtered for nothing.'

The civilians exchanged a brief look. Cromwell stared at the defiant youngster.

'We can but praise God's mercy the entire army was not slaughtered and our cause undone,' he said soberly.

'What I saw, God had nothing to do with it,' Sparrow retorted. He blinked, cursing his loose tongue. 'I mean, God would not have ... you know, I mean ... the battlefield was ...'

'I fear you are not a godly man, Captain Sparrow. A godly man is never forsaken, sir, no matter what hell in which he finds himself.'

Sparrow straightened up, silent. He nodded absent-mindedly, unable to concentrate, sweat breaking out in fluid streams over his chilled body. Cromwell breathed deeply.

'Why do you fight, Captain Sparrow?' he asked shortly.

William blinked back at him, beads of moisture stinging the corner of his eyes.

'You seem to have found yourself commanding a company, with no reason as to what you do or why you do it.'

Sparrow felt himself shaking now. Whether in anger or outrage he did not know.

'You were commissioned by Sir Gilbert Morrison into your village militia, and then transferred into Sir William Waller's cavalry, is that right?'

Sparrow nodded dumbly. Battles and skirmishes, long marches and wet weather. By God it was as much as he could do to remember anything else! How dare they question him like some common coward, he'd never run away, not once!

'Colonel Fulke,' he said carefully, 'will vouch for my

service, sirs. He made me captain after the siege of Bristol.'

'We know full well what Fulke says. I'm not questioning the fact you fought, I am questioning why you did so. To what purpose, to what end do you fight for Parliament?'

Sparrow was silent for a moment, opening his mouth before his reeling brain had formed a considered response.

'Because the King, sir, is in the wrong. If he will not see it, then he must be shown. I'm only a captain so it's not my place to point out the error of his ways.' He held his breath for a moment, remembering the *Messalina* and its maniacal master. 'But if I haven't come across the King, I've come across some of the men who serve him. Maybe he doesn't know what they do in his name, I don't know. I hope for his sake he doesn't. But I've seen something of what they're capable of – that's the men I'm fighting.'

He paused, more awkward than ever.

The civilian clerk resumed writing, his quill scratching loudly across the report. The chairman glanced at Cromwell.

'Simple revenge is no fodder for godly men,' the burly soldier said crossly. 'Captains like you, inciting their men with base and callow motives, with plunder and sack in place of good heart, have been stoking the fires of war in Germany. Godless marauders, sir, have turned their lands to a wilderness! Their men no longer remember the reason they went to war in the first place. I will have no such captains serving in my forces,' he concluded, slapping his broad palm into the table with surprising force. He paused, colouring up like some fiend of the underworld.

'However, Colonel Fulke speaks well of you, and we note you have remained with the colours despite your various misadventures on the field. We thank you for your previous good service. But it seems to me you have been advanced beyond your ability or wit, and cannot, therefore, be expected to act with the necessary authority over your men.'

William's ears burned red, hellish bells ringing through his head. What kind of inquiry was this? Hadn't he done enough?

Cromwell pursed his large lips, nodded. The civilians rearranged their papers. The chairman looked up, looking straight through the mortified youth.

'You are hereby relieved of your command. This tribunal feels no further punishment is required.'

No further punishment was required. True enough.

They adjourned to the Paradise, the last repository of their hopes (and belongings), Tobias Fulke tottering along in his super-annuated armour, William Sparrow staring at the cracks in the road as if they held the key to his corrupted fortunes, three pounds seventeen and six in his purse – for all he had done that summer.

The pair of them stumbled back along the Embankment towards the bridge, gangs of filthy children caterwauling in the mud below, throwing stones or hauling driftwood from the slimy margins. A couple of adults in threadbare coats were waiting on the slipway beside a rickety wagon, supervising the mud-splattered harvest. Good wood would fetch good money, in London's frosty streets. The Royalist blockade of the north had cut the capital's coal supply to a trickle.

Nicodemus Burke had met them in the street, trotting along beside his commanders as they retraced their steps toward the noisy, overcrowded inn.

'Whatever is it? Are we to be sent to Ireland?' the imaginative youngster enquired, following them indoors. The red-haired boy had been sent down from their billet near Hemel Hempstead with their clothes and personal effects, and had been hoping their new assignment might take him back nearer home. One look at old Fulke's gaunt features convinced him otherwise. 'What is it, Captain Sparrow?'

William shook his head, running his thick tongue over his teeth before summoning up the energy to reply. 'They've chopped the pair of us. I'm too stupid, and the colonel here's too old.'

'Old?' The officer in question was as ancient as his armour, everybody knew that. He hadn't exactly been a spring chicken when the war had broken out, and Nicodemus couldn't see his recent service had taken much further toll on his faculties.

'Old, aye,' Fulke quavered. 'Too old for field service. I'm on the reserve list for garrison duty. Garrison duty,' he repeated with disgust, baffled by the afternoon's vicious twist of fate.

The tribunal had been a sight kinder with Fulke than they had with Sparrow, assuring him they valued his long and loyal service to Parliament's cause. But the winter was coming on and there were tough campaigns ahead. Surely a younger man would be better suited to the rigours of the field.

'You know who they've got in mind, don't you? That bastard Slaughter,' Fulke rasped, recovering somewhat as he took a seat beside the busy public bar of the bustling tavern. Sparrow pulled a shilling from his new hoard and slapped it on the ale-puddled table.

'We'll have a jug of that sheep piss and a couple of bottles of porter to go with it,' he barked at the bad-tempered landlord. Their sour-faced host looked as if he was going to offer another waspish witticism from his well-tried collection, but thought better of it when he caught Sparrow's eye.

'Bad day, 'ave yer?' he enquired.

'Bad enough. Now shut your trap and set 'em up,' William snarled.

The landlord obliged, thrusting a brimming tray and a brace of beakers over the bar at the scowling ex-soldier. William lifted the tray down to their table, poured each of them a generous measure. Nicodemus eyed the jug hungrily. Sparrow relented, motioning to the boy to hold his tankard up. He poured him a tot of foaming ale and raised his own beaker in an ironic salute.

'To the swift victory of Parliament,' he called. The noisy Londoners peered over their shoulders at the loud-mouthed cretin, but raised their glasses in case the bloody oaf had connections over the river. They didn't want to be frogmarched off to the Tower.

'To the early victory of Parliament,' they retorted sheepishly.

Sparrow sighed. 'Five bloody months,' he growled. 'They've had me finger and half the muscle of my right arm, and all I get is a few measly shillings,' he complained, gulping his ale noisily in a bid to blot out the vile memory.

'Five months, aye. And I've been with them from the beginning. Edgehill, Brentford, Cirencester, Lansdown, Bristol,' Fulke agreed. 'But the thing that grips me, they'd give my regiment to a damned Irishman. Even his own side turned against him.' Nicodemus nodded in the hope the old duffer would elaborate, but Fulke lapsed into silence once again.

'I did all right, I've stuck with it good and bad – mostly bad,' Sparrow went on self-pityingly. 'I could be back in Bristol writing pamphlets for the King now,' he declared, rather loudly as it turned out. The mob of Londoners near the bar peered over their shoulders once again. Turned traitor already, had he? Typical bigmouth from down country.

'Make yer mind up, squire,' a lean soapmaker in a greasy apron called cheerily. ''S no use backin' both 'orses for this one!' Sparrow glared at the undernourished cockney, who raised his own glass in greeting.

'Garrison duty,' Fulke wailed. 'Pensioned off like a broken-winded gelding,' he whined.

It was going to be a long night.

Sparrow and young Burke couldn't follow the verses, but they joined in lustily as Fulke warbled the chorus.

'We be soldiers three . . .'

'PARDONNY-MOI JE VOUS ENPREE!'

'Lately come forth from the Low Countree . . .'

'WITH NEVER A PENNY OF MONEY!' Bang crash, as they hammered their drinking pots down on the table.

The landlord wiped the bar down for the hundredth time, watching the merry drunks rocking back and forth around their beer-drenched table. The game old bird in the shirt had given the entire inn a selection of his favourite battle songs, picked up during the wilder days of his youth. The other two had joined in wholeheartedly when they could, or slipped back against the soaking-wet bench to catch a moment's shut-eye.

'That's enough now, sirs,' he pleaded, reaching over to pick a couple of beakers from the frothy lagoon. 'There's folk waiting to get to their beds!'

'And the only reshun they're safe in the firsh playsh is cush we're here to defend 'em!' William told him with a belch, eyes rolling horribly in his ale-addled skull.

'And never a penny of money!' Nicodemus sang, lifting his young head from the table for a moment.

'Come on now, gents, up to your rooms with yer,' the landlord urged through gritted teeth. The doors swung open, admitting a draft of chill air and a flurry of snow.

William squinted up at the newcomers, recognizing the grimly stacked features of Hurst and Renwick, their former jailers. The two cavalrymen were wearing felt hats now, and had exchanged their buff coats and breastplates for rather more comfortable black cassocks. Sparrow nudged his former commander in his emaciated ribs.

'Look out, Toby,' William called familiarly, 'they'll have ush on a charge for drinkin' out the wrong shide of our cupsh,' he drawled.

The sober soldiers stalked over to the noisy corner, nodding at the exasperated landlord.

'We'der thought you'd dally up yere,' Baab Renwick called.

'Another round on us, me beaut, no hard feelings loike,' his companion called. They pulled up stools and joined the red-eyed trio around the table. Sparrow frowned, trying to give them his most ferocious stare, but his eyes didn't seem to want to do anything but cross comically.

'Ah, fair dos, lads,' Baab toasted, 'you done yer bit down yer way, and nobody in this yere man's army could think ill of yer,' he went on in his outlandish accent. 'Taam 'n' Oi thought we'd drink to yer, ter show yer thur wur nothin' personal about it, loike. We jus' 'ad do az we wuz tole.'

Sparrow's head hit the table with a thunk. Tobias wiped his white moustaches, nodded vigorously. 'No hard feelings at all, lads. You only did your duty.'

'That we did, uncle, and tweren't pleasurable neither. But Old Noll, mind, who you come across seemingly, he's a cracker for the roights and wrangs o' things. Seems he weren't too struck with matey's work down at, what wuz that place agin, Taam?'

'New-summat or tother.'

'Newbury. You weren't there, then?' Fulke enquired.

'Be Gaad no, zor, we bin up tother end of the country, loike. G' 'em what-for at Winceby, eh, Taam?'

'Surely did, Baab. Our man struck up with the Yorkshire feller in the black 'at, wass 'is name 'gin, Baab?'

Baab pulled a tattered news-sheet from his pocket, squinted at the smeared script. 'Sir Thomas Fairfax, that's the feller.' Tobias Fulke nodded appreciatively.

'We've heard great things about Mr Cromwell and Sir Thomas,' he agreed.

'Who?' William asked, opening an eye. Nicodemus had curled up on the bench beside him and was snoring like a young hog as they downed their drinks – rather more thoughtfully than previously. 'My head hurts,' William moaned. The two cavalrymen exchanged grins.

''E canna take 'is ale, that one,' Baab commented.

Fulke sighed. 'We've had bad news, as you've obviously heard. I've been at it since Edgehill, William here since the summer. Apparently, though, we've not worked hard enough.'

''Ad it 'ard down yer way, 'ave yer? We 'eard about that feller Waller, losing all his guns at ... what's it called?'

'Roundway. I missed it, but William was there. He was taken prisoner and shipped off for service with the Spanish,' Fulke said.

''E gets aboot a bit, I'll gi' 'en that!'

'The damned pirate who was shipping them was chased by a man-of-war, and so he started throwing his prisoners overboard in the hope of putting them off the pursuit.' The hardbitten cavalrymen glanced at each other as if they couldn't quite believe what they were hearing. 'William and a handful of others managed to swim for it, and they were picked up. The rest were drowned. They were dropped off in Bristol, just before it fell.'

'Ah, we 'eard all about that. Yer feller wossisname up before 'em 'isself!'

'That droopy bugger who had the bad cold? Oh ah, I remember,' Thomas Hurst nodded. 'They say 'e'll get off the death pennully cuz 'is old gaffer's one of them lordy fellers.'

Tobias wiped his eyes.

'There was nothing more he could have done. I'd wager Rupert himself couldn't hold Bristol against that sort of attack.'

'Ah, well. We'd best get on, we're off 'gin termorrer, back 'ome.' Fulke nodded as the cavalryman rose to their feet. 'See you again, uncle, somewhere, eh?'

'Aye, come up our end o' the world sometime, we'll show you some fightin'!'

Sparrow and Burke snored on.

BY

THE PARADISE INN,

LAMBETH, LONDON

The crudely cut quill quivered over the rough paper, leaving a ragged tear of spilled ink.

Williom Splodgeraw.

Will-iam Splatrag.

Sparrow hissed through his teeth, tossed the useless instrument aside, and hurled the balled paper into the corner with the rest of his pitiful detritus. He flexed his aching fist, wiggled what was left of his fingers. He'd started the war with ten but could only count nine and a half now. He examined the wrinkled pink stub of his right index finger, a small price to pay for survival in half a dozen fights perhaps, but grievous enough for William. What with the tip of his finger missing and the rather more serious gash across his right forearm he had picked up at Bristol, he would have to learn to write all over again – if he was to make a living at something other than fighting.

God's bud, they'd robbed him of the only skill he had ever had – reduced him to a second-rate cudgeller in an army of misfits and fuming fanatics. He had been taught to read and write at an early age, and in return had been indentured to his tutor, Master Percival Greesham, a Printer by the Grace of God. Greesham had set his store on the highest possible standard of work, loudly insisting his apprentices practised the very neatest secretary hand.

'If you must scrawl, go and find a privy wall,' he would tell his smarting charges as they presented their inky efforts for his inspection. William grunted with resentment. Secretary hand? Italic? He could barely scratch his own name now. He chose another piece of paper, dipped the awkward quill into the ink, and tried with his left hand.

Warlim Spallgrow.

Willliim Slapworth.

Nicodemus Burke strode up behind the toiling scribe, shivering in his shirtsleeves after his visit to the washhouse. He whistled disjointedly, accompanying himself with snatches of the tunes he had picked up from Old Toby. 'Pardonny-moi, la-la, la-la.' The under-aged ensign peered over Sparrow's arched shoulder, sniggering to himself as he rubbed his face bright in a grubby cloth. 'Trying to disguise your signature, then, Will?'

William put the pen down and glanced balefully at the inquisitive boy.

'You've seen the bill, have you?' the youth asked, unabashed.

'Bill?'

'Bed, board, bawds, and beer for a week,' Nicodemus chimed on. 'With old Toby off visiting his lady friends looks like you'll be picking up the tab, I mean, you can't expect me to.' The youth chuckled.

William rolled his eyes, ran his tongue over his furry teeth. 'What bawds are you talking about?' he enquired, with serene indifference.

'That one with the eyepatch. What did she say her name was?'

'Never mind that. God's wounds, we'd all nicked the pin,' William countered, 'you didn't even wake up for a day and a half, as I recall, so don't go slanderin' your elders!'

Nicodemus laughed woodenly, temporarily unnerved by the memory of the fearful headache he had endured following his first brush with beer. A suitable penance, he thought with a shudder.

Sparrow frowned, lifted his purse from his broad leather belt, and tipped the few coins he had left into his palm. Barely a pound now. He dreaded to think what the bill might be. Well, the bastard landlord could get in line with the rest of his creditors. Christ knew the gap-toothed screw had had enough of his cash the last seven days. William had drowned – bloated – saturated his tortured spirits with alcohol, extinguished the punishing realities of his diminished circumstances beneath three inches of frothing ale. The moment he got to the dreary depths of his tankard he had clambered to the bar and refilled his pot from the bottomless jug. Faces and funny hats, voices and jabbing elbows had occasionally broken the shifting pink mist he stared through, but he had sealed over the cracks with another mouthful, staggering off into the welcoming oblivion of the drunks' den.

William considered his plight for a moment, glanced sourly at the fresh-faced youth peering out of the frosted window.

'You've not spent a penny of yours so far, you scrawny prickster!' Sparrow accused, balling another scrap of paper and hurling the missile at the youth's distinctively spiked red crown. 'They paid you off same as the rest of us!'

Sparrow and Fulke had not been the only ones to fall

victim to the energetic new lieutenant colonel of Mercer's regiment of foot – their closest friends and comrades had also been given their marching orders, sent back to new assignments in the capital. Nicodemus had been amongst the second wave of soldiers who had fallen foul of Michael Slaughter's draconian purge. Ranters, drunkards, whore-mongers, and thieves had followed, dismissed from the regimental base at Hemel Hempstead. The chosen men had been paid off and replaced with a steady stream of stocky dullards Parliament had recruited away in the depths of the south-east, in the hope they would prove more malleable than the trouble-making veterans. Slaughter, determined to stamp his authority on his new command, had dismissed all but two of the old captains, the under-age ensign from Sparrow's company, a one-legged sergeant from Fulke's former company, and the entire (and unofficial) sharpshooter platoon. The few old sweats who had survived the vicious purging knew Slaughter – a former King's man – had already fled one regiment. Rather than face the prospect of a second mutiny in their already divided ranks, Slaughter's superiors had decided to place the experienced officer with the most reliable regiment they could find. Steady men who would do what they were told, not string their colonel up like a starved cat as their colleagues on the other side had attempted to do. Nicodemus had been given a handful of shillings, and more importantly, had been allowed to keep his prized possession, an outsized red Dutch coat with blue and gold cuffs. Nobody had managed to part him from the coat – or any of his precious hoard of coins, for that matter.

'If you can't pay your way, piss off out of it,' Sparrow snapped, barging past the youth, hauling up the sash, and hurling the innocent ink pot out of the window.

'OY!'

Sparrow slammed the sash back down, wrapping his arms around his chilled body as a blast of cold air sobered him up even further.

What was he going to do now? He could barely write his own name, let alone sort and set a tray of type. The only career he had ever had snatched away by a chance blow from a rusty sword. It was enough to make you puke. How would he feed himself – labouring? Droving? Hedging and ditching? He thought for a moment about Mary. Thank God she wasn't up there expecting him to find for her and the alleged baby. If only he had stuck at what he knew – printing – he would in all probability have taken over the shop from old Greesham by now, brought in some likely lads to learn the business while he put his feet up and counted the cash. Taking it easy while the hotheads got on with the wretched war. What thanks had he ever got for all his sacrifices? None!

The loud rap at the door jogged the morose soldier from his gloomy contemplations. He looked at the boy, held his finger to his lips, and impersonated Nicodemus's high-pitched falsetto.

'Captain Sparrow's away to the town! He said you'll get your money when Parliament pays him what he's owed!'

The door was flung open by a pair of brawny cavalry troopers, buff-coated crab-men in their lobster-pots and burnished breastplates. Sparrow groaned, wondering what further tortures the bastards over the river had devised for him.

'Good Christ above, haven't you had your pound of flesh?' he enquired, as the leader stepped into the room, looked around the squalid quarters, and tutted under his breath. He jerked his head and caught the loose helmet in his broad palm, examining the squall of black splashes which had defaced the highly polished steel. Sparrow squinted at the red-haired intruder, half recognizing the cavalryman's weather-pickled features.

'Ye've not amended yer ways yet, then, ye great pock-pudding?' Archibald McNabb enquired in his broad Scots brogue, wiping the worst of the ink away on one of Sparrow's discarded shirts.

'Archie! By Christ, I'm glad to see you!'

'Lieutenant Colonel McNabb, laddie, lieutenant colonel now,' the squat, bow-legged officer announced. 'And ye ken me man here, Culverhouse, from Lansdoon?'

Sparrow nodded at the second rider as he removed his helmet and loosened his scarf. Matty Culverhouse was as dour as his colonel, a hard-bitten veteran of a dozen battles. Five months before he had been a grown-up soldier among a gang of noisy children, a gaunt warrior patiently explaining cuts and thrusts, swerves and lunges to his pitifully eager charges. At least Sparrow had narrowed the gap somewhat with his brutal experiences that summer.

'Matty! You're still in one piece, then!'

'Thank God!'

They shook hands warmly, the Scotsman as usual torn between smacking the lumpen Sparrow in the mouth with his gauntlet or throwing his arms about him. He settled on his usual sardonic grin and a shake of his bright red head.

'Ach, look at yeself, man, half the beggars in Newgate could make a better show of themselves!'

'I sometimes wish I was with them, the set of back-stabbing bastards they've put in charge of us,' William moaned. 'I've done all right for myself, and would have gone on if that tub-thumper Cromwell hadn't put his ugly mug in.'

McNabb chuckled vindictively. 'I heard all about it,' he admitted, rubbing his palm over his pale red bristles. 'You and old Fulke, eh? He told me the worst of it.'

'Where did you see him? He's been off calling in favours from his old pals from Bohemia.' He flicked his last remaining coins towards Nicodemus, who had remained silent in the corner as the old friends made themselves comfortable in Sparrow's sorry garret.

'Pop and fetch us a couple of jugs,' Sparrow ordered. 'And if you haven't enough tell him to put it on the slate.'

'He'll be scrawling your bill on the roof tiles, if it gets any longer,' Nicodemus muttered, ducking out of the door.

They had emptied three of the stone jars, and reclined against the peeling plasterwork, pleasantly reduced by the strong, frothing ale.

'A fine set of scoundrels we're going to end up with, soused like herrings,' McNabb complained, rubbing his knuckles into his pale blue eyes. Sparrow belched, swinging an empty jar on his remaining index finger.

'Beating the drum again, then, Archie? I well remember what happened the last time you were short of a cornet or two. And what became of my horse?'

McNabb's flushed features turned to granite and his discoloured lips curled back from his tobacco-stained teeth.

'That bleary-eyed beastie? That blee and white shitesack? See you, William, ye did me no favours handing over yon cock-eyed nag to me that day!'

McNabb had made the mistake of lending William his charger to speed his cornet's courting the day before Roundway. William had not returned by the time the furious Cavaliers had attacked, and the Scotsman had ridden into battle on Sparrow's piebald gelding Jasper – a beast altogether more suited to war and rampage, although not capable of the speeds the Roundhead horse required when they were forced to quit the field. Jasper's broken-winded gait had in fact saved McNabb's life – the swiftest of the refugees had plunged over a hidden ravine, killing themselves and their horses before the horrified back markers could pull up.

'I left him in Warwick, if you want to know. In the care of some dragoon major at the castle there. Nae doubt they've set the beast to work the fields, it's no more use for war than a sack of sheep lights!'

'Never did me any harm,' Sparrow said, prickling up all over again at the implied slight. McNabb guffawed, and even the somewhat more sober Culverhouse was moved to snigger a little. 'You can laugh, but you'll not find these Londoners too eager to take our place! Half my last lot have buggered off home, and the new colonel's weeded out a dozen and more.'

McNabb nodded. 'Aye, so the auld deevil was saying. But they'll not be idle long, see you. Sir William's about ready to take the field again, and we've a fine set of Kent men to make soldiers out of now.'

'And you're in need of a cornet, is that it?' Sparrow enquired. It would mean a drop in pay if he took up his former posting with McNabb, but he couldn't live on air and water, could he?

The burly Scot grimaced. 'I've cornets enough, William, but no flag for the fools to carry,' he said woodenly.

William frowned, wondering what the veteran soldier was talking about.

'Ye ken the rules, laddie – we lost our standard on Roundway, we'll not be permitted to carry another until we pluck one from the Shagpolls.'

'Roundway was a long time ago,' Sparrow said uneasily, all too aware the lost standard had been in his keeping when the disastrous battle had been joined. It had been unusually tactful of McNabb, neglecting to remind him of it.

'Not long enough for us to recover the honour we lost,' the Scot said carefully.

'We? I was carrying the cornet that day,' William growled, determined to face up to whatever slurs came his way – if only to save what little face he had left.

'You couldn't be blamed, laddie. The troop's job is to protect the standard. If the cornet's lost, it reflects on the troop, not the trooper. And besides,' McNabb went on brusquely, 'Waller lost three dozen and more colours that day.'

Sparrow frowned, thinking hard. 'And until you take one from the enemy, you ride without a flag,' William said flatly.

The Scot slapped his thighs. 'Aye, and we'll have plenty of opportunity to remedy our deficiency, once we get out for another bout at Hopton.'

Sparrow looked perplexed. If they weren't recruiting, why were they here?

'You've a saddle for me as a cavalry trooper, is that it? Stripped of my company *and* my rank?'

McNabb pulled at his blunt chin in agitation. 'If it was up to me, laddie, we'd find a troop for you and ye could keep your rank,' he growled.

'But?'

'Well, it's the colonel, see you, William, he's a damned forward fellow, one of these damned fine independents ye've heard so much about. We don't always see eye to eye as it is, me being of the Presbyterian persuasion, if ye take my meaning.'

William didn't. They were all on the same side, surely?

'He's mickle choosy over his officers, he only took me because yon Waller put a word in for me!'

William frowned. 'I don't mean as a cornet,' he spluttered, alarmed. 'I mean as a trooper of horse.'

'Ach, laddie, you'll be better off with your own sort, there's dozens of West County men in Essex's army.'

'I've just been thrown out of Essex's army!' William cried. 'What am I supposed to do, go up north? I'll tell you something for nothing, Cromwell wouldn't have me in his bloody fine regiment!'

The cavalrymen exchanged glances. They knew all about the stamp of men the Huntingdon squire was insisting on for his 'Ironsides'. Sober, God-fearing individuals who put Christ, then cause, before every other consideration. Cromwell had welded a unit more coherent and determined – and immensely more disciplined – than any other formation in the field, whether it served King or Parliament. Its military reputation was spreading across the country as quickly as the news-books could be printed. It was widely accepted that it had been Cromwell's buff-coated Crusaders who had protected the eastern counties – the bedrock of Parliament's war effort – from Royalist invasion at the end of that long miserable summer. McNabb's superior had clearly taken a leaf out of Cromwell's book, and was studying the antecedents of every officer he appointed. They all knew full well Sparrow's military record wouldn't stand up to much scrutiny. A hulking great oaf from Somerset carrying grudges in place of a cause and with little time and no taste for the religious squabbles of the day would have been tarred and feathered for his fearful impudence.

'Well, that's his loss. They made out I'd panicked at Newbury, see, but we'd stuck to it all day and we'd have been slaughtered if we'd stayed where we were!' Sparrow exclaimed. 'They weren't there, Archie, it was total chaos – horse and foot and guns all around.' The Scot clenched his teeth, displaying unusual patience with his distressed protégé. Sparrow paced back and forth, waving his arms as he demonstrated the various manoeuvres on that stricken field. 'You might just as well have commanded a flock of turkeys as men!'

'I'm sure ye did yer best, there's no straight lines or angles on a field of battle, God knows.'

'And it wasn't just me they blamed! Old Toby was worn ragged, we had to carry him off. They say he's too old for field commands!'

'Aye, we've just seen him. At smoke wi' a passel of seamen back from the Continent. Looked like yon Fulke's taking service abroad, or joining the fleet!'

William shook his head, not really listening. It hadn't occurred to him he would have to start from scratch once more, a common pikeman in some rabble militia. No money for himself, let alone for Mary if he ever saw *her* again. The broken captain gulped the sour dregs from his tankard. Thrown on the dustheap, cashiered, unwanted. A summer of toil and turmoil for nothing.

'What about horse boys? Do you need someone to shovel your shit?' Sparrow asked resignedly. McNabb sucked his off-colour teeth.

'I'm sorry, laddie. It's gone hard on you, I ken. Mebbe things will pick up a little in the New Year? Now we're proper allies?'

Sparrow looked blankly at his red-haired mentor.

'Ye've not heard? The Covenant, laddie, by Christ ye're an ignorant Sassenach after all! Yon Parliament's forged a truce with Argyll and his cronies, they've signed a treaty against the King!'

Sparrow nodded. He'd read something about it in one of the news-books, but as usual the string of complex clauses regarding methods of worship and who knelt where to whom had left him completely cold.

'Cromwell was right enough, Archie, I'm not exactly a godly man now,' Sparrow breathed.

'It's not just a religious covenant, laddie, it's a covenant for war as well! Twenty thousand Scots, veterans all, ready to cross the border!'

Sparrow imagined a horde of red-haired McNabbs swarming south. He sniggered a little.

'It's no laughing matter, laddie!'

Indeed it was not.

Practically the whole of Scotland had been galvanized by the National Covenant, a sacred oath which governed their entire existence – regulating their clerical and secular lives to a strictly controlled regime as never before.

Every village had its council of elders, local synods that maintained an iron hold on the morals and politics of the people. Fanatically Protestant, the Lowland Scots found the Covenant especially appealing, binding their nation against what they saw as the insidious approach of Popery, a bulwark against the rascally Irish who had been busy

171

butchering their colonizing kin over the water. The unsmiling Scottish elders had forced the moderates and Royalists out of government. Only in the semi-barbarian Highlands were there men enough – and determined enough – to resist their rule.

The Scots had already gone to war on two occasions against King Charles, refusing to adopt the Book of Common Prayer His Majesty had decreed they must adhere to. The King's mouldering army had been given a thorough trouncing by the battle-hardened Scots, commanded by veteran generals who had learnt their trade in the great German wars. Men as well known in Pomerania and Westphalia as they were in Midlothian and Stirling. Whipped up into fanatical frenzy by covens of black-suited preachers, the Scots had shown their heathen neighbours what a godly army could do if it put its heart and soul into a fight. Charles had eventually been forced to back down but as soon as he had damped down one fire another had sprung into life. The Parliaments he had been obliged to call to finance his disastrous invasions had hindered rather than helped – snapping at his heels with their petitions and remonstrances – urging the King to amend his ways and govern the land through Parliament, not despite it. The King had ignored the mounting pressure – and sparked the bitter conflagration which had engulfed his unhappy kingdom.

A year on, John Pym, chief architect of Parliament's war on the hounded King, had sent his trusted aide Sir Henry Vane to the north, charging the brilliant politician with cementing the treaty at virtually any cost. Parliament needed a new army and new hope, or the entire rebellion might be crushed by the King's fiercely triumphant lieutenants. Vane had locked horns with the equally fanatical

and every bit as cunning Marquess of Argyll, a wily Camp-
bell laird fiercely loyal to the Covenant, determined to
bring the heathen English into line with his own country's
strictly imposed sense of order. Argyll's price was high:
the abolition of Episcopacy and the imposition of the
Presbyterian Church south of the border. At last, the
precious deal had been struck. After endless months of
intense negotiations, the Parliamentarian grandees who
had balked Charles had finally forged a treaty with those
same Scots grandees who had defeated the King on the
borders.

It had been a difficult engagement and nobody anticipated the marriage would prove to be trouble free.

The new Covenant between the English rebels and the
stout patriarchs in Scotland might have been an eminently
sensible compact to righteous Presbyters like McNabb,
but to Cromwell and his new breed of fighting men it was
a hateful imposition on an individual's freedom of worship. But this time, twelve months into a war without an
enemy and without a foreseeable end, Cromwell and the
independents had been forced to shut their mouths,
swallow their pride, and agree their side of the treaty,
knowing the Scots could tip the delicate balance of power
one way or the other.

Argyll, playing to his strong hand like the magnificent
politician he was, had insisted on one further clause
pledging the English to bringing the Churches of God in
England, Scotland, and Ireland into conformity with one
another. The wily Scot had meant conformity with the
presently perfect Church of Scotland, but Vane insisted
on a subtle addition to the text, so that the planned
reformation should be 'according to the word of God'.
The Scots had agreed Vane's small point, failing to realize

that 'according to the word of God' might be interpreted in half a hundred different ways.

'See you, William, these damned independents, as they call themselves—'

William waved his ink-smeared hand in annoyance. 'All right, all right, spare us the sermon,' he growled. Sparrow hadn't paid much attention to the infinite and subtle shadings of the remarkable undertaking, the sacred binding of two great peoples into one colossal force. If McNabb was anything to go by the Scots wouldn't give up the steam off their piss unless there was something in it for them. As far as he could make out it came down to this: twenty thousand hairy Scots were coming to England to fight the war for them, and in the meantime William Sparrow, pikeman and part-time pamphleteer, could go to hell. 'In other words, it's sackcloth and ashes and cold oatmeal all round,' he said sourly. 'Three-hour sermons every day and extra on Sundays.'

McNabb looked aghast at the blasphemous Sassenach. 'To think I've taught ye all ye know, God's bones I've gan bluddy wrong somewhere!' he swore, shaking his bullet head in dismay.

'Never mind all that, Archie, this treaty of yours might look fine on paper, we might even teach the King a lesson or two. But if we ever get him out of the reckoning it'll end up as it started: us at each other's throats, mark my words.'

DIVERS INNS AND HOSTELRIES

He thought for one shuddering second he was back in the sea, crushed and coshed by the relentless, maniacal waves. A ferociously vivid nightmare of heaving deck and splintered rails, of crudely tattooed arms and leering faces. William fell away from the red belly of the *Messalina's Purse* into the fearful embrace of the raging depths, watched the masts sprout like treetops from the wild green jungle of the waves, the life-swallowing cascades of boiling foam. The sudden, bone-jarring chill set him thrashing like a mackerel, kicking his legs and clawing at the sky.

Tobias Fulke stood over him with his legs splayed, an empty bucket upended in his white-knuckled fists. The gallant old gentleman had filled the bucket from the partially frozen rain butt beside the front door of the quiet inn, carried the brimming pail up the stairs to William's noisome garret.

Sparrow coughed and blinked, his heart crammed in his throat like a sack of sand. He gasped and spluttered, wiping his face on the ruckled bedclothes he had recently vacated.

'Christ's bones,' he croaked, 'you could have stopped my heart!'

'On your feet, William, lying there daydreaming all

afternoon! There's work for us yet, my lad!' Fulke exclaimed, clanging the pail onto the dresser and standing away from the saturated soldier, still ensnared in the blankets he had tumbled out of bed with. The bedraggled captain hauled himself to his feet, shivering and shaking as he hopped from one bare foot to the other, his filthy shirt clinging to his large, clumsy frame. Fulke regarded him for a moment before tossing him clean linen.

'Get changed. We're off to meet the lads!' he announced, his eyes gleaming with malicious intent.

'What day is it?' William asked, bewildered by his abrupt rescue from the all too familiar nightmares.

'The day of our revenge, or as good as. Come along, lad, you'll catch your death in that.'

Fulke busied himself locating stockings, breeches, baldric, and buff while the shivering captain picked at his sodden underclothing.

'What lads? From the regiment?'

'As was. I've sent Nicodemus along to Holborn after Muffet. He'll know where the rest of them are holed up.'

'What is it?' Sparrow asked, yanking the sodden shirt over his head. 'Slaughter's been done in and we've been reinstated?'

'Slaughter's untouchable, William. Orders from the top. But another old friend has just sailed into our sights.' He clicked his tongue in exasperation. 'I'll explain on the way, are you coming along or not?'

'Where?'

'The Dog and Compass in Greenwich, for a start, and after that Chatham Dockyard!'

'Chatham? Why Chatham?'

'That's where Gallen Fey's found himself a new ship!' Fulke exclaimed, as if annoyed his hulking captain had not already divined as much. 'Now get your breeches on!'

Fulke fairly skipped along through the early evening crowds, as anxious as a spotty-arsed youngster hurrying to meet his first lass. He had thrown a Dutch coat over his canary yellow suit, and had replaced his usual ornate helmet with a wide-brimmed black hat supporting an enormous green feather. Sparrow lurched along beside him, nursing a cruel hangover and belching as if he'd swallowed a bucket or two of bilge water. The hideous odours wafting up from the mudbanks along the teeming river would have knocked over a horse. A hundred hawkers were shouting their wares, pushing their way through the throng with their evil-smelling trays brimming with assorted shellfish and eels.

Sparrow took one look at the gritty red and yellow pulp and the thrashing mass of dark green snakes, turned into an alley, and threw up over the greasy cobbles.

'Ye darty barstad! Puke in yer own yard, why doncher?'

Sparrow straightened up, wiped his mouth on his sleeve.

'William? Come along or we'll be late!'

Sparrow traipsed on after the avuncular colonel, wondering how far they were supposed to be going. Luckily, Fulke managed to persuade a carter to give them a ride along the bustling Embankment. Sparrow huddled in the back of the wagon, hemmed in by a selection of stinking casks. He couldn't guess what they contained. Fulke seemed immune to the terrible stench, squatting on a soap barrel with his hat on his knees to bring his protégé up to date with developments.

'Hawker's an old friend of a friend of mine. You remember good old Tilly from Exeter? Well, he's her uncle.'

Sparrow opened one bloodshot eye and studied the diminutive warrior, happily swinging his shoes to and fro like a child on a picnic. Uncle? That was a new one on Sparrow. Matilda Dawkins – Fulke's fondly remembered Tilly – was one of the most charming, unscrupulous, and hard-working whores in the West Country, a grinning red-haired harlot who ranged from port to garrison and back again in a seemingly ceaseless crusade to part as many men as possible from their money. This Hawker fellow was another of her damned customers, not some long-lost relation. Sparrow frowned, wondering who the old duffer was trying to fool. For an old soldier who had campaigned from one end of Europe to the other, he could be as naive as a cross-eyed goose-girl sometimes.

'Well, Hawker's in town after his latest trip out, and he bumped into another old friend, you remember Gallen Fey, of course, from the *Conqueror*?'

Of course Sparrow remembered him. If it hadn't been for the quietly spoken, infinitely determined seaman, William and his friends would have been feeding the fishes by now. Taken prisoner back at Roundway, Sparrow and a hundred or so other unfortunates had found themselves loaded aboard the *Messalina's Purse*, bound for service with the Spanish Tercios at so many shillings a man. The bastard master of the misbegotten pukepot was setting a course for Antwerp when a storm blew up, bringing Fey and the *Conqueror* with it. Doomed to destruction under the man-of-war's guns, Captain Cruickshank jettisoned a score of his human cargo in the hope of putting his enemy off the pursuit. Torn between continuing the chase and saving the helpless victims from drowning in the storm-racked seas, Fey thankfully decided on the latter course and ordered a boat over the side to haul the few shocked survivors to safety.

William had read that the *Conqueror* had been lost during the recent siege of Exeter, but he knew better than most you could never trust the news-sheets – no matter what side they favoured. According to the Royalist scab sheet *Mercurius Aulicus,* the brave vessel had already been scuttled, sunk (twice), driven aground by a drunken helmsman, and sold to the French by its mutinous crew.

'No, well, this time it's true,' Fulke went on as Sparrow voiced his reservations about the accuracy of his information. 'Fey's just back from Plymouth after being exchanged. The thing is, most of his crew are still down there.'

'Where? Plymouth? I thought we still had Plymouth?'

'Yes yes yes, we still have Plymouth – thank God! I'm talking about Penmethock. Penmethock, you remember it, don't you?'

Nathaniel Hawker's riotous crew might have been Parliamentarian by persuasion, but there wasn't a Puritan amongst them. They had staggered into the *Honest John*'s boats and made straight for the Rummer, as wild an inn as could be found in Roundhead territory. The seamen and shorehands who frequented the hideous hole had fortified it against watchmen, constables, and all the forces of Parliament. So long as the fleet remained loyal to the cause, their scrofulous crews could have their fun – safely away from the distressed stares of the goodwives of Chatham. Hawker and his senior officers had left them to it. They had been taken on up the Thames Estuary in a pinnace, to make their reports, collect orders and provisions, and reacquaint themselves with any number of whores and other men's wives.

'Thank God the fleet sided with us,' Fulke reflected as the wallowing wagon pitched and creaked along the crowded street. 'I'd rather have them behind us than agin us.'

'You're bleedin' welcome to 'em,' the driver called from the running-board, 'bleedin' shower.'

The garrulous driver had finally dropped his passengers outside the Dog and Compass in Greenwich, a slightly more respectable inn within spitting distance of the great bend of the Thames. The busy quays which had been thrown up over the muddy banks were packed with boatmen and hauliers, hawkers and whores, tinkers and rope-makers. Sailors in grubby canvas jackets with distinctive blue or red stripes, leather hats, and pinching clogs made their way up and down the noisy boulevards, busy about or frantically searching for work. A dozen fat merchantmen were lying at anchor just offshore, serviced by a flotilla of lighters and skiffs being rowed to and fro beneath screaming squadrons of gulls. Dusk had hurried up from the sea, and the merry lanterns the steersmen had hung from their bows cast shimmering nets of silvery scales over the gently ebbing water. Masts and rigging clanged hollowly, a sombre accompaniment to the rackets being kicked up in the streets. Closely packed hovels and vast, yawning warehouses seemed to be pressing in on the fierce activity, eavesdropping on the hair-raising oaths and scandalous gossip being bawled back and forth across the gloomy alleys. Dark lanes bisected the docklands, leading the unwary out of the bright-eyed glare of the street entertainments and into the sinister nether world of London's teeming underbelly.

The hustle and bustle reminded Sparrow of his home town of Bristol. The sights, the smells, the same cheerfully coarse conversations. Fishwives and slouching apprentices, ranters and ravers. Fickle crowds which mutated into screaming mobs one moment and melted away the next, carried this way and that like the wandering platforms of weeds and refuse washing up under the barnacled jetties. He ducked his head and followed Fulke into the crowded inn, pushing and shoving their way through to the brightly lit interior of the reeking barn.

Hawker turned out to be every inch as raucous as his garishly lit surroundings. Alert with nervous energy, he jumped out of his seat and waved the newcomers through the vulgar congregation of drinkers and drabs, clasped Fulke by the hand, and clapped Sparrow on the back hard enough to loosen his teeth. Hawker was of medium height, slightly stooped by his long years on deck. His small head was framed by an immensely tangled mane of grey and gilt hair, tied back in a queue with a faded red ribbon. Tropical weather had turned his gaunt features the colour of well-beaten copper, and his permanently narrowed eyes might have been nut-brown or almond – leaving the fearful Londoners with the impression they had a half-tamed native of the Indies roaming their streets. Sparrow noticed he had buckled a large cutlass to his broad leather belt, worn outside his square-cut seaman's jacket, discoloured and stiff with salt and spray. He had tucked his canvas trousers into a pair of elaborately worked Spanish leather boots, clearly taken from the chest of one of his unfortunate victims. He looked more like one of old Cruickshank's cronies than a Roundhead captain-at-sea.

John Grey, his mate, more than made up for his strikingly flamboyant master. He wore a plain, weather-worried broadcloth suit with a matching hat pulled down severely over his protruding ears, like some absent-minded clergyman. The immense collar of his grubby shirt looked as if it had been cut from one of the sails. The rosy complexioned mate was smoking a foul-smelling pipe, lifting his cleanly shaven chin to blow wobbling smoke rings into the all-pervading fogs which had jammed themselves against the rafters. Grey sat patiently beside his captain, peering over the charts Gallen Fey had brought with him as if to make up for his captain's inattention to the detail of the operation. Sparrow dragged up a stool and sat down, feeling sick and bewildered, ill at ease in the company of such vastly experienced old sweats.

'Make yourself at home, lad, and get this down yer!'

Sparrow nodded soberly, allowing his chief to do all the talking while he poured himself a short measure and glanced about the packed bar. Customers in various states of inebriation hauled themselves up on one another's clothing, serving girls with swinging hips and brimming trays moved to and fro as if caught up by some invisible tide. Foaming tankards rose and fell, spilling more slops onto the slippery stone floor.

'Toby! How long's it been now? Seen much of that niece of mine?'

'Not since the siege of Bristol,' Fulke called back, reaching over the chart-strewn table to shake hands with the rather more reserved figure of Gallen Fey.

'We rather lost touch, what with half a dozen brigades of Rupert's best foot to worry about!' Fulke crowed back. 'I'm sure she'll find her feet though, you know Tilly!'

'Find her feet?' Hawker bellowed over the din. 'Aye, no doubt she'll bounce back, eh, Toby?'

Fey ignored the witticism, busy flicking through the charts he had taken from a mouldy leather case. Sparrow's unsmiling saviour had certainly done a fine job of concealing his intense pleasure at meeting his former passenger once again.

'I'm glad to see you are still in one piece, Captain,' he said carefully, straightening his black leather sea-hat and leaning to one side as Hawker prised himself to his unsteady feet. Hawker banged his tankard on the table to bring the extraordinary council to order.

'Gentlemen. We all know one another now, so it's high time we got down to the matter in hand. Gallen?' Hawker crashed down onto the bench, almost catapulting the shorter, paler Fey to his feet. The captain cleared his throat and leaned forward like a schoolmaster instructing a set of particularly obnoxious students. Fey's cold, dispassionate manner seemed strangely at odds with the tale he had to tell. Ordered by the Earl of Warwick to transport vital provisions to the hard-pressed city of Exeter, he had taken the *Conqueror* up the long, narrow estuary of the Exe, under the noses of hundreds of Prince Maurice's troops. Fey pursed his lips, nodded at the bewildered officer squatting on the stool opposite him.

'Captain Sparrow will recall we took the same risks at Bristol, and with God's grace survived, aye, in and out.' Fey's colourless features seemed set like stone as he pondered his fluctuating fortunes. 'The King's men had better sport at Exeter. They had set up batteries on either bank, and they took away our masts with the first shots. We ran aground and they pounded us to matchwood.'

Hawker looked suitably downcast by the man-of-war's end but he raised his tankard anyway. 'Here's to the *Conqueror*, and all who sailed in her – living or dead,' he called.

William raised his glass with the others, wondering what old Fulke had dragged them along for. What had any of this to do with him?

'There were a few dozen survivors all told, pulled out of the Exe by Prince Maurice's bloody Cornishmen,' Fey continued. Hawker leaned over to spit on the filthy floor. 'Exeter surrendered a day or two later, and we were marched off with some of the garrison. We had no idea where we were going, but I eventually worked out where we were by the landmarks along the coast. William here walked that road before me. Through the coomb and down the cliffs, to Penmethock by the sea.'

Penmethock. The shabby little fishing village had been a Royalist outpost since the beginning of the war. Now, with Prince Maurice's army demolishing Roundhead resistance up and down the coast, it was the jewel in the crown – its bloody inhabitants loudly proclaiming they had been loyal from the first. They crowed and preened and spied on their neighbours, denouncing the folk inland as traitors and rebels. William had often wondered what had driven the tiny village to such extremes of belief. Fanatics were ten a penny up and down the country, but here was a whole vile nest of them. A stinking crab pot, a barrel full of snapping congers. Home to the most ruthless gang of swivel-eyed bastards Sparrow had ever had the misfortune to come across. The interbreeding weevils had

owed fierce allegiance to the all-powerful Dyle family –
and had been pathetically eager to do their dirty work for
them, however bloody. It had been the eldest son, Lord
Clavincale, who had sold the Roundhead prisoners into
slavery in the first place; a one-way passage to the Spanish
Netherlands and service in the grim, multinational ranks
of the Archduke's war-weary Tercios.

Sparrow knew the place – by Christ, he would never
forget it.

'They carted me off to their Assizes with the officers,
but the common men were marched off to the quarries,
put to work like convicts,' Fey went on. 'I protested to
their officers and village elders, to the Earl of Dartland
himself – but they laughed in my face. It was to my
everlasting shame and damnation that I was exchanged,
and forced to leave my men behind.' He studied his
audience for a moment, his grey eyes as cold as a washed-
up corpse. 'I have sworn by God's book to have them
back.'

The officers were listening carefully now, as if mesmerized by Fey's stony-eyed report. The sea captain rifled
through the charts, found his mark with a short-tempered
flourish. 'I was taken down to the harbour, here, and put
in a boat. They forgot to blindfold me, and I was able to
look around and map the place in my head.' Fey tapped
his furrowed brow. 'Then I saw a ship, a red ship tied up
next to their fishing fleet like a pure-bred Arab in a field
full of nags.'

Sparrow knew the name of that damned ship, and
realized in a moment why he had been dragged along to
the assembly.

'The *Messalina's Purse*,' Fey breathed, turning the foul

name into a serpent's hiss. 'Cruickshank himself, if you'll believe me. As bold as brass and not thirty miles from our garrison at Lyme.'

Hawker sat back against the bench, sighing with frustrated rage. John Grey picked up the chart which had been cast down in the dregs on the table.

'Where is this place? Near Lyme? I've not heard of it.'

'I have,' Hawker said. 'A poky little hole, John. A regular harlot's web.' Fey took the map from the mate and held his finger to a tiny notch in the Dorset coastline.

'From what I saw, it is clear the enemy high command is using Penmethock as a major supply depot for Prince Maurice's army. I saw warehouses stacked to the eaves with barrels and provisions, far more than Major Brinks' garrison would ever require. And the *Purse* was just one of three ships ferrying supplies around the coast. Two of them were captured by our squadron based off Poole, stuffed full of all manner of goods; cloth and coin and plate and powder. Three shiploads for a backwater like Dorset? To my mind, gentlemen, it can mean but one thing.' Fey tapped the map, the few remaining Roundhead strongholds red-ink islands in a sea of Royalist blue. 'Maurice is presently moving westwards to blockade Plymouth, but the enemy is clearly intending to finish affairs further down the eastern coast, our last garrisons between Maurice and the southern counties.' Fey ran his finger along the jagged peaks and sudden sweeps of the coastline. 'The King is bogged down in the Thames valley, but we know he has sent Hopton into Hampshire with a new army, obviously intending to build up pressure on the capital from the south. Now if Maurice should turn back along the coast there's barely a garrison worth the name between them. The Prince can storm or even bypass our strongholds, link up with Hopton, and together they can swing up towards London.'

He regarded the perplexed councillors for a moment, heads tilted to one side as they attempted to frame the desperate manoeuvres he was describing on his ruckled chart. Fey drew a heavy breath. 'Gentlemen, as we know the Earl of Essex is having trouble enough dealing with one army. God alone knows how he'll contain three.'

Even Hawker seemed slightly overawed by the horrifying prospect. A vast trident of bloodthirsty Cavaliers thrust into the sagging underbelly of London, the heart and soul of the cause?

John Grey looked dubiously from the charts to the gravely earnest captain.

'There is no reason to suppose they are intending any such thing, sir. Maurice is squatting outside Plymouth, a good fifty miles from this Penmathick place with our garrison at Lyme in between. It's another forty or fifty as the crow flies on to our other garrison at Poole. If the King had ordered such an operation surely Maurice would be screening Plymouth and marching east as fast as he was able?'

Fey nodded. 'Or the King, in his overweening arrogance, might believe his irresistible nephew can take Plymouth as quickly as he captured Exeter and Dartmouth. Then he would be free to turn back, deal with Lyme and Poole in quick succession, and *then* link up with Hopton.'

'Presumably you have already thought to communicate this intelligence to the Admiralty?'

'I tried,' Fey said, colouring slightly. 'They were most interested in my report, and promised to give it their full and undivided attention just as soon as they had the time.'

'Typical!' Hawker sneered. 'The earl's as much idea of waging war at sea as I do about growing apple trees. He sees ships as a means of moving men from one bit of dry land to another. Drake and Howard would have keel-hauled the old soak, trying to fight with one foot planted on the shore.'

Fey scowled, reluctant to cast aspersions on the Admiral of the Parliamentarian fleet. 'They did promise to alert the earl to the possibilities of a fresh descent on Poole. As you know we have a warship or two anchored in Brownsea Roads against such an attack.'

John Grey twitched uncomfortably, running his broad hand over his head. 'Aye. The place would have gone long since, without the fleet keeping watch and ward over it.'

'You can't use warships as floating fortresses, John! Good ships lying at anchor trying to stop an enemy in command on the land? Athens tried it when they fought the Spartans, look where it got them!'

Hawker wiped the froth from his mouth on his sleeve. 'Tied up with one hand behind your back, it's against all we've ever known!' he grumbled.

'Well, whatever your present opinion of the good earl, he has his hands full dealing with the Dunkirk privateers, without considering punitive expeditions against insignificant little fisher-towns in the heart of enemy territory,' Fey interrupted briskly, beating a tattoo on the faded chart with the gnawed stub of his pencil.

Sparrow squinted at the lush green interiors and the jagged coastlines, the fanciful creatures emerging from the carefully painted waves. He'd seen those coasts from the deep end and didn't relish the prospect of going back – if that was what the jabbering magpies were proposing.

'So why have you called us all here?' he thought aloud, startled at the sound of his own gruff voice.

Hawker grinned wolfishly.

'A man after my own heart! The earl might not be contemplating getting off his landlocked arse, but it doesn't mean to say we have to stick in harbour picking grit from our belly buttons!' Fulke glanced around at the bewildered Sparrow, his merry grey eyes sparkling with mischief. 'Think of it, William! A chance to have a crack at that dunghill lynch mob!' he exclaimed. 'We'll sail in and pull the floor out from under them!'

John Grey seemed to share William's misgivings, frowning at the vast empty spaces on the fanciful chart as if superimposing the massively superior enemy forces in the vicinity. Hawker and Fey seemed to be taking rather too much for granted for his liking. But he would relish the chance to cut that notorious butcher Cruickshank down a peg.

Fey had unrolled a second, rougher chart; a sketch map of the harbour and its stranglehold cliffs, various buildings marked in black ink.

'A dozen good men on this crossroads, and you could hold the place against an army,' he predicted. 'Cliffs here and here, there's only one way down into the village, along this path here. The quarry is over towards the west, hidden in the hills a mile or so from the harbour would be my guess. Dartland has a house somewhere in this coomb here, the quarry road runs right past it.'

'So they think they're safe enough,' Hawker added with relish. 'From the landward, anyways.'

Fey pointed to the harbour, the broad black bulk of the mole protruding from the cliffs like a broken rib.

'They think they're safe from the sea and all. They've set up batteries here and here, to command the harbour entrance.'

Sparrow's uneasy dislike of the hare-brained scheme was rapidly turning to outright contempt. 'You've just told us how you lost your ship running under Prince Maurice's culverins,' Sparrow pointed out, 'and here you are proposing to try the same again? Parliament must have more ships than it has sense.'

Fey showed his teeth, transformed into an imp of Satan by the thought of his crew toiling in that hastily pencilled quarry back in Penmethock. 'You haven't been listening. Parliament has not yet found me a new command. And even if I had been provided with a new ship, I would not be at liberty to risk it in such an endeavour.'

'So you're going to steal a fishing boat and sneak in after dark,' Sparrow snapped. 'And you're expecting me and my men to come with you.'

Hawker frowned, glanced enquiringly at the silent Fulke. 'I thought you said he was up for it, Toby?' he snorted derisively.

Fulke cracked a smile. 'He hasn't heard the plan in its entirety,' he said.

Sparrow wasn't sure he wanted to hear their damned plans. The way he'd been treated, he would do better to try and build his bridges with the King than risk his life and all the others in some cock-eyed gamble like this. He was surprised old Fulke had even countenanced such a ridiculous scheme.

'We do not propose to force our way into the harbour,' Fey explained patiently. 'We will simply sail in on the tide, right under their noses.' Sparrow shook his head, took another soothing swig at his beer. 'Penmethock is a known pirate base, a smugglers' hold. So we shall become pirates for the day.'

This was beyond sensible argument. Sparrow drained his tankard noisily. 'They'll spot us a mile off,' he scoffed. 'We'll be—'

'He's a bell-wether strunt after all, this captain of yours,' Hawker called, lifting his sharply angled chin. 'We've been at this a damned sight longer than you have, son! Don't you think we haven't thought this through? They'll spot us all right, the *Blue Doubloon* out of Dunkirk. One Captain Terrence Gable in command. I caught her, lock, stock, and barrel, on my last trip out. She's sitting back at Chatham now with a few holes here and there – a missing mast or two, mebbe. We'll look as if we've been chased home by some interfering bastard of a Round-head, and they won't know what's hit 'em!' the excitable captain exclaimed.

'You see, William? We'll be at their throats before they realize what's afoot!' Fulke called, digging him cheerfully in the ribs. Sparrow grinned back at them, completely unconvinced.

PART THREE

TO CROSSBONE QUAY

'God be my witness, you yourselves are the destroyers, the wasters, the spoilers of your fatherland. My heart sickens when I look on you.'

Gustavus Adolphus, King of Sweden, berating his looting troops, September 1632

FLAXPITS MILL,

BLIND MAN'S MOOR, DORSET

Hugo Telling had suspected Sir Gilbert Morrison of many things during their brief and bitter acquaintanceship, but he had never imagined the garrulous old soak was a rune-writing warlock, able to converse with the birds of the air and the beasts in the field. The snowy-muzzled old mongrel crouching beside the door must have been a hundred years old, and yet the vile merchant had filled it with new energy and purpose, set it outside his daughter's door like Cerberus himself. A growling familiar to keep the randy Cavalier away from Bella's rather overcrowded quarters.

Telling paused on the landing, his bare feet chilled to the bone. What was the wretched creature's name again?

'Shushh, boy,' he breathed. 'Nice dog.' The nice dog bared its yellow fangs, its rumbling growl climbing another octave. Telling peered at the formidable portcullis behind its drooping head, completely at a loss.

Sir Gilbert had insisted they stay within eyeshot if not earshot, hadn't let Bella stray any further than Maynard's weed-infested backyard. When the cunning merchant had been too busy to stand guard himself he had set Mrs Pride on them, forever bustling and cleaning and whistling to herself.

If not Mrs Pride, Mary Keziah, alternately pale and

flushed, holding her swollen belly as if she expected it to explode at any moment, or Anneliese and Jamie, arms linked and laughing like larks. Sir Bloody Gilbert Bastard Morrison hadn't appeared too bothered by the amount of time those two spent with one another – he seemed glibly unaware of his own son's existence.

Telling, though, was another matter.

Sir Gilbert could read the thoughts as they unpeeled from his fevered brain. He could sense the minute tremblings of his heart every time Bella so much as sneezed in his company. The merchant touched, sniffed, stared, and imagined exactly as Telling touched, sniffed, stared, and imagined. He knew what he was thinking, what he would say, and had a fair inkling what he would do if he ever let the youngster out of his beady-eyed sight.

Damn him to hell! He hadn't even had the common decency to inform Hugo of the arrangements being made on his and Bella's behalf.

None of his business? How did the blasted turncoat make that out – Hugo was to marry his damned daughter, for God's sake!

Hugo bit his raw bottom lip, fretting over the spider-web strands of his uncertain future. Sir Gilbert's ghostly brother had driven to the coast with the laden wain, and ridden back on a bony black cob. The wagon and team must have brought in a few pounds, let alone the hoard of trinkets the merchant had borrowed from Kilmersden Hall. The anxious Cavalier had spied the miller in hushed conference with his grasping brother, but hadn't been able to pick up the faintest clue as to what had been decided. As far as he could see the canny miller hadn't brought back a sack full of coin from his mysterious trip. It was more likely he had agreed a price with the master of some ship for Bella's passage abroad. Where abroad? France? The Americas? Sir Gilbert wouldn't say when his sweetheart was due to embark, let alone whether Hugo would be joining her or remaining behind. Perhaps the cunning old buzzard was intending to sneak Bella away out of the mill, and get her aboard before Hugo was aware of his antics. He nodded shrewdly. Yes, that would be it. With his daughter safely abroad he could cock a snook at Hugo all over again.

A door shrieked open behind him, sending a shiver of apprehension up the captain's spine. He leapt around and saw the Machiavellian merchant's milky bulk emerge from the room he shared with his brother.

'Down, Griper,' he hissed. Telling thought for a moment he was referring to him. The dog in question slouched back down on its ancient grey paws, eyelids drooping.

'Off to pluck a rose, Telling?' his intended in-law asked maliciously. Hugo grinned sheepishly.

'That ale's gone straight through me,' he whispered. Morrison stepped closer, peered into his pale face.

'Ale, my arse. What were you thinking of doing? Getting in there and cutting my Bella out of the pack?'

'I was thinking no such thing,' Telling hissed. 'How could you imagine a gentleman would behave in such a—'

'Gentleman? When it comes to my daughter you forget your manners quick enough! If it wasn't for Mrs Pride keeping her eye on you I dread to think what you might have tried,' Sir Gilbert leered.

The guest-room door clicked open, and Mary Keziah appeared, clutching a dish brimming with melted wax and a tiny glimmering candle.

'He hasn't woken you all up, I hope, mincing around the house at the dead of night?' Sir Gilbert wondered, stepping aside as the maid frowned, then waddled out onto the landing.

'I was not mincing!' Telling snapped back.

'Creeping, mincing, peeping,' Sir Gilbert allowed. 'I'll not split hairs over what it was you were up to.'

'They're both out cold,' Mary sighed, tugging her shawl about her shivering shoulders. 'Now let me pass.'

'Where are you going?'

'Where do you think?'

Sir Gilbert waited for the pair of them to complete their midnight toilet, and watched Telling all the way back into the small room he shared with poor Jamie. Telling looked over his shoulder, spied the belligerent bulk of the merchant in the shadowed hallway.

The bastard must be a light sleeper, or he has the ears of a bat, Hugo thought grudgingly, closing the door quietly on his nocturnal reconnaissance.

He tiptoed towards the blanket-tossed pile of the bed, paused when he heard the tiny tap against the window. Damn the merchant, had he trained a nightjar to peer through the shutters at him? A black-eyed raven to squint through the keyhole of his heart?

Telling padded across to the window, opened the shutter, and practically shouted with fright.

Bella Morrison was clinging to the frame, a spectral angel-witch come to steal his manly liquors. She was swaying back and forth in her transparent nightdress, her hair flashing silver in the pale moonlight hanging behind her shoulder.

'Well, open the latch, or I'll fall,' she whispered, her breath forming a film of vapour over the cracked glass.

Telling was galvanized into action, yanking the shutters back, tugging the window open, and standing back as a stream of cold air lifted the shirt from his bare legs. Bella ducked her head and swung herself into his room, shivered with delighted fright as he clamped his arms about her chilled body.

'You could have fallen to your death,' he complained, his lips brushing her ears.

'I don't care!' she hissed.

'You could have swooned and broken your neck,' Telling complained, clamping his lips over the item in question. 'You're hardly healed as it is, without clambering over people's houses!'

He'd had the window up a dozen times, but the precarious wooden ledge his sweetheart had negotiated hadn't looked likely to bear his weight.

'I could have hung on to this,' she whispered with a throaty chuckle, reaching down between them to grasp him in her hot little fist. He squirmed in agonized delight, maddened by her careless caress. 'I told you, it was nothing more than an unlucky ricochet. Oooh, you're all hot!'

'Get into bed!' he croaked, shivering like a reed in a gale. Bella pulled herself away from him, squinted over her lover's shoulder at the snoring form of her brother.

'I'll not lie backwards next to Jamie, daft or not,' she exclaimed crossly.

Her brother had spreadeagled himself beneath the heaped covers, and Telling would have been lucky to slip back in himself, let alone bring his sweetheart with him. He snatched up his cloak from the settle instead, draped it about them as they stood shivering in the fractured moonlight lancing through the shutters.

'I tried to get to you, but your father's clinging closer than a rash! He won't tell me what they've arranged!'

'Nor me. That's why I came to you,' she replied, taking a deep breath as they clung against one another. She groped lower, lifting his ruckled shirt to spread her palm over his taut belly.

Telling closed his eyes with a tiny sigh of ecstasy. The room seemed to buckle and warp as if it was made of molten glass, every surface reflecting his dazed features. Bella watched his pinched features contort in apparent agony as she gripped him harder.

'No, don't,' he pleaded, his knees buckling beneath him. 'Not yet ... Bella!' She gave a little shiver as he bucked and gasped before her, amazed as always by the ridiculous ease with which she dismantled the strutting Cavalier. Turned his spine to honey and his bones to butter with one touch, one teasing caress.

He coughed hollowly into the fragrant cleft of her collarbone.

'Bella!' he sighed, clinging on to her like a salmon. The girl held her slim finger to her lips, her eyes twinkling with mischievous delight. Hugo stood away from her, his trembling hands hovering in front of his soiled shirt.

She tilted her head to one side as if studying his reactions, puzzled by this upright ape who charged troops of dragoons but wilted before defenceless maidens.

'What is it, where are you going?' he quailed, as she stepped forward, kissed him on the cheek, and turned toward the heavenly illuminated window.

'They'll miss me if I'm away long. With three in a bed you've only got to scratch and we're all wide awake in a moment,' she said simply, opening the shutters and gazing out over her uncle's shimmering fields. The white stones in the walls glowed like piled skulls.

He came after her, shirt bunched in front of him, grasping for her slim back.

'Let me go! Hugo!' Raising her voice now, as if the youth had recovered enough of his manliness to reassert his flagging will over her immaculate, unimpeachable designs.

'Bella!' he wailed, watching his sweetheart duck out of the window and cling to the damned ledge. He watched her slide along the wall like a phantasm, her soft white shift fusing with the rough whitewashed walls.

'Bella!' he sighed. With a twist of her hips she was gone, back into her own room. He watched her slim hand reach out and close the shutters after her.

Bella.

He blinked, wondering if his overwhelming lust for the bewitching creature had misled him. His fingers crept lower, through the ruckled shirt and over his cold, oyster-backed belly.

No.

At least, he hoped not.

Maynard Morrison felt the bed yawn to one side as his elder brother swung his legs up and under the ruffled covers. He was a light sleeper, and well used to lying awake listening for the scuttle and rush of beast and insect in the loft. He liked fresh air, whatever the season, and had set the shutters open so the room would be light enough for his brother to find the pisspot without stubbing his toes.

'Brrrrr. A fire wouldn't come amiss, Maynard,' Sir Gilbert observed, tugging the covers back over his frozen frame. Maynard doubled his hands under his head, sighed heavily. By God, his niece hadn't seemed overly bothered by the boisterous winter weather. He had heard the window grate next door, and had watched her flit along the beams, a creature of air and darkness in her silky shift.

'She's a rum 'un, your lass,' he said to the hanging counterpane. Sir Gilbert opened one eye, studied the brightly illuminated form of his brother, lying out like a stone knight on a sleepless tomb.

'What d'yer mean by that?' he asked at last.

Hugo slept late. Bright wintry sunshine flooded the barely furnished room, bars of gold slanting through the opened shutters. He blinked, propping himself up on his elbows and peering around the room for his absent bed mate. The heap of clothing Jamie had left the night before had gone. Hugo tilted his head, caught the excited shouts from the yard. He leapt out of bed in his shirt, grabbed his pistol, and tugged the shutters back. The three of them were sitting along the drystone wall bordering the miller's threadbare orchard. The girls were pressed together against the chill wind, their cloaks ruffled up behind them and their bonnets billowing like faraway sails, barely restraining their alternately light and dark hair. They were rocking to and fro, watching Jamie's hare-brained antics in the trees. The daft youth had spoilt his best suit rolling in flour, and was dashing from one arthritic trunk to another, touching the bare branches, dabbing his white pawprints over the ancient bark. Telling could hear his shrill voice as he cried and whooped.

'I'm Jack Frost, my breath to freeze, the melancholic spirits of these trees! Hush the bud and still the root, my summer harvest farmers loot!'

'Be careful, Jamie, you'll give yourself another turn,' Anneliese called, wiping the frigid tears from her eyes.

'Another turn? He's more turns than a broken compass,' Bella cried, waving her brother away as he dashed in at them, flapping his arms like a plucked crow. 'Pester someone else with your tomfoolery!'

For a second Hugo thought he might leap down and join them, run and caper in the orchard just as he had with his bullying elder brothers in those dwindling days before the war. The cold pistol seemed to have grown out of his fist, a warlock's tool grafted onto his arm, sewn into his strained sinews in place of a bat or fishing rod.

'What time is it?' Telling called down, his loud enquiry startling them from their childish pranks. The girls peered up over their shoulders at him, aloof in the window in his flapping shirt, scowling at their noisy banter.

'Oh, don't shoot Mr Telling, sir, we'll promise we won't wake you tomorrow!' Mary Keziah called, screeching with laughter. Anneliese covered her mouth, giggling despite her concern at Jamie's mad antics. Bella turned away with a tiny flick of her chin which Telling felt as a boot in the balls.

'Come on down, Hugo! There's a pond behind the sheds!' Jamie called, pointing over the wall.

He lowered the pistol, shook his head. 'In this weather? You'll catch your death,' he called, frowning.

'Yes, mind you keep clear of it,' Mary Keziah added, waving her finger at the pale boy in a ridiculous parody of parenthood. Telling shook his head. He and Mary Keziah had never seen eye to eye on her role. She was supposed to be Bella's maid, a family servant, but she had always taken more liberties with her mistress than Hugo thought proper. He had refrained from crossing swords with the impudent girl, however. She had a temper to match Bella's and a store of common sense which he had a horrible suspicion might considerably outweigh his own. He thought of the girl's absent sweetheart, that hulking prick Sparrow. Wondered what he was up to this cold morning. How was it fate had decreed their paths should cross – more than cross, intertwine like mating snakes? Here he was miles from home, a fugitive from the King's justice, helping to safeguard the big-mouthed rebel's pregnant wench. It didn't make any sense. Any of it.

'You'll get the pip sitting on those stones,' he called down, irritated by the dark-haired maid's teasing smile.

'I got a sight more than a pip sitting somewhere softer!' she bit back.

Bella and Anneliese shrieked with laughter, clawing at each other as they attempted to avoid toppling over the back of the wall. Bella's blue gown billowed in a sudden mischievous gust, and she made a great play of smoothing the ruckled material back down over her stockings. Telling licked his lips.

'Where's Sir Gilbert?' he called, placing his pistol back on the dresser.

'Gone off with Uncle Maynard. They'll be back this afternoon.'

There! More bloody arrangements! How dare they plot

behind his back, leave him snoring while they settled his fate!

'Where?'

'Horn's Cross. Down the coast road somewhere.'

Horn's Cross? Where the devil was that?

Blind Man's Moor was a desolate wasteland of poor grazing and sudden, switchbacked slopes. Narrow dales criss-crossed the drab heather and gorse uplands, rocky escarpments prising holes in the harsh turf like dirty elbows through a fustian shirt. Boulder-strewn streams stole waters from the stony ridges, draining the long expanses of windswept bog and linking the deep black pools which were scattered here and there about the wilderness. There were no signs of war this far away from anything an army might want. The few inhabitants scratched a living from sheep, the bloodily daubed creatures wandering over the vast down seeking a digestible meal. Away inland, there were odd clusters of villages along the main Dorchester to Lyme road, which wound between the ancient tumuli where long-dead tribes had buried their fallen. A finger-post in the middle of nowhere directed the traveller south towards the coast, the isolated villages of Fib's Corner, Tubbleton, Horn's Cross, and Penmethock. From a distance, the tiny outposts would look no different from the standing stones or exposed bedrocks. Harsh grey angles carpeted by lichens and moss. Here and there a grainy window or a rash of imported tiles.

The church was squat, Saxon, workmanlike. A stubby tower and a narrow nave. A doom-laden bell which might attract the hardy folk in off the hills for their endless Sunday sermon from Mr Moulton, their warrior preacher.

The grey fortress had been built on a small tump away from the road, the drystone wall around the churchyard a stockade against pagan invaders swarming up from the creeks and coves along the coast. The gravestones had been tilted this way and that by the frightful, mindless winds, and the ring of battered elms which had been planted as a break looked as formidable as a bank of sorry winter sedge. Rooks and crows cawed from the branches, as they eyed the steaming horses tied up in the yard. Indoors, the church was a frozen whitewashed mausoleum, a fort against thought, a sanctuary against God's bounty.

Sir Gilbert eyed the grimly vaulted ceiling and returned his attention to the grimly vaulted clergyman. Isaiah Moulton was long and large, misshapen, and wont to scowl and frown. His thick hair was as greasy and curled as any black sheep's, his complexion mottled, a riot of bright choleric reds and unhealthy lemon. His mouth appeared to drain his head, slick and stringy with excess spittle.

Sir Gilbert had allowed his brother to do all the talking, and a poor bloody job he was making of it and all. Moulton would need some encouragement, that was certain.

'This girl, she is with child?' the clergyman enquired in his queer, sonorous voice.

'No, she certainly isn't,' he snapped indignantly. 'She's a respectable girl same as her mother, sadly deceased.'

'To be wed to a soldier.'

'Such are the times, sir,' Sir Gilbert agreed.

'Away from her own parish church?'

'Forced out by circumstances,' the merchant agreed. 'Chased from one home and another by lewd, godless men, sir. Wounded even unto the brink of death by our frightful excesses.'

'Indeed. Chipping Marleward, you say?'

'On the Fosseway towards Bath.'

'The King's forces would appear to have assumed jurisdiction over the West Country. I cannot imagine what lewd or godless troopers you can be talking about,' Moulton said, his wet mouth like a conger's gape.

The fellow was pulling his plank, that was for sure. Was he some damned Papist who had lost his trail? Sniffing out the few Puritans who had remained behind?

'Alas, not every man who fights for the King is worthy of his service,' Sir Gilbert said smoothly. Moulton grunted something.

'I've yet to meet one who was,' he said. 'On either side,' he added as an afterthought. Sir Gilbert saw a chink of light at the end of the tunnel. This was no Papist. He'd spoken his mind about Royalist excesses and then tried to dilute the comment.

'The fact of it is, sir, I'm not keen on this liaison. He's a captain in Rupert's lifeguard, and terrible to behold at your door, sir, I can assure you.'

'Rupert's lifeguard, you say?' Moulton asked distractedly. Last heard of two hundred miles away, surely? That Rupert, though, he could move quick enough, when provoked.

'Aye,' Sir Gilbert agreed, watching the clergyman's wandering eye. 'But ours is not to reason it out. Family ties, sir, can string us up either end, in times like these.' Moulton agreed this was true. 'But I owe my first duty to the great

God who gave me the girl in the first place. He has told me, through my conscience, that I can't alter her nature, that I'll never subdue whatever it is she sees in him.'

'Indeed?'

For a moment Sir Gilbert had strayed into the uncharted territory of truth. Well, half-hearted lies and bluster hadn't got Maynard anywhere, that was for sure.

'If I could just see 'em wed in the eyes of God, I'd know I'd done my duty,' Sir Gilbert wailed. Moulton relented a little.

'It's not usual. There's proper procedure, banns to be read . . .'

The merchant shivered in his borrowed coat, glanced up at the arrow-slit windows. 'And a nice congregation for you. I don't imagine the plate goes round to much benefit out here, eh?' Moulton's watery eyes narrowed, squeezing tears into the puffy creeks about the sockets. 'Maynard will be turning his household out, I know. And then there's my own servants and lifeguards to think about. They wouldn't want to miss a good winter wedding!'

Moulton pondered the pecuniary advantages of such a union. God knew there were heathens enough on this moor without turning honest Christians away from their church. It was nothing more than his Christian duty to relax the rules and get these folk wed. He smiled, his discoloured teeth slick with saliva.

'There's a war on, after all,' he allowed. 'I couldn't in all conscience turn your youngsters away. God knows there are more than enough straying from the proper path as it is.'

'Capital!'

'Of course, there is one small problem.'

Sir Gilbert frowned.

'The church is, as you are no doubt aware, somewhat chilled.'

'I've been warmer,' the merchant admitted guardedly.

'The coal supply being what it is . . . it becomes difficult to warm one's heart to do one's sacred duty.'

'You want a fire in the chapel?'

'No, sir. The house of God is not a Turkish harem, sir, the congregation will sit and freeze, if God wills it, aye, and roast in the summer!'

'A change of air never did anybody any harm,' Sir Gilbert agreed readily. In and out, he wasn't planning on spending a week kneeling in a pew.

Moulton looked somewhat pained. 'But I fear my own quarters, being rather cramped and wanting, would not be conducive to Christian thought, to the texts I will have to prepare and the service I will surely be needing to study.'

'A sack of coal for Mr Moulton's house? Maynard, what do you say?'

The miller looked glum. 'A sack, I dare say.'

'Newcastle coals.'

'Newcastle coals it is!' Sir Gilbert exclaimed.

'There we are, then, a properly ordained service, with all the trimmings.'

'Trimmings, sir?' Moulton asked dangerously. 'A simple service as God intended, sir, surely.'

'Of course. By trimmings I merely mean . . . a bride and groom, gathered together with the . . . good book.'

Moulton nodded. 'You can have your man send the coal around,' the clergyman said dismissively, his smiling mouth crammed with strings of spit. Cant and hypocrisy were meat and drink to Sir Gilbert. But this mealy-mouthed toad, rubbing his dry white hands in this barren house of God, made him glad of his own grime.

HORN'S CROSS,

BLIND MAN'S MOOR, DORSET

The garish caravan had set out early that morning, coats and shawls thrown around their best clothing. Telling had taken the grey cob he had ridden down from Chipping Marleward and gone ahead in his care-worn coat, brushed and soaked and daubed and stitched by the excellent Mrs Pride. He had added another clutch of feathers to his hat, polished his boots and all his equipment. Telling glanced over his shoulder at the chilled cavalcade, their spirits somewhat dampened by the reckless breeze gusting in over the wilderness of moor. Thackray rode just behind him on a borrowed pony, carrying the ridiculous duck gun as if he was about to fire some heroic salute to the heavens. Behind him came Miller Morrison on the newly exchanged black cob and his scowling brother astride a one-eyed bay mare. The miller's own dog cart was creaking on its ancient hinges under the weight of the bridal troupe. Bella was in her best blue gown. Anneliese had arranged Bella's hair in intricate ringlets, fixed a small strip of calico about her rapidly healing head wound. Her hair bobbed enticingly about her rather pinched features. Mary Keziah had also crammed herself in the uncomfortable cart, packed in with the bonnets and bouquets and holding her abdomen against the jolts. They had lodged the coal-sack behind the seat, Bella insisting it was covered with a blanket. 'I'm going to my wedding delivering a hundredweight of nutty slack!' she had snapped.

Starling was driving in his tall black hat, Jamie was striding along whistling like an idiot, with Mrs Pride and the millhand Sebby Boyce bringing up the rear, baskets and bottles under their arms.

Saturday morning, and heavy rain clouds were hurrying in from the sea as if they intended to race the bedraggled party to the church. Trees and bushes bent double in the scouring winds.

What a hateful wilderness, Bella thought. She winced as her maid's thrusting elbow caught her under the ribs.

'It's no good, you'll have to let me out,' Mary Keziah complained, levering herself out of the peeling leather bench seat. Anneliese made room as the maid manoeuvred herself to the side, Sebby Boyce doubling forward to help her down. Bella peered around at her, concerned and irritated at the same time.

What a grand affair this was turning out to be! Arriving at a tumbledown church in the middle of nowhere wearing a filthy dress at the head of a procession of tinkers! A few weeks before she had been engaged to poor Anthony – Lord Clavincale – looking forward to a sumptuous wedding in Gloucester's newly conquered cathedral. But Clavincale was dead – done in by her own hand as much as Hugo's furiously aimed bough – and the cathedral remained in the care of Sir Edward Massey's stubborn Roundhead garrison.

Her errant knight was riding alongside the jolting carriage, his pale features lit up with impatient excitement. Hugo looked as if he would climb down and haul the wretched wagon himself, in his gnawing haste to get his bride to the church on time. She realized he had waited an age for this moment, bent all his youthful energy towards overcoming the obstacles thrown in his path and finally making her his wife.

She had hardly lifted a finger to speed the union he had set his young heart on.

Bella felt a pang of guilt at her own bad temper, and favoured the earnest cavalier a beaming smile. Hugo grinned back, throwing out his chest and straightening his back. One look from her and he was as stiff as a poker. Bella stifled a giggle which her panting maid completely misinterpreted. She hoicked up her skirts and prepared to walk back to the mill.

'Don't you go bothering about me,' she cried. 'I won't hold you up.' Mary Keziah tugged her shawl about her drab brown gown. 'Go on without me if you like,' she invited her mistress.

'Don't talk such nonsense, Mary, we'll do no such thing!'

'We said eleven, that old bugger won't hang around,' her father called, turning the mare's blind head around to see who had caused the delay.

Telling halted, peered about anxiously. He would have preferred the preacher to come to them. By God, they'd be visible for miles around, strung out like this. Luckily there didn't seem to be any high ground, nor worthwhile cover, for a trouble-making spy. He gazed around the barren moor, a few pitiful shrubs cowering over clumps of crabgrass.

'How much further is it?' he asked the morose miller.

'Fair way yet,' the carefully preened and startlingly flour-free miller replied, nodding down the road. Did he mean a mile or one hundred?

'I just need to catch my breath,' the maid called out, settling her aching bundle on a large stone beside the road. She spread one white hand over the mossy pillow, closing her eyes with pain.

'What is it, Mary dear, is it coming already?'

'Little bugger's turning over, is all,' Mrs Pride declared, settling her basket on Jamie and striding over to help the distraught maid. 'Sebby, less 'ave that bottle of yours,' she demanded.

Bella sat up in the dog cart, drumming her fingers on the running-board. 'We'll never get it over with, at this rate,' she muttered.

'Over with?' Telling called, leaning over his pony's neck and scowling at his wild-eyed intended. One moment she was beaming at him, the next she was throwing her weight about like a slimline version of her damned father! He wondered for a moment if marriage would settle her raging temper. 'You make it sound as if we're going into battle!' he called dejectedly.

Bella tossed her shoulders, looked away over the horrid moor. Her fingers strayed to the bandage, making Telling wince in sympathy. 'Let's just get on, can we? Before we all freeze to death?'

'You go on,' Mary Keziah sighed. 'I'll follow on when I've me breath.'

'Aye, I'll stay with her, the poor splinter,' Mrs Pride cooed, cradling the pale maid in her strong arms. 'We'll see you at the church.'

Bella was furious, her cheeks flushing with fury and then dimming dangerously. She glared about the rotten church, the stone-cold chamber and worm-riddled pews.

She had never seen such a beastly place. Her head throbbed horribly, and her blistered vision blurred for a moment. She blinked rapidly, releasing a single silver tear. Why, it wasn't fit for hogs, let alone for decent folk to get wed in. Her father, standing behind her left shoulder, was thinking along the same lines, wondering why the dribbling oaf Moulton didn't get on with it. Much more of this and he'd see the error of his ways and call the whole wretched wedding off again! Moulton muttered and sighed, flicking through his moth-eaten prayer book, the tallow pages greasy with age and extensive use. He'd turned his red nose up at the mention of trimmings, and yet here he was going through the entire book as if he was some bishop officiating for one of the royal Princes! Get on with it, man, he muttered under his breath.

Telling stood erect beside his sweetheart, swallowing nervously and glancing around at the fuming girl. He wished Moulton would hurry, so he could claim his prize at last.

The rest of them had taken up the front pew, Anneliese sobbing, Jamie staring at the ceiling with his mouth open, the miller, Starling, Sebby, and Thackray looking glumly dignified alongside. Half a dozen local crones had appeared out of the woodwork to witness the fun, crouching in their pews like so many superannuated witches.

Moulton peered between the two lovebirds in front of him, trying to avoid eye contact with the ferocious calico-wrapped spitfire in the crumpled dress or the scowling Cavalier beside her. As soon as one of them spied the other they seemed to bristle up like a pair of gamecocks. There would be fireworks in their house, that was for sure. He lifted his fleshy chin, rolled his eyes heavenwards.

At least there would be some compensation for his sacrifice, with a few hours beside a proper fire to look forward to.

'We are gathered here in the sight of God this day to join Bella Marguerite Morrison and Hugo Telling as man and wife. If any man can show cause why they should not be so joined, let him stand forth now, or for ever hold his peace.'

Might as well be married in a barn, Bella fumed.

I'll hold me peace, all right, Sir Gilbert growled.

Please God don't change your mind, Telling wished. Just repeat the words and . . .

The sudden, deafening bang tore the air from his lungs and the spine from his back.

The church seemed to shiver, rocked to its foundations by the elemental attack. The iron-ribbed oak door crashed open under the weight of four sets of shoulders and numerous boots. A sudden gust of wind lifted skirts and ruffled prayer books, startling the tiny congregation from their uncomfortable pews. They peered over their shoulders in alarm, squinting against the thin sunlight slanting through the ancient arch. A dark figure strode forward brandishing a pair of pistols. His boots rang on the chilled stone floor.

'Stop the wedding! They're murderers and traitors, the pair of them!' Compton Speedwell called nasally, half a dozen of his men spreading out behind him with muskets and carbines ready, match fuming sullenly in their eager fists.

Telling was paralysed with indecision. So many conflicting emotions his fevered brain couldn't begin to process them, a rush of sparks to an empty pan. He stared down the barrels of the hobbling dragoon's pistols, lifting his arm across Bella's as if his thin limbs could protect his staring bride from the intruder's bullets.

Compton Speedwell tore the scrap of paper from his coat, grinned maliciously at the terrified congregation.

'Orders from Sir Ralph Hopton, commanding officer of the captured counties of Somerset, Dorset, and Wiltshire, viz., the immediate arrest of known traitors and rebels. To wit, Bella Morrison, Jamie Morrison, Mary Keziah Pitt, Gwen Pitt, laundress, and Mordecai Pitt, rebel deserter.' He held the order between his index finger and thumb, still clutching the pistol, and allowed himself a scowl of delight. 'Along with any others who may have aided and abetted them, to wit, Captain Telling of Rupert's horse!'

His scarred face had suffered further indignities when he had tumbled from his horse back on the causeway. The nose had been broken and badly set on a flaking foundation of dried blood and mucus. He had lost three teeth from his lower jaw, torn his cheek raw so it resembled a poultice of diced liver. A broad and grubby bandage had been tied about his left ear, practically torn off by the impact on the rough road. His coat bulged over a tightly wound breastplate of bandages they had secured around his broken ribs. He had split his left boot up the side because of the vicious swelling between ankle and knee, secured the flapping sections with string.

His eyes, however, glittered with undiminished violence, as if his fearful injuries had merely whetted his appetite for revenge.

*

Speedwell had picked himself out of the ditch beside that damned causeway, his angry but rather muffled shouts eventually attracting the attention of his terrified men. He had crawled halfway to Wells before the bastard cowards had risked approaching him, as if they were convinced he was a supernatural sprite from the marshes. Graves looked as if he had fallen beneath the hoofs of an entire cavalry regiment. Martin Pike was yelping with agony, his leg twisted horribly beneath him. One by one the rest of the command appeared out of the shadows, leading their panting ponies.

They had spent the rest of that filthy night in a reedsman's cottage before making their sorry way back up the gorge they had searched the day before.

Speedwell, propped up on a hunchbacked pony, had gritted what remained of his teeth, his features distorted with rage, the maniacal roaring in his ears building up with every jog and jolt. The sorry procession rode straight through the silent village of Chipping Marleward, their eyes stung by the lazy smoke rising from the wrecked wash-house. They had spotted the terrified civilians running away over their back gardens, taking cover in the woods and hills.

Two brown bundles had been lifted from the ruined laundry and placed in a couple of wheelbarrows, what was left of their charred limbs stacked like kindling on top of the roasted trunks. The unexpected return of the dragoons had clearly halted their grim burial, the unfortunate villagers who had set about the grisly task joining their neighbours on the far side of the stream.

Speedwell had ridden on by, leaning over to spit a mouthful of bile over the scorched heaps of flesh. He smiled grimly as his phlegm hissed and rolled around the blackened stumps, imagined he was desecrating Telling's grave.

One day, my friend, he thought viciously. One day soon. Blind Man's Moor wasn't that big a wilderness. He'd search every blade of grass, turn over every stone to find the despised Cavalier.

They rode on. Every step now a symphony of searing pain, relentless burning sensations up and down his torn arms and legs. His hands shivered like some gin-blossom's blue-veined paws. The rasping reins ran with blood.

Nobody spoke.

Speedwell crossed the stream and pointed the way up the hill, to the big house in the woods. That old battleaxe Ramsay was as guilty as the rest of them, she'd tend their wounds while he figured out what to do next.

Back to Bristol to admit he had been humbled by a scrawny Cavalier and a few women, that his brave command had been given the run-around by a gang of straw-munching hill folk for the second time in as many months?

He would never live it down.

He had lain on his back, tears stinging his protruding eyes as the miserable old widow daubed his wounds and bandaged his seeping cuts, teeth set as he contemplated his revenge. Yes, she stared all right, but her bitch of a daughter had ridden off with them, that much was certain. A regular coven, he thought vindictively. When he returned he would burn the place to the ground and set the old widow on the road.

He would catch up with Telling and deal with that smirking upstart himself.

Two days later he had been able to walk – after a fashion. By that time seven more of his renegades had decided they had urgent appointments at the other end of the country. Pike was limping about nursing a swollen knee. Auld Guppy and a handful of the older men had remained at the hall, happy enough to pick the widow's threadbare larder clean. With Graves and that wandering simpleton Mitchell he had about a dozen men left.

The depleted troop had resumed its journey that afternoon, their ponies refreshed by the rest and Widow Ramsay's lush lawn. They trotted back down the hill and out through the deserted village, straight down the causeway, and on over the levels as far as Glastonbury. Next day they turned east across the Polden Hills to pick up the Fosseway. He took them via Yeovil to Crewkerne before calling a halt, a blistering pace which had left his men moaning and his own barely healing wounds shrieking torments to his numbed skull.

But he welcomed the pain, the torn flesh, the rasp of the saddle against his flayed thighs. It helped him concentrate, focus all the pain and hurt on one person. Hugo Telling.

Telling had ruined his mission, spoilt his play back in the gorge, and made him and his command look fools into the bargain. He had lost a good half of them without so much as a sniff of the enemy, and would be obliged to go through the whole distressing incident with some jumped-up magistrate down west – he could hardly go riding into neighbouring counties without so much as a by your leave from the local authorities. He would either have to stop off in Yeovil and report to the justices for a new warrant, or continue on towards his final destination with a crude counterfeit. He had chosen the latter option, deciding to risk everything on a sudden sortie, riding directly to Blind Man's Moor.

He rolled the sinister-sounding name around his mouth, wondering why it should have struck a chord in him.

Penmethock. Of course. It was only a few miles on from the barren wilderness. The cracked-up old bird who ruled the roost down there was notorious all over the west for his draconian punishments, his vile treatment of any person tainted with the disease of rebellion. Black Bob Dyle wouldn't take much convincing as to the importance of the dragoon captain's mission. Together they would ensure that greased eel of a Cavalier was brought to justice – preferably at the end of a hemp rope.

It had all worked out precisely as he had anticipated, except for the justice's tomfool of a son John, the deceptively delicate and stubbornly willed Lord Clavincale. The candle-wasting spark wanted to know the ins and outs of everything, why had he done this, why hadn't he done that? Speedwell had been forced to bluster, and the more he blustered the more suspicious and critical the boy had become. He thought for one ghastly moment his forged documents might be countermanded, that the son might delay matters by insisting on some time-wasting inquiry into the whole affair. But luckily for Speedwell the sire had overruled the youngster and allowed him to serve the warrant for the apprehension of the fugitives. Speedwell had limped across the courthouse to collect his precious order, but the grinning boy had snatched it from his hands, insisting he went along with the dragoons to see the warrant was properly executed.

Oh, it would be executed, all right.

And in any case, a few extra muskets might come in handy, with that bastard Telling on the loose and armed to the bloody teeth.

'Stay exactly where you are,' the youth called, his voice shrill in the echoing church. Speedwell cursed under his breath. The interfering teenager wouldn't keep still or silent. Young Lord Clavincale stepped alongside the dragoon as he displayed his creased warrant to the dumbstruck congregation, spoiling his triumphant entry.

Hugo Telling had recognized the scowling dragoon at once, but wondered at the identity of the stranger alongside his old enemy. He seemed better dressed than most of Speedwell's dragoons, although he was obviously a deal younger than the filthy veterans.

'We are authorized to convey the aforementioned to the nearest garrison, where you will be held until your trials,' the youngster called, his voice rebounding over the empty pews. 'Captain Speedwell, escort the prisoners into the yard.'

The battered dragoon glanced sideways at his gallantly turned-out assistant, his scarred flesh peeling from his teeth in a savage smile.

'They're my prisoners,' he leered. 'Fetch the ropes, we'll save this turkeycock a hard journey back, obstructing an officer of the crown in the course of his duty!'

The blushing youngster stuck to his guns, holding the dragoon's crooked glare for a moment. 'They are under my father's jurisdiction,' he grated, his bare cheeks flushing red. 'They will not be harmed before they have been properly tried.'

'Properly tried, yes,' Speedwell argued, wrinkling the torn warrant in his grubby fist, 'but he's not on any warrant! I brought you notice of 'em, I'll take care of 'em, especially him,' Speedwell breathed menacingly. Still the boy wouldn't budge.

'You will escort the prisoners to the Assizes as we agreed. My father will decide whether they are to be returned under escort to Bristol or tried where they are.'

Telling glanced at Bella, sobbing with outraged frustration beside him. 'Don't worry.'

Speedwell grunted with anger, limped away from the plucky youngster as if galvanized into action by his mortal enemy's whispered encouragement.

'No talking there! Silence, the lot of you!' He hobbled down the aisle with his pistols aimed at the Cavalier's astonished face. The youngster in the blue suit doubled down the aisle after him, knocking the pews aside in his agitation.

'Captain Speedwell, remember you are acting under my father's jurisdiction,' he insisted. The guards hurried into the frozen church after their chiefs, powder pots clanking merrily on their chests.

Telling glanced over the furious captain's shoulder, recognized the giant dragoon with the flaxen hair and the frightened youth with the red Montero. The boy he'd warned off on the causeway, he thought furiously, limping like a wounded stag. Should have killed the bastard while he had the chance. As well as half a dozen ruffians in their civilian coats there was an equal number of foot, hastily turned-out countrymen wearing miserably faded blue coats. He presumed the strangers belonged to the determined youngster.

Speedwell pressed his hate-racked face against his.

Telling leaned away, refusing to breath the same sour air as the determined dragoon.

'One move, one fart, and I'll drill you, so help me,' Speedwell snarled. He stood back on his heel, his repulsive double smile rippling the scarred flesh below his mouth. 'Not so cocky off your horse, eh, Telling? And this is the legendary Bella Morrison? Reports of your death were clearly rather premature.'

The girl staggered a little, clutching her hand to the bandaged wound. Tiny saws seemed to be at work, severing her right eye from her coiling brain.

'What is the meaning of this outrage? How dare you interfere with my daughter's wedding!' Sir Gilbert called, sliding in behind the richly appointed youngster. 'Stamping about shouting your orders, in a house of God and all,' he said blusteringly.

The boy concentrated hard, gathering up all the authority he could muster. 'We regret the intrusion—'

'Hah!' Speedwell shrieked with laughter.

'—but we are come on a warrant from Sir Ralph Hopton, authorized by my own father, the Earl of Dartland,' the young pup went on, gamely ignoring Speedwell's murderous glare.

Dartland? The merchant wondered, thinking furiously. Why would that ring a bell?

'Dartland?' Bella asked, alarmed. She glanced guiltily at Telling, biting his lip in mortification as he stepped from one boot to the other. Not *the* Dartland? Poor Anthony's notoriously cranky father, here?

'Pissed yerself, I reckon,' Speedwell leered, shoving his brutally used features into Telling's suddenly fearful face. 'Bit different, eye to eye, isn't it, my little coxcomb?' The shrivelled Cavalier blinked, licked his dry lips.

'You have no authority here,' he said hoarsely. 'Sir Ralph Hopton is unaware of the true facts in this case!'

'Hah! That's what you think,' Speedwell snapped, curling the prized paper under the candle-waster's nose. 'A properly made out warrant, authorized by the earl, just as this lordling says.'

The lordling in question was clearly unaccustomed to being referred to in such an offhand manner. He was about to say so when Speedwell darted forward and cracked the walnut butt of his pistol on Telling's wrist.

'Hugo!'

'Captain Speedwell!'

'Keep your mitts where we can see them!' Speedwell shouted, making Bella jump with fright. Sir Gilbert had pulled her by the shoulders, trying to pick her away from Telling's twitching side.

'Sir Ralph Hopton would never have issued such a warrant had he been in possession of the facts! I am a captain in Prince Rupert's lifeguard and this young woman is to be my wife!' Telling shouted.

Speedwell's bloody features darkened with fury. 'On the scaffold, mebbe!'

Telling nursed his bruised wrist and stared dumbly at the young nobleman, desperate for his support.

'Leave out your fancy talking, Telling, we can all see you've beshit yourself again!'

'When I arrived to get to the bottom of the matter, I found these dragoons sacking the village. They tried to—'

Speedwell's furious backhander sent Telling spinning over the altar. He cracked his head and slipped to his knees.

'Hugo!' Bella wailed. Sir Gilbert clamped his sausage fingers about her arms, pulled her away none too gently.

'Captain Speedwell!' the youngster shrieked, his voice shrill with anger. 'You will refrain from manhandling these prisoners! Have a care, sir, they are under my father's jurisdiction now!'

'He claims he was getting to the bottom of the matter, and we find him marrying the cross-eyed doxy! Use your brains, man!' Speedwell snarled, anxious not to have to reveal the precise details of the sorry incident back in Chipping Marleward. The rebel screws had done his men in and that was it and all about it, he thought furiously.

'Doxy?' Bella repeated, her pale features pinched with sudden colour.

The young nobleman ground his lips together in fury as his muttering troops eyed their bedraggled counterparts. Two sets of men, two sets of loaded muskets, two sets of sullenly burning match, filling the church with the bitter incense of battle.

'You damned horse thief, who do you think you are talking to? I am John Dyle, Lord Clavincale, and I am not accustomed to being insulted by brigands from Bristol!'

Clavincale! She prayed she had misheard the name! Bella peered over at the blushing youth, picking out some shades of resemblance in his somewhat leaner features. Anthony's younger brother. Of all the people she could least afford to meet. The youngster was standing his ground in front of the older dragoon, refusing to be diverted by Speedwell's dreadful mutterings. His men, buoyed up by their master's tenacity, eyed their counterparts across the aisle. Like Speedwell, the dragoons seemed slightly awed by his prickly outburst.

'Gentlemen, this is an outrage,' Moulton piped up – more for appearances' sake than any heartfelt desire to get involved with these dangerous strangers. He held his Bible in front of his chest as if it would deflect their bullets. Nobody paid any attention to his half-hearted protest, and the clergyman relapsed into agitated silence.

Speedwell realized he had gone too far. Upsetting the little strunt in his own backyard, his father an earl and a justice of the peace and all. He grimaced, watched Telling haul himself to his feet. Clavincale glowered at the truculent dragoon for a moment.

'There is no need to trouble yourself, sir,' the youth said levelly. 'We will put the entire matter before my father. It will be for him to decide how we are to proceed.'

Speedwell, who knew he had already said too much, lowered his pistol a notch. 'You're right, sir,' he added as an afterthought. He looked up, expecting to see the youth preening his ruffled feathers. Instead the young nobleman strode forward and slapped the bigger dragoon with his gauntlet. Speedwell staggered, his men tense as the Cornish infantry menaced them with their muskets.

'Agh, God damn,' Speedwell muttered, wiping his wounded mouth.

'You dared to insult me, sir, you'll answer for it,' the youth snarled, pressing home his advantage. Speedwell looked over his shoulder, realized his men had allowed the Cornish pricks to get the better of them. He tried to grin. 'You push me too far,' he said out of the side of his mouth.

'Not far enough, sir. Once we have dealt with these prisoners I shall send my second to call on you, sir,' the supercilious lordling rasped. 'You may of course present your humblest apologies before all these presently assembled witnesses.'

'Well, I meant nothing by it, sir,' Speedwell said shakily.
'I mean . . .'

'Sergeant, escort the prisoners out into the yard!'

'Yuz, my lor'!'

Speedwell glared from the impudent lordling to the
shaken Cavalier.

They would pay for this, by his oath, they'd pay.

PENMETHOCK ASSIZES,

DORSET

The ground floor of the courthouse had been constructed in locally quarried stone, but the lately completed first and second storeys had been finished with red brick, giving the new building an uncomfortably alien appearance against the sea-bruised, wind-chipped coastline. The handsome foundations had been laid before the war to grandiose designs drawn up by the late Lord Clavincale. The Assizes had been intended as a scaled-down, rather more practical version of their own family seat at Fib's Hall, a mile or so further up the hill. An ambitious public work funded by the immensely rich Dyle family for the punishment of felons, protection of the peace, and encouragement of public morals. The new structure had been designed to further the family's hold on the village, and, rather more shrewdly, to serve as a valuable source of income for the canny earl. Black Bob would be entitled to oversee the imposition and collection of fines, rents, and taxes, as well as superintending harbour tariffs and import duties. After his son's untimely death, however, the increasingly bitter earl had ordered the two new storeys and bricked up half a dozen windows, bought up great lengths of chain, and dug deeper dungeons. The avaricious landowner had ordered cheaper materials, ugly imported bricks rather than the pale stone from the hills, and set unskilled labourers and petty criminals to work on his dead son's once proud design – turning a monument into a malignant mausoleum. Anthony Dyle's lofty and precisely drawn plans had been perverted and poisoned by vengeful necessity.

With the outbreak of the war the Assizes – dreaded destination of poachers and horse thieves – had been hastily extended to cope with the sudden crop of rebels, whores, and deserters netted by Black Bob's eagle-eyed constables. A scatter of outbuildings had been tacked on to house a rapidly expanded company of guards and jailers, cooks and clerks, as well as laundress, carpenter, bailiff, locksmith, and hangman. The red-brick monstrosity had been built beside the crossroads where everybody – seafarer, traveller, farmer, or felon – could see it. The ugly keep might have been built by robber barons or marcher warlords: highly visible, highly practical, it dominated the gorse-green landscape just as effectively as the towering stacks of the Hare Rock overshadowed the nearby harbour. Its wind-blown walls were protected by a stone palisade topped with iron spikes. In its turn the arched gatehouse might have been designed by trolls; roughly hewn and rugged, it dwarfed and demoralized the unfortunates who passed within. Hugo stared at the crudely chiselled greeting above the arch: 'Amend thy weys or Ryde the Mare.'

His hands had been bound behind him, his right foot roped to the dirty girth like some common horse thief. Captain Speedwell's bearlike sergeant had bunched the hemp leading-rein in his enormous fist, alternately tugging Telling's foaming beast on and then savagely kicking it in the snout to send it rearing and plunging beneath the pale Cavalier.

Twelve miles they had ridden, every jolting step a torture, far worse than any of the battles or hardships he had ever faced. His whole life, his hopes, his sweetheart, his dreams and future, trussed and tied and then set adrift on this stranger's sea. Everything he was, everything he wanted being dragged behind an overgrown oaf in a pea-green coat. He could have wept with frustration, but he had determined not to weaken before Speedwell's sardonic smile. A week which should have seen him wed and happy now looked likely to end in him being hanged and hurled into a pauper's grave with Bella's still beautiful corpse.

He shuddered with terror, horrified by his rapidly collapsing horizons.

Stupid, pointless, squalid death.

He could have faced a regiment of Roundheads in an open field, charged a battery of guns with a grin and good cheer. But the homicidal Speedwell would shoot him in the back – even if this backwater court cleared him of these trumped-up charges.

Perhaps they would free him and hang Bella? Would the deranged dragoon or this lunatic judge realize there were worse punishments for him than death on the scaffold? What was life without his almost wife? What pleasure would there be in breathing air Bella had not shared?

'Get on, boy, duck your 'ead or ye'll spoil our fun 'anging yer,' Graves leered over his shoulder.

Winded, wet, and deeply alarmed at the vile turn of events, Telling held on with his legs and endured the thumps and the bumps, peering over his shoulder at the rest of the sorry procession.

Sir Gilbert and Miller Morrison were back on their

ponies, but Speedwell hadn't thought it worth tying their hands. Martin Pike kept an eye on them, his tightly bound leg hooked over the pommel of his saddle and the bright red Montero set at a rakish angle on his dark brown curls. Thackray, Sebby Boyce, and Algernon Starling walked behind, muttering to one another and staring about, their arms tied behind their backs and the loose rope slung under Auld Guppy's gnarled fists. Four more dragoons escorted the overcrowded dog cart, Anneliese and Bella huddled together behind one of Clavincale's men slouching over the bunched reins. Jamie sat beside the driver, whistling to himself and grinning at the bewildered guards as if they were all off for a picnic beside the sea, a pleasant interlude in a triumphant progress along the coast. The rest of the dragoons followed, with the last of Clavincale's men bringing up the rear – match burning and muskets ready. The young lord himself was back on his thoroughbred chestnut just to the left of his troop, staring over the shuffling files at the impudent dragoon who had taken up station on the far side of the column.

Compton Speedwell looked no happier than Telling. He had wondered about putting spurs to his horse and escaping over the ugly moor, but cowardly flight had never been his way and he wasn't intending to break that rule now – not for the sake of some whiskerless boy like Clavincale, at any rate. He'd kill the shit-breeked wretch quick enough – if it ever came to that – but the captain did not relish the prospect of explaining the oafish lump's death to his father the earl. Black Bob was madder than a pitful of rats – that was clear enough to anyone. Speedwell was beginning to wonder whether he had done the right thing calling the damned family in on his little mission. Far better if he had gone by night, located the miller's nest, and stormed in with muskets blazing. Brigands or deserters would have been blamed for the killing, and as soon as it was realized the victims had been wanted by the Royalist authorities – well, not many people would have lost much sleep over their shocking fate. A shot in the dark, a knife in the back, ambushed on the lonely moor – so long as Telling had ended up dead he wouldn't have cared. He seethed and fumed on his horse, propped up uncomfortably with his wounds crying havoc up and down his arms, legs, and trunk. The wet wind seemed to be flaying his exposed cheeks, rubbing salt into the ruts and lashes where his skin had been.

Speedwell glanced over the weary, blue-coated escort at their flushed chief. He was sitting his horse like a sack of slops, the skittish chestnut tossing its head as if embarrassed by its master's inelegant posture. He looked up. The Morrison girl was peering over her shoulder at them again, her ravishing features mottled with cold, undermined by insinuating seams of uncertainty. The wound in her head was troubling her too, by the way she kept picking at the bandage as if it had been tied too tight. By God, no wonder Telling had put his neck in the noose for her. She was worth fighting for, that one. A bit of rough treatment, a damn good fright, and she might be worth cultivating, he thought to himself.

The unrepentant captain urged his horse along the marching column, pulled in easily beside the creaking cart. He noticed with irritation that the nobleman had copied his manoeuvre as if he was scared of missing something, urging the chestnut up on the blindside so he could keep an eye on his erstwhile ally, no doubt.

'I must say, I've been looking forward to making your acquaintance, Miss Morrison,' he said easily, forgetting his pains for a moment and delighting in her closed-mouth response. 'How many is it now you've potted? Seven? Eight? My men weren't the first to fall beneath your pistol, were they, Miss Morrison? Must have come as a bit of a shock, taking a ball back for a change, eh?'

Bella stared straight ahead, the dark-haired girl beside her clutching at her arm in feverish anxiety. Speedwell felt the familiar sickly surge of excitement clog his throat. A year before these two fine young sluts wouldn't have given him the time of day. Now he had them at his mercy – virtual mercy, anyway. If he'd acted sooner he could have shot down the lordling, scattered his dozy escort, and snatched the prisoners back off for himself. How would they have found him, back in Bristol with two thousand others just like him marching off to all points of the compass? You might just as well try and keep your eye on a pint of sea water in the middle of an ocean as one wanted dragoon.

'Miss Morrison will have a chance to answer your charges in my father's courthouse, just as you will answer for your own errors to me,' Clavincale called from the other side of the cart. Speedwell grimaced, nodded his head with exaggerated respect.

'A misunderstanding, sir, in the heat of the moment, you understand.'

'Is that your apology?' the young lord crowed.

'Apologize, apologize, a thousand eyes all stuffed with lies,' Jamie Morrison piped up from the running-board. The driver glanced sideways at his unhinged passenger. Bella gritted her teeth, turned to the young man riding alongside her.

'I'll answer any charges he cares to bring,' she said stoutly, tears pricking her eyes. 'But if there *has* been any fault then it has been mine – none of these people had anything to do with it,' she insisted.

'Shot five of my men by yourself, miss, is that it?' Speedwell called nasally. 'By God, it's a good job old Pym hasn't too many more like you.' He gave her a juicy wink.

'As I said, sir, Miss Morrison and her party will have a chance to put their side of events before my father.'

Speedwell sniggered, wiping his face on his bloody coat sleeve.

Further proceedings were interrupted by their arrival at the courthouse.

Bella peered ahead, watched the big dragoon in the pea-green coat tug Hugo's pony under the horrible gate-house, and lead him off into a corner of the courtyard. The column filed under the leering sign and formed up in the shadow of Black Bob's Mare, a gaunt oak gallows, worn smooth as a fragment of the true cross by long and continual use. Bella shivered in its vile shadow, stared beseechingly at poor Hugo, hatless and hopeless on the bloodily beaten pony. He tried to smile back at her, gloomy as a guillemot on a crowded cliff.

Speedwell followed the ragged column through the gate, his double smile slipping from his scarred face as he watched the courthouse guards file down the steps to reinforce the blue-coated escort. God damn it all, his case wasn't all that much more promising than Telling's. Trumped-up charges and a crudely forged warrant? Careful scrutiny of his mission would expose him as a liar and renegade, if he didn't look sharp.

Abraham Bacon, the lugubrious clerk, paused on the courthouse steps, his large hands clasping the iron balustrade as he surveyed the twitching catch. He lifted his black hat from his swept-back hair and bowed to the young lord – as if it had been Clavincale who had cornered the fugitives after some miraculous pursuit across the moor. Speedwell breathed a plume of cold vapour, watched the lordling dismount clumsily from the fresh chestnut and stride up the steps, pausing to confer with his father's clerk. Clavincale looked over his shoulder, reporting the captain's many misdemeanours in a supercilious undertone.

Speedwell grinned back. He didn't like the look of the place, or these bumpkin judges. By God, he wished he'd cut and run while he had the chance. There would be no getting out now, not without Black Bob's bloody permission, at any rate.

The dungeons proved every bit as uninviting as the grimly utilitarian courthouse. The entire party had been led into the barely furnished hall and immediately separated. Bella and Anneliese had been left with Lord Clavincale while the men were shoved and prodded down the stairway to their left, bundled out of sight as if their very existence above the ground was an act of contempt. Bella watched them go, her pinched features draining.

'You and Miss Ramsay need not be detained below stairs,' Clavincale muttered, ill at ease with the women. 'There is an ante-room on the second floor,' he said thickly.

Telling had peered back over his shoulder, caught one last glimpse of his sweetheart as she stood shivering beside the gesturing nobleman. John Dyle. Lord Clavincale!

He closed his eyes for a second, horrified by the spiteful twist of fate which had left them all at the mercy of the awkward, headstrong boy. Younger brother of the

Clavincale who had died by their hands outside Gloucester! By Christ, it was like some wretched drama by that Shakespeare fellow. A tragedy in five increasingly hateful acts.

The younger Dyle's features might have been leaner but he had the same lazy, pale grey eyes as his dead brother. He had seemed stern enough standing up to Speedwell. He might have looked like a spoilt boy, but he had held his ground as the devious dragoon blustered and threatened.

Telling swallowed, reassured himself that neither the boy, nor his notoriously cracked father, could possibly guess at his connection to the murdered brother. How could they possibly find out Telling had been moments away from being charged with bludgeoning the elder Clavincale to death in the woods near Brockworth those brief weeks before?

Telling shuddered as he followed the grinning jailer down the steps. The newly laid stone flags were coated in a treacherous film of algae, growing vigorously up and down the walls despite the constant stamp of the guards and the chain-laden shuffle of the unfortunate inhabitants. They ducked their heads under a chipped stone arch and waited in the passage while their jailers shuffled by, clanking their keys against the rusted iron bars of the straw-strewn cells. Abraham Bacon stood by with the lantern, tilting his head to read the names from Speedwell's clumsily folded warrant. Starling, Thackray, and Boyce were unceremoniously shoved into the first cell. Sir Gilbert's black-suited clerk looked around his new surroundings as if he found them quite acceptable to his station. Thackray slumped down on a filthy pallet, his head in his hands.

'Ye'll be comfy in there, boys, but mind ye those rats,' Humphrey Gale called vindictively, closing the cell door on the bewildered trio.

Telling, Jamie, an unusually silent Sir Gilbert, and his wretched brother were prodded into the next cell. Abraham Bacon peered through the bars at the strange company. The scowling Cavalier, the morose miller, the grinning idiot, and the hectic merchant – shuffling in the straw like common pickpockets. Bacon smoothed the warrant in his large palm, peered down his nose at his prisoners.

'Where are the rest of your party? Mesdames and Master Pitt? Well?'

Telling shrugged. 'I've not seen any of them in weeks.'

Bacon snorted. 'The laundress and her children? Are they back at the mill?'

'Captain Speedwell never said anything 'bout any . . .' Humphrey Gale protested.

Bacon held up his hand, pained by his jailer's surly outburst. 'It is of no matter. We seem to have the principal players and a few others besides,' he reflected, apparently satisfied.

Sir Gilbert shook off his profound sense of misery for a moment, grinned good-naturedly at the round-faced clerk. 'My good man, there really isn't any need for this,' he began. Bacon nodded his large head, brow creased in concentration. 'As you are no doubt aware, neither my brother here nor myself appear on the original indictment, whatever that rogue Speedwell reckons to the contrary. We were on our way directly to the courthouse when that oaf Speedwell burst in upon us accusing us all of God alone knows what.'

Bacon sucked his drooping lower lip for a moment.

'Directly to the courthouse, via the church at Horn's Cross?' he enquired. 'In company with the fugitives already mentioned? I believe we have grounds enough for your detention, Sir Gilbert.'

'A simple ceremony joining my son-in-law to be, here, with my own daughter, Bella, light of her poor dead mother's life,' the merchant scoffed, beginning to get into his accustomed stride.

'Yes, well. I am sure the judge will be looking forward to your explanations as much as I will,' Bacon snapped, tucking the folded warrant back in his pocket. The clerk strode off down the gloomy passage taking the lantern with him, the grinning guards falling in behind.

Telling stared at the agitated merchant. 'You realize who the boy in blue is, do you?' he hissed.

Sir Gilbert frowned. 'Of course I realize, you damned plover,' he snapped. 'So you'd best watch what you say, or we'll all be done for. By God, we'll need a slippery Johnny to get us out of this damned mess,' he went on, reddening. Telling shrugged his narrow shoulders.

'I was a student at law before the war—' he began, silenced by the merchant's sudden snort of derision.

'Oh, well, that's all right, then. No doubt you have already picked holes in the prosecution's case large enough to sail a galleon through!' Sir Gilbert exclaimed.

'I'd be in a better position to protect her if she was my wife! She would have been before now if it hadn't been for your tomfool interfering!' Telling snapped.

'Don't try your lawyer tricks, muddying the waters with all that nonsense now!' the merchant warned, his fleshy jowls set. 'That warrant was signed by Hopton himself! Bella, Anneliese, and the rest of them! It wouldn't matter a fig if you were married to Prince Rupert, he couldn't get my Bella off a murder charge any more than you imagine you can!'

Telling strode into the tiny pillar of light beneath the barred grate, clenching his fists with frustration.

'Jamie can put his side of it, and Anneliese is heir to the Ramsay estate,' the student of law turned soldier reasoned. 'They can hardly argue with one of their own, can they?'

'Kilmersden Hall's a long way from this shitpit,' Sir Gilbert growled. 'And who's going to pay any attention to what Jamie's got to say?'

His son grinned stupidly at his ferocious father. Telling stared at the lousy wall, the teeming algae scored by scratches and scrawled names. All dead now, he wouldn't wonder. An oyster of doubt was beginning to fester at the back of his mind.

Morrison knew all about the business at Brockworth, how Telling had been caught by the elder Dyle playing popnoddy under a tree with Bella – his fiancée. Clavincale had drawn his sword and pursued him into the woods, where by a series of lucky tricks Telling had managed to get the drop on him and club him down with a broken bough.

That information might be the merchant's ticket out of here, Hugo thought, horrified by the insinuating possibility. Morrison could make up some cock-eyed tale that Hugo had pounced on his delectable daughter, and that the outraged Clavincale had been stabbed in the back as he went to her aid. The damsel in distress rescued by the errant knight, only to be cut down by Telling, the loathsome serpent. It would go down Black Bob's ears easier than a spoonful of honey. Talk about killing two birds with one stone!

Hugo glanced around at his furiously thinking cell-mate. 'They'd never believe a word of it, I swear I'd take you down with me,' he breathed.

'What? A second ago you were saying we'd be able to talk our way out of it!'

Hugo frowned. The merchant was as slippery as a jug of jellied eels, but his surprise had seemed genuine enough.

'Well,' the miller said from his untidily stuffed pallet, 'ye'd best get your stories straight, cuz Black Bob'll get to the bottom of it, aye, if any man will.'

PENMETHOCK ASSIZES,

DORSET

Cornered, she snarled and spat like a scalded cat. Pitied, she cracked up like an overboiled milk pudding. But the awkward boy hadn't got much out of the tantalizingly distressed girl whatever ham-fisted tactics he had tried. It was a good thing in some ways poor Anthony wasn't there – he would have been fawning all over her by now, the young nobleman thought ruefully.

John Dyle – Lord Clavincale now, he remembered with a flicker of shame – was very much in awe of his exotic prisoner, Bella Marguerite Morrison. Bewildered by her predicament, she was bewitchingly innocent. Imploring the boy as if he was her saviour, not one of her executioners. The thoughtful youngster shuddered again. God forbid it should come to that! He could no more execute the forlorn maiden than he could extinguish the stars from the sky. Clavincale squirmed as he contemplated his own role in her imprisonment. There had to be something he could do – without arousing his father's ire. If Black Bob felt his whippersnapper of a son was being unduly lenient on the poor girl he would be doubly hard on her himself, that was for sure.

Clavincale almost envied Telling.

Moments from marrying the girl despite all his obvious

troubles – he must be eating his own innards in frustration by now. He chewed his fleshy lip in jealous agitation, shaken to the core by his unenviable dilemma. He ought to have been inviting the girl to a dance at Fib's Hall, not discussing the terms of her forthcoming trial.

Clavincale closed the door on the distressed maiden, nodded as authoritatively as possible to the drowsy guard. At least Bella wasn't suffering the same indignities as her sweetheart, stuck in a cell beneath the Assizes. Still, a feather bed in heaven would be the equivalent of a rack of nails if one had come so close to possessing a treasure like Bella only to have her snatched out of your hands.

Clavincale was sixteen and three-quarters years old. He was inquisitive and clever but rather subdued, largely because he had dwelt so long in his elder brother's all-encompassing shadow. Ignored and neglected, he had taken to spending longer and longer periods in his room, avidly digesting the few worthwhile books he had inherited from his brother or studying the flora and fauna he collected during his long walks along the cliffs. He had been due to go up to Cambridge, but the war had interrupted the orderly progression of his education, kept him cooped up at home.

A few short months ago John had been little more than a ghost in the cold house – but now Anthony had taken his place, forced him out of the shadows and into the cracked-up glare of his surviving parent. John had become his half-dazed father's prop at home as well as at the Assizes, eager to set his quick wits to the complexities of the courtroom. He had thrived on the responsibilities he had been given, relished the challenge of filling his dead brother's shoes. But he would never take Anthony's place in his father's heart. He would often come upon the old earl bent beneath Anthony's full-length portrait, staring at the lifeless oil eyes as if he could think his absent heir down from the cluttered wall, recreate his precious flesh and blood from the cracked canvas.

The Dyle family had bred sound statesmen rather than strong soldiers. Eminent Royalists in a strongly Royalist district, neither father nor sons had ever had much time for the military. Anthony had been a gifted, cunning courtier, a clever diplomat and useful agent. Young John had been destined for a quiet career in the Church or law – until his elder brother's squalid death outside Gloucester had brought his world crashing down around his ears and confirmed all his father's long-held mistrust of soldiers and soldiering.

Now John had been forced to take up the great majority of the household affairs, as well as assisting his father at the Assizes and helping Abraham Bacon with the miscellaneous clerical work. A lesser youth might have cracked under the strain, hidden away from the pressing realities of life without Anthony with blind bouts of drinking and whoring. As it was, the elder son's death had brought out the best in his brother, hastened his progress toward responsible manhood. As much as anything else, he felt it was his duty to try to curb some of his father's worst excesses. Black Bob they called him, the terror of all wrongdoers who had the misfortune to fall into his clutches. But some lousy Roundhead deserter or a half-drowned sailor could not be held responsible for Anthony's death. They could not punish the innocent in some perverse bid to dilute their own all too bitter bile. He felt Anthony's loss as keenly as his father, but he wasn't the first elder brother who hadn't come home, and he wouldn't be the last. If anything was to blame it was the war itself. And so, the unusually thoughtful youth reasoned, they should make it their business to finish the wretched business as soon as possible.

He sighed heavily, walked across the landing, and descended the broad stair to the lobby, torn every way at once by conflicting emotions, divided loyalties, and desire.

Bella Morrison, revolt ringleader and principal offender in this deplorable assault on the King's peace, was driving him to distraction just as rapidly as his brother's untimely death had catapulted him toward his various and unexpected destinies.

The rest of the hastily convened tribunal was reviewing what little evidence they possessed in the Earl of Dartland's robing room, a small but comfortable apartment immediately behind the main chamber. The newly appointed members of the panel were relaxing now, sipping wine and discussing their oddly assorted catch in the lazy warmth from the well-tended fire.

Major Brinks, as senior military commander in the area, had reluctantly accepted the assignment. He was a soldier, not a damned magistrate, and would have preferred to be back with the bulk of Porthcurn's regiment outside Plymouth. This was his first independent command, however, and he had been given the rank – and therefore the responsibilities – to go with it.

Abraham Bacon attended in place of the earl. Black Bob was busy entertaining his good friend Captain Cruickshank from the *Messalina's Purse,* and had left his clerk to attend to the tiresome minutiae of the case. Bacon would be expected to know every detail of the various indictments forwards and backwards, and woe betide him if he failed to come up with a suitable response to his master's shrewd enquiries.

Shoved up into the dock, the blinking prisoners would barely recognize their own names before they were sentenced and taken down. The more they argued, the more they tried to muddy the waters, the worse Black Bob's moods would grow.

The third member of the tribunal was Michael Keeler, the shifty, slightly seedy town solicitor, a tousled, overripe Cornishman in a distressed black suit. He got by on his cynical wits rather than any real mastery of the law he represented, but he and Black Bob had known each other long enough to understand what was required.

Brevity.

The trouble was, there was little evidence of anything, on their prima facie examination of the facts.

The drowsy trio watched Clavincale help himself to the wine and sit down heavily in his father's seat. He wouldn't have dared do so if Black Bob had been in the building, Bacon thought, raising his bristling eyebrows.

'My lord,' he said, with a short, stiff bow. 'We were presently examining this rather preposterous warrant. An inelegantly presented indictment, whichever way one chooses to look at it.' The clerk examined the ragged document as if it was a tobacco leaf fresh from a Virginia plantation, the fragrant forerunner of a highly speculative shipment. 'Three of the accused listed in the warrant are still at large, while we seem to have acquired half a dozen more suspects who don't appear at all! Most unsatisfactory, it would seem.'

Clavincale had been sceptical of the warrant from the moment he had heard about it. He had argued that as Dorset was well beyond Speedwell's jurisdiction, the insolent dragoon's involvement should have ended with his presentation of the document to officers from the local assizes. His father's men should have assumed responsibility for serving the warrant – not a pack of ragged-arsed hounds from up country. Typically though, the eager youngster had been overruled by his scowling father. The earl had given Speedwell permission to serve the questionable indictment, so long as all the accused were immediately returned to his courthouse. Suitably chastened, Clavincale had simply gone along with the dragoons for the ride – and it had been highly fortunate for this Telling character that he had. Speedwell had made it perfectly clear he would have dealt with the careworn cavalryman in an even more arbitrary fashion than Black Bob.

Clavincale pictured Bella's distress, imagined the girl's grief if her intended had ended his wedding day swinging from Speedwell's rope. Purple tongue clenched between his teeth rather than exploring Mistress Bella's delicately heaving cleavage. Her . . .

'What of the girl, what does she say to it?' Bacon enquired, an ironic smile playing about his rat-trap mouth. It was obvious to the clerk the boy was smitten with this auburn Amazon, this murderer of the King's dragoons who had wandered into their territory.

Clavincale gulped his wine, feeling the heady brew warm his already overheating frame.

'All she will say is that the rest of them had no part to play in the incident at the village. She insists she should answer the charges herself.'

'According to the dragoon fellow, it was the missing laundress who whipped the rest of them up. It's her we ought to be looking for.'

Clavincale nodded – a little too eagerly.

'On the other hand,' Bacon went on, 'Miss Morrison would seem to occupy a rather superior social station. I cannot imagine some village washerwoman ordering this young lady about, can you?'

'Hah! I'd like to see it,' Brinks leered. 'A ball scrapes her head and she's up and about in a few weeks? Some of my lot could do with her grit!'

Clavincale gave him a wan smile. Of course Bacon was right. If Bella had been there she would have been expected to exercise some authority over her revolting neighbours.

'Well, in any case I have ordered the release of the servants,' Bacon said shortly. 'They don't seem to be implicated in anything more serious than following their masters' instructions, and their pointless prosecution will only prolong matters. My lord your good father will not take kindly to being bogged down with irrelevancies such as these. He will want someone to make an example out of. This Morrison girl should fit the bill nicely.'

Clavincale could hardly help looking glum. Bacon's simplistic solution would clear the otherwise muddy waters, but expose Bella to their blunt allegation: that she had organized and led a village rebellion which had seen five of the King's loyal soldiers done to death. He sighed heavily to himself.

'What troubles you, my lord?' Bacon asked innocently. 'Perhaps the unfortunate words which were exchanged between your good self and this Captain Speedwell at Horn's Cross?' Bacon had already received a full report of the highly amusing dispute. 'I fear your initial judgement of Speedwell's character was all too shrewd,' he simpered. 'However, I clearly do not need to remind you,

my lord, what your father the earl would make of any . . .
unpleasantness stemming from the regrettable incident.'

Clavincale sucked his cheeks at the warning, gnawed
his lower lip in exasperation. He swigged his wine and
ran his finger under his constricting collar. Bacon rubbed
his hands, delighted to see the posturing youngster
squirm. Far too big for his boots, even with his dolt of a
brother gone, he thought, well satisfied with the afternoon's debate.

Compton Speedwell had made sure to keep out of the
young lord's path while he and his lawyer cronies decided
how to proceed with the perplexing case which had come
their way. Maybe if he let the lad alone he would forget
all about their little falling out back at Horn's Cross.
Insulting Black Bob's son in his own backyard? That
hadn't been a wise move at all – the youngster had far
more pluck than he would have given him credit. Speedwell was still debating whether to ride out and leave them
to it – while he was still at liberty to do so.

The dragoon lifted his tankard and drank the warm
dregs.

Speedwell had taken up a comfortable billet at the
Mermaid, a rollicking tavern on the Crossbone Quay well
suited to his robust tastes. Gah, let that pisspot Clavincale
send his second after him – if he dared set foot over the
blood-splattered, puke-rotten threshold. He wasn't going
anywhere, not until he was square with that house dove
Telling, at any rate.

He sat back on the worn bench, eyed the tavern door.
A pair of fishermen in baggy cotton smocks smeared with

dead scales and old guts ducked under the low beams and made their way to the bar. Like every other beef-witted bastard in this stinking shambles they seemed no more than half alive, shuffling about with drooping lips and wandering eyes. Little Lord Clavincale would need a sight more than these dullards in the village band if they meant to arrest him for his ill-considered insolence.

Henry Graves, Martin Pike, and Auld Guppy were slouched over the table in the reeking alcove, gloomily addressing their empty cups, while the rest of the troop were within shouting distance in case of trouble. Not that he would make the mistake of relying on that damned shower to back him up if things got nasty. Frightened villagers were one thing, soldiers and sailors and the full majesty of Black Bob's backyard justice were quite another. He tapped the tankard on the table, attracting the attention of the drowsy barmaid in the stained bodice.

'Now then, Debra, my dove,' he called. The girl glanced around angrily, but rearranged her features into a winning grin when she realized which of the shifty-eyed strangers had hailed her.

She swept out from behind the bar like a galleon under sail, her voluminous breasts bouncing beneath her bodice. The half-crippled dragoon looked like shark bait but seemed well bankrolled, treating his doubtful disciples to round after round of ale.

'It's thirsty work, tracking Roundhead fugitives from one end of the country to another,' he said, cracking his repulsive double smile. She grinned back, displaying a wet mouthful of variously decayed teeth.

'Tracked 'em down 'ere, then, 'ave you?' she asked,

collecting the tankards as the semi-drunk soldiers ogled her businesslike chest. 'It's funny, cuz I ent seen no Roundheads in yere for a long time!'

'We left them up at the Assizes. They'll not go far,' Speedwell told her, reaching up laconically and coiling a curl of her frazzled red hair around his finger.

'Now then, Captain,' she said, husky now. Wishing he'd stop looking and offer her out.

'How much to put a smile on my lads' faces, eh?'

Debra arched her awkwardly painted eyebrows. One of them bell-wethers, was he? She'd thought as much, with that creepy face of his and all. She glanced around at his loose-tongued lieutenants. The old one and the boy wouldn't take her beyond three strokes each. The big bugger in the green coat, well, he could have it on the house, for all she cared.

'A shilling each,' she sighed. Speedwell pursed his disfigured lips.

'Here's two.' He slapped the coins on the rough table. Debra placed her meaty palm on top of his torn knuckles, tried to entice the stranger with her sauciest smile.

'You can go too, if we call it three,' she offered. 'Now I can't say fairer than that!'

Speedwell shook his head, cold as a dead pollack. Still, two shillings. Not a bad evening's work, all things considered.

'Come on, then, you bulls, let's see what ye've got,' she said, leading the way toward the suicidally steep staircase.

Standing a few rounds and laying on a whore would clear him out in another day or two, and even if he had all the coin in the world, it wouldn't buy their fickle loyalty. He hadn't forgotten their pitiful performance on the causeway – only old Griffin had showed any spunk that night, and look what had happened to him.

Speedwell picked his way along the greasy cobbled quay, his nose assaulted by the oily stink of the evening's catch. A few older netsmen were sitting cross-legged along the harbour wall, the stone bollards flattened by years of use into so many lichen-mottled mushrooms. The gulls kept up a fearful squall, ducking and diving out over the water for the scraps they tossed over their shoulders.

They might have imagined he was enjoying the view, but the ever watchful dragoon was merely eyeing escape routes. He could be across the quay and into one of their little bobbing boats in five minutes, if necessary. He snorted under his breath. Clavincale wouldn't dare renew his challenge. The blow across the face had stung like buggery, but he would be damned if he was going to risk his neck righting *that* wrong. The candle-wasting whoreson was just another spoilt brat, a common or garden rake just like that bastard Telling. But Telling didn't have powerful fathers and pots full of money. Telling didn't have half the population of the county waiting to do his bidding. Nobody would mind if he filleted him!

He paused to take a piss, the amber arc splashing noisily into the emerald-green water.

Now his lady friend, well, he was beginning to regret the fact her name had been top of his warrant. Maybe he should have gone along with the pretence she had been killed back in that lousy village street, written her off in his report. It would have been more fun to take her back to Bristol for himself, set her on trials of a rather more earthly nature. He grinned at the enticing prospect. Maybe he should tell Black Bob he had made a mistake?

Substitute the dark-haired doxy for Telling's intended? The look on that clown's face when he walked down the aisle, interrupted his little game – hah, it was worth a hundred cuts, a thousand blows.

'The evening air has clearly gone straight to your bladder.'

The startled dragoon spun round on his heels, arranged his features into a genial grin as he adjusted his clothing.

Young Lord Clavincale had shadowed him along the quay, watched him staring out to sea among the coiled nets and stacked pots. He had concealed his rather conspicuous suit of rich blue velvet and red silk beneath a threadbare travelling cloak which had belonged to his dead brother. Speedwell gave the youngster an ironic bow.

'Indeed, my lord. I was taken short whilst admiring the view. How is it sunsets are never the same, away from the sea?'

Clavincale ignored his unusually poetic observation.

'I sought you at the tavern. Your men told me you'd stepped out.'

'As you see,' Speedwell smiled, holding his open hands away from his belt to ensure his young rival knew he was not reaching for his weapon. Fools like Clavincale respected things like that, always making a point of allowing their enemies to arm themselves. The drooling pup didn't have the balls to simply run him through and worry about it later. Clavincale took a stride forward.

'Understand, sir, that I mean to put aside our own personal quarrel until we have settled the matter in hand, namely the fate of our prisoners.'

Our prisoners, eh? Speedwell grinned amiably.

'Very good of you to say so, my lord, but as I have already made clear, any remarks uttered by myself were in the heat of the moment, and not meant in any degree to be taken seriously by your honour,' the dragoon lied easily. Clavincale's cheeks seemed to quiver with irritation or uncertainty. Apologize to this wallowing prick?

'I have discussed the matter in detail with my father, Mr Bacon, Mr Keeler, and Major Brinks.' He nodded over his shoulder toward the merrily lit town. 'We are of the opinion that this is a military matter, and as such should not fall under civilian jurisdiction.'

Long words now, what was the fellow blathering about? Were they intending to ship his catch off somewhere else? Back to Bristol as per his original instructions?

'My father has therefore agreed to hold a special tribunal tomorrow morning, where he will sit with Major Brinks and Captain Cruickshank to judge all matters before them, beginning with the facts alleged against Miss Morrison.'

Speedwell nodded. So that bile-bellied, bald-headed bastard of a pirate was still in town then, eh? Captain of the *Messalina's Purse,* the sleek blockade-runner tied up over the far side of the harbour? Perhaps the devious old screw was looking to give himself a veneer of respectability, judging other people for once. The filthiest robber in the Channel, sitting on a military tribunal? That would be worth a laugh, at any rate. He frowned.

'And what of Telling? He obstructed me in the course of my duty,' the dragoon objected, forgetting his manners all over again.

'Telling has applied for permission to represent Miss Morrison in court. He will be dealt with once we have . . . decided her fate,' Clavincale said faintly. The lordling coughed, as if the cold night air had finally gotten hold of his chest.

'All I ever wished, my lord, is to see justice done,' Speedwell observed piously. 'Mind you, the sight of that pompous weasel wheedling over his precious sweetheart, trying to—'

'Captain Telling is an officer and a gentleman of Prince Rupert's lifeguard,' Clavincale snapped. 'It will be a matter for the court to rule on his involvement in this matter.'

'Of course, my lord. I merely meant to observe that it was Telling as led the fugitives out of the dale and over the levels! He shot one of my men!'

'My father the earl will be deeply saddened to hear all the distressing details, how it was one man was able to disable an entire troop of His Majesty's brave dragoons,' Clavincale said with leaden irony.

'He obstructed my men as they went about their duty, he's as guilty as she is,' Speedwell muttered.

Clavincale stepped closer, his patience at an end, and spoke in an urgent undertone. 'Well, as I said, these are matters for the court to decide. The other matter is between you and me, sir. Should you feel yourself unable to apologize, I will see you on Plum Hill this time tomorrow eve, and we shall settle the issue once and for all.'

Speedwell's dark eyes flashed. He thought about grabbing for his sword but Clavincale's paw was already twitching at his hilt. He was no soldier, but he'd probably learnt to fence a little by now. The dragoon eyed the smooth-tongued serpent. The nosy boy was far more dangerous than he had looked, that was for sure.

'I never meant no offence to you, my lord,' he said thickly.

Clavincale knew it was as close as he was going to get to an outright apology. And besides, if he did force the issue, he doubted he could get the better of the dangerous, scar-faced fanatic – not fighting fair at any rate. There was little to be gained being slaughtered by some murdering cut-throat with a sharpened bilbo under his shirt – as his late lamented brother had apparently been murdered up at Gloucester.

'In that case I accept your withdrawal,' he said quickly, before Speedwell could regain his balance. 'We will say no more about the matter.'

Speedwell peered after him as the youngster made his way back along the Crossbone Quay, strangely unnerved by the preposterous oaf's self-confidence. He frowned, tried to remember if he had actually apologized for anything. He was buggered if he could, and yet this nobleman had given every impression he had grovelled at his feet like some gin-blossomed bloat slung out of the Mermaid's fetid cellar! Cheated and ridiculed, but off the hook. Perhaps it might be better to let sleeping dogs lie after all, he thought.

Across the water, the *Messalina's Purse* swung to and fro on her ropes, as if trying to free herself from the hateful confines of the harbour. A yawning sailor aboard the hungry privateer clanged the ship's bell, the mournful tone echoing out over the sea, stilled and stifled by the endless roll of the waves and the last, guttural complaints of the gulls.

LYME BAY,

OFF PORTLAND BILL, DORSET

The bare few of them who had survived being thrown overboard from the *Messalina's Purse* stared at the grim grey bay with a mixture of simmering resentment and apprehension. To starboard, the rocky shore and striding green downs which had witnessed their cruel fate. To port, the open sea which would have swallowed them like a woman's tears, dashed them up on the wide strands weeks, months later.

The survivors had instinctively sought each other out as the rapidly re-equipped *Blue Doubloon* skimmed the waves, two or three miles offshore. The patched sails billowed and banged as they rounded Portland Bill and entered the enormous arena of Lyme Bay – the deep green amphitheatre where the vicious tragedy had been played out five months before.

Some of them watched in awe as the great sabre-edged sweep of the Chesil Beach was unsheathed along the shore, electrified by the all too familiar panorama. A pleasant enough view when there was several inches of stout oak planking beneath your boots, but an impossibly nonchalant and untouchable horizon when you were bobbing in the troughs with several pints of salt water sloshing in your lungs.

Some of the others hardly seemed aware of their

traumatic return, sharpening weapons on the foredeck or chattering to the ruffians they had brought aboard at Chatham. They hadn't needed much persuasion to join Gallen Fey's unauthorized enterprise, the promise of a free hand looting the vile hornets' nest more than enough to tempt the freebooters, deserters, and common criminals from the harbourside taverns.

Fey would have preferred to pick a sober, God-fearing crew, but his own men were even now toiling in that damned Dorset quarry, and the Parliamentarian Navy had long since press-ganged their more respectable comrades into its desperately undermanned ships. Fey had been forced to take the dregs and the drunkards, the scum of the shore. Nathaniel Hawker would have given his right arm to come with them, but he had already been ordered back to sea in his converted merchantman, charged with patrolling the Channel. He could not be spared from his duties against the rampaging Dunkirk pirates.

But he had lent his old friend the next best thing – his sourly staring mate, John Grey. The miserable Jonah seemed transformed the moment he had stepped on deck, from dour Puritan elder to snarling tyrant. His large, fleshy ears twitched as he strode about the newly refitted ship, eavesdropping and encouraging the muttering mutineers. He had been setting about the more reluctant volunteers with a length of knotted rope before they had left the Thames, stamping his authority on the doubtful Roundheads. He didn't seem to require any rest – getting by on a jug of grog and some maggoty ship's biscuit – and he hadn't taken his beady black eyes from the crew since they had left Chatham.

'Who are you lookin' at, boy?' was his universal greeting

for the grumbling raiders. He was hardly any more considerate with old Fulke's veterans.

Pissed their drawers because some bugger had thrown them overboard? He'd been tossed in the oggin more times than he cared to count, but he'd always managed to swim and kick his way to safety. He had heard all about their little escapade off Penmethock, but the candle-wasting clods had got no worse than his crews had meted out to the privateers and Irishers they had cornered in the Channel. Roped together and over the side with them like a string of mackerel feathers, bobbing heads swallowed like black pearls, one by one in the fearful chop. Grey had heard all about Valentine Cruickshank – most seafaring men had – and it had been the opportunity to put one over on that notorious slack-bladder which had persuaded him to join the *Blue Doubloon*'s desperadoes. Grey strode down the foredeck, eyeing the pale landlubbers as they lurked beside the gunwales, sick as kittens in a drowning-bucket.

'Not far now, boys,' he growled. 'Still glad you came along, eh?'

The lean, grey-haired veteran slouching on his sacking-wrapped musket nodded soberly. 'Wouldn't have missed it,' Colston Muffet said curtly.

Grey thrust his stubbled chin out in defiant salute, stamped off towards the forecastle to chivvy along a gang of ruffians who had been assigned to repairing rigging. The heaving deck was still scattered with odd swirls of planed wood, sticky pools of pitch where the Chatham dockhands had patched the battered ship. Several smashed guns had been disembarked and replaced, new carriages hauled aboard to mount the scarred barrels. Fey didn't have enough gunners to man every weapon – but he was not intending to shoot his way into the guarded harbour at any rate. The *Blue Doubloon* didn't need to be completely seaworthy – as long as she could limp along the coast the privateer's distressed condition would be an advantage. Still flying her tattered black pirate colours, she would give every impression of a blockade-runner fleeing some Parliamentarian squadron, taking refuge in the nearest friendly harbour. By the time the enemy gunners realized their mistake Fey would have landed his shore parties and it would be too late for them to offer any serious resistance.

Or so he hoped.

Although she had not been restored to her original seaworthy state, the *Blue Doubloon*'s hasty renovations had not come cheap. There had been no question of going cap in hand to the Navy Board – this was a private venture, a personal feud between Fey and the despised town. Parliament would have refused even to countenance such an expedition, and would have locked the furious captain in irons if they had suspected what he was up to. They had enough on their hands with the King's privateers running amok along the coasts.

But Fey had been undaunted by meaningless minutiae like finance. He had simply sold his fine (and practically virginal) house in Chatham for two hundred pounds cash. The various proceeds of his many voyages and expeditions had raised another two hundred, and the contents of his household another fifty. Armed with this fortune, he had persuaded carpenters and joiners, sailmakers, caulkers, riggers, gunners, and sawyers, to complete the necessary repairs in days rather than weeks.

While he was busy aboard, his officers had scoured London for men and munitions. Tobias Fulke had pitched in with his entire household armoury of halberds, swords, pistols, and carbines, which, together with the arms they had taken from the *Blue Doubloon*'s magazine, went a good way towards equipping the shore party. He had rustled up another half-dozen volunteers from his own contacts in the capital: a couple of wounded sergeants who had been weeded out of their city Trained Band regiments as too old for further service had proved willing enough, as had a couple of strapping lads from their muddy delvings beside the Thames. Fulke's old friend and mentor Henry Mercer, cheesemonger and Roundhead (in that order), had contributed five stone of his best cheese to feed the eager Argonauts.

William Sparrow, roused from his resentful, drunken lethargy by Fulke's continual imprecations, had ridden from one end of London to the other, gathering his scattered (and sometimes sceptical) command.

He had at first been reluctant to commit himself to the desperate venture, but he had not managed to unearth any alternative employment and the all too likely prospect of starving to death in a London alley had not appealed. Parliament didn't seem to care for his services and there were more than enough beggars looking for work to prevent him from earning an honest crust in the capital. He had no home to go to now the army had finished with him, and had little idea where he might find his sweetheart Mary. He might have bombarded every hamlet in the West Country with letters asking after her and the babe – but Mary had never learned to read. A well-known (and easily recognizable) Roundhead, he would have been arrested as a spy before he had a chance to find her for himself.

Fey and Fulke had attempted to inspire the sulking

youth with lurid descriptions of the revenge they would inflict on their bitter enemy, but it had been the pressing question of William's growing debts which had finally resolved him to action. He would either have to take ship with Fulke or pay his bills at the Paradise. Sparrow had spent three-quarters of his back pay on wine and women – and wasted the rest. There was no immediate prospect of any further emburement, and the landlord had already warned he would call in the constables if he didn't settle his outrageous accounts. The furious crusader had even been obliged to force young Nicodemus to hand over a shilling so he could get his cutlass sharpened for the mad voyage west.

Sparrow, as large and clumsy as any of the sandpaper-handed dockhands, had always been blessed – or cursed – with a vivid imagination. He had had his fill of Lyme Bay back in July, and could not conceive how they could attack and defeat a large and well-equipped garrison in the heart of the enemy-held west. Those bastards down in Penmethock would be fighting like wildcats in a barrel, desperate to defend their homes against their infidel invaders.

By Christ, they would need some surprise to get the better of them, he sighed to himself. William's obvious reservations had not gone unnoticed by his hastily assembled comrades.

'Colonel Cromwell was right all along,' sneered their agitator and conscience, Hereward Gillingfeather, his shirt billowing around his wiry frame as he was buffeted by the winds. 'You lack faith, William,' he accused with a shake of his head. 'Put your trust in God and we will wash our swords in their bowels.'

'It's a good job some bugger's paying some attention

to what's being planned,' William snarled back. 'I'll wager your precious Cromwell wouldn't have risked his neck on this damned jaunt.'

'Jaunt?'

Long Col, hastily summoned from his home in Holborn to lead the shore party musketeers, sucked at his cold pipe, lost in his own thoughts as his colleagues bickered. He had weighed the risks with his usual clinical detachment, concluded that the Royalist crab pot could be taken – given the right combination of tides, daylight, and reasonably accurate timing. As long as those guns could be knocked out, they could land the raiding party in the heart of the defences before they were even aware.

And besides, he had a score to settle with those slave-trading bastards the same as the rest of them.

'You'd think that captain had done you a favour, throwing you overboard,' he said, jabbing his pipe-stem at the brooding, scowling Sparrow.

'Ah, the flabby bastard needed a good swill!' Billy Butcher cackled.

William showed the cockney sharpshooter his teeth. 'Well, revenge is one thing, suicide's another,' he retorted, cracking his fist against the salt-stained gunwale.

'Hah! If you've no heart for the business you should have stayed in your sty back in London, with the gin-blossoms and the polecats,' the agitator snapped, the frail threads of his patience stretched by the captain's grumbles.

'I've a heart for the business, and a head as well, luckily for you mumming clowns. This has to be properly planned or we'll all end up back on the *Purse*! And I tell you this, we won't be as lucky a second time!'

Gillingfeather, who had spent what little recreation

time he had been allowed attending the endless, increasingly agitated debates at the House of Commons, turned his furious, salt-spotted face away from the worthless rogue. He stood like some hairy figurehead, bending the waves to his stare, raising his chin now and then to look up through the patched rigging to the hurrying clouds as if he was guiding the vessel by power of prayer alone. His younger colleague Billy Butcher – renowned as the best shot in the entire regiment, not least by himself – was as usual squatting cross-legged below the rail, calmly cleaning his fowling-piece. He had already stripped the firing mechanism to its constituent pieces, lifting the intricate ratchets to scrape the debris from the steel teeth, blowing the grime from the powder pan. He had wrapped the rest of the tricky mechanism in sackcloth to keep it from the blowing spray. The tousled youth closed one pale blue eye to peer down the long barrel, and resumed whistling the irritating jig he had picked up from one of the volunteers.

'You'll be awoight, mate, when we're in amongst the bleeders. Just like Bristol's walls, eh? 'Member that time that mad bastard was standing in that cart? Went arse over tit when the dozy buggers pushed it in the bleedin' moat!' The huddled soldiers grinned at the memory, one of the few victories they had earned during the siege which had ended with Prince Rupert's forces blasting their way into the defiant city – and Sparrow's men marching out like so many miserable vagabonds.

Sparrow refused to be carried along by the thoughtless young killer's bravado. He gripped the shrouds as if the rigging was his lifeline, his umbilical link to dry land, then glanced around as his young runner was violently ill over the side.

Nicodemus Burke was standing a little way off, sick to his stomach as the privateer breasted the waves and chopped through the crossfire of currents which switch-backed the seas around the reefs and rocks. He had gathered up the immense sleeves of his prized red coat and was hugging himself in abject misery, wondering for the hundredth time why he had joined their desperate adven-ture. It wasn't as if he owed any money to anyone. The strange coastline slipping away to his right was as foreign as the shores of Africa, the misty headlands of Newfound-land. The young runner, brought up in the slums of Gloucester, had joined the regiment after the famously successful siege, and although he had heard a dozen different versions of his comrades' horrible ordeal aboard the *Purse*, he could not share their determination to exact revenge. But what else was he supposed to do? Walk home? Join the noisy battalions of urchins roaming the streets of the capital? Nicodemus might not have relished the dangerous expedition, but drowning aboard this stinking tub was preferable to starving among strangers.

Caleb Cruickshank, the dumb giant who *had* shared their miserable fate aboard the *Purse*, was standing beside him, his legs splayed against the violent pitching of the deck. He hardly said a word to anyone at the best of times, and nobody could guess what was sliding through his slow mind now. Did he share Long Col's cold-hearted determination for revenge? Butcher's unquenchable drive to add to his long tally of kills, or Gillingfeather's fanatical faith in their westward crusade? How would he react when he worked out the prime target of the expedition was his own father, the renegade privateer Valentine Cruick-shank, captain of the despised *Messalina's Purse*?

The daft boy's capering devil of a father had treated his own flesh and blood as he had his lousy prisoners, throwing them overboard like so much refuse in an attempt to throw off the pursuit which had appeared as if from nowhere off his port bow. The poor boy had been sent aloft as lookout in the teeth of a howling tempest and had failed to spot the rushing man-of-war which Gallen Fey had been steering through the storm. Captain Cruickshank's fearful officers – all too used to his insane tempers – had pleaded with him to send the boy below, but Cruickshank had thrust them away and ordered his idiot son to stand with the prisoners on the heaving deck. Nicodemus shuddered with revulsion. Thrown overboard by your own father? It was too horrible to even think about. No wonder poor Caleb wouldn't say much.

William thrust his water bottle in the boy's sour face. Nicodemus lifted his pale hand and took the bottle, sipped uneasily at the brackish contents.

'I don't know how you stood it,' Nicodemus complained, spitting another vile mouthful over the side. 'Tossed like a pudding from the pan to the fire.'

'We didn't stand anything. Never mind what this lot reckon, they were all as scared as me.'

'I knew the Lord would deliver me from the waters,' Gillingfeather said coldly, perfectly confident of his own invincibility. William frowned, patted the poor youth on the shoulder.

'I told you, stop staring at the horizon, it'll make you feel worse,' Sparrow advised, although in truth he wasn't feeling any better himself. Brought up a stone's throw from the muddy Avon, William had always been a strong swimmer. But his ghastly nightmare aboard the *Messalina's Purse* had cured him of any love for water.

Gallen Fey had been used to a lumbering man-of-war, and was concentrating on steering the lighter privateer through the swirling offshore reefs. The slightest flick of the whipstaff and the graceful vessel would slide off obligingly on her new course. Devil take her, but she was a sweet little thing. It reminded him of his dim and distant youth, sailing his home-made yacht around the harbour.

He frowned, glanced up at the hurrying clouds once more. No time for daydreaming, with these damned currents.

Tobias Fulke clutched the rail beside him, lifting his hat to wipe the spray from his face. The feverish preparations and relentless pounding of the waves had sucked his strength, drained his spry complexion to that of an ulcerous old man's. For once, Fey thought, Fulke looked his years.

'You'd best get below for some rest,' the captain advised, nodding his head towards the roundhouse.

Fulke straightened his back as if he were on parade, redoubled his grip on the slippery rail. 'Ah, a bit of sea air, freshens the blood,' the ancient warrior told him. 'And besides, I wouldn't want to miss anything.'

Fey nodded quietly. 'Your lads know what they're about. It's the other lot I'm worried about.'

'Your mate seems to have them well in hand,' Fulke replied, nodding on down the heaving planking toward the indestructible Grey, who was helping the volunteers haul a cannon into a shot-splintered gunport along the deck. 'I'm glad he'll be fighting on our side,' he said with feeling.

Their plan of campaign, for what it was worth, was fairly simple. They had no idea of how many enemy troops or armed civilians might oppose them, so speed and surprise would be of vital importance if they were to take their objective. Gallen Fey would bring the *Blue Doubloon* as close to the shore as possible, trusting to his expert knowledge of the reefs and shoals to approach Penmethock from the east, around the colossal, gull-crowded cliffs of the Hare Rock. They would haul up the shot-blasted colours and torn sails they had stored in the hold in a bid to convince any observers the friendly privateer had been chased in from the Channel by a Parliamentarian ship. They would lower the longboat on the eastern face of the Hare Rock, putting one party ashore a mile or two from the enemy outposts, and then sail on around the headland to approach the closely guarded harbour itself.

Captain Sparrow would lead the first landing party, guiding his contingent up the narrow shingle beach and around the cliffs to attack the enemy battery beneath the Hare Rock. With the cliff battery silenced, the *Blue Doubloon* could hug the eastern flank and penetrate the inner harbour, out of the effective range of the second battery built under the cliffs across the far side of the bay. Once inside the harbour, Fey would open fire with every single gun he possessed, hoping to disable any opposition with double-charged round- and chainshot. He would then land Colonel Fulke's party on Crossbone Quay. They would charge straight up the main street driving the confused enemy before them, rendezvousing with Captain Sparrow's men at the Assizes by the crossroads. A second party would then turn west and hurry up the coomb, to release any prisoners still being held at the quarry. Once they had finished mopping up, the men would have an hour to collect what loot they could carry and make their way back to the ship. They reckoned to be in and out in under three hours.

'On second thoughts, Gallen, old man, I think I'll take your advice and get below for a spell. Haven't found my sea legs yet, you know,' Fulke said, interrupting Fey's train of thought. The captain nodded, watched the old man stagger aft towards his temporary quarters beneath the poop. Fey caught a splash of surf in the corner of his eye, and peered around as yet another spear of barnacle-encrusted rock reached from the depths for his borrowed ship. He ordered the helmsman to correct their course, and peered through his glass at the obstreperous sea.

Nicodemus Burke found him when he went below with the colonel's supper, a frugal meal of bread and cheese to be washed down with a flagon of good cider. He was welcome to it and all. Nicodemus wouldn't have been able to touch a thing.

Tobias Fulke was lying in his narrow bunk with his long arms by his sides, strangely shrivelled without his burnished armour and ornately engraved helmet. Nicodemus peered down at his white-whiskered face, the old man's flesh as coloured as any fresh-featured youngster's. Apart from around his mouth, that was. The lips seemed strangely dark, almost blue. The boy looked closer, noted the strange tallow shadows about the corners of his mouth, the striking grey rings under his closed eyes.

Wasn't looking too good, but then neither was Nicodemus, with this bloody swell.

'Supper, sir. Captain William says to tell you we'll be ready to lower the boat in another half-hour.'

Nicodemus held on to the oak bulkhead as a particularly big wave lifted the privateer bodily from the sea and rammed her under once more. The water thrummed and washed against the creaking planking, making the boy twitch with anxiety. Never again, he vowed.

Old Toby must have been reading the battle plans when he'd fallen asleep, the rolled parchment clutched in his scaly, blue-veined fist. Nicodemus reached down and shook the old gentleman by his bony shoulder, and knew at once the gallant old warrior was dead. Dead as his own father had been those three years before. He stood back, swallowing nervously, glancing about the bare cabin as if all the medicines in the world were racked on shelves waiting for him to administer some life-saving spoonful.

The boy had seen his fill of corpses at Newbury. Slashed and trampled, pounded to mush by cannon or torn and gouged with whistling musket balls. The old man looked almost angelic in comparison, a granite relief on a cold tomb in St Mary's Church back home. His frail body, horribly naked without its lacquered armour, was chilled to the bone. He turned and ran for the stairs.

'He must have been suffering, all this time,' Sparrow said around the ashes of mortification which seemed to have choked his throat. 'He would never have let on, even if he knew.'

Gallen Fey, standing beside him in the deathly quiet cabin, nodded gravely. 'Ah, he knew all right. But it wouldn't have mattered, not to Toby.'

Sparrow turned his head away, horrified to find himself on the verge of tears. The bloody boat wallowed and swooned around the reefs, tipping them this way and that as they crowded around the pale corpse. Fey had lifted the tightly rolled parchment from the old man's gnarled fist, worked it free from the dead fingers. He unrolled the note and scanned it quickly, sucking his cheeks as he did so.

'See you, it's his will.'

William hardly dared look the captain in the face, staring at the indecipherable, upside-down scrawl.

'Another fifty pound, his worldly fortune, to be divided equally amongst the men after the successful capture of Penmethock. His armour to Nicodemus, as he's the only one it'll fit.'

Sparrow heard the wretched boy sob behind his back, but dared not turn round to offer any comfort.

'His ivory pipe and all his baccy for Colston Muffet, in lieu of many a shared smoke. His pistols one each to Gillingfeather and Butcher.' Fey looked up, his thin features ghastly pale. 'The last entry is for you, William.'

Sparrow took the note, peered down at the filmy characters. At last he was able to make out: 'To my friend and comrade William Sparrow of Bristol. Carry my sword, and remember me. You'll never be reckoned a gentleman with that meat cleaver you carry. If you should bump into young Matilda, give her a shilling or two for me, for old times' sake. Your friend, Toby.'

'Now then, William,' Fey sighed. 'You've got his sword, you'd best see you wear it well. He wouldn't want to see it given up, lad.'

*

The variously sceptical crew took old Fulke's death as an ill omen for their westward adventure. The game old bird who had insisted and inspired them since they left Chatham, pegging out not ten mile from their destination? It didn't take a warlock to work out there were dark days ahead. Even Gillingfeather, who would normally have praised the heavens for granting the old fighter such a fitting end to his martial career, seemed strangely subdued, chewing the ends of his tawny beard absent-mindedly as Fey called the crew together to inform them of the hastily revised plans.

Sparrow stood just behind the diminutive, bow-legged captain, holding on to the shrouds and staring out to sea as Fey's high-pitched shout was picked up by the wind and dashed out over the foaming wavetops. John Grey stood to his left, his arms folded over his chest, sea-coat pulled up around his thick neck.

'And so Captain Sparrow will lead the main party through the village. Mr Grey will take his contingent to the quarry to release the prisoners, and Elder Sergeant Muffet here will lead the advance party to disable the guns.'

The miserable crew, bunched up on the heaving decking below him, glanced at one another as if they had been assigned to serve under the Devil and his imps.

'Colonel Fulke died as he lived, serving the cause he had in all conscience taken up. He would have expected you men to do the same,' Fey went on, desperately trying to animate the sullen mob. 'His death is a blow to us all, but we must complete our mission.'

The reluctant shore party muttered and nodded, their variously brown- and black-hatted heads shifting and tilting like a gale through a cabbage patch. Hardly any of them had heard much about Sparrow – certainly nothing any good. The ship's gossips maintained he had deserted Waller's army and been thrown out of Essex's. He had moped about the *Blue Doubloon* as if he was sailing to his own funeral, not preparing to lead the men into a fight for their lives.

'Colonel Fulke has also made arrangements for a bounty to be paid to every man once the village is taken,' Fey called, his steel-grey eyes flaying their wretched faces.

'How much?' one rogue at the back called.

'You'll get your money, you damned marauder,' Gillingfeather snarled, wheeling around to glare at his fickle comrades. William was trembling with frustrated rage, stuffed so full of conflicting emotions he thought he might burst. Tobias Fulke was dead, worn to the bone by his continual efforts on behalf of the Parliamentarian cause, and here were these dogs griping over a few pennies. Money hadn't mattered to Toby – as long as he had a few spare shillings to feed his men he had been happy enough. These worthless cunts weren't fit to stand on the same deck, gutless vultures perched along the rails of his funeral barge.

'Put the lousy bastards ashore, if they haven't got the stomach for it,' he shouted, choking with blind anger. 'I'd rather fight alongside one true-hearted man than you turd-skinning shits!'

Gallen Fey stared at the furious youth, taken aback by the captain's outburst. Muffet, Butcher, and the rest of the sharpshooters, already fully armed for their mission, seemed to close in behind their red-faced champion. His sacred band, ready for a bloody last stand on the rollicking privateer.

'There's more than one shit aboard this tub!'

'Aye, and you've shit your breeches often enough, by all accounts,' the sharper at the back called out over the growing tumult.

'I've shit bigger things than you for a start,' Sparrow called, gripping the hilt of his cutlass as he took another threatening step towards the mob, standing on tiptoe to peer over the murky swamp of sea-sickened faces. 'You were quick enough to sign up when you were stuck in a bloody tavern with a few fat-arsed wenches for company. Well, we're here now, that rock you can see there, that's where we're going.'

The reluctant volunteers flinched away from him, stepping out of the angry soldier's way as he shoved his way through their sticky-fingered ranks. Captain Fey stood on the poop deck, drumming his long thin fingers on the rail as he wondered what to do. Their fickle mood had swung from sullen to ugly. One spark now and they would be fighting for their lives. Thank God they had had the sense to delay distributing the arms!

He wondered whether to order his few trusted men to get amongst them. Sparrow, though, one of the few reliable officers he had left, was lost in the middle of the surly gang, surrounded by hostile stares and jabbing elbows. He would be dead before the few loyal men he could count on could leap to the fool's assistance.

Sparrow shoved another grumbler out of his path, intimidating the ragged recruits with his bristling bulk. His stare and defiantly set jaw seemed to overawe the unbelievers, identifying and isolating individuals among the cowering pack.

'That was you bawling, was it? Well, what about it?' Sparrow shoved the smaller man aside, elbowed another who had half-heartedly attempted to hold him back. 'Ah, you fancy yourself as a fighter too, eh? And what about you, you cross-eyed cowflop? I don't know why we picked you up in the first place, you wouldn't worry a convent full of crippled nuns, let alone a regiment of King's men!'

For a moment Fey thought the blundering idiot had gone too far. He had stamped and shoved his way to the gunwale, and turned at bay beside a fuming brazier. A shorehand in a leather apron seemed alarmed to have attracted the hulking brute to his workplace, and swayed from side to side uncertainly, his grey eyes flicking from his friends to the suddenly dangerous stranger.

'And what are you looking at?' Sparrow demanded, snatching the crude iron tongs from the nervous worker's frail grasp, as if the bewildered stranger was about to attack him with them.

Sparrow flinched as the hot iron burned into the wet creases of his broad hands. He was used to dealing with hot lead and heated ladles, but the burning tongs still blistered his callused palms. He felt a surge of panic. If he threw the wretched tongs overboard he would break the spell, look a complete fool as he blustered and raged. The bloody deckhand must have been using the tongs to pour pitch from the sticky pail beside his feet.

Do something, he thought feverishly.

The entire company had turned to stare at the posturing officer, watching the barely perceptible tremor in his bare arms build up and up until he seemed ready to fall down in a fit.

'We're out for revenge, not money!' Sparrow brayed, sweat breaking out on his cold brow. 'I'll show you bastards what we mean!'

He held the burning tongs in one white-knuckled fist, held his arm out in front of him.

'Anybody who wants to come ashore with me had better get himself marked! Aye, a mark for our suffering, to mark us apart!'

His mind was lurching and slipping like egg white. He swore he could smell his own flesh, roasting on the hot irons. No time to lose. He must get rid of these tongs!

'Any of you lily-livered house doves with me? Eh?'

Before he could summon another sentence into his bone-dry mouth, Sparrow lowered the glowing tongs onto his bare forearm. The matted black hair stank and sizzled as the searing metal scorched his trembling flesh.

The disbelieving seamen gasped in shocked sympathy as Sparrow lifted the hot tongs from his arm and shoved them back into the brazier. The deckhand fainted in an untidy heap, the leather apron flapping over his unwashed bulk like a well-tanned shroud.

Sparrow held his scarred arm aloft, the horrified sailors staring open-mouthed at the obscene kiss burnt into his livid flesh. The captain hung on to the gunwale with his right hand to steady his legs.

'There you are, her bloody forget-me-not! *Messalina*'s bite! I'm going ashore to sort those bastards, even if I have to go alone!'

There was a sudden blur of movement through the agonized crowd. Gillingfeather shoved his way through the ghoulish spectators, tearing the carefully buttoned shirt from his own hairy arms. The deranged musketeer lifted the tongs from the brazier, glared maliciously at the glowing metal mouth, and lowered it onto his own arm as if he was slipping himself into a ten-shilling whore.

He sighed with ecstatic contentment, shivered with pagan pleasure.

'I'm with the captain!' he croaked, his tongue turned to sawdust by the searing pain.

There was a moment of silence before all hell broke loose on the plunging privateer.

Gallen Fey stood on the poop deck and watched the bright-eyed mob roar their approval, shoving and barging themselves to the front, crowding around the scorched zealots as if they would have given everything they owned to hurl themselves bodily into the flames.

Sparrow leaned back against the gunwale, white faced and blowing hard as the demented volunteers fought one another for the privilege of handling the awesome tongs. The dozing deckhand, raising his head from the creaking planking for a moment, imagined he had woken up in the middle of some terrible cannibal feast, and promptly fainted away again. Some of the men scorched themselves until they toppled over or had to be held up by their friends, others simply took the tongs, winced in horror, and passed them on to the next eager recruit. But in two minutes Sparrow had turned the mutineers to fanatics bent on the blood of the Antichristian heathens of Penmethock.

Colston Muffet worked his way through the shouting, screaming, screeching madmen, and placed his hands on William's broad back. 'By Christ, Will, we thought you were a goner!' he said, awed by the captain's display of bravado. He glanced down at the smoking wound on Sparrow's forearm, shook his head at the terrible brand. William, tears springing into his eyes, seemed almost light-headed now. Muffet held him up by the elbow as the big man collapsed into his arms.

'I've got to make it look good,' William hissed into Long Col's grubby ear.

'Look good?' Muffet repeated, stunned by the doubtful captain's sudden conversion.

'Aye. Well, ever since I got that wound back in Bristol, I can barely register hot or cold, not on my forearm at any rate,' Sparrow whispered.

Muffet straightened, completely speechless. 'You mean that was all a bit of mummery for these damned fools?' he asked through gritted teeth.

Sparrow allowed himself to be helped back towards the poop deck, the white faces of his fellow officers looking down from on high. The cheering seamen clapped him on the back and called his name, delirious with enthusiasm for their captain and cause.

'To tell you the truth, Col, I hardly felt a thing,' he said, grimacing with pain now. He lifted his hand, looked at the angry red weal across his palm. 'My bloody hand hurts, though.'

PENMETHOCK ASSIZES,

Bella had been left in the ante-room by herself for so long she could barely think straight. Gnawed by doubts, terrified of the trumped-up charges they might bring against her, she alternated between fits of frustrated fury and bouts of self-pity. She paced the bare room and stood on tiptoe to peer out of the window, stepping back dizzily as if her brain was pitching violently inside her skull. The puckered skin was tightening now, and the tearing pain far worse than the actual impact had been. She could barely remember being shot at all. A cloud of white smoke and a sudden, jarring silence, before the endless descent into darkness. She remembered feeling weightless, as if the lead ball had ploughed into a mass of downy feathers. The blood-splattered roadway a handsome four-poster into which she sank like a stone. Fragments of faces, hissed observations louder than shouts in her ringing ears. She didn't remember feeling frightened, hadn't seemed concerned she might be witnessing the last gasps of her own life.

Bella wiped away a tear on the grubby arm of her gown, blinked rapidly to disperse the red mists crowding in from the corners of her eyes.

Her wobbling horizons were dominated by the gloomy shadow of the scaffold, that brutally businesslike structure which seemed to dominate the courtyard. Please God she wouldn't find herself studying the courthouse's hideous architecture from that damned platform. They couldn't hang her. She couldn't die before she'd done anything! The wound in her forehead glowed with pain, a white-hot brand sizzling about the fault lines of her skull. She sat back down again, spread her palms over the plain table as if stabilizing herself.

Bella had been cut off from all her friends and family and left to stew. If she kept quiet and tilted her head to the worn oak she could hear the patient shuffle of the guards outside the door, their muted conversations when the officers had wandered off elsewhere. A scowling old crone with an impossibly thick accent brought her meals on a tray and collected the barely touched plates. There had been no sign or word from Hugo or her father, and her tearful friend Anneliese had been removed from her company – without explanation – the day before.

Bella recovered slowly, and returned once more to her lonely vigil by the window. She stared at the monstrous triangles which made up the oaken gallows. Guards in blue coats were pacing to and fro, workmen with sacks of clanking tools were busy about their tasks, the old crone with the soup tureen ladled brown slops into their bowls and pewter pans. Beyond the wall, she could see the tops of the houses and beyond the bright-red tiles, the silvery green sheen of the sea, as still and perfect as a knight's breastplate. Little boats went out in the gloaming and returned at dawn. White sails like nail parings flickered on the edge of the horizon, free as gulls as she raged helplessly in the sterile cell.

The young lord came and went, asking questions from the side of his mouth as he looked at the walls, stared at the ceiling. If she had been able to catch his eye for a moment she might have attempted to persuade him to her cause. The other man, Bacon, let his eyes stray where they wanted, unembarrassed by her expertly heaved cleavage. He might relish her milky flesh, but he would no more spring to her assistance than that scar-faced dog of a dragoon would rush to defend Hugo.

What had they done with him? Where was her father? If anybody could get them out of their dire straits it would be Sir Gilbert.

Bella chewed at the battered shreds of her nails. The merchant had strayed out of his depth. He couldn't influence these hatchet-faced hounds any more than she could. He would have enough of a job explaining his own part in the affair, let alone assisting his distressed daughter. She turned and wandered back to the door, listened for a moment, and then strode back to the window, as if drawn by the leering totem crouching like a servant beneath her barred balcony.

'Answer to yer name, missy,' the guard encouraged, leaning over to hiss in her ear. The leering brute stank like a marl pit, and his reeking breath seemed to have rotted the teeth in his gums. He had clenched his fingers about her arm so hard her pale flesh had turned a lifeless yellow. She looked up, blinking into the phalanx of sunlight filtered by the windows above the bench. A brightly painted coat of arms made up of mermaids and unicorns and bound chests and rolled charts. Carefully furled flags had been propped up either side of the emblem, forming a bloody backdrop for the silhouetted shape of the Earl of Dartland and the tribunal members.

'Well?'

'Bella, answer your name!'

The bewildered girl glanced down at the earnest features of her counsel, his white-knuckled fingers clutching the barred dock.

'Hugo?'

'Answer your name,' he insisted, his grey green eyes glittering with intent, his pinched features as pale as death. The downy moustache which seemed about to blow away at any moment. Hugo!

'Yes,' she mouthed, smiling distractedly at her lost sweetheart. What was he doing down there? Standing in the well of the court with the clerks and the lawyers in their ridiculous powdered wigs, the grumpy serjeant-at-arms and the smirking witnesses. Speedwell tilted his hateful head to one side, gave her an ironic bow. She looked around at the public gallery, crammed with Penmethock's finest, all drooling for her precious blood but restrained by the roving eye of the judge. To her right, at the end of the row, the wonderfully reassuring faces of Thackray, smiling awkwardly, and Anneliese, wiping her red nose in a grubby handkerchief.

'Bella Marguerite Morrison, you stand before the court on two charges,' Abraham Bacon went on waspishly, his long dark hair gathered up under his misshapen headdress. 'Firstly that you did on 18 September last conspire with others to obstruct officers of the Crown in the collection of the assessment for the village of Chipping Marleward, Somerset, by divers actions and exclamations intended to foment the said villagers to resistance. Secondly, that you together with others did murder Joshua Lawton, Simon Crabtree, Timothy Calderwood, Michael Wilkes, and John Chetworth, said officers of the Crown, as they went about their duty, contrary to the King's law. How say you, Bella Morrison?'

Bella bit her lip, tilting her head to follow the clerk's vindictive accusations.

'Not guilty!' she mouthed at last.

'Not guilty, my lord,' Telling seconded, in case the decayed vulture who chaired the tribunal had missed her strained denial. Bacon gave him a supercilious sneer, glanced over his shoulder at his master.

'Mr Keeler will present the case for the Crown, my lord.'

The Earl of Dartland waved his veined claw distractedly.

Keeler, his wild hair protruding comically beneath his wig, jumped to his feet as if he had but five minutes of the court's time to press his case. He threw his brief notes onto the stand, bowed shortly.

'If it please my lord, I will outline the bare facts of this grim crime. The young lady who stands before you is the daughter of Sir Gilbert Morrison, of Chipping Marleward, in Somerset. On 18 September last, Miss Morrison encouraged and commanded the said villagers into an act of rebellion against the collection of their assessment, properly set by the acting Governor of Bristol Sir Ralph Hopton, in the name of His Majesty King Charles. In the ensuing action,' Mr Keeler rasped, glaring significantly at the pale angel in the dock, 'five dragoons were killed, either by Miss Morrison's own hand or at her encouragement.'

'If you're accusing her of murder, accuse her!' Telling cried, jumping to his feet. 'Who did she murder and how? A strip of a girl kill five dragoons? Pah!'

'Silence!' Bacon roared from his desk beneath the

judge. 'Sir, you will restrict your hysterical outbursts or be escorted from the court!' Telling glowered at the clerk, his broad face framed by his viciously parted black hair. 'You will have your opportunity to address the court, sir, kindly resume your seat.'

'Miss Morrison, as daughter of the said merchant, was the natural ringleader of this revolt, aided and abetted by known Parliamentarian sympathizers, and as such, she stands before you. The rest of her co-conspirators are presently at large.'

Telling felt as if he was ready to explode, as if his ears and mouth had been stuffed and prodded with charges of black powder. One after the other, Keeler's lying witnesses had trotted out the same damning tale, of angry Roundheads issuing out of their homes to surround poor Sergeant Lawton's brave patrol. Of furious laundresses wielding washing paddles like broadswords, of straw-chewing country folk running defenceless dragoons through on their rusty pitchforks. And at the centre of the whole whirling inferno, Bella Morrison, shouting and screaming and egging the murderers on, until felled by a chance shot from one of her dying victims. Captain Speedwell told how the terrified remnants of his troop had arrived back in Bristol, how they had organized a punitive expedition against the revolted village. How they had returned to find the surly villagers making sport with their butchered colleagues' equipment, singing and boasting and swearing they were for the Parliament.

At last, after excruciating hours of enforced silence, Bacon waved the apoplectic Cavalier to his feet. Telling called Anneliese Ramsay to the stand, and the dark-haired girl made her way down from the gallery under the hostile stares of the villagers, the muttered comments of the smirking guards. She dithered and stumbled over her oath, but gripped the rail as if she was prepared to endure everything on her friend's behalf.

'Miss Ramsay, you are the daughter of the late Sir Marmaduke Ramsay of Kilmersden Hall, Somerset?'

Anneliese nodded, her dark eyes filming with tears.

'And is it right your father and brother have already given their lives serving in King Charles's armies in the west?'

'She won't be the only one here to have lost kin, Telling,' Bacon warned.

'Even so, I must be entitled to establish the witness's family background and political persuasion, to prove Miss Ramsay and her family are as staunch for His Majesty's cause as the members of this court.' There was a murmur of approval around the packed galleries. The earl, who didn't appear to be paying any attention to the proceedings, flicked his quill in annoyed agreement. He leaned over and whispered something to the grinning pirate who sat to his left.

Captain Valentine Cruickshank was bored to distraction by the endless to and fro. He was grinning sardonically at their intended victim – chewing her lip ragged in the well of the court while her friend gave evidence. Cruickshank wondered how he could persuade his friend the judge to allow him to take her off aboard ship. By Christ, she'd wish she'd hanged rather than spend the rest of her beauty time chained up in his cabin!

When he bored of her, he would throw her to his men in lieu of back pay, save himself a fortune – and the dogs from plotting mutiny. Ah, Black Bob might owe him several favours, but releasing this flirt-gill into his care would stretch their symbiotic relationship a little too far.

Cruickshank was a Dunkirk privateer, a pirate in all but name who served King Charles by preying on the generously loaded ships of his revolted fleets. But if he served King Charles one day of the week, the other six he served himself. Blockade-running and smuggling brought him a pretty penny, supplemented by variously dubious dealings with Royalist and Parliamentarian alike. This Bella girl, for instance, why it wasn't four days since that miller fellow had made enquiries to his mate Edward Callow about her passage to France. Fifty pounds on the nail if he had taken her aboard. Ah, it was a pity she'd fallen into Black Bob's clutches. She would have been a sight more fun on board the *Purse*.

Cruickshank rolled his eyes back toward the uppity Cavalier who was pacing in front of the tribunal like a young colt. He'd missed the gist of the captain's precious speech, but then, Telling could no more save Miss Bella from the gallows than he could himself.

'Miss Ramsay, perhaps you would like to tell the court what really happened on 18 September.'

They had hurried her through her evidence, brushed aside her observations, ignored her conclusions. Anneliese, already strained to breaking point by the horrible events of the last few weeks, had been unable to shift their vindictive view of the clash in the village.

Bella, alternately pale and then flushed, had swayed and blinked, nodded confusedly as Telling had tried to take her through the day.

'Your witness was shot in the head in the act of

rebellion; it will not surprise the court to find she has no real recollection of the events you are asking her to describe!' Mr Keeler had crowed, stripping his frail defence to the bone in a moment. 'And besides that, her account does not appear to tally with the version rendered by Miss Ramsay!'

Telling had called up his heavy artillery: Sir Gilbert himself, clearly subdued by the unenviable fix in which he found himself. The merchant had nevertheless confirmed his son's fantastic absurdity, and agreed the two aforementioned distressed maidens, horrified by poor Jamie's plight, had been rushing to his defence, rather than organizing a deliberate attack on his tormentors.

'What sort of soldier makes sport with a daft lad like that?' Sir Gilbert had appealed to the reptilian court.

'If your villagers hadn't done them in with their household tools, we would be in a position to make enquiries of their nature,' Bacon had replied, silencing the blustering merchant's sallies.

Keeler hadn't let Sir Gilbert off the hook, confronting him with his tarnished war record. The turncoat merchant's frequent changes of heart set the piously Royalist public benches hissing in disgust.

'Isn't it right, Sir Gilbert, that before you raised this regiment of foot of yours for the King you raised the village Trained Band for the Parliament, and took their gold for it into the bargain?'

'I saw the error of my ways,' the merchant growled. 'Good fortune in war don't grow from seed, you have to seek it out as you may.'

'Indeed.'

'I've paid my debt to His Majesty a dozen times over! I led a regiment of foot – paid out of my own pockets, mind – to join his army outside Gloucester. You can ask anybody,' the merchant blundered on, unaware of Telling's panicked stares. The florid clown was straying toward dangerous territory, if he kept bringing Gloucester into it . . .

'They're serving still, with Colonel Nybb, as I believe is known to some of you,' Sir Gilbert went on.

Cruickshank opened his bored eye a notch. Colonel Nybb had taken over the old fool's men, eh? He wouldn't care to wager how many of the poor buggers were left, with a mad bastard like Nybb in charge of them.

'He is known to us, as is of course your late and bitterly lamented ally, Anthony St John Dyle.' Bacon's carefully aimed dart struck the merchant square in the chest.

The young Lord Clavincale, sitting in the well of the court beside Mr Keeler, glanced from the red-faced father to his ethereal daughter, sitting forlorn in the court.

'The late Lord Clavincale and I worked ceaselessly to raise and equip the regiment, it is true,' Sir Gilbert said warily. The court erupted with frantic whisperings. Bacon was silent, allowing the merchant to blunder on into the biggest trap of all. The earl himself, barely able to keep his eyes open until now, looked up sharply. 'We were in the saps before Gloucester two and three times a day, encouraging the men.'

'And you were also present when the late Lord Clavincale was murdered, is that correct?'

Sir Gilbert swallowed nervously, the colour draining from his fleshy features. His quick eyes moved around the court, from Telling and back to the grim clerk.

'I was with Lord Clavincale's party when we were set upon by a party of enemy deserters in Brockworth wood, it is true,' he lied uneasily.

He wondered frantically what reports they had received about the dreadful incident. If they knew the truth, he, Telling, and Bella would have already been stoned to death by now.

Clavincale – Black Bob's own flesh and blood – had caught his fiancée Bella under a tree with Telling, that lecherous snake of a Cavalier. The overweight cuckold had waded in with his broadsword, but the younger man had evaded his brutal strokes and felled him with a bough. But he could hardly give the nobleman's own father that version of events, could he?

Not without incriminating Telling, at any rate. Well, the way this was going, he would have no choice but to sacrifice the captain to save his daughter. The bastard judge might just show some mercy if . . .

'It would seem you bring disaster down on all partners save yourself,' Bacon observed. 'For while two expert swordsmen in your company were butchered, you managed to escape these vagabonds without so much as a scratch.'

'I defended myself as best I could! I had the hand off one of the brutes!' Sir Gilbert invented again. If they had read the report, they would know one of their alleged attackers had lost an arm in the bloody struggle beneath the dripping trees.

'You saw my son die?' the earl asked, his ghastly features clenched like iron, his voice the rasp of a file on a hot horseshoe. Sir Gilbert collected himself with difficulty.

'I did not see the fatal blow struck, my lord. I was being set upon myself at the time. All I could do was fetch help and assist in their pursuit.'

'Which was reportedly unsuccessful.'

Sir Gilbert paused, his fleshly lips moving this way and that. Hugo Telling looked up at the merchant, his breath a bag of razor blades in his constricted throat.

'Well?'

'Well, my lord . . .'

Bella Morrison peered over at her father, suddenly aware of the vicious game of cat and mouse being played out before her, and of Hugo's tremendously precarious position. One word from her father and he would be hanging from the gallows which had haunted her dreams these last dreadful days. She glanced over at her pale-faced father, imagined she could see the greased cogs and complex mechanisms clanking and clicking inside his fevered brain.

'My lord, I believe I may have some information for you about your son's tragic death.'

The entire court was hushed, as if the mice under the panelling were holding their tiny breaths in expectation. Black Bob seemed to be trembling on his shabby throne, his eyes bitter jewels in his wasted skull.

'Well?'

Sir Gilbert teetered on the brink of the precipice, frantically weighing the odds of his intended betrayal. The slender Cavalier in front of him seemed to shrink and squirm, as if he could already feel the hemp knot under his chin.

'Well?'

Bella closed her eyes, crucified with terror. He meant to betray Hugo in some cock-eyed bid to save her. Sending Telling to the scaffold for his part in the wretched fight in the woods wouldn't trouble the merchant, it would simply be another of shabby deal to him, a fair exchange.

'I hesitate to divulge the details in public, my lord.'

Black Bob pushed his chair back with a nerve-grating scrape.

'Indeed? Then we will retire to my robing room. Be aware, sir, I do not appreciate unnecessary delays. Be assured you know your own mind before you deliberate with me!'

'I know it, my lord,' the merchant replied, avoiding Telling's gaze.

'Then this court stands adjourned.'

'Father!' Bella warned, clutching the worn rail, her heart crammed into her throat. Sir Gilbert waved his hand at the distracted girl. Black Bob rose from the chair like a bloated vulture from a rack of ribs, strode along the dais with new found energy.

'It was me, it was me all the time!' Bella wailed. 'Don't listen to him, sir, he'd perjure himself to save me! He'd say anything, blame anyone!'

Black Bob had taken the merchant's bait and meant to run with it. He ignored the pale beauty's hysterical shout, climbed down the steps, and swept towards his chamber. Abraham Bacon left his post beneath the dais and waved the frowning merchant out of the witness box. The public gallery erupted with whispered opinions, the drowsy guards predicting verdicts as if they had spent years at the Bar themselves. Telling eyed the exits with despair. The merchant meant to betray him after all, then. Sell him down the river in some naive bid to save his daughter. He was too tired to argue, and in any case, he would have gladly given his life in place of . . .

Boom!

The court fell silent, heads turning this way and that as every man, woman, and child present stopping talking and listened hard. One of the guns across the harbour perhaps, signalling an incoming ship.

The sudden splutter of musketry outside the barred window had them on their feet in seconds.

Black Bob halted beside the door, stung by the sudden fusillade. He peered round at the devious fiends in the dock, wondering for a moment how they could have summoned up such an assault on his court. The merchant was already making his way past the lawyers' benches, as amazed as the rest of them.

'Well? What of the pursuit? You seem to be holding something back,' he snarled over the rising hubbub. Cruickshank was already on his feet, his pistol in his fist. Major Brinks, sitting alongside, looked around the court for his bewildered guards.

'Well?'

'Turn out the guards! We're under attack!'

'What of my son?' Black Bob shrieked, striding back toward the dumbfounded merchant as the public stampeded from the galleries, knocking the dozing soldiery aside. Bacon hurried over to the demented judge, throwing out his arms to shoo his master from the court. Cruickshank and Brinks followed the bawling earl into the ante-room and clapped the door shut.

Hugo Telling breathed an enormous sigh of relief and listened to the guards on the wall open fire against their mystery invaders. In another moment, everything was in an uproar. He pushed past the terrified Keeler and clambered up the rail towards Bella, standing forlorn in the dock.

'Turn out the guards! We're under attack!'

A mass of muskets snickered and popped and the screaming started, drowning out the furious screeches of the gulls.

THE HARE ROCK,

PENMETHOCK, DORSET

The oddly comical towers of gull-splashed stone seemed to beckon the privateer towards the secret harbour nestled between its outflung limbs. Squalls of kittywakes and guillemots, puffins and fulmars heralded their arrival with raucous screeches which set the nervous invaders' nerves on edge. The peculiar shadow cast by the Hare Rock seemed to engulf the boat, enticing the sour-bellied crew to their doom on its massive seaweed-racked haunches.

Muffet's heavily armed advance party had already clambered down the rigging into the wave-tossed longboat and paddled with difficulty towards the shoreline. Their departure seemed to have sobered the remaining volunteers, subdued their all too brief display of fierce bravado. The few who had actually followed their mad captain's example and branded themselves were fussing over their blistered limbs, holding their cudgels and swords under their armpits while they tied grubby cotton bandages around their scars. The rest of them were munching dejectedly on Mercer's donated cheese, washing the creamy paste down with the last of their rum ration.

By God, they'd need it where they were going.

Sparrow paced to and fro shouting himself hoarse and soothing his throat with the precious amber fluid – as if he could hold them together with his own furious energy. He had taken off his buff coat in a muck sweat, rolled up his sleeves, and then absent-mindedly thrown it back on again. But despite his loud-mouthed efforts to inspire his rascally Huns, his doubts and apprehensions came seeping back, insinuating themselves through the spongy bedrock of his rum-laced courage.

Who was he trying to fool? The cloud of breeze-blown chaff he was relying on to follow his lead, Gallen Fey, or himself?

He cursed under his breath, summoned up another vision of poor old Toby, lying cold in his winding-sheet below the well-trodden deck. He let the anger and hurt boil up in his brain all over again, extinguishing his qualms and fears like a bellows full of woodsmoke through a hive. Tobias Fulke's courage wouldn't have evaporated at the critical moment, left him high and dry and hesitating on the gunwale. He would have leapt into twenty feet of water in his armour and waded ashore along the seabed if necessary. Age and the elements were no obstacle to his dogged spirit. He must not – he would not – fail Toby, or these ignorant apes he had tempted aboard with promises of loot and liquor.

Sparrow watched Muffet's boat ride the tumbling waves between a broad gully, jagged weed-slimed rocks precious feet from the keel. As he watched, the longboat was lifted like a barrel and carried into the narrow cove, dark figures popping up and dropping over the side. In another moment they were lost to sight, hidden behind the hanging gardens of rock and their canopies of glistening kelp.

The Hare Rock dwarfed the *Blue Doubloon*, towering hundreds of feet above the privateer. Seabirds wheeled and rolled through the spume and spray, as Fey brought the ship in tight to the reefs and shoals.

A lesser captain would have stayed in deeper water offshore, entered the harbour by the front door. Not Fey. The dapper little captain stood straight on the quarter-deck, altering their furious course by a quarter-point here and there. The water had soaked his hat, swollen the brown leather around his pale head. John Grey was staggering along between the gun carriages on the fore-deck, bent double against the spray and the waves. He hurried from crew to crew like a Druid priest administering to a doubting flock, ensuring the great cannon were loaded and ready and the powder and match was being kept dry under sacking and sailcloth.

Sparrow stared at the enormous vaulted chambers which formed the belly of the mighty headland, the fluted columns and triumphal arches which had defied the sea for thousands of years. Half a point out and Fey would dash them against the rocks and that would be an end of it. A few bodies swirling in the flotsam, giving the despised villagers something to think about the next time they checked their nets. William glanced over his shoulder. At least Fey seemed to know what he was doing. Sparrow bent over and peered back the way he had brought them, a mad crescendo of waves and rearing rock. Treacherous shoals Fey had negotiated as if he had been in super-natural communication with Neptune himself. Surely any lookout on top of the formidable cliff would be staring out to sea, not examining the deadly network of rocks and reefs between his feet?

Sparrow turned and watched the great bay open out before them. Away on the horizon, a long blue spur of land. To his right, the rearing cliffs beneath the Hare

Rock, staggered and shelved, variously coloured strata piled this way and that. He followed the mad geology of red and grey rocks until it collided and merged with the black cliffs formed by the green downs rushing in from the north. The lush fields had hurled themselves over the bare bones of the cliff, forming weird slides and coombs leading down to the steeply shelved shingle beaches. The biggest fissure had been worked and mined by a busy stream, emptying into the wide bowl formed by an ancient glacier. It was around this natural anchorage that the village had grown up, stacking itself around the shelves of rock in grey and merry red tiers. The fishermen had attempted to seal themselves off from the sea by constructing an enormous black breakwater across the narrowest neck of the bay. Sparrow could see piled baskets and crab pots, heaped nets drying in the afternoon sun.

Fey brought the *Blue Doubloon* about, trusting to the energetic currents to carry the privateer into the inner harbour. The wind changed, a smart breeze whipping Sparrow's crusty hair across his face. The sails boomed and cracked, so loud the dozing guards must have been aware of them. He listened hard for shouts or shots or clanging bells, but the noisy wind and screaming gulls which had formed a towering white tornado above the ship drowned out any disturbance from the land.

'Shore party, have a care,' Sparrow roared, his mouth dry as the planking under his boots. 'Another few minutes and we'll be inside the harbour, they can't miss us then!'

The two elderly sergeants Toby Fulke had recruited in London were hounding and harrying the men, taking their minds from the fight to come by bawling nonsensical and contradictory instructions into their pale faces. Goodrich and Jameson had tried to rekindle the spirit they had shown after Sparrow's foolhardy demonstration, although they had refrained from taking the hot tongs to their own forearms. The bearded veterans were heavy, fleshy men who had been with the colours for years. In the days before the war militia service with the London Trained Bands had been a pleasant diversion from their trades, a chance to leave their troubles and families behind and get off for a weekend with their like-minded cronies. In between their frequent debaucheries, however, they had learned to march and knew musket and pike drill off by heart. There would be little chance to use either tactic here, though. This would be a street fight, impure and simple, a vicious brawl which would result either in the shore party being thrown into the sea and slaughtered or in their mastery of the spiteful little nest. It was for this reason that in the new plan caused by Fulke's death most of the musketeers would be sent with the equally experienced Muffet: his squad would attack the gun emplacements and then storm into the village from the eastern slopes. Sparrow and his sergeants would lead their men in from the Crossbone Quay, pistolling and cudgelling any bugger who got in their way. If they met a body of foot drawn up with pikes in the centre and shot on the flanks, or even worse, a body of enemy horse in an open field, they would be shorn to the bone in a few minutes. But clumsy great blocks of pike would be unable to manoeuvre in the narrow confines of a village street. Sparrow had had a gutful of street fighting back in Bristol. He knew it was quick, brutal, and bloody, with no pattern or shape, no flanks or centres or reserves. A soldier couldn't look around to gauge how the battle was going, stuck halfway up a broken staircase with a platoon of enemy sharpshooters plugging the doorways. He had a few tricks up his sleeve, though, in case the enemy force managed to organize some resistance in the squat red-tiled hovels leading up the hill from the quay.

If Fey could just get them ashore . . .

'Captain Sparrow, sir!' Nicodemus Burke had hurried down from the poop, tacking across the heaving deck between knots of anxious soldiers. Sparrow glanced down at the red-haired urchin in his outsize coat, the enormous sleeves rolled up so he could get to grips with Fulke's personal banner, a square of fringed blue silk with an angel descending from a fluffy white cloud. Strikingly inappropriate in a hold full of spewing, cursing, reluctant Roundheads. Nicodemus — Sparrow's ensign — would carry the colour in place of the regimental banner they had been forced to leave back at Hemel Hempstead with that brigand Slaughter. 'Captain Fey says take cover when we come under the mole. They might start shooting from the quay.'

Sparrow nodded. 'And mind you keep that red head of yours down, too, when it gets hot,' he ordered, giving the youth's spiky mop a brisk pat.

Nicodemus tugged back in embarrassment. 'Will you stop doing that, Will? They think I'm a little house dove as it is,' the youth complained bitterly.

'Ah, you've already proved yourself, lad, don't you go showing off in front of this lot.'

If there was showing off to be done Sparrow would have to do it himself, whatever the consequences. He would be in charge, after all.

Colston Muffet could have thrown himself down and kissed the damned rocks. Long days and sleepless nights on the *Blue Doubloon* had drained what little love of the sea he had left, and he was mightily glad to feel the shingle scrape under the longboat's barnacled keel. He had been the first out, lifting his musket well clear of the spray and boosting himself nimbly over the gunwale. He slipped, steadying himself with his left hand with a curse. Gilling-feather had leapt into the slipping shingle and scrambled away towards the sandy bluffs which encircled the rocky cove, the crumbling strata pocked and holed by rabbits and sand martins. The wiry agitator doubled up the slope toward the path in the left-hand corner of the smuggler's hideout, furiously blowing on his match as he went. Billy Butcher was squatting in the boat, his fowling-piece trained on the over-hanging cliffs. A dozen musketeers disembarked clumsily from the narrow boat and followed the elder sergeant up under the lee of the cliff.

'Get that boat secured, we might need the bugger getting off,' Muffet called. The sailors who had accom-panied the raiding party leapt over the gunwales and dragged the boat up the bank. Butcher climbed down and followed the others up the narrow path, dotted and dashed with hundreds of rabbit pellets. The lush turf had been cropped close by the plentiful rodents, exposing dusty soil and elbows of grey rock. The lean veteran led his men along the rising path, ragged ghosts in their salt-encrusted coats of many colours. Their burning match fumed and fizzled, releasing ribbons of white smoke.

They doubled around the lower slopes of the massive headland, following the jagged contours higher and higher. To their right, they could see the empty downs rolling away toward the east. To the north, the long kidney-shaped ridge of Bay Hill, with its squat black church and stubby tower. The main road passed along the far side of the hill, crossing a small brook and dropping away sharply toward the village buried in the coomb below. Muffet, shielding his eyes with his long hand, couldn't see a living thing, save for a few sheep away on the far slopes. Billy Butcher grinned, his teeth dazzling white against his sunburnt features.

'Caught the buggers napping, Col. Just like that village back at Bristol.'

'And we all know what happened at Bristol,' the elder sergeant replied, nodding the sharpshooter on along the treacherous path. The dusty track led them in a wide arc around the Hare Rock, bringing them out on a level plateau with a stunning view of the bay. Muffet hurried them on, pointing the party down the slope towards the long strand which ran along the inner cliffs.

There was flash of light on steel.

'They're looking the wrong way, Col,' Butcher gasped, hurrying to keep up with his sergeant's long-legged lope. 'We'll catch 'em 'avin' one off the wrist, whilin' away the afternoon,' the sharpshooter boasted.

Muffet ignored the boy's nonsense, peering down the strand for the gun emplacement.

Suddenly he saw it.

A cairn of large pebbles plugged with sacks of sand and gabions, a monstrous nest at the foot of the cliff. Some vast iron eagle had laid a couple of long bronze cannon in the rocky crevice, the barrels pointing out over the shimmering emerald bay. It was shocking to think man could desecrate such a paradise, bringing his guns and powder to such an Eden. Muffet frowned. Well, it wouldn't be an Eden for long, if those gunners managed to get a shot on the *Blue Doubloon*. He could see the privateer now, edging around the headland.

So could the gun crew, wallowing about their weapons as they slept off their dinners. The first drowsy lookouts had scrambled up on their emplacement for a better look, shouted for the glasses to study the intruder.

Muffet waved his men on, timber wolves creeping down from the wild hills to stalk victims in the village. They hugged the cliffs, moving from boulder to outcrop to stunted hawthorn. They were so close they could hear the gun crew shouting to one another, see the lazy officer climbing up beside the cannon to see what all the fuss was about.

A shot-blasted privateer, torn and scored to the white wood where the red-hot balls had struck her. Rigging askew, sails torn and flapping. The black colours blowing raggedly above the wounded decks.

The officer sent a runner back along the strand. An errand boy in a baggy sea-coat and bare feet, making nothing of the rough flints and grit which made up the exposed strand. Hurrying back to the village to warn the major there was a ship in the harbour.

Gillingfeather rose out of the rock like an avenging angel, his tawny beard crackled and frosted with salt spray, his mad eyes gleaming with malice. The terrified boy stopped in his tracks, flapped his arms in shocked silence as the agitator darted forward and crammed the butt of his musket into the boy's forehead. The pole-axed youth fell into the pebbles, blood bubbling from his split head. Gillingfeather ducked down and dragged the boy under cover, rejoined Muffet's party as they completed their approach. The gun crews had built themselves some rude shelters from the winds, pebble walls and thatched roofs, buttressed with lengths of timber they had found along the shore. The officer had a slightly grander apartment, a tiny one-windowed cottage built into the lee of the cliffs. Muffet signalled two men to the cottages, while he waved the rest into a line. They stalked across the last few yards, checking their muskets and blowing on their match. The loose shingle seemed to grate and slide under their boots. Surely they would be discovered.

'It's the *Doubloon* out of Dunkirk, I'd know that tub anywhere!'

'By Christ, she's in a bad way, listing like that!'

The Roundhead renegades crept closer while the gunners pointed and stared, intent on the battered intruder across the water.

Muffet hauled himself up the turf wall of the rear of the expectant emplacement, raised his musket, and squinted down the barrel at the shirtsleeved officer.

'Turn around now, sir, nice and steady.'

The lean veteran watched the bewildered officer swivel around awkwardly in his roll-top boots, blinking sleepily in his dishevelled finery at the unexpected intruders. His long black hair was hanging in dark ribbons over his unbuttoned shirt, stained with the rich red wine he had taken with his dinner. He groped for his sword, realized he was staring down the barrels of half a dozen muskets. His men, swarthy militia from the hills round about, had left their arms stacked against the bulging pebble wall of their emplacement.

'Who the devil are you men? What's the meaning of this?'

Butcher and Gillingfeather had already slid away from the wall and were gesturing the puzzled crew away from their pieces.

'Never mind all that, you damned coxcomb, just drop that cleaver before I drill you,' Muffet said out of the side of his mouth.

The angry officer stared from the grey-haired veteran to his own open-mouthed men. Yards from any available weapon, they would be shot down before they had gone two paces. And that stone-eyed bastard would put a ball in his belly for the simple pleasure of seeing him squirm. The wide-eyed crew swallowed nervously as their commander twitched with mortification. His gun position taken from him without a single casualty. He hadn't even raised the alarm! Muffet took another two steps closer, lowering the musket a notch. The officer pulled the first six inches of blade from his scabbard.

'That's better. Careful, now. Now get over by the wall with the others.'

'I don't know who in hell you are, or where you came from, but you won't leave this bay alive. I promise you that,' the semi-drunken Cavalier vowed, swaying slightly as he let his sword clatter to the stone floor of the emplacement.

'We'll see,' Muffet mouthed. 'We'll see.'

The black-slime walls of the mole reared up around the privateer like the jaws of some enormous sea monster, a vast whale ready to swallow the impudent Jonahs who had ventured into its lair. Sparrow peered over the splintered gunwale at the gaggle of dirty urchins who had been fishing from the end of the breakwater, waving their arms as they welcomed the 'friendly' vessel. A few old men among them, burnt like copper by sun and wind and fish oil, peered under their palms at the battered ship, noting the extensive damage to the superstructure, the knotted rigging hanging lazily from loosely swinging yardarms. She'd been in a fight, sure enough.

But the half-dozen cannon which menaced the breakwater from the shot-torn deck seemed solid enough. The gun crews who squatted behind the vast pieces seemed lively and alert and the officers who directed them clearly knew their business. The *Blue Doubloon* glided under the barnacled shadows, slipping into the harbour on the tide. Sparrow raised his head over the gunwale once again, taking in every detail of the overshadowed anchorage. To his left, the mole swept away like a vast black jawbone, linked to the looming cliffs by colossal boulders set like dull stones in an iron crown and great yawning seams of variously grey mortar. The cliffs collided, concertinaed in on themselves to form the coomb. A snug haven for the hovels and houses stacked neatly above the broad sweep of the Crossbone Quay. He could see the busy main street running off behind the wharves and on up the slope towards the converging hills, Pen Point, Sully Hill, and Cairns Hill to his left, Plum Hill broad and bald in the centre, and Bay Hill curving protectively about the precious town to the right. Crossbone Quay was alive with fishermen and goodwives, shouting children and squawking chickens, penned cattle and heavily laden carts. Many of them had stopped work, paused over their nets as the slim intruder glided over the rising tide, stark black lines against a jewelled sea. Below the stone quay the fishing fleet, a couple of dozen boats gaily painted in greens and bright blues, seemed to add further animation to the bustling harbour. The merry flotilla reminded Sparrow of a flock of garish hatchlings, bobbing and diving under the slow, watchful eye of the brooding red dragon moored behind them.

The *Messalina's Purse.*

'Beat to quarters!' The sudden command electrified crew and spectators alike, and as the drum rolled the ship turned from a mysterious apparition to an armed intruder. The guns were trundled out into their ports. Gun captains peered down the gleaming barrels at their prime target, moving gently against her moorings. She might just as well have been shackled to the seawall, her defenceless stern exposed like a bare-arsed whore.

The last time Sparrow had been this close to her he had been kicking his lead boots in a ferocious swell, riding the waves as the despised ship made her getaway across the rearing and plunging bay. Here again in all her impudent glory, lashed to the quay like a greyhound in the slips, her curious crew hanging from the rigging as they watched their sister slip into port beside her.

'Open fire!'

Sparrow ducked back down as the deck heaved beneath him. He felt the terrific force of the recoil through the groaning planks, felt the ship tilt as the big guns were brought to bear one by one. The gunners could hardly miss, hurling double-charged roundshot down the red dragon's throat from point-blank range. The *Doubloon* righted herself in a fog of foul smokes, dim red flashes sparking in the sudden, man-made murk. The first shots smashed through the enemy ship's stern, demolishing the decorative glasswork and streaking the length of the deck – destroying everything in their fiery path. Fey had aimed low, hoping to tear the guts out of the formidable warship before her own guns could be brought to bear on the intruder. The raiders snatched up their weapons as Fey let the *Doubloon* drift in on the tide, sliding across the *Purse*'s broken stern.

As soon as his ears had stopped ringing Sparrow made out the sudden shrill yells of fright and hurt across the harbour. He raised his head, and saw how the red ship had staggered under the sudden broadside, splintered planking and spars flying into the air and splashing into the deep green water, men running this way and that over the deck.

'Shore party, make ready!' Grey bellowed from the quarterdeck.

Sparrow gripped his halberd and prised himself to his feet, his compacted knee joints and calf muscles shrieking with cramps. He glanced around him, nodding encouragingly at the press of grubby faces which seemed to surround him. There was no going back, no way off without shame and a stab in the back.

'Shore party, make ready!' Sparrow repeated, finding his voice in the depths of his parched throat. 'Any moment, lads. Let the captain bring us in to the quay and then in and at 'em. Don't give 'em a moment to think about it, rush straight through 'em,' he advised.

There was a squall of ill-aimed musketry from the alerted privateer, a clatter of lead balls on the broad oak bows. Fey's gunners opened fire into the drifting white cloud thrown up from the enemy vessel, ending the one-sided duel in a crash of lead. Sergeant Goodrich stood with his legs spread, manhandling the swivel gun on the bow. The slim barrel had been double loaded with grapeshot, to cut a swath through the screaming mobs on the quay. He lowered his fuming match to the touch-hole and stood back coughing as the fierce explosion sent a bucketful of iron slugs hurtling across the smoky water. Some scored the rough jetty, others embedded themselves in the wooden pylons. But the bulk of the point-blank barrage swept over the exposed quay, finding softer targets in the press of terrified humanity. Shouting fishermen and screaming women went down clutching spurting wounds. A burly shorehand lifting a crab pot above his straw head was caught in the face, and collapsed to his knees, braining himself with his own missile. The rest of the shrieking civilians fled down every alley and open door and gateway, leaving the exposed quay to the maimed and the dead.

There was a juddering crash as the bows came round and collided with the harbour wall, skittling Sparrow's men about the smoky deck. More shots rang out. A scorched black hole appeared as if by magic in the limp sailcloth above William's head. He cursed, rolled over, and jumped to his feet. The bows were rasping along the stone as the *Doubloon* was carried about by the swell, away from her intended victim across the water.

By Christ, they could jump for it!

'On your feet, with me!' Sparrow bawled, hurrying over to the starboard bow. Goodrich pushed the swivel gun away and joined the captain clambering over the bullet-raked gunwale. The two men leapt clear of the awkwardly docked ship, landed heavily among the pots and the nets. Sparrow caught his breath and looked up, saw a crowd of terrified villagers squeezing themselves down an alley between the flung open doors of a well-stocked warehouse. A tall man in a dark-blue coat was aiming a pistol at them. The man fired, and Sparrow hurled himself down in the stinking trap of nets and lines, eye to eye with the undersized pouts left stinking in the sun by the sea folk. The bullet whined overhead and struck the *Doubloon*'s bows, singing off into the water.

One of the musketeers who had remained with the shore party took a snap shot but couldn't hit the warehouse, let alone its cursing defender. Sparrow leapt up once more and half ran, half stumbled through the fiendish mantrap of pots and nets, floats and lines. His boots tangled and his breeches snagged, but he ducked his head down and charged on, scattering the flimsy wickerwork baskets in his wake. The man in blue turned to run, thought better of it, and hurled the smoking pistol at the buff-coated bull. The heavy pistol glanced off Sparrow's arm, jarring his elbow. He redoubled his grip on the halberd, brought the heavy blade down on the man's crouching head. The screaming man ducked his head out of the way, but the savage blow cut deeply into his shoulder. He yelled, shrill with terror, and scrambled away on his haunches as Sparrow dragged the blade back. The captain heaved the halberd free, kicked the groaning man aside, and looked over his shoulder.

To his everlasting relief, he saw Nicodemus, Goodrich, and the whooping shore party burst through the maze of nets and pots and charge over the quay after their champion.

'Shore party, follow me!' Sparrow yelled, ducking his head as a bottle sailed through the air and smashed on the ground. One of the barefoot sailors howled and hopped as the glass tore and slashed his callused soles. He turned from the maze of hovels and alleys, waved them on to the left, down the long exposed sweep of Crossbone Quay.

'Don't stop for any bugger till we get to the top! Don't let them regroup!'

The leading raiders had reached the safety of the warehouse and were breathlessly peering into the cool, dim depths, examining its precious hoard. 'By Christ, they've loaded her to the rafters!' The eager crew leered into the mysterious cavern, their bright eyes misting over in contemplation of the loot they might find within.

'Shut the doors and we'll go through her later,' Sparrow ordered. 'It's no good trying to empty the warehouse with a townful of King's men at your backs!'

The belligerent shore party saw the cruel logic of the captain's argument. If they went in now they could find themselves surrounded by the vengeful inhabitants. The knowledge sparked their martial ardour all over again.

'Come on, you bastards, the quicker we rout these drunken swine the sooner we'll be filling our sacks!'

The murderous men turned behind the furiously shouting captain and pursued the lumbering officer up the quay, scattering townsfolk hurrying out of their way. The vindictive raiders clubbed, wounded, and kicked the bleeding bodies, axed cables, and cut mooring ropes with malicious glee. More shots were fired from the town, ill aimed and at extreme range. They did no damage but inflamed the shrieking banshees to further outrages. With a terrifying whoop of animal fury they swerved away from the bloody quay and began the deadly charge up Penmethock's main street, rabid wolves going for the throat of the paralysed town.

Edward Callow would rather have faced a hundred more broadsides from the damned intruder than explain his error to his master. Callow, the dour and hitherto unshockable mate of the *Messálina's Purse,* would have wagered the lives of his grandchildren that he had correctly identified the bloody, fire-breathing raider. Why, it was no other but the *Blue Doubloon* out of Dunkirk, one of the *Purse*'s own sister ships. Terrence Gable's. Shot-blasted and battered, rigging hanging and sails limp, the privateer had clearly cut and run from some fight out in the Channel, just as they had been forced to do themselves that fateful summer.

Aye, it had been a black day for all of them, when the *Purse* had come up against the *Conqueror* that time. But the *Conqueror* had been beached and breached off Exeter, and the last he had heard the *Doubloon* was blockade-running around the Wash. What was she doing here, running into harbour like a ghost ship, tattered colours hanging like rotting weeds from the maintopmast?

He cursed under his breath, felt the *Messalina's Purse* lurch chronically beneath his feet. They were taking water fast, the hull holed by half a dozen carefully – cruelly – aimed shots. By God, that gunner had known his business, turning in on the tide and sliding across their stern, crippling the *Purse* before they had lit their match.

'Get those guns about!' Callow bawled at the deafened, bloodied, smoke-scorched survivors who scuttled to and fro on the listing deck. The dazed crews hauled and pushed at their pieces, straining and cursing as they attempted to manhandle the remaining cannon to bear on the drifting fugitive. Callow peered through the drifting smoke, saw the shore party dash along the quay. Further up the hill, armed men were milling uncertainly in the street. God only knew where his master, Valentine Cruickshank, had taken himself off to. Bedding some whore in a filthy garret somewhere, or gambling away the crew's cut in the tavern. But woe betide him if Cruickshank returned to find his pride and joy wallowing under three fathom of water! He might as well hang himself now as face that. The grim-faced mate ground what were left of his teeth, eyes streaming with smoke and fury as he watched the few gunners that were left struggle with the guns. Callow ignored the throbbing wound in his thigh – he had been caught by a vicious splinter as the galleries below had been pounded to ruin – and hauled himself down the steps from the poop deck. He hung on grimly to the gun-wale, squinted through the foul fogs drifting over the water. It was now or never.

'Fire!'

The broadside rocked the crippled privateer, left her foundering beside the quay. Callow hung on grimly as the crucified crew readied themselves to leap overboard. The waterlogged hull was flooded by fresh torrents forced in through its splintered ribs, accelerating the chronic list.

Two guns on the *Doubloon*'s stern roared in reply, and Callow threw himself down as the screaming iron sang over the sea and impacted against the gutted privateer. Callow's men were throwing themselves over the sides, jumping from the torn rigging. The wounded mate clawed at the deck, pulled himself across the slippery planking towards the cross-eyed devils who had remained beside one of his precious guns.

'Is she loaded? Is she loaded?' he bawled. The shell-shocked crew shook their heads dumbly, their wits scattered by the sudden tempests which had scoured their ship away from under them.

'Hurry up, you dogs! Double load her! Roundshot!'

The terrified crew hurried to their posts, sponging the smoking barrel, ramming home the powder charge, and scooping the heavy iron ball down the barrel. A painfully thin gunner, his bare chest scored with burnt powder, rammed the ball home and stood back.

'Faster, you scum-throats! She'll sink beneath us if you're any longer!' Callow roared.

'Pull her back!' Callow hauled at the waxy rope tackle, gritting his teeth in fury. One by one, the bewildered gunners joined in, sinews stretching as they hauled the great carriage against the increasing list back up to the smoky gunport. Callow threw himself over the gun like a monkey climbing a palm tree, squinted along the barrel through the sulphurous mists which obscured the hated trickster. He felt light-headed with pain, sick with loss of blood, and had to blink to clear his vision. At last he made out the battered shape of the *Doubloon*, broadside-on now, her mainmast splintered like rotten timber, her rigging hanging over the splintered decks like some hateful ivy. Figures were moving drunkenly across her crippled decks, busy about their remaining guns.

'Fire!' Callow pushed himself away as the vast cannon spouted flame. He was hurled aside, landing with a groan against the burning gunwale. The last gunners fled, leaping over the flaming decks into the harbour. Men were screaming, swimming, and splashing in the bobbing litter, clinging to the floating spars and scrapped masts, friend and foe alike coughing and retching on the churning brine.

Callow felt his coat scorch, the greedy heat eating up his arms. A desperate explosion fractured the crisp air as a powder barrel went up.

A moment later a rain of wooden splinters clattered and splashed around him. He lifted his arm, saw his canvas coat was burning merrily. He knelt up with a wince, tearing the burning coat from his back, the flames licking and biting at his fumbling fingers. He hauled himself to his feet, just as Gallen Fey lowered the linstock to his last gun. The roundshot bucketed through the smoke and tore a breach in the battered gunwale, lifting the screaming mate from his feet and hurling him against the mainmast, his opened belly splashing blue and red streamers over the resilient oak. Callow, his steaming entrails hanging from his hands, collapsed to his knees, and groaned in shock. Agonized moments passed as he felt his mistress die beneath him. The forecastle seemed to rise out of the smoking wreckage as the bows sank slowly beneath the lapping green waters. A cauldron of bubbles escaped from the breached hull. Callow, whiter than chalk, his bloody hands splayed over his torn belly, lifted his head from the burning deck, the last of his tangled hair smouldering and stinking. He watched the splintered figurehead swim below the lapping waters as the harbour tugged the broken toy below the surface. The eager wavelets swallowed the deck, the lopsided guns, and the slumped bodies. It coursed over his splattered feet, devoured his scorched legs, and swirled around his raw neck. He propped himself up on his blistered elbows, but could not lift himself out of the flood. With one final heave of agony, the *Messalina* rolled under the sea, taking her dying mate with her.

CROSSBONE QUAY,

PENMETHOCK

The semi-drunken remnant of Speedwell's troop of dragoons imagined their mad captain had finally gone too far – antagonizing these in-bred cretins on their home turf. The sudden fusillade of shots and shouts had them throwing back their stinking bedding and leaping for the weapons they had left lying in the corner of their noisome garret, convinced they were under attack. Big Debra, hurled off the horribly sunken pile of fetid bedclothes like a vast pink jelly, squawked her protests as her erstwhile customers grabbed their breeches and dashed to the windows. A whining bullet and a puff of pulverized stone sent them diving to the floor. Auld Guppy, hand on heart, sucked great lungfuls of agonized breath. Martin Pike, mewing with terror, squirmed over the floor like a decked conger. Graves, the giant sergeant who Speedwell had left in charge, tore his coat from the back of the door and tugged it on, stood beside the window eyeing the mad cavalcade in the street below. Half a hundred screaming villagers were charging up towards the Mermaid, others were issuing out of front doors and windows as if their reeking hovels had been chalked for the plague. Stumbling fishermen were staggering out onto the tavern steps, shouting and bawling as they tried to detain the desperate fugitives. Henry Graves bit his lip, paralysed by uncertainty. The big man jumped with fright as the cannon boomed over the water to his right, an intense barrage heralding another panic-stricken flight from the exposed quay. This time, the street was filled with a gang of well-armed men, led by a snarling brute in a buff coat. As he watched the leader pointed the furious mob on up the main street.

'By Christ's bones, it's the enemy!' Graves realized at last, jumping back as another ill-aimed pistol shot struck the crumbling masonry beneath his observation post.

'Here?'

'Hundreds of the bastards,' Graves answered, snatching up his musket. 'Get the rest to bar the front door, we'll keep the back way open in case we have to leg it,' he ordered, feverishly searching for his bullet bag and bandolier in the tangled mess at the foot of the warm bed. Martin Pike had crawled back over and peeped down into the chaotic street fight, closed his eyes as Graves hammered the grimy pane out of the window with his musket butt.

'Guppy, get them moving down there!' Graves roared. The electrified dragoons ran for the door, the distraught whore tugging the bedding around her abused bulk.

Roundheads? Here?

Two miles further west, bewildered militiamen taking their shift guarding the prisoners in Penmethock quarry took off their hats and tilted their heads to catch the faint echoes of bloody battle. They could make out the muffled crump of large-calibre guns, and every now and then a sea wind blew up the fainter strains of musketry, an angry, insinuating crackle like an enormous wasps' nest being stirred with a stick.

The puzzled guards exchanged anxious glances, shielded their eyes, and peered back down the steep coomb towards the village.

'What's Black Bob doing, using cannon for a firing squad?'

'I heard tell that honey blob might catch it hot.'

'Firing squad?' their bristling sergeant called angrily. 'That's no firing squad, that's a culverin or I'm a Froglander!'

Further down the dusty bowl, the ragged prisoners paused over their boulders and stones, listening to the growing tumult. Sixty men and a handful of women, smothered from head to foot in pulverized rock, their iron chains rasping red-raw weals around their wrists and ankles. A legion of ghosts in a rocky limbo.

'What is it, John?'

'Have they come for us, then?'

'Come for us? They've forgotten we're even here!'

The distracted sergeant whistled his men to attention, sent them doubling around the rim of the quarry to keep an eye on their famished slaves.

'Bob Simmonds, get yourself along the path there and have a scout out. And hurry about it!'

The sudden booming barrage died away. Sergeant Titus Beam tilted his head, strained to pick up the threads of the distant fighting over the angry squalls of the gulls. Damn it all, what was happening back there? He looked down into the hard-worked quarry, eyed the surly prisoners who had stopped hammering, gawping in wonder.

'Get on with your work! We haven't brought you here to stand about jaw-wagging!'

It had taken them going on half an hour to cover the distance from the cliff. Gillingfeather had been all for cutting their prisoners' swinish throats and chucking their bodies in the sea for the dogfish to chew on, but Muffet had insisted the captured gun crew be locked in the cottage – despite the furious officer's protests. Let the buggers think he was having trouble restraining his murderous men – their understandable anxiety would be as effective as a few hundredweight of iron chain.

A blow from Gillingfeather's musket butt loosened several of the mortified officer's fine white teeth and persuaded his surly crew cooperation would make more sense than futile resistance. They were kicked and shoved into the salt-crusted hut like so many cattle, and Butcher slammed the feeble door on their packed bodies. The raiders had hauled sandbags, lengths of planking, and several large rocks up to try and seal the breach as best they could, and tied the door handle with an old belt, ignoring the increasing tumult from within.

'Let us out! We can't breathe stuck in 'ere like this!'

'Shut your trap, you malignant shit!'

'Let us out, you rebel bastards!'

It was clear the shattered, wind-blown wood and hastily improvised barricade wouldn't hold them for a moment, though. Muffet pulled at his long chin distractedly. Killing them without a sound? It would have to be knife work, a right shambles. And the cold-blooded slaughter of their prisoners wouldn't look too good if anything went wrong with the highly dangerous expedition. The veteran gave the anxious agitator a broad wink.

'Gilly, you stand there and shoot the first bugger who sticks his head out, Smith, you shoot the second. But I don't want you slaughtering them behind me back, d'you hear me now? Not after the last time! Just stay here and keep an eye on them until we get back!'

Gillingfeather opened his mouth to protest at being left behind, but Muffet held his long finger to his lips and waved them away. The hairy musketeer finally realized what he intended, gave the barricade one last vindictive kick, and crept off on his toes.

'I'll drill the first bugger who risks a fart,' Billy Butcher added for good measure. It was a calculated risk, leaving seven of the bastards behind them, but they had little time or opportunity for anything but slitting their throats. And Muffet wouldn't kill men as if he was drowning kittens – not without good reason, at any rate. The raiding party had collected the stacked arms, hammered soft-headed nails into the touch-holes of the guns, and thrown their match and linstocks into the sea. They might not be secure, but the fear of being shot down by a fanatic Roundhead might keep their heads down just long enough, Muffet thought ruefully, leading the way back along the rocky strand toward the coomb.

Thirty breathless minutes later, the raiders had reached their second objective, the squat, ugly courthouse, dominating the crossroads at the head of the cloven coomb. By Christ, what a fright they had given those blue-coated guards, shambling about beside the main gate like animated scarecrows. The first volley had dropped the trio by the gate, sent the rest of them dashing for cover.

Billy Butcher took steady, deliberate aim down the endless barrel of his fowling-piece. His grubby forefinger tightened about the iron trigger, and the long gun leapt against his shoulder. He closed his pale blue eyes and waited for the stinking fog to clear, opened them in time to see his intended victim topple back down behind the assizes wall. His long-range shot attracted a flurry of musketry from the courthouse walls and windows, all of it falling at least twenty yards short. The angry fusillade tore up gouts of turf and clipped the grit from the well-maintained road, but didn't harm the rest of Muffet's platoon, advancing deliberately along the road from the bridge which they had secured without a shot being fired.

Butcher reloaded his musket at the double, hurrying to keep up with the rest of them as they ran to take advantage of the sudden slackening of fire from the fortified courthouse. The cursing blue-coats along the walls were priming their pans and ramming down new charges, with one frantic eye on the massed attackers swarming up the slope at them. Miles from any Round-head garrison, they had believed themselves safe and secure in their coastal fastness. Their leader, a wolfish veteran with a shock of grey hair, lifted his floppy black hat, and waved it towards the walls.

'William Waller's dragoons, charge!'

William Waller's dragoons? Here? The frantic musketeers trembled and sweated as they reloaded, threw their pieces back over the brick stockade, and squinted for a target.

William Waller's dragoons? The last they had heard Waller was in London, forming a new army in place of the one he had lost on Roundway in the summer. If Waller's dragoons were attacking, the Night Owl must be hiding over the ridge with the rest of his command! It wouldn't be the first time he had caught the Royalists napping, either!

The panic-stricken defenders searched the open field and deserted road for the devilish advance party. There they were, lying doggo in the ditch which had been dug beside the highway by generations of Penmethock Assizes' miserable patrons. The blue-coated recruits blasted the shadows, a squall of bullets tearing at the flimsy cover their attackers had taken refuge behind. One man fell aside, his musket rolling out of his shivering fist and clattering down the slope. The survivors knelt up and gave them a stinging volley in reply, clipping three more of the blue-coats as the inexperienced musketeers peered over the rampart to see what damage they had inflicted.

'Get down, you damned plovers!'

Another long-range shot caught the bawling corporal in the ear. The pitiful puppet staggered along the rampart and then fell head over heels, landing in a cloud of dust beneath Black Bob's gallows. His terrified platoon had had enough. New to the colours, they couldn't be expected to hold off William Waller's entire army by themselves! The raw Royalists scrambled down from the rampart and joined the race for the rear gate with fleeing tradesmen and terrified courthouse employees, ladies and gentlemen in their Sunday finery whose business had taken them to the court, and a hundred and more common people who had been trying to squeeze their way in to the assizes in the hope of witnessing a good hanging. The eagerly anticipated execution of that wondrous young beauty from up Somerset way who had shot all those dragoons in the village there. The surging mob careered away from the vicious musketry, pushed and shoved a passage through the narrow back gate buried in the rear wall, and galloped off down the steep slope towards the village. Others, panicked by the mad stampede in the courtyard, had redoubled their efforts to force their way into the massively squat assizes building itself, but were being held off by confused court officials and quailing blue-coated guards. Even as they pushed and prodded the invaders from the courthouse steps, the Roundhead sharpshooters used the suddenly deserted brick walls as cover, forced their way in through the main gate, and aimed a torrent of lead at the squirming, pushing, screaming mass of fugitives on the steps.

The shrieking mob flung up their hands as the slugs tore through their Sunday best, puncturing lungs and shattering bones. The few shots which had missed the writhing targets clattered against the wall in a deadly tattoo. Wounded men and women fell over the railings, splashing the steps with their blood, clawing at one another's agonized faces as they were trampled by their friends. The guards tugged the massive oak doors to, trapping the fugitives on the bullet-thrashed threshold. Musket and pistol shots from the tiny courthouse windows forced the Roundhead party back from the yard, giving the dazed survivors time to stagger away around the corner of the main building to join the last of their friends escaping via the back gate.

Colston Muffet tore another pot of powder from his bandolier and tipped the contents down his smoking musket barrel. The panting veteran added a ball and rammed it home with his scouring stick. He had pressed himself against the formidable brick wall, his men taking cover as the defenders poured a furious fusillade against the gate. Billy Butcher doubled up along the wall, his fowling-piece clutched in his fist. The youth threw himself down, wiped his powder-smeared mouth.

'The rest of 'em are pissin' for it, back down the hill,' he reported, jerking his thumb over his shoulder. Muffet frowned.

'Right back towards William and the rest of the buggers,' he snarled. 'Better if we could have holed 'em up here awhile,' he concluded, spitting into the rank weeds which flourished in the slight dip below the sheltering wall.

'We'll never force our way in now,' Butcher growled, 'not with all that lot ready for us.' Another patter of musketry scoured the wall and gateposts, as if to underline the sharpshooter's gloomy summary of the situation.

'Then we'll have to pin 'em down here until William gets to us,' his sergeant replied, ducking down to aim his musket around the bullet-scored oak gate.

The siege of Penmethock Assizes had begun.

The shrieking mob fleeing the packed public gallery had at first stampeded towards the main vestibule. Turned back by the shouting musketeers and the horrible screams of their fellows from the other side of the formidable barricade, they had fled back down the hall towards the cold heart of the building, spreading panic and confusion and preventing the few officers who had kept their heads from directing their men to the thinly held frontage. Young Lord Clavincale, bewildered by the sudden squalls of musketry, was knocked aside by the thrusting, cursing villagers. He cracked his head on a bench, reached behind his ear to find his scalp bleeding profusely. He scrambled to his feet and drew his sword as the clerks and lawyers fled for their lives, forgotten in the absolute, stomach-cramping panic which seemed to have stolen all their wits at once. He pushed his way through the terrified fugitives and grabbed a couple of the equally terrified guards by their coats.

'Back to the door, you dogs! Pick up your weapons!'

The trembling soldiers pushed and shoved at the irate youngster, but Clavincale held on like a limpet, turning them back the way they had come.

'Who is it? Who's firing?' he bawled in their bewildered faces.

'Roundheads!'

Roundheads? Here? The red-faced boy shoved and prodded the reluctant musketeers back out of the court and into the hall, where their more courageous colleagues were busy reloading and firing wildly out of the smashed window. Every ill-aimed shot seemed to attract a fusillade of well-aimed fire in return. Another blue-coat had already been hit in the shoulder, and was squatting against the steps, his breath coming in deadly rasps.

'Who's firing there? How many of them?'

'Hundreds.'

'Hundreds? You damned fools! There can't be that many of them, not here!' Clavincale insisted, ducking down as another shot screamed into the crumbling plasterwork behind his head.

'Best keep down, m' lor'. There's a poacher man with

'em!' And no poacher worth his salt would miss a chance to drop a justice of the peace.

The well of the court had emptied as quickly as if a sack of grenades had been lobbed in through the grim windows. The screaming survivors had kicked, scratched, and bitten their way through the logjam of humanity at the rear door of the court and poured down the staircase, fleeing the gloomy mausoleum by the unwatched back door.

The dumbstruck tribunal had been hurried into the Earl of Dartland's ante-room, where Major Brinks and a brace of wide-eyed musketeers were acting as bewildered bodyguards. Cruickshank had drawn and checked his pistols and was standing beside the narrow window, squinting into the rear courtyard as the mindless mob steeplechased down the bare slopes. Keeler – minus his tawny wig – and Abraham Bacon – his thick brows creased in scowling concentration – hurried in after them, directing the few fools who had followed them to hold the hall against all comers. Bacon flattened himself against the door, catching his breath as Black Bob fumed with rage at the inexcusable interruption.

'They must have slipped out of Plymouth, or Lyme,' Major Brinks thought aloud, wiping his forehead on his trembling forearm. 'Whoever would have guessed they'd strike here?' he asked, pole-axed by the shocking onslaught.

'They're letting the common folk run back home,' Cruickshank called from the window. 'The back gate seems open.'

The maniacal earl didn't care who they were, where

they had come from, or where they intended going. His only thought was for the merchant, hesitating in the dock as he described his son's squalid death outside Gloucester. What had he been about to say? The fat oaf had been glancing about the courthouse as if a flock of birds of paradise had been released for his amusement, clearly about to divulge some hitherto overlooked detail. He had grasped at the merchant's tumbling straws, only to see them blown away by the invading tempest. 'And who,' he asked waspishly, 'is watching the prisoners?'

Brinks looked up at Bacon, at bay with his back to the door, and Keeler, clutching the table and breathing heavily as if he had run a mile.

'Well?'

'My lord, I left the prisoners in question in the custody of the officers of the court,' Bacon said uneasily. Black Bob bristled up all over again, his hatefully shrivelled features curling and flushing with outraged spite.

'It would appear,' he growled, 'that the principal officers of the court are here with me.' Bacon swallowed, running his pale hand through his dark snakes of hair.

Major Brinks nodded soberly, waved the clerk away from the door. 'Now your honour is safe and secured here, I will return to my men,' he said crisply.

Black Bob waved his claw distractedly, and watched impatiently as the soldier sallied out into the tumultuous courtroom.

The first thing Brinks saw was Telling and Speedwell, locked together beneath the oaken dock in a murderous embrace. Bella Morrison was clinging to the rail, throwing her head back, shrieking and kicking, as her anxious parent and howling servants attempted to pull her away.

'Come away, girl! Whatever's the matter with you?'

The red-eyed wretches were crying and cooing to one another like a flock of chickens taking shelter from a prowling fox. The ghoulish villagers who had turned out to see the proud beauty hanged had fled for their lives, leaving the token force of soldiers and militiamen to hold the front of the court against the unexpected assault. Brinks strode across the well of the court towards the cursing rivals, tearing at one another as if they were fighting for the girl's fickle favours. Papers and petitions had been scattered all about, wigs and gowns flung over the overturned seats. He picked his way through the chaos and grabbed the cursing dragoon by the shoulder, just as the bloody-nosed Cavalier freed his left fist and struck his attacker on the side of his scarred head.

'Leave that prisoner be, Telling,' Speedwell fumed, redoubling his attempts to smother the younger man's attacks by pinning him in a bear-hug.

'Stand off! Let him be, Telling, or I'll run you through, you may have my word on that!' Brinks cried.

'That's his friends out there, I'll wager!' Speedwell bawled, kneeing the struggling youth between the legs. Telling, winded and with tears springing into his eyes, folded up, whistling in agony. Brinks pushed the dragoon away from his victim, sending him crashing over one of the upturned chairs. Speedwell, floundering among the discarded papers and warrants, seemed to explode with rage at this new setback. Cheated of his prize, he kicked out with all his might, sending a chair crashing into the angry major, who was hurled back over the bench. Speedwell scrambled away on his bruised backside, tugging his sword from its bent scabbard. Telling, who had not been allowed to retain his weapon during the trial, lifted the wooden stand from the bench and hurled it at his enemy, cross-eyed with rage. Speedwell lifted his arm, deflecting the missile into the dock with a screech of pain. Brinks menaced the fighting cocks with his own sword, gesturing Telling away from the downed dragoon.

'Get back with the rest of them, Telling, or I'll run you through,' he vowed. The prisoners crowding into the dock held on to the rail as if they were all at sea, watching the drama unfold under their feet like Roman nobility at a gladiatorial arena. Sir Gilbert had no thought but to flee. He was tugging at his daughter's arm, trying to drag her away from the fight. God only knew who it was at the door, but as the merchant had no friends left in this damned world, they could only mean trouble. 'Come away, Bella. For the sake of your poor mother's memory!'

'Hugo!' Bella cried, her bewildered brain reeling from one appalling shock to another.

Speedwell hauled himself to his feet and advanced to the attack, one bleary eye on the major and the other focused on the retreating Cavalier.

'He was trying to run off with her, in all the confusion,' Speedwell accused out of the side of his raw mouth.

'I was protecting her from these brigands,' Telling snarled back.

Brinks took another step between the furious combatants, tickling Speedwell's blade away with his own.

'Stand aside, Major, this isn't your concern!'

'Major Brinks, arrest that man! He is a murderer and a liar!' Sir Gilbert advised from the dock.

Speedwell glowered up at the red-faced merchant,

slashed at the rails with his sword. 'Shut your trap, you scheming shitbag! I'll deal with you later!'

Bella, alarmed by the ringing blow on the worn oak, screamed with fear and slumped back against Anneliese. Telling, horrified the dragoon might have struck his sweetheart, launched himself into the attack once more, propelling the blinking major against the dragoon. Speedwell parried the surprise blow, thrusting his sword at his despised rival. The blade flicked beneath Brinks' dithering steel, embedded itself under the astonished officer's armpit.

'Gah!' Brinks staggered back, his sword clattering to the courthouse floor. Telling picked it up in an instant and stepped around the groaning major. Speedwell glanced from his blood-smeared sword to his enemy, grinned with furious delight despite the major's sudden collapse.

'There now!' Speedwell cackled. 'You've skewered the major here trying to get away! You'll hang for that, if nothing else!' He paused, sucking in his breath. 'You'll not fox me a second time, Telling, I promise you that!'

The young Cavalier lunged forward, jabbing the borrowed blade at the scar-faced cut-throat. 'You stabbed him, damn you! They all saw it!'

Speedwell ignored the rabble pressed up against the rail above, tapped Telling's furious thrust aside, and lunged for his face. The youngster jumped back, his feet constricted by the tightly packed courthouse furniture. He backed into the witness box as the mad dragoon slashed and parried, his black eyes sparkling with fierce determination.

'This is it, Telling, me and you! There's no judge nor jury to interfere for you now!' he cried. Speedwell ducked down, swerved onto his right foot and then back to the left in the blink of an eye. Telling lashed back in desperation, horrified by his rival's snake-eyed skills. He parried a series of ever swifter blows, feinted to his right leaving his left side unprotected again. Speedwell stepped under his sword and thrust, skewering the back-pedalling captain through the shoulder. Telling screamed, collapsed against the witness box as the dragoon moved in for the kill. Speedwell kicked the Cavalier's borrowed sword aside, raised his own for the killing blow.

The pistol shot rang around the court, deafening the horrified spectators in the dock. Speedwell staggered around, glared balefully at Brinks – propped up in the debris behind him, his smoking pistol clutched in his bloody fist. The dragoon cracked a demonic smile, turned to face his attacker.

'Damn you to hell, sir, I knew you for a rogue from the first!' Brinks whispered. Speedwell stumbled back along the compacted benches, picking his way with difficulty through the clutter. Brinks eyed him with bloody minded contempt.

Telling had scrambled away between the benches, lost to sight for a moment.

'I'll be back for you, Telling, when I've done with this prick!' Speedwell called, winking at the swooning women in the dock, the miller, and the merchant. They wouldn't dare come down and fight him. By Christ, he'd finish with these poltroons and take the girl for himself! Ride hard for the north and bugger the lot of them! The pistol ball had struck his bottom rib, the blow absorbed and deflected by his thick coat, heavy leather belt, and his grubby bandages. A dry wound, but a hard enough jolt to kill a lesser man. Like that dog Telling. Where had he got to? He peered over the benches, saw the youth scuttle up the steps toward the judge's raised dais.

'Running for justice, eh, Telling? I'm here to tell you there's none, beyond the justice this allows you.' He held the bloody sword up in ironic salute, glared down at the wounded major. 'And as for you,' Speedwell snarled, resting the bloody point against the major's pale neck, 'the next time you shoot a man, make sure you finish him off, or by Christ I'll—'

Telling had ducked behind Black Bob's moth-eaten throne and torn the ceremonial halberd from the colours standing against the wall. He turned, sucked in a giant breath, and hurled the heavy spear at the chuckling Caliban. The heavy steel blade was not absorbed or deflected by the dragoon's bloody coat or filthy bandages. It bit ruthlessly, deep between his ribs, lacerating his lungs and puncturing his foul heart. Speedwell took one tottering step forward, raised his sword a notch, and collapsed into the dock without a sound.

Brinks closed his eyes, his breath coming in short, ragged gasps. Sir Gilbert was first to recover his wits. Scared stiff by the hideous trap in which he found himself, he knew they must get out, out of this damned place, damned quick.

'Don't stand there gawping, girl, get out of the way!' He elbowed Anneliese aside and lifted his vaporous daughter by her loose arms, propelled the dizzy girl down the steps. Maynard and Thackray, peering over their shoulders at a fresh clatter of musketry, lent a hand, helping the distraught girl to stand as Sir Gilbert climbed down and lifted Speedwell's sword from the clutter. He had anticipated Telling's frenzied stare, and clearly felt it prudent to arm himself in case his would-be son-in-law felt inclined to settle matters there and then.

'Now then, Telling,' he said warningly, twitching the blade this way and that as the panting captain turned his baleful stare on the merchant. 'You know I was bluffing. I had to say something, Hugo,' he said encouragingly, using Telling's first name for the first time in his life. 'God's bowels, you saw the way the wind was blowing.'

'I saw which way you were blowing, all right,' the captain growled.

Sir Gilbert took cover behind his distraught daughter, holding on to her shoulders to manoeuvre the blinking girl before him like some slender human shield. 'You could have had us all strung up, the way you were going on! Training for the Bar? No wonder you joined the cavalry!' he told Telling, following some cock-eyed notion that attack would be preferable to defence.

The chalk-faced Cavalier stumbled across the court towards his bewildered lover and her anxiously staring sire. Bella seemed to recover from the punishing shocks long enough to free herself from her father's fearful grip and throw herself at her bloody champion, clinging to his neck like a mermaid dragging her sailor victim under the waves. Sir Gilbert struck while the iron was hot, pushing and prodding the distracted pair toward the rear door, the deserted staircase.

'There's no time for that foolishness now! Get a shift on or they'll be back and catch us!' he snapped, pointing the bloody sword toward the door. 'Down the steps, everybody!'

Telling hung back, holding his limp sweetheart under the armpits and refusing to budge.

'You would have sold me down the river to that damned tyrant!' he accused, looking up from Bella's rapt features for a moment.

'I did what I had to do. You would have done the same if you'd been wearing my shoes, young man!'

Telling thrust out his chin in defiance. 'By Christ, you'd best mark that well, old man, the next time we come to such a pass,' he vowed.

'For God's sake, come along, all of you!' Anneliese shrieked, snapping them out of their ferocious contest of wills. The blinking Cavalier shook his head as if rousing himself from a nightmare.

'You go on, I'll catch you up,' he said thickly, disentangling his limbs from Bella's cloying embrace. Anneliese helped the shaken girl away. Sir Gilbert glared at Telling.

'More damned heroics? Haven't you seen enough?' he bawled.

Telling recovered his scattered nerves, ignored the blustering merchant's fevered shouts, and picked the major's sword from the floor. He strode back through the lopsided benches and bent down to help the wounded officer. Brinks opened his agonized eye for a moment, smiled grimly at him, his teeth clenched.

'I thought you'd legged it,' he winced, thin streams of blood running through his clawed fingers. Telling grimaced.

'That murdering swine brought this down on us,' he said, nodding his head at Speedwell's hideously battered corpse, face down in the aisle beneath the deserted dock.

'They've caught us napping, Telling. Won't look good when Prince Maurice reads the report.' He tried to laugh, but only managed to retch a little blood over his white wrist. Telling nodded distractedly. He had already come off the worst in one brush with the dour Prince. He'd get no sympathy from Maurice, whatever happened now.

The appalling clatter and patter of musketry seemed to intensify over the shouts and screams of the soldiers in the hall. Brinks' dimming eyes roved over the plainly plastered ceiling as if he could make out his men, feverishly reloading their muskets as they defied the presumptuous invaders. He lifted his right hand weakly, clutched at Telling's arm in desperation.

'They're standing their ground, Telling, the boy's with them but they'll not hold out for ever. You must take command for me,' he implored, squeezing Telling's sore arm.

'Are you coming, boy?' Sir Gilbert boomed from the staircase. Telling looked up, his thin lips set in a stern blue line.

'You go on, I'll catch you up,' he called.

CROSSBONE QUAY,

PENMETHOCK

Gallen Fey felt the *Blue Doubloon* slide and settle against the soft pillows of sand and mud beneath her battered keel. The tide which had carried the longship into the quiet harbour had ebbed, exposing racks of sand and slimy mudflats. The privateer had been deposited against the quay, her sleek, V-shaped hull held more or less upright by compacted beds of shingle and sand. Without the slimy sandbank, the battered ship would have toppled over completely – Dunkirk privateers weren't built to take the ground on an ebb. Fey had sent the few trusted men he had left to inspect the damage below decks while he and a brace of wounded laboriously laid their remaining gun. The unexpectedly severe exchange of shot with the slowly sinking *Messalina's Purse* had crippled him, he knew it in his bones. The ship sagged as if its back had been broken; he had sensed the water running over its trembling sinews, the thrum of the tide as the water boiled back and forth beneath its shattered bulkheads. But now the *Doubloon* stood high and dry, teetering on a slimy sandbank, besieged by armies of red-backed crabs. Fey lifted his hat and wiped his sticky scalp, peered through the smoke at his enemy.

The *Messalina's Purse* had gotten the worst of the exchange. She lay in a deeper channel half a cable off, her bows submerged in the slack, scummy water the ebbing tide had not managed to carry off. She shared the *Doubloon*'s fast hull – but lacked her supportive sandbanks. Without the slimy cushion to hold her the *Purse* had simply keeled over, her yawning hull washed by the sullen waters. Fey took little comfort from her bloody demise. His own ship had been fatally punctured in the deadly exchange, and without the *Doubloon* he could see no way out of the hellish trap. He eyed the wrecked privateer across the harbour. The guns which had broken the *Doubloon* had snapped loose and slipped over the splintered deck: some had become entangled in their cat's cradles of rigging, adding to the clutter on the splintered deck. Some of its corsair crew were still hauling themselves about the stricken monster, clinging to her splintered teats as she buried herself in the harbour silt, her smashed stern standing proud of the flotsam-splattered water. The survivors had hauled themselves ashore and fled to the cover of the tavern which dominated the approaches to the quay, where they were no doubt reorganizing themselves for the inevitable counter-attack. Half a dozen of his own men – blown into the water by the mutually destructive broadsides – had swum back to the ship or limped along the quay, dodging the ill-aimed bullets being fired from the hovel beside the packed warehouse. One of Sparrow's raiders, crawling back on bloody feet, had already been hit in the thigh and hand by the hidden sharpshooters, and was lying amongst the scattered crab pots, pleading for help over the spiteful fusillades. As he watched, a platoon of wary villagers doubled out of the alley alongside the hovel, kicking the nets and pots aside as they searched for their pitiful victim.

God's nails, these people were no better than demons in human form!

'Covering fire!' Fey bawled to the few bewildered musketeers he had left, crouching lame and lifeless behind the damaged gunwale. The shell-shocked raiders peered over the rail, fired a volley at the cackling wolves picking their way through the harbour clutter. The villagers ducked down as the stray shots scoured the stones, then howled with delight as they located the unfortunate seaman, frantically hiding himself under a heap of lousy netting. Fey limped to the gunwale, lifted his pistol, and fired at the screaming banshees. A woman with a mad mane of grey hair shrieked in pain and hopped off, clawed hands clutching her holed thigh. Her colleagues, ignoring the desultory fusillade, threw the crab pots aside, grabbed their victim by his bloody feet, and hauled him across the cobbles, banging his shaven head on the glistening rocks. Fey watched, twitching with helpless rage as the witch-whelped swine dragged their prize off to the leaning hovel. He squinted, made out other shadowy figures gesticulating behind the smashed windows.

'Haul the gun about! We'll put a shot through that God-damned sty!' Fey croaked, tossing the pistol aside and lending a hand with the gun's greasy harness. The powder-caked, bloody boned gunners heaved and strained at the brooding iron monster, hauling the smoky barrel around inch by bloody inch.

Away over the quay, they could hear the wounded man screaming with terror – soul-shattering cries like a hog being singed and bled for slaughter. One of the deckhands, his loose limbs trembling with outraged sympathy, couldn't stand the shrieks of torment. He stood up and shouted, shaking his fist over the gunwale. He coughed and then fell back with a grunt, caught by a spent ball. The iron slug rolled over the cluttered deck as the dazed seaman sank to his knees, holding his bleeding head in his hands, cursing and spitting over the waxy planking. Fey peered around the abandoned ship in desperation and noticed a gang of wounded volunteers sitting with their backs to the rail, bloody limbs splayed out over the decking. Caught in the furious exchange of fire, they had been splashed and gouged by flying iron, and wanted no further part in the hare-brained invasion.

'Those that can move, help with the gun,' Fey ordered. The bloody survivors eyed the fanatical captain, crouching in the flimsy cover provided by the shot-blasted forecastle. 'Get over here or I'll have you all flung to the sharks!' the capering captain ordered, lifting his pistol from the deck and menacing the reluctant volunteers with its grimy eye. It wasn't loaded, but the wounded weren't to know that.

One by one, the half-drowned, savagely mauled seamen crawled over the leaning deck, leaving trails of gore and bloody handprints behind them. The battered crew reloaded, coughing on the smoke, rubbing their red eyes on their bloody sleeves, wincing and sighing at the agonizing effort. Fey darted to the gunport, picked up the discarded sponge, and reamed out the barrel ready for the charge while one of the cursing wounded tore the leather seal from the powder barrel. He held his cupped palm against the blowing sparks, poured a measure onto the ladle, and resealed the barrel while the second gunner, his hand already shattered by a wicked splinter from the hounds of the mainmast, laboriously fed the powder down the hungry barrel. Fey rammed the charge home and held his thumb over the vent while a third gunner added the wadding. Three of the cursing scarecrows lifted the iron ball between them, rolling it down the barrel and standing back as a burly deckhand in a filthy shirt rammed the round home, added another handful of wadding and nodded to the mad-eyed captain. At Fey's signal they took a frail hold on the gun harness, bent their backs once more, closed their eyes, and heaved with all their might. At last the heavy gun carriage creaked and shrieked over the worn planking, the solid wheels squealing as the gun began to move up the cruel camber of the deck to the gunport. Fey leaned down over the piece, squinted up the barrel towards the compact hovels. The upper storeys seemed to be bulging out over the top of the lower, bellies inflated like overbaked cakes. He closed his mind to the gut-wrenching cries which rattled the tiles on the monstrous pit, climbed down, hauled the carriage a fraction to the left, and bent to pour some finely milled powder into the touch-hole.

He snatched the fuming linstock from the floor, waved the crew back, and fired. The heavy cannon crashed back, bouncing over the creaking deck as the heavy round ploughed through the smoke and sailed through the smashed window of the enemy strongpoint. There was a shattering crash and a geyser of dark grey smoke. Tottering figures emerged from the doorway and fled as best they could. Deafened by the enormous recoil, Fey's battered gunners could still hear the enemy villagers, screaming in frenzy as they were buried in the rapidly collapsing house.

Drained and exhausted, it was all the pitiful survivors could do to stand watch, peering toward the eerily deserted main street. Up on the hill, somewhere beneath that climbing column of shot-blasted smoke, was Fey's captive crew. Chained like slaves in some Caribbean swamp, they toiled night and day in Penmethock quarry. The thought of his own men being put to work like beasts gnawed his soul, tempered his determination. Their sacrifice would be worth it, if he could release his stricken men.

Fey swallowed with difficulty, wiped his trembling hand across his mouth. And what then? What if Sparrow's shore party succeeded in securing the village? The *Blue Doubloon* was done for, just as that accursed privateer settling across the harbour. Fey peered at the tiny flotilla of garishly painted fishing boats, becalmed now under the bullet-scarred quay. They would have to secure those boats, or the whole expedition would be stranded thirty miles and more from the nearest friendly garrison. He looked around at the red-eyed shadows who had flung themselves down about the smoking gun, more dead than alive. They couldn't hope to hold the quay any more than they could conquer the moon, Fey thought bitterly.

It was all down to Sparrow now. If he didn't return soon, the whole expedition would have been in vain, and the bloody survivors would have to face the all too predictable consequences of their impudent invasion.

William Sparrow, streaming with cold sweat and half blinded by the smoke pouring from some flaming hellhole behind them, was crouching down behind an overturned wagon, the bulk of his raiders coughing and spluttering around him. Nicodemus, his bright red hair standing on end, looked as if he was wearing some fanciful Grecian helmet. His ragged colour was draped over his lap, Fulke's personal banner holed and singed by shot and flame. Caleb Cruickshank was squatting beside him, his great clumsy bulk balanced on his stubby fingertips. He was panting heavily, but seemed unconcerned at their desperate plight. William grunted, turned his head to peer through the wheel spokes toward the top of the bitterly contested road.

The fanatical inhabitants had turned the quiet High Street into an Alpine pass, a mountain redoubt which would have turned Hannibal himself aside. Emerging from their sparse hovels with whatever implement came to hand, they had sallied out in mobs of seven or eight people, fallen on his party like drunken banshees until beaten back by clubs and swords. Women as well as men, clawing and kicking and screeching they were rebel bastards and Londoner scum, glassy eyed like the fiends chained up within Bedlam's bruised walls. William had waved his men on, urging the raiders up the hill to the squat assizes beside the crossroads, but they had been held up at every alley, attacked on every doorstep by more of the wild-eyed Scythians. The furious villagers had rushed out to meet them with hoes and pitchforks, curved filleting knives and crude clubs. A gang of netsmen had hauled a large cart into the road and turned it over in front of them. William and his panting sergeants had slashed and hacked their way across the barricade, but the raiders had been bombarded from the surrounding windows with chamber pots, bottles, loose tiles, and various items of furniture.

William, who had fought to hold the crucial Christmas Steps in the ferocious battle for Bristol, had never seen anything like it. Lacking any effective musketeers, the raiding party had been obliged to ward off the vicious counter-attacks with swords and belaying-pins, enmeshing themselves in bloody hand-to-hand combat which slowed their progress as if they were dragging anchors behind them. Half a dozen of the hard-fighting shore party had already been brained, the poor fools who had been left behind surrounded and dragged into the nearest alley by the screeching fishwives. Goodrich and Jameson, appalled by the desperate resistance, had redoubled their efforts to break through, chopping and hacking at the ill-armed netsmen until they were forced back from the wagon. William had leapt over the splintered poles and jabbed the cursing fishermen back with his sword, but he could already see more villagers throwing up a fresh barricade further up the hill.

Cudgelled, kicked, and cornered, Sparrow's sinking heart pumped fitful bursts of lukewarm blood around his exhausted body, his straining muscles going limp with despair. His belly squirted with bitter biles and his dust-dry throat ached, sucking and blowing the spark-tumbling smoke. He leaned against the heavy wain, panting hoarsely as the villagers dithered before him.

'A pox on you cut-throats! You've made sport with me once before!' he bawled at the bronze-faced fishermen hanging back uncertainly beside a narrow alley.

The roaring brute in the buff coat was armed to the teeth with two swords and a pistol, clearly determined none of them would survive the vicious street fight.

'Throw us overboard like scrap fish, you beef-witted bastards?' He thrust his blade at a frightened boy brandishing a grappling hook, forcing the youngster to take a fearful step out of the invader's way.

'We'll throw you overboard, you dirty whoreson!' A grey-haired grandfather loped up with a rake held over his sun-bleached head, brought the steel spikes down in a whistling arc. Sparrow levered himself away from the wagon and hacked at the wooden pole with his heavy cutlass, fracturing the frail shaft and biting into the old man's arm. Goodrich seconded him, striding forward with his sword and beating the shouting youngster back. The old man fell to the cobbles, clutching his slashed arm. His bony, blue-veined claw was hanging by slender tendons from the bloody stump of his wrist. Sparrow kicked the cursing elder aside, chased the rest of them down the alley. It reeked of stale fish and cat piss, boiled cabbage and rotting vegetables. The sooty walls towered over him like a hellish canyon, broken shutters gaping like a conger's mouth over gloomy windows. He looked up just in time to see a brimming chamber pot sailing through the smoke, covered his face as it landed with a stinking splash in front of him. Splattered with dung and urine, the furious officer retreated, ducked back behind the wagon as the battered raiders exchanged hair-raising insults with the fearful faces at the windows. The few musketeers he had left kept up a desultory fire, forcing the villagers to take cover and reloading furiously as the hidden defenders threw down anything which came to hand. Goodrich crouched down beside him, wiping his creased forehead on his threadbare coat sleeve. The bearded veteran was puce with anger and effort, his lips pulled back in a rictus of agony from his teeth.

'We'll get no further, Captain. Not against a dozen muskets,' he gasped at last. Sparrow nodded, fighting to catch his own breath. He could hear the distinctive cough and spit of small-arms fire further up the hill. That must be Muffet's party, attacking the assizes and wondering where the main party had got to.

The trouble was, the main party was stuck like a mouse in a greased bottle.

John Grey's platoon had already loped off down a likely looking alley, hoping to work their way through the tangled vegetable gardens and rickety sheds at the back of the houses and find their way to the quarry. Sparrow's rapidly diminishing command would have to fight their way on or sit there and be surrounded. So far they had been fighting surprised villagers and screaming women. Further on, they could expect more organized – and better armed – resistance.

Sparrow cursed under his breath, his mind in turmoil as he desperately attempted to think what to do. Take cover in one of the houses? They might as well surrender what little advantage they had right now. Retreat back to the ship? That would leave Grey and Muffet's sections high and dry, stranded and surrounded by these swarming demons.

What to do? Tobias Fulke would have thought of something by now, kept their momentum going. Lurking here behind a barricade, it would only be a matter of time before the enemy brought up massed muskets and pikes, a troop of horse perhaps. By Christ, a squadron of cross-eyed dragoons could have charged right through their perilously exposed position.

Jameson, his forehead split open by a carefully aimed three-legged stool, collapsed beside them, his blood-flecked sword lying in his lap. He jerked his chin back the way they had come, over the fantastic pile of debris and the huddled bodies of the fallen.

'They're back in the tavern, at least a dozen of them, and well armed too. They've been taking pot-shots at the men at the back,' he reported. William ground his grubby palms into his eyes. They had dashed straight past the busy inn, leaving a valuable strongpoint in their rear. So much for his brilliant generalship! The overweight sergeants didn't seem overly concerned at their plight, scratching their beards and wiping their swords on their coat sleeves as they waited patiently for William to come up with something.

'This cart'll save us one way, but if they sally up at us from this side . . .' Jameson shrugged significantly.

Sparrow thought for a moment, feverishly patting the heavy ribs of the overturned wagon as the flimsiest ribbon of a plan began to unfold in his head.

Bristol. William recalled their stand on the long earth wall overlooking the truncated church of St Mary Redcliff. A legion of howling Cornish had pushed an enormous wain up to the ditch, the vast hold stuffed with bundles of firewood to fill the broad trench. They had all the ingredients lying at their feet!

'I want all the powder that's left, every stick and rag lying about thrown in the back,' he ordered, licking his charred lips in excitement. 'We'll right the wagon and set fire to it, look, push the bugger up the hill at the bastards,' William informed them, his glistening green eyes scanning their broad, blank faces. 'It'll cover us on the way up, and the flames will force the swine out of our way!' The sergeants shrugged, apparently satisfied with the captain's simplistic solution. It might not be Caesar, but it might just work. 'We'll need every combustible we can get in the back, double quick! Get them working!'

'Right you are, Captain,' Goodrich said cheerfully, turning to the wide-eyed mob crouching behind them like frightened rabbits stuck in the middle of a harvest crop. 'On your feet, you fornicators! Get this wagon right-side up, and look alive!'

*

The quarry guards were fingering their weapons nervously, blowing on their match as the crescendo of battle rolled this way and that according to the fickle wind. The contrary breeze would silence the furious musketry for a moment and then carry the racket back to them, reminding the bewildered guards of rollicking waves driving pebbles up a steep shingle beach.

The guards were ranged about the steeply sloped stone bowl, keeping one eye on the dusty prisoners clumped together below them. The scrawny wretches had ignored the jumpy soldiers' bad-tempered instructions to get on with their work. Sergeant Titus Beam had doubled up the path to the collection of simple stonemason's huts at the head of the valley. He shielded his eyes and peered down the coomb, saw the smoke hanging above the village. He swallowed hard, crucified with uncertainty. Surely the last enemy forces had retired into Plymouth, abandoned their strongholds to Prince Maurice's all-conquering buccaneers? Yet here was the evidence to the contrary, right in front of his eyes. Musketry crackled angrily away to his left, centred on the ugly, smoke-wreathed bulk of the assizes. To his right, a swirling cauldron of flaming fogs coiled and pulsed above the gaping mouth of the harbour, trapped by the ridges and cliffs which encircled the anchorage. He shook his head, then spotted the sudden movement in the bushes beside the stony path. Bob Symonds, hatless and harmless, was bounding through the bracken and gorse, his long legs lifted comically from the dense vegetation. He stared dumbly as what looked like a handful of white dandelions puffed up behind him and a split second later poor Bob tripped, measuring his length in the crisp brown fronds. Beam heard the pop and crackle of their muskets, and saw the men hurry along after their escaping victim.

Titus raised his musket and blinked to clear his filmy vision. His fat finger trembled on the trigger as he swung the barrel to and fro searching for a target in the shifting Sargasso of bracken.

The enemy musketeers had ducked down into cover to reload, hidden in the undergrowth while he stood there like a statue in the middle of the path. Titus lowered the musket and took a step backwards, peering into the twitching undergrowth.

'Drop it, Father, and tell your boys to do the same,' a broad London accent invited from the silent scrub. 'I've a bead on your belly right now, it's up to you,' the sharp-shooter advised.

'I've a platoon of men down the hill there!' Titus called back, wondering if he should risk a quick look over his trembling shoulder. They might have got behind him now, cut him off from the quail-bollocked plovers in the quarry. By Christ, it could be tricky if the mysterious raiders intended to set his charges free. He'd been hard on them in the past, that was true enough. Gripped by panic, his courage drained by the hideous uncertainty of the sudden, unexplained danger, Titus turned on his heel and sprinted for the bracken over the far side of the road.

John Grey let the red-faced bandit charge straight at him, rose from the brush like an overweight imp from hell, and fired his horse-pistol into his face. The lead slug hit the fleeing fugitive in the neck, sparking a fine spray of bright blood. Beam staggered on, dropping his musket and panting like a bloody throated dog. He swerved to the left, trying to escape the avenging angel, lost his footing, and collapsed into one of the innumerable stone gullies which lined the coomb like a dogfish's gills. Grey bent down and lifted the musket from the trampled bracken and then scrambled down the gully after his choking victim, relieving the malignant viper of his keys, powder flask, and bandolier. Five minutes later the dour mate led his men around the rim of the quarry, down the slope to the clutter of huts beside the pit.

The rest of Titus Beam's men, alarmed by the sudden shots and tortured silences which followed, had taken to their heels over the steep slopes, leaving their red-eyed prisoners hammering and tearing at their bloody shackles in a fever of anticipation. They looked up to see John Grey's men hurrying down the rocky shelves, waving their arms and shouting as they hurried to embrace their long-lost comrades. Eyes streaming, voices hoarse, they praised God until they were blue in the face, like ancient woad men dancing around stony cairns. The thin grey wraiths capered with delight as the sweating newcomers hurried amongst them with hammers and chisels. John Grey, tears in his eyes at their sorry plight, went from one to the other unlocking their shackles with the keys he had lifted from Beam's gory corpse.

'Take up your picks and hammers, there's plenty of work for you all yet,' Grey called encouragingly. For once the pitiful company, tears cutting jagged trails down their dusty cheeks, would not need to be whipped back along the all too familiar path. Ragged and barefoot, red brace-lets around their wasted limbs, the freed prisoners stumbled and fell, crawled on all fours through the grit and gravel after their rescuers.

Captain Sparrow's hard-pressed battalion had just doubled its numbers.

PENMETHOCK ASSIZES,

'It's Waller's army! They've marched past Hopton and they're out after Maurice!' the nervous blue-coated guard insisted, stepping from one holed boot to the other as the prickly young nobleman interrogated him. 'We saw hundreds of 'em, coming up the main road!' Lord Clavincale shook his head in disbelief. Hugo Telling, crouching beside the smashed window across the hall, risked another peep over the shattered sill. The long gun cracked in immediate response, tipping the inquisitive captain back on his scrawny behind as the round splintered the frame. The wavering soldiers eyed the foolish intruder with disgust. They had run across his type before, chronically eager to prove themselves they would fight to the last drop of their blood. He'd be the death of them yet, carrying on like that. The gloomy recruits had thrown themselves down behind the pock-marked walls, squatting in a glittering sea of pulverized glass. Blackened with soot and grime, their eyes shone eerily from their sweat-plastered skulls as they brooded and muttered, muskets clutched between their knees. Clavincale crawled from window to window, urging the men to keep firing, but the surly soldiery hardly dared raise their heads, let alone take aim against the bullet-splattered gate. Telling peeped out of the window once more, hoping to Christ there was just the one sharpshooter. As far as he could see, the road was deserted either way. He ducked back in as a wildly aimed shot thumped into the wall several feet from his lookout post. Hugo scrambled back over the floor, shaking his long head in agitation.

'That's no army,' he accused the dithering musketeer. 'There's a dozen of them at most. We ought to make a sally and flush them out, stuck in here like constipated hens!'

The blue-coated soldier cocked his jaw indignantly. 'You weren't there, sir. You never saw 'em. Hundreds of 'em, horses and flags and drums and all!'

Telling's thin lip peeled back from his teeth. 'Hundreds of them? Take a look for yourself, there's not as much as a cat to be seen!'

'Well, then, they're hiding out, waiting for us to do something daft!'

One of the musketeers across the room muttered something to his mate, who nodded his head vindictively. Clavincale glanced at the bristling captain, wishing he shared his apparently boundless confidence. The courthouse had been riddled with bullets, four of his men had been hit and God knew how many had run off. There had to be a company of them, at least.

'They wouldn't attack a village with a garrison this size with a dozen men,' he snapped. 'They might very well be fanatics, but to assault us with anything less than a company would be suicidal.'

The thin-faced Cavalier, desperately drawn by the tortuous uncertainties of the last week, appalled to find himself at the merchant's mercurial mercy, turned his eyes on the nervous nobleman.

'That's what they're hoping we'll think,' he snorted.

'I'll wager there's not more than a dozen men in that ditch. There's more of us stuck in here,' he sneered.

'Well, why don't you piss off out of it and even things up, then?' one of the musketeers murmured behind his back.

'That's enough!' Clavincale ordered, glaring at the miserable remnants of Brinks' company. He looked up at Telling, ran his tongue over his thick lips in distraction. 'What do you suggest?' he asked in an undertone, tacitly acknowledging the captain's greater experience.

Telling studied the cowering wretches crouching below the holed windows, reckoning their worth in a moment. 'There's not that many of them. If they were stronger they would have risked a charge on the door by now.'

'Or worked their way around the back,' Clavincale added, anxious to prove his own grasp of tactics. 'Do you think they might be after my father?' he asked at last.

Telling raised his pale eyebrows. God's wounds, he couldn't blame them if they were at that. The vicious old bastard must have made whole brigades of enemies over the years, lording it over these backwater cretins like some feudal warlord. God only knew what hideous tortures the judge would have decreed if the mealy-mouthed merchant had betrayed him – described Telling's part in his son's squalid death.

Clavincale must have read his mind. He smiled awkwardly.

'My father can, on occasion, be somewhat overzealous in his punishment of rebels and wrongdoers,' he said uneasily.

'They've come back for revenge,' one of the anonymous musketeers hissed under his hand. 'It's Black Bob they wants, not us!'

'Silence!' Clavincale bawled, stung by the logic of the remark. All this pain and death, shooting and burning, compressed like a wound spring and then released in a furious tempest of revenge. In the name of his own father. The young nobleman paled, biting his lip in agitation. Somewhere, deep in his slowly maturing consciousness, he could have predicted his father's heavy-handed approach might spark a vicious cycle of punishment and revenge. That his draconian punishments would one day reap their deserved whirlwind.

'Tweren't owt to do with us, any of it,' the stubborn soldier observed for the benefit of his doubtful neighbours. Telling eyed them, ranged around the room, twitching with resentment. The treacherous curs were no better than Roundheads themselves, foully infected with the dread disease of rebellion. No bugger did what he was told these days, that was the trouble. He nodded slowly. Exercising command over scum like this was like trying to skate on a crackling winter pond – you never knew when the ice would turn back to water beneath your feet.

'We'd best get back to your father. You men can carry Major Brinks.' The blue-coats looked doubtful, wondering what the skinny stranger was up to. Telling ached with uncertainty. If he challenged the craven swine right out, they might shoot the pair of them down dead and run for it. Hugo wondered for a moment whether Bella had gotten safely away. Away where? Into the hands of the bastards lurking outside the court? He prayed to God to keep her safe, until he could catch up with her and get away from all of them. Back to the army, back to the camp where life was sweetly simple in comparison to this monstrous nightmare.

He flicked his eyes warningly at the bewildered lord-ling, stepped back to the main door. The soldiers watched him like mesmerized hens, fingers tense about their weapons. The sharp stink of fuming match filled the room, overpowering the equally strong odours of blood, sweat, and fear. Telling reached down and opened the door into the main courtroom, held it open while Clavin-cale stepped heavily across the littered floor, boots crunching the scattered glass.

A sudden shot from the wall made them all jump. Telling pulled the youngster by the slashed sleeves of his doublet, dragged him over the threshold as the surly soldiers crouched ready for action. None of them dared raise his weapon, not while the thin streak of piss had his cleaver in his paw, at any rate.

'You men hold the hall,' Telling told them curtly, closing the door on their sneering faces and leaning against the cool wood to steady his nerves.

'They won't stand a moment,' Hugo told Clavincale, who was staring about the partially demolished room in utter astonishment. His father would have thrown a fit if he could have seen the state of his domain. The court looked as if a herd of elephants had stampeded through it. Major Brinks had propped himself up beside the dock, methodically winding the pistol clamped between his knees, bloody fingers fretting over the intricate wheels and ratchets. The colour had drained out of his face, leaving his features tallow. His eyes burnt with feverish, unhealthy intensity. Clavincale spied Speedwell's corpse, thrown down like a sack of laundry beside him. It was the first body he had ever seen, and the bloodily bruised features brought him up short, knocking what little wind he had left out of him. Brinks looked up as Telling hauled the nearest bench across the door, the old oak shrieking over the tiled floor.

'Are they all dead?' Brinks asked, his pale head lolling on his shoulders.

'As good as,' Telling rasped, stacking chairs and dragging tables around to form a rough barricade, wincing at the hurt in his own shoulder.

'There's another door into Father's ante-room,' Clavincale said woodenly, nodding his head at the plastered walls which separated each compartment of Black Bob's partially demolished hive. Telling strode back over the floor, took a quick look down at the wounded major. Brinks, perhaps guessing his own men had run out on him, grinned foolishly, patted the pistol.

'Aye, well. You go on, I'll watch the damned door,' he croaked feebly.

Telling glanced at the horrified lordling, nodded him on through the clutter.

'What happened to him?' he asked at last, pointing at the dragoon's brutally battered corpse.

'He attacked Captain Telling. I saw it all. Ordered him to put down but he . . . wouldn't have it,' Brinks gasped.

Further discussion was interrupted by an acrimonious exchange of shouts from the other side of the rough barricade. Telling knew what they were doing well enough. 'We'll be back directly,' he promised the dying major. Brinks waved his pistol in bitter resignation as Telling prodded Clavincale across the room, hurrying toward the ante-room.

'What is it? What are they doing?'

'They've just surrendered to the bastards outside,' Telling hissed, rapping on the ante-room door. He listened for a reply, reluctant to walk into a room full of trigger-happy amateurs.

'Father! It's us, don't shoot,' Clavincale called.

There was no reply. Telling gingerly pushed the door open. The ante-room was deserted.

'Where have they gone?' Clavincale wailed, peering around the empty chamber. His father's desk, strewn with curling papers. Wine jugs and goblets in a glistening red lagoon. The door to the main staircase was standing ajar.

'Father! Father!' Clavincale hurried down the steps, his shrill calls rebounding around the cold stone landing. Telling doubled after the frightened fool, hauled him back by his coat-tails just as the heavy-set nobleman was about to dash out of the back door, swinging eerily on its rusted hinges. Surprised, Clavincale toppled backwards, sending his desperate saviour sprawling as a furious splatter of musketry sparked and chipped the ornate doorway. The two men scrambled back into the hall, caught their breath in the questionable cover of the alcove. Telling peered out into the enemy held yard. The shots had come from the drab outbuildings built in the lee of the sea wall. Workshops and stables, a shabby smithy under a tarpaulin lean-to. He could see a gang of musketeers clustered about the abandoned sheds, feverishly reloading their pieces as their colleagues attempted to master a pair of prancing chargers. The horses, terrified by the madhouse racket of shot and shell, were rearing and snapping, the unfamiliar soldiers grasping and tugging at their bridles.

'They're taking the horses,' Telling reported, throwing himself back down into the lee of the door.

'Where's Father? Is he away?' Clavincale enquired, his fearful features mottled with sweat and creased with anxiety. Telling was about to reply when an enormous intruder sprang up the cell-block stairs, boots clattering on the bare flags, a curved sword glimmering in the smoky light like some genie of the lamp. The panting giant spotted the officers cowering in the hall, bent down to grin broadly at them.

'It's you, my lord,' the piratical jailer observed, bowing shortly as Clavincale levered himself to his feet, back to the hall wall. 'You'd best get upstairs with the rest, they're barricading themselves in now!'

Clavincale recognized Humphrey Gale, the leering turnkey he had complained to his father about on so many occasions in the past. The man was nothing but a beast in baggy breeches, merrily content to torture and beat whoever he was bidden – and any other bugger besides. The nobleman nodded with all the dignity he could muster, glanced up the deserted staircase.

'There's nobody in the court but Major Brinks,' he snapped.

Gale wiped his nose on his sleeve, to show all he thought of the Plymouth man.

'Yer father's taken up hold on the top floor, his personal quarters, my lord,' Gale replied with an easy smile. 'He's half the muskets in the county stored up there, for one thing.'

The armoury! Of course. The second floor of the courthouse had largely been taken over by Bacon's administrative offices, with another small but sumptuously appointed set of rooms for the judge. But Black Bob had completed the building's crude design himself. The drab pile also housed the town's plentiful collection of firearms. If the damned townsfolk had needed to be armed, the judge had insisted on keeping the weapons under lock and key – where he could keep an evil eye on them.

The well-stocked armoury had been located in a specially strengthened strongroom at the back of the building. There would be musket, ball, and powder enough to withstand a siege by William Waller's entire army, if necessary.

'What about Brinks? They're in through the front door already?' Telling snarled, swinging his bloody sword in agitated circles as he peeped around the pock-marked doorframe.

'Won't do 'em any good,' Gale theorized. 'This damned pile won't burn, not in a thousand years.' He stamped his boot for emphasis. 'And they'll never get up the stairs, not past me and Captain Cruickshank! We'll come back for your fancy major!'

Clavincale nodded sourly, apparently satisfied by the jailer's crude assessment, and waved the sickeningly loyal servant on up the staircase.

How was it that his father had managed to inspire brutes like these to such devoted service while better men fumed and fretted, gnawed by their chosen allegiances? How could the King ever convince his people he meant them well when he employed such devils as his favoured persuaders? Clavincale sighed with misery, followed the turnkey's bulging backside up the broad steps. Telling hurried behind, stopping on every other step to peer back down into the stairwell.

'Don't you worry, sirs! Take a passel of the buggers to put the captain off his mark, eh, my lord?'

'What's that? Oh, yes. Of course.'

The dejected lordling traipsed up the cold stair, toward the site his father had chosen for his defiant last stand. Every step felt as if he was lifting his weight again of lead ingots. Damn Telling for holding him back! He should have ducked out of the hated building and run for it. Let them slake their thirst on one another's blood.

It would all have been so much easier, he thought, if he could only convince himself such a sacrifice might be worth something. If what they were standing for was right.

'Back? Go back? We'll go back when all this has blown over and not before,' Sir Gilbert Morrison vowed, his florid features colouring up like boiled beetroot. He clamped his paw around Bella's white arm, tugging her beside him as he huffed and puffed along the narrow stone-crowned gully. Maynard, Anneliese, and Thackray picked their way through the rubble, glancing fearfully over their shoulders for signs of the inevitable pursuit. Jamie Morrison bent to pick up stones, hurling them at the flock of choughs hopping around the jagged gap. Starling trotted ahead, a mincing imp in his threadbare black suit, his broad-rimmed hat bobbing on his over-large head. The shrivelled clerk pointed on down the canyon toward the belt of firs and pines which had been planted on the slopes opposite as a fanciful windbreak. Sir Gilbert wiped his streaming brow, squinted at the cool canopy of tall trees. They were hatefully exposed in this damned cleft. One dozy bugger on a horse could run the lot of them down, plug them like trout in a barrel.

'Go on, man, don't stand there gawping!' the distracted merchant bawled, waving the capering fool onwards.

'Don't pinch! You're hurting,' Bella protested, trying to free her arm from her father's punishing grip. The cool sea air seemed to have restored some of her usual spirit.

'Never mind pinching, young woman! They would have done a sight more than pinched your bloody arm if we'd stayed there much longer!'

The terrorized fugitives had fled the court by the back door, followed the last of the whooping villagers over the rear wall of the complex. But Sir Gilbert hadn't followed the panic-stricken herd on down the hill. He had led them off to the west, taking a narrow rabbit track across the scree-littered slope and leading them over an outflung spur of Cairns Hill. The track had risen steeply, then turned sharply to the left, entering the sudden gully via a ragged fissure in the rock. The panting renegades had squeezed their way through the narrow crevice, grateful to get off the wickedly exposed hillside for a moment.

'Get to the trees! We'll hide out there until nightfall and try to get back,' Sir Gilbert called, boosting his protesting daughter on along the pellet-strewn path.

'Back where? The mill?' Maynard enquired anxiously. Helping his brother out of his 'little fix' had caused him a deal of trouble already, he thought ruefully.

'I'm not leaving Hugo back there!' Bella shrieked, the watery sunlight bringing on a near-fatal headache and preventing her from throwing her father off. For once in his life Sir Gilbert aimed to exact some obedience from his wretched daughter. It was her damned forwardness which had got them all into the horrible mess in the first place.

'Stop your squalling and get on, there's others here to think about apart from that woolly headed candle-waster you've lavished your time on!'

Bella squinted at Anneliese, her dark features sour with fright, and the gloomy miller, whose dolefully turned-down mouth was slack with the effort. Sir Gilbert himself seemed on the verge of bursting like an overripened seed pod. Purple with rage, his bedraggled best suit scuffed and torn, stained black with his long hours of hateful imprisonment. He wasn't setting foot in that foul nest again, not for any bugger. That dolt Telling would either perish with the rest of them or find some unguessed exit – just as he usually did.

'You heard the man, he'll catch us up later!'

'How will he know where to find us?' Bella wailed.

'He'll find a way,' Sir Gilbert muttered, thinking grudgingly he might at that. God knew he hadn't managed to shake the damned burr off yet. Bella tore at her clothing, wrenched the broad green band from her tangled hair. She tossed the memento onto the path as a mark Hugo might follow, ground her teeth in resentful supplication, and allowed her father to steer her back up toward the waiting trees. She looked back once, saw the grubby twists of smoke smudging the jagged ridge, and deflated with despair.

When would it ever end? she wondered, sick to her stomach with the frights and fights and perilous adventure. Had it really been her? Those few brief months before, sitting up on Anneliese's bed at Kilmersden Hall, swooning and fretting for some excitement, a little adventure in their tediously straightforward lives? The sight of a horseman clattering over the bridge on some warlike errand, the long files of soldiers toiling up Bitterwell Hill, had left them breathless with anticipation. They had willed the war closer, prayed the bloody armies would come their way. The armies had come their way all right, swallowed them up and spat them out. Torn their families in shreds, ransacked their homes, and carted off the precious possessions they had moped and sighed over bare weeks before.

Bella realized with a start she had been rendered as rootless as the rogues fighting on the ridge. Torn from her village and set adrift on a swirling, spume-racked sea which set them down and picked them up on some lunar whim. She had always been headstrong and decisive, making plans for her future as if she was the prodigal son. War had stolen whatever scrap of independence she might have achieved for herself at home, and set her adrift on these hateful adventures. She had been beaten and chased and shot and accused, rebounding from one damned man to another from one end of the country to the other.

As dependent as a child on the foolhardy fighter, the hopelessly devoted hero they had left behind.

The Trained Bandsmen had unearthed a couple of drums and were banging them for all they were worth, raising the village and the hills round about. The snarling, saturated survivors of the *Messalina's Purse* had rescued what was left of their flag from the splintered mast and fled the partially submerged ship. The waterlogged corsairs had nailed a quarter of the torn colour to a pikeshaft and were frenziedly waving it back and forth in the broad square outside the Mermaid, bringing bewildered survivors out of the holes into which they had scuttled. Benjamin Callard, the lanky, raw-boned village drummer, had rolled up his sleeves to beat out violent tattoos, a primeval throb which seemed to shake the shocked town to its foundations with its elemental, warlike racket. The urgent drumming had brought men running from hovel and inn, quayside and boat. The foul-tempered menfolk had worked their way back through alleys and across tangled vegetable gardens to answer the call, ordering their equally deranged women to stay indoors and restrain the shouting, bawling children. Thirty, forty, fifty of them had gathered beneath the dripping black banner, clutching whatever weapon came to hand. A dozen blue-coated soldiers crowded together, anxiously wondering what had become of their officers and friends. They jumped in fright at the sudden clatter of hoofs on the cobbles as Speedwell's brave dragoons sallied out of the stable yard on their fiery nags, muskets and carbines clenched in their fists.

Henry Graves – mightily relieved the villagers hadn't been planning a lynching party for his shag-daft riders – had led his men out to join them, peering over the sea of anxious faces for an officer. The villagers and superannuated sailors stared back, imagining that as he sat on a horse the giant in the pea-green coat must be in charge. Graves, whose muscled bulk had long since outstripped his cranial capacities, walked his pony in circles, realizing with a start he outranked the desperate gang. The enemy raiders had charged on up the High Street, he knew that well enough, but what was he expected to do about it? Benjamin Callard stopped drumming, tilting his head for further instructions. The sailors peered through the crowd of strangers for their officers, Mr Callow or Mad Val himself.

'Nah, I saw Callow go down with the *Purse*!'

'Captain Cruickshank was away to the town, I tell 'ee!'

'They were all up at the courthouse to try that flirt-gill!'

'Ah, that's where the buggers were off to, mark my words!'

'They knew where they were off and all, some bugger's blabbed!'

The furious drumming had knitted the diverse crowd together. Without its constant, mesmerizing pulse, the band fell apart once again, a gang of belligerent, bewildered strangers, as suspicious of the man standing next to them as the rampaging raiders who had scoured the quay.

The sudden cannon shot might have blown the entire clan away like chaff in a tempest. They peered back over their shoulders to see a ball of white smoke rise from the broken-backed deck of the *Doubloon*, the treacherous impostor which had landed the invaders on their shore. The few fanatical fools who had remained on board were firing a swivel gun at the small skiff being energetically rowed across the harbour, apparently intent on blasting the little craft to matchwood. The first round had sent up a column of sea water and drifting debris, drenching the unfortunates who crouched fearfully over their feverishly dipping oars.

'It's Captain Took! From over the water, look!'

'That's him all right, nicked the pin as usual, I'd wager!'

'He must have been pissed as a crock-dick dog to miss that bloody ship sailin' in as fine as you loike!' The mob surged over the quay toward the steaming wreck of the *Blue Doubloon*, but the angry fighters were stopped in their tracks by a feeble volley of musketry. Captain Took, the drunken devil with the flowing black locks, stood up in the soaked skiff, waving his arms as if he feared the villagers might not recognize him. They rowed towards the outer mole, perilously exposed to the enemy ship bottled up inside. Took's grim-faced galley-slaves were

361

tugging and pulling at the oars, propelling the boat through the slack water and sullen beds of drifting wreckage. Their broad-bladed paddles set the scorched bodies of drowned sailors bobbing once more.

'It's me, you damned carrion! Give me covering fire!' Took roared, cupping his hands to his wide red mouth. His baggy white shirt was streaked and spotted with blood. Startled musketeers hurried to the side of the quay, took what cover they could amongst the pots and crates, and fired an equally ragged volley at the treacherous *Doubloon*. Their bullets scoured the deck, clanged off the haphazardly hauled cannon, and whined through the hanging rigging. Shrill screams told them their shots had also found softer targets. By Christ, there couldn't be too many of the rebel tricksters left alive now. The moment's respite gave the toiling oarsmen the vital seconds they needed to steer the skiff across the mouth of the harbour and under cover of the quay. Took leapt out and doubled up the steps in his shirtsleeves, waving his men after him.

The miserable crew who had lost their gun emplacement earlier that vile afternoon had stood in the cramped hut for thirty hateful minutes, imagining every moment the mysterious raiders meant to break back in and shoot them all down like dogs. They had strained their ears listening for any movement before they had risked calling out to their cruel captors. Eventually they had convinced themselves the cunning raiders had moved on. They had knocked the barricade aside and searched the looted emplacement for their weapons. Finding none, they had set off down the strand, hurrying to return to the embattled town.

On the way they had found their errand boy Thomas Callard, brained by a musket butt and half hidden under a bush. His bare feet kicked and twitched on the pebbles, his clenched fists leaking frail runnels of sand. A little while later, they had come across John Neeson's skiff, drawn up under the cliff. Took had ordered them aboard, and pointed the way across the bay to the smoking harbour.

'Well? What are you standing here for?' the suddenly sobered captain bawled, relieving one of the blue-coat musketeers of his crude, mass-produced sword. 'Where have the bastards got to?'

'Up the town, sir! Hundreds of 'em!'

'And more further up, I heard.'

'Waller's dragoons,' one of the blue-coats added helpfully.

'Waller's dragoons?' Captain Took snorted.

The village drummer pushed his way through the gang and peered at the newcomers, recognizing his neighbours despite saturated clothing and matted hair.

'Where's Tom? You've left him back over there, have you?' he enquired. Took, Major Brinks' second in command, had no idea of the identity of the dead boy.

'The bastards brained him and locked us up,' he said simply, pushing past the pale villager to make a preliminary reconnaissance of the stricken village. Callard searched the faces of his friends, who turned away wiping their noses or twitching in shame.

'Your boy couldn't have felt much, I reckon,' one of the erstwhile gunners said out of the side of his mouth. The drummer peered over the emerald water in mortification, as if he could see his son lying on the strand opposite, beneath the brooding grey cliff.

'There they are, cowering by a wagon halfway up the street!' Took yelled from beside the hovel on the corner. 'There's not more than fifty of them all told!'

CAIRNS HILL,

PENMETHOCK

The exhausted fugitives had thrown themselves beneath the cool skirts of the fir trees, leaning against their rutted trunks as if they were reclining on feather pillows. Bella had drawn up her knees and folded her arms beneath her head as a makeshift cushion, and was dumbly wondering what might have become of Hugo. Her skin crawled as she imagined the fate which might have awaited him – if her father had carried out his intention and betrayed the boy to Black Bob. Hung, drawn, and quartered, his steaming entrails set alight before his slowly closing eyes. She shuddered with revulsion. Anneliese crouched beside her, murmuring encouragement to the sobbing girl. Miller Morrison and his brother were standing a little way off, peering under the eaves at the deserted gully. Starling was sitting cross-legged on his own, face furrowed with concentration as he offered up a short prayer of thanks for their unlikely escape. Anneliese realized Bella wasn't paying any attention to her quiet encouragement. She looked up slowly, watching the merchant and miller debate their next move.

'He owes me, Maynard. Fifty pound for Bella's passage, plus all this aggravation. A fine house and a steady business, I shouldn't need to tell you it didn't grow from seed, brother!'

'Neither did the mill. And I'm not risking my neck trying to get you your money back!'

Sir Gilbert seethed with frustration at his brother's typical lack of initiative. 'Well, he's a sight more than my fifty locked up on board that wallowing crab pot, you said so yourself,' he called accusingly.

The miller shook his head, hammered hollow by the heart-stopping turmoil of the past few days. He hadn't seen Gilbert for twenty years, and by God he wouldn't care if another score went by before he saw him again.

'Aye, and there's been more than a few floaters who tried parting him from it,' the miller scolded. 'Cruickshank don't take kindly to folk trying to part him from his hoard.'

The merchant fumed and fretted, tugging at the sagging flesh beneath his chin. 'We can't just walk away and leave it,' he growled.

'We can walk away, though. Get off while the going's good. Christ Jesus, Gilbert, they were going to hang your girl back there. We've got her out and there's an end to it.'

'Got her out for what? To spend the rest of the war wandering the roads? We've no home, no money, no prospects.'

'Then you're square with the best portion of the rest of the population. You'll get by, you always did, Gilbert.'

As well as the fifty pounds for Bella's passage the miller had paid Callow Sir Gilbert had lost the last of his carefully nurtured fortune. Wrapped in a leather pouch, it was in all probability safe where he had left it – nailed beneath the wagon which was presently parked in the courthouse yard in the middle of a vicious firefight! He meant to retrieve the money, if it was at all possible – aye, and anything else he could lay hands on besides.

'I shan't leave it,' Sir Gilbert concluded.

'Well, that's all very well, Gilbert, but it won't take 'em long to figure where we've gone!'

'You don't reckon I'm going to leave my last few bob lashed under that cart, do you? For some snivelling horse boy to come across? There has to be some way, there always is, if you look long enough.'

'Pah!'

The dark-haired girl wiped her eyes on her sleeve, sickened by his relentless avarice. She looked up sharply, wondered where Jamie had got to. Anneliese leapt to her feet in panic, peered around the quiet copse.

'Jamie! Jamie?'

Sir Gilbert glanced over his shoulder, irritated by the noisy interruption. 'Where's Jamie?'

'I thought he was with you!'

Algernon Starling looked up from his prayers. 'I believe he stepped out to pluck a rose,' he said nonchalantly.

'Pluck a rose? Where did he go, Cornwall?' Sir Gilbert blustered. 'Jamie?' he hissed into the surrounding trees. 'Jamie!'

Anneliese ran around the ring of firs, peering behind the mossy trunks for her absent sweetheart.

'Don't get lost now! Maynard, for God's sake go with her!'

Anneliese dashed into the deep wood, scrambling up cool earth banks and slipping down sudden stony gullies. She called his name, louder and louder despite the pressing danger and the furious imprecations of the missing boy's father.

'Keep quiet, girl, you'll have those bandits on us again!'

Anneliese ignored his furious warning, slipped through

the closely packed trunks as if she was trapped in some vile dream, the lofty firs towering higher and higher overhead. She did not know how far she had run, but she had left the men behind her. The trees were thinning out now, weak winter sunlight filtering through the gaps in the canopy. The fertile mulch which had cushioned her progress gave out over beds of clattering grey rock. She was at the edge of the wood, looking over a deep broad valley toward the massive headland of Pen Point. A stony path ran past her hideout from right to left. There was no sign of Jamie. She groaned with despair, worked her way along the edge of the plantation towards her right, following the great coomb delved out of the towering hills.

She smelt the smoke before she saw it. A thick, boiling soup of burning woods and resins. Anneliese hurried on, peering over the perfect green canopy at the massive black mushroom which stained the sky. Jamie would have been drawn to the trouble like a wasp to a jam jar, she knew that by now. And he would tug her along behind like a Judas goat, she thought with a flicker of resentment.

John Grey had ordered them under no circumstances to loot the hall. He had pleaded with them to confine their search to gathering arms they might use to complete the rout of their hated tormentors. But within two minutes of waving the dusty legion up the long gravel drive toward the Earl of Dartland's fine house on the side of the hill the screeching devils had put out all the windows and built a bonfire with the splintered remains of his household furniture. He had trotted up the path after them, panting and coughing as he tried to keep up with the ruffians from the *Doubloon*. The delay might destroy them.

Flames and screams, servants running over the impeccable lawns. A blue-coated soldier pursued by a mob of vengeful skeletons. Smoke billowed from the upper storeys as the mad gang ran riot through the despised judge's personal quarters. Paintings and vases and assorted ornaments sailed out of the fractured windows. Embroideries and bedding were flung from the balconies like massive dun streamers. Grey stood in the ruin and groaned aloud, watched the eager-eyed looters from Chatham dash off to join the orgy of destruction.

'Collect their weapons! Arm the buggers or they'll slaughter us all,' he bawled, hurrying after the shrieking fiends, stepping over the smashed glass over the steps. He was forced back by a grubby tide of sooty humanity, coughing and retching as they stuffed their faces with hams and cheese, great feathery lumps of new-baked bread they had snatched from the abandoned kitchens. They tore at the food like starving beasts, leaving black teeth marks in Black Bob's stolen vittles.

'That's enough! Never mind that table, grab those pikes! You can't fight the bastards with candlesticks, man!'

The boiling smoke belching from the demolished drawing room forced the crowd back out onto the lawns. Some had torn off their ragged shirts to carry their loot. Others were struggling under the weight of intricate clocks or hiding great silver plates under their clothing. Hardly any had thought to snatch a weapon. Grey had left them to it, taken a couple of the more determined prisoners off around the back of the smoking ruin. A tall sailor who claimed to be a naval lieutenant was cursing his fellow fugitives, pleading with them to hurry. Poor food and long hours had wasted the flesh from his frame, loosened great clumps of his braided hair leaving him with bald and pulsing sores. The howling mob didn't seem to pay the scurvy officer any more attention than they had the dour mate. The two of them had found half a dozen good horses in the stables and a large hay wain in the yard.

'Get those horses in the traces, we'll carry their loot in the wagon for 'em or they'll never move.'

'Never mind the loot,' the monstrous sailor snarled. 'Let us at those bastards back in the village!'

'They'll not take kindly to being parted from their goodies now,' Grey replied, peering around the deserted stables for anything of use. 'We'll march 'em back behind the wain, where they can see it.'

'Rather like dangling a carrot in front of a donkey?' the balding seaman asked.

'It's called soldiering,' Grey growled.

The noisy cavalcade had finally left the flaming ruin behind them, struggling along the road behind the creaking wagon. They were in high spirits now, ecstatic with destruction, drunk on shallow mouthfuls of looted wine. Stolen bottles passed from hand to hand amongst the merrily singing mob. Everything that could be rescued from Black Bob's pile had been loaded aboard the cart, and there was no shortage of helpers to push the great galleon along the track. A dozen of the more belligerent prisoners clutched halberds and swords they had taken from the looted house, and had formed an impromptu advance guard along with Lieutenant Rhodes and Mr Grey. The gruff mate peered over his shoulder in concern,

grimly aware he would have the devil's own job in per-
suading the delirious band to do anything more than
protect their spoils.

'Gallen Fey, he's come back for us,' Rhodes repeated
in astonishment, as his worried rescuer gave him a brief
description of the hair-raising invasion. 'And Sparrow and
Muffet with him! Huzzah for all of them, and you too, Mr
Grey!'

The object of the skeletal youngster's praise scowled
back at him. 'They need a sight more than huzzahs to
help them now, sir. They're stuck back in the village
fighting for their lives, while this lot quarrel over trinkets!'

Rhodes looked suitably chastened. 'I'll speak to them,'
he promised.

Jamie Morrison watched the merry mummers hurry along
the track below him, pushing and pulling at an enormous
cartload of furniture. He smiled brightly, hoisted himself
to his feet, and trotted down the slope, waving his hand
in greeting. The trigger-happy guards raised their muskets
and took aim at the daft boy as he skipped from boulder
to boulder down the slope.

'Helloing, helloing. Have you come with a fair?' the
deranged youngster enquired.

Grey raised his pistol, aimed it at the trickster's laughing head. 'And who d'ye think you are, jumping out on
us like that?' the mystified mate demanded, watching the
silent trees for the rascal's cronies.

'It's a trap!'

'Shoot the bastard, he's one of 'em!'

Jamie beamed at his would-be executioners. 'Have you
come to play?'

'Play, aye!'

'And loot!'

'And revenge ourselves on you worthless shitehawks!'

The tightening ring of nervous musketeers cordoned the boy off from the precious wagon, bobbing barrels levelled at his carefree head.

'NO! Don't shoot!'

Anneliese dashed down the path toward the stalled caravan, waving her arms above her head as the bewildered musketeers menaced the mysterious stranger.

'We're unarmed!' Anneliese shrieked, tripping over her skirts as she sprinted to intercept the capering boy.

The shot came from the far side of the stalled convoy. A pale wraith still smothered in dust from the quarry lowered his stolen musket, twitching with excitement at the deafening retort. He coughed on the acrid smoke as if in astonishment at what he had done – what his new toy was capable of doing.

Anneliese threw out her hands and crashed into the stony path with a single groan of anguish. Her left shoe rose once, and fell back, kicking up the dust.

'Hold your fire!' Grey called angrily, hurrying forward to the girl's side. A steady stream of bright blood was already pulsing out over the gravel, soaking into the parched surface. She had been hit in the stomach, falling onto the bullet which might otherwise have clipped her leg. Her face was caked with dust, her mouth gasping air like a landed fish. Rhodes stared down at the ghastly wound as Grey tore at her patched dress, ripped her underclothing aside to examine the smoky hole the lead ball had punched in her skin. He growled with exasperation as he inspected the deadly hole.

'Don't shoot,' Anneliese gasped. 'Don't shoot him, he's proper daft. He won't hurt you. Daft, I say.'

The boy in question seemed as stunned as the rest of them. He walked sideways over the path, averting his head from the dying girl, tilting his chin as if he suspected the downed Samaritan of some kind of wicked jest. Rhodes looked around at him, squinted at the thin youth's senseless face.

'Who are you? Who is she?' he asked at last.

The daft boy pursed his lips, narrowed his eyes at the stranger. 'The one as looks out for me,' he said woodenly.

'Get her up on the wagon,' Grey barked, his unblinking eyes filmed with a red mist of fury. There had been no need. No need at all. Rhodes and a couple of the other men lifted the lifeless bundle up onto the running-board. They had to haul a broken-legged desk out of the way to make room for her. None of the gloomy looters dared gainsay the furiously sobbing Rhodes as he rolled the broken desk down the rocky slope.

'Well, you can shoot maids well enough,' Grey told the miserable rabble. 'But we didn't bring you down here to slaughter virgins.'

The dusty mob looked away, unable to hold the mate's furiously accusing stare. The girl's blood was dripping through a rent in the running-board, forming a dark lagoon on the stony track.

'The people who put you here,' Grey continued, striding through the ranks of wraiths, 'are back down the bottom of this hill. Captain Sparrow's men are already there, fighting your battles. They came back to free you, now it's up to you to help them!' he snarled, his booming voice hoarse with fury. He flicked his broad paw at them, choking on his own disgust.

The chastized crowd set off again, heaving and hauling the heavy wain, pulling at the enormous spokes as if they could speed its progress down the rocky slope.

Jamie Morrison followed the creaking cart, reaching out absent-mindedly to touch the wounded girl's hanging arm. He brought his hand up to his face, mesmerized by her lifeblood slipping over his fingertips. He raised his fingers to his lips, glanced sideways as Lieutenant Rhodes grimaced in horror.

'The damned fiend's drinking her blood!' Grey stared at the miserably bewildered youngster, shook his head in shocked sympathy.

'She's given her life up for him. A lick of blood ain't going to make much difference to her now,' he said quietly.

Down the hill, the crescendo of battle built up once more, echoing out along the steep-sided coombs which radiated away from the embattled hub. It was beginning to get dark now, and the dusty warriors cast great shadows over the white road. An evil wind was sidling up over the coomb, bringing the first frail dabs of snow to wet their dusty faces. They reached the summit of Cairns Hill, and saw the village scattered about the vast bowl below them. Half a dozen bright fires lit the hellish scene, illuminated the continuing carnage. Grey waved them on, the heavy wain creaking and rolling as it picked up speed. A pack of half-starved stone wolves, released from the iron spell of some country clever-woman, they capered and twitched with manic energy, filled with the heady liquor of battle. The chilled corpse on the running-board might have been their totem, a black flag laid out with due care and ceremony to oversee the vicious slaughter. The villagers clustered about the improvised barricade hardly knew what hit them. Squinting into the swirling snow, all they saw were pale half shapes blowing like leaves down the undefended alleys, phantoms in the gathering murk. The sudden bloody onslaught caught them unawares, drove them back against their own defences. Only their own abject terror saved them – they took to their heels before the chain gang from the quarry had time to trap all of them against the upturned tables, the sandbagged wagons. The half-dozen villagers who stood and slogged it out were quickly overwhelmed by the wild mob, who then set about helping themselves from the clutter of discarded weapons. The rest of the bewildered defenders fled while they could, working their way through abandoned houses and scrambling over rickety fences to escape. Some took to the hills, the wild, rocky cliffs and ledges which encircled their doomed village. Others doubled through the blizzard towards the crossroads, obeying some ancient instinct by taking refuge with their lord and master in his great stone cairn. His courthouse of a keep.

Somebody was blowing a horn from the upper-storey windows – a furiously urgent summons which echoed down the embattled coomb, alerting the survivors. They could hardly turn their backs on the old man now. They couldn't ignore the call to arms.

To Black Bob's last stand.

PART FOUR

CRUICKSHANK'S HOARD

'Men of our profession ought to be well prepared, having death ever before their eyes, they ought to be ever ready to embrace it.'

Robert Munro, Covenanter Colonel

PENMETHOCK VILLAGE CROSS

The deadly rattle of the drums vibrated through the bones of the basilisk village, setting every hovel rattling on its foundations like mouldy teeth in a set of stony grey gums. The cobbles seemed to lift beneath William's feet, the tired mortar ruptured and cracked by the violent rhythms of war. Every splintered shutter and hanging door seemed to be gaping open around them, mouthing the same murderous message, the heart-stopping pulse of battle.

Drum-du-dum, drum-du-dum, the evil echo of their doom, getting louder every wasted moment in that treacherous alley between the leaning houses. William peered over his shoulder as the mournful tattoo resumed, squinting back down the steep High Street through ribbons of acrid smoke and confusing swirls of snow. The white powder was scorched and smeared the moment it made landfall, bruised and blackened by the battle-boiled stones. He could see a black banner swirling piratically above a great mob of soldiers, cursing and shoving themselves some room around a small troop of horsemen. Horsemen?

'Have a care! They've behind us,' he yelped unnecessarily, ducking back down behind their loaded wain. His sooty-faced raiders had already deciphered the rumbling racket, watched the dreadful approach of the Royalist porcupine, half a hundred spearpoints glimmering in the man-made mist. A fire-breathing dragon plugging their only line of escape from the rat-trap village street. They seemed paralysed with doubt, frozen like icicle-men as they gathered the flotsam and jetsam for Sparrow's funeral-pyre wagon. Splintered planking and broken doors, old pots and rustling nets had been thrown on the bonfire, household furniture smashed and hurled over the rim.

The throb of the drums brought them up short, looking from one to the other and finally at Sparrow, their equally dumbfounded leader.

An enemy regiment, blocking the damned street behind them? Where in the bowels of Christ had they sprung from?

The coiling smoke rings were gathered up and scattered by a freshening sea breeze, revealing the Royalist force in all its deadly glory. They were striding out, giant with their own invincibility, shouting and whistling their friends and neighbours from the cellars where they had taken refuge. Seventy, eighty, a hundred. Riders as well, bawling like devils for Roundhead blood.

Sparrow spat in the road, eyeing the available exits from the blind gorge they had charged into with such reckless determination. Open doors and smashed windows, crooked alleys where they would have to go in single file. Scattered like a band of cut-throats fighting it out in some city stew.

'Turn the wagon around, we'll push it down the hill at them!' William barked, his running eyes glistening with ferocious invention. The rejuvenated sergeants caught on at once, cuffing and bawling the slack-mouthed survivors into order. A dozen of the raiders manhandled the heavy wain about in the narrow street. There was a splutter of ill-aimed musketry from the bastion beside the village cross, but most of the shots howled overhead, striking sparks from the battered houses.

'Come on, you slack-bladdered monkeys, it'll roll a sight faster the other way!' Jameson roared, pushing and kicking the frightened mob into a frail testudo behind the wagon. They bent their backs and braced their legs to the vast cart, loaded to the gunwales with splintered timber and household trash. Jameson flung a looted bandolier and a handful of discarded powder flasks into the bonfire hold and trotted alongside as the heavily laden wagon began to pick up speed, wheels sliding on the slick cobbles.

'Push, push, you kill-calf bloats!' The entire shore party seemed galvanized by their terror, packed in behind the unlikely war engine and praying to Heaven the mad captain knew his business. William himself, panting with exhaustion, paused in a shattered doorway, urging the anxious Argonauts to greater efforts. 'Run the bugger right through 'em, it's your only chance!' he bawled. The words were barely out of his scummed mouth when he was hurled aside by a savage blow from behind.

The worm-eaten stool shattered in pieces against his broad back and crested helmet, almost braining the shouting captain. William dropped his sword in surprise, staggering under the furious householder's attack. His jarred frame crashed to the ground as the frantic attacker grabbed the longest stool leg and crouched for the kill. Sparrow kicked out with all his remaining might, catching the man in the knee. He rocked back against the wall, giving the winded captain a moment to scramble to his feet. The demented villager rushed back to the attack, the two men grappling with one another in the narrow, dimly lit passage. The wiry rascal seemed to be twisted from iron, his ragged beard a sparse blaze on his bony, pock-marked chin. His breath reeked through the blackened stumps of his teeth as he snarled and spat.

God's nails, to be murdered by a back-stabbing rogue in his stinking cabbage patch of a hallway! Sparrow felt the anger surge through his tingling nerves, animating his bone-tired limbs. He stepped back, tempting the cursing villager into pressing home his attack. Sparrow grabbed him by his shirtsleeves and spun him around, using his own momentum to hurl him into the brickwork. The villager grunted with pain and fury as his face collided with the wall, splintering his teeth and shattering his nose. William snatched his sword from the floor and brought the heavy iron hilt down on the back of the spluttering rogue's neck. His knees gave out and the bloody wretch collapsed to the flags, further infuriating his accomplice, who had hurried down the passage brandishing a viciously curved filleting knife. William hurled himself sideways as the screaming banshee tripped over the writhing householder. William lunged with all his might, skewering his attacker on the brutal blade. He lifted the cutlass, feeling the bloody weight sag on the curved steel, and wheelbarrowed the shrieking villager back down the passage. He tore the blade free and shoved his assailant into the gloomy pit of the pantry, bracing himself in the doorway to steady his legs. His breath came in great gut-wrenching sobs as he stared down at the disembowelled housewife, her plain shift drenched and splattered in horribly bright blood. The red-haired woman was whistling through her pale lips, clutching her ruined belly. Her dirty fingers grasped the impossibly spouting slash as she stared at the ceiling, panting asthmatically as her eyes glazed with agony.

William shuddered, blinking fearfully at the fatally injured woman. He backed away on unsteady legs, his skin crawling like a maggoty shroud over his screaming bones. Her husband had propped himself up on all fours, and was staring through his spread legs at his slaughtered wife, his mouth moving sideways as he uttered idiot gibbers. William felt a surge of panic, an overwhelming tide which washed through his mind, taking the last of his shocked reason with it. His mouth filled with bile as he stood there above his silent accuser. He felt like a ten-year-old caught stealing pies from the market. His tumbling vision frosted and fractured, a thousand shouting faces, tearing hands grasping at his aching neck. William brought the dripping cutlass down in a whistling arc with final, punishing force. A cleansing blow, exorcizing the ghosts of war which had boiled out of the hatefully crammed cauldron of his brain. The cutlass broke the screaming victim's neck, the greedy blade biting through the side of his head, just below his gold-ringed ear. The ferocious blow fractured a handful of his vertebrae, slicing clean through muscle and gristle and clogged arteries. The man slumped forward, arms splayed like a Muslim at prayer, his partially severed head hanging grotesquely from the twitching trunk. His life-blood squirted and pulsed over William's boots, an arc of gore rainbowed over the dirty brickwork above the hewn body.

Goodrich peered into the shambles from the bright doorway. The grizzled veteran grimaced, sickened by the slaughter. The savagely wounded villager was kicking feebly and hissing through his clenched teeth, his eyeballs protruding like a freshly caught cod's, clawing at the brickwork as his lifeblood lagooned under him. William was spreadeagled against the wall as if he had been trapped by some terrible tempest, caught up by the bloody tornado which had scoured the demolished home. He was struggling to swallow, his breath coming in hideous rasping gasps. Goodrich stepped past him, bent down quickly, and dispatched the man with a blow from his pistol butt. A merciful release which cracked his skull like a rotten goose egg and stilled his agonized struggles for ever.

William was aware of his hoarse breathing, a lurid, lusty echo in the blood-splattered hallway. Goodrich showed his teeth, in some peculiar rictus of a horrified disbelief.

'He came out at me. I didn't know,' William gasped at last. Goodrich peered down the hall, nodded slowly, and gently propelled the captain away from the carnage.

'Come away. There's no more to be done here.'

William blinked as he stumbled out into the daylight. He squinted up at the uneven rooftops, convinced the narrow street was slowly closing in, imprisoning him in the hellish canyon. He stared at the crabby, lead-bound windows, imagined glassy eyes piercing his soul.

He thought he might have been standing in that bloody doorway for days, but he realized it could only have been a few moments. The panting sergeant cuffed and kicked him, terrorized the pale captain into bewildered obedience.

'It's no use fretting now, lad, they're deader than a pair of bloaters! Nobody asked 'em to run out on you!' Goodrich screamed over the howling storm which seemed to have blown itself up out of William's fractured heart. Sleet and ice, stone and blood. William was about to consider the awesome implications of the sergeant's observation, but the gruff veteran was having none of it.

'That's what war is, lad, a godforsaken mess. Don't let any bugger tell you otherwise.' Goodrich gripped him by his bunched coat and frogmarched him down the street, hurrying the dazed officer after the screaming wagon, which had left twin trails through the slowly pitching snow.

One by one the filthy raiders had fallen away from the speeding hulk, left behind like thrown jockeys at a steeplechase. The great wain had careered from one side of the street to the other, its huge wheels spinning and shrieking over potholes and steps, the feverishly piled load hurled up in the air like autumn leaves in a bonfire.

Jameson pursued the mad juggernaut, his fleshy face trembling as he panted in its churned wake. He threw his hastily rolled torch into the back and hurled himself into a doorway as the powder ignited with a smoky orange flash, setting the wretched detritus alight in a moment. Fanned by the brisk winds funnelling over the shrieking galleon, the fire gobbled up the loosely heaped trash, turning the cart into a blazing meteor which sent the panic-stricken Royalists running for cover.

Goodrich was charging like some bearded bull, Sparrow's halberd in one fist, the other bunched behind William's neck. They had to run to keep up with the blazing load, showering sparks and belching smuts into its foul slipstream. The sergeant harried the panting survivors, lashing out at the gasping wretches crouched in the ash.

William rubbed his fists in his eyes, desperate to see

through the choking smoke, the ghastly logjam of images crowding his fevered brain. He stumbled, Goodrich cursing as he yanked the incoherent youth to his feet once more. The wild-eyed mob stampeded down the street, hurdling the huddled bodies of the unfortunates who hadn't managed to shove themselves out of the way or claw their way up a blisteringly hot wall.

A mad dash through a shambles of shattered bodies, lying like roast rabbits trapped in a blazing stubble field.

The enemy drummers stared in mute wonder, their fingers frozen about their sticks as the flaming juggernaut careered down the steep street towards them. It seemed to grow larger with every tortured revolution of its blazing wheels, filling the narrow street with a thousand furies.

Speedwell's renegade dragoons tried to turn their prancing mounts out of the terrified press of men, hurling themselves at gaping windows, clawing at crumbling ledges to escape the diabolical onset. Their apple-eyed ponies reared and snorted in terror, throwing riders into the jumble of arms and legs packed into the running gutters. Henry Graves was stricken with dread, convinced he would be burned black beneath the hellish wagon. He would never kick his way out now, jammed in the street by the panicking soldiers. And then his roving eye focused on a frail lifeline hanging limp in the rolling smokes above his head. A clothes line, by Christ, strung between the abandoned hovels ready for a washday which would never come.

Henry boosted himself out of his saddle a moment before his pony was struck down, grasping the washline in his great meaty paws. The rope yawned under his weight, tugging at its frail fastenings beneath a crumbling window ledge. He grunted with the effort, lifting his feet as the blazing wagon passed beneath, closing his eyes at the sudden rush of boiling smokes. He swung to and fro through the fearsome heat, locking his fingers around the precious line, believing for a split second he had saved himself.

Next moment he heard the sudden shriek of metal as the crude fastening broke, heard the tired screws pull free even above the insane roar of the wagon. He turned his head to see the pulley explode out of the crumbling mortar. The frail washline sagged under his enormous weight, sending the screaming dragoon plunging into the crackling inferno. His primeval roar of agony was swallowed up by another pulse of fire and brimstone, his coat, clothes, hair, and cheese-rind skin pared from his red frame in a moment. He writhed and kicked, surrounded by the eye-melting fires which consumed the air in his bursting lungs, dried the blood in his withered veins. And still he tried to force himself to his feet, engulfed as he was, dwarfed by the giant, greedy fires.

His appalling struggles stunned the dazed Roundheads tottering through the wreckage behind him.

'Christ Jesus!' Goodrich mouthed, closing his eyes and averting his face from the burning monster. He threw his arms over his head against the sudden roasting glare, ran straight into a frightened shadow soldier who had ducked out in front of him. Goodrich opened his eyes and clubbed the wild-eyed youngster out of his way. The youth fell to the cobbles as if pole-axed. In another moment the burning wagon wheels impacted with a well-scrubbed step, shattering like matchwood. The enormous cart turned over, spewing its hellish load over the market square, a molten river of sparks and flame which pursued the luckless Royalists over the cobbles like a fiery broth. The wreckage careered into the inn, demolishing the porch and bringing the door down. The fire leapt over the splintered woodwork like a sackful of snakes, sparking the cloud of powder dust thrown out by the dreadful collision. A villager crouching in the porch was crushed to a red and black paste in a moment. Horrified townswomen who were watching the carnage from the snug were thrown back like rag dolls, crawling away on their hands and knees through the greedy, choking smokes.

The survivors picked themselves up as best they could, stumbling through the smoking wreckage, hopping over the molten cobbles to escape the hellish raiders. A catatonic cabin boy clung to their scorched standard, staring at the bloody carnage as if he had been whisked into hell's deepest torture chambers by black arts. A moment ago he had been surrounded by shouting, screaming men, armed and ready to trap the Roundhead dogs at the top of the street. But his friends had been blown away like chaff, shorn from their standard like rancid wool. Their closely packed, sweat-sleek bodies had been replaced by eerie flurries of snowflakes, blowing in over the hateful wreckage. The villagers and soldiers packed in on the fringes of the Royalist schillitron had been able to escape, to run off towards the smoky quay or dart into one of the alleys which led away from the main street like so many fish-bones. Terrified by the flaming chariot, they gibbered and sweated and choked in their hovels, or sprinted across the fields like rabbits.

Captain Took shook his head, tried to clear his streaming vision. His men had been swept away, crushed like ants under a sledgehammer. He was too stunned to speak, to bawl his shattered battalion back to its colour. Took peered around the square, the blackened corpses and fuming spars, tangled equipment and hollow drums. He lifted his sooty hand to his mouth, felt the scorched crack of his mouth and his crisped cheeks. His hair, his vain-glorious pride and joy, raven black and as fine as any woman's, had been chewed away to vile ropes, ashy hand-fuls which cracked under his fingertips. He groaned in shocked humiliation, looked up as pale shapes danced in the fog before his eye. Slim scarecrows wandering through the slinking, sullen tails of their firestorm, laughing and jabbering and spearing the writhing wounded. Took stood still, mouth agape, as a bearded bear tramped through the smoking rubble of his command, hauling an equally dumbfounded commander with him. Took peered at the man's mobile red mouth, but his words were lost in the angry growls vibrating inside his head. Took watched in helpless fascination as the staring stranger shook himself free from his mentor, strode over a charred corpse towards the cabin boy.

'Take quarter, surrender the town,' the buff-coated ruffian with the singed beard bawled, shaking Took by his trembling shoulders. 'D'you hear me now, sir?'

The bewildered Cavalier turned aside, watched the rebel chief pick the cabin boy's black fingers from the standard with peculiarly tender care. The gentle giant leaned the tattered flag over his shoulder, patted the youth on the back in encouragement, and stared back at the captain.

'Call your men in now, or they'll slaughter the lot of you,' he said heavily, as if dismayed to find himself giving such an order. Took swallowed, baffled by the sudden and utter disaster which had overtaken his brave assault.

It was as if an avenging angel had flown down the narrow canyon, cracking a flaming whip and scattering brimstone like seed corn, the triumphant counter-attack which might have cemented (or at least spared) his reputation swallowed up by the slumbering dragon of war in less time than it took to peel an apple. Took jumped with fright as the big sergeant cuffed him about the shoulder.

'D'you take quarter or not?' he asked, holding a bloody dirk to Took's parched throat.

The wretched captain nodded, too demoralized for any further futile gestures.

Clavincale had drifted away from the others, isolated by a growing sense of unease, a morbid dread he had found himself in the wrong place at the wrong time. He had taken up a position at a barred window overlooking the courtyard, the clustered outbuildings glimmering white, much improved by the mantle of snow. The sullen blizzard had played relentlessly about their spluttering battle, large fluffy flakes blowing in from the sea, powdering the cake-tin coomb. The marauders who had caused such mayhem in the village had left bewildering trails through the thin canopy, as well as the occasional splash of blood where one of his father's chattering guardians had gleefully found a mark.

The first floor of the battered courthouse had changed hands twice now. The triumphant band of Roundhead musketeers which had spearheaded the assault had taken the horses from the stables, isolating the garrison while their friends fetched willing helpers from Black Bob's notorious quarry. Reinforced by fifty and more ravens in dust-clogged clothing, the raiders had forced their way into the hall and erupted into the main courtroom, where they had been met by a furious charge led by the redoubtable Captain Cruickshank and his beer-bellied cronies under the equally piratical Humphrey Gale. The glassy-eyed bandits had rushed down on the startled Roundheads as they picked through papers and examined the huddled bodies of the fallen. Swords, clubs, and musket butts had sent the gutless swine tumbling back outdoors.

Clavincale glanced at Telling, lost in his own thoughts at the next window along. He had fought like a wildcat in a sack, slashing and hacking at the dismayed invaders, forcing his way past their feeble sword strokes. He had run one man through and lopped the callused hand from a second.

Why?

It hadn't been Telling's fight. The judge had been moments away from sentencing the captain's hopelessly devoted sweetheart to hang by her pretty neck, and yet Telling had remained behind with him, ready to risk his life in their fight. Perhaps he was hoping Black Bob would be gnawed with guilt, dismiss the ridiculous charges against the girl there and then. If so he would be sadly mistaken. Black Bob wasn't in the habit of showing mercy, not since poor Anthony had been taken from them.

The rebels had been daunted by the ferocity of their counter-attack and had evacuated the courthouse leaving half a dozen cruelly hewn rockbreakers behind them. The cheering Royalists had been further encouraged by the timely arrival of more than a dozen refugees from the rather more costly encounters in the village – driven from their barricades by the Roundhead main body.

'Main body? There's not more than a company of 'em, all told,' Cruickshank had concluded, absent-mindedly wiping his sword on a discarded coat sleeve. 'They scarpered soon enough, when they got a taste of this,' he boasted.

Major Brinks, unexpectedly rescued from his miserable outpost in the courtroom, clamped his teeth over another sour mouthful of agony. Parchment-pale and beaded with tiny pearls of sweat, he nevertheless understood the leering captain's insinuation.

'My men fought well enough, while they were able,' he griped.

Cruickshank raised his tawny eyebrow in mock surprise. 'I never doubted it for a moment, sir. Their charge was quite spectacular, straight out of the door and over the hill! I'll wager they're halfway back to Plymouth already!'

The surly pirates who had survived the sinking of the *Messalina's Purse* grinned at their energetic commander, stalking back and forth over the littered floor.

'And what d'you mean by that?'

'Well now, sir,' the captain said, every trace of humour evaporating from his voice, 'the majority of them have gone over to the enemy. What are we to make of that?'

'They were new-raised men, new to the colours,' Brinks growled.

'And newer to the cause. I would have slept a sight lighter if I had known the stamp of your men, Major.'

Brinks seemed stung by the slur. He raised the sodden rag he had clamped to his punctured chest, presented the bloody bundle as if it was evidence of his own good service.

'Is this not enough for you, Captain? I'd have slept a

sight lighter if I knew the stamp of your blackguard friends!'

Cruickshank frowned with impatience. His filthy corsairs formed the backbone of the defence now, he was in effective command of the rabble who had remained. Blasted from their hammocks aboard ship or roused from their stinking pits ashore, the crewmen had stuck together in the chaos and confusion, not taken off for the hills like so many lost sheep. He eyed his ruffian bodyguard with unusual fondness. 'They stick by me, my boys,' he declared.

The Earl of Dartland, drumming his skeletal fingers on Abraham Bacon's commandeered desk, snapped them in frustration. 'They had nowhere else to go,' Black Bob snarled, interrupting the acrimonious exchange with a flick of his wrist. 'They are pariahs, sir, just as the dogs who abandoned these works will have no place here when we have settled with these unwarranted intruders.'

Clavincale swallowed nervously, anxiously imagining the fate which awaited the unfortunates who had left their posts. Those misguided recruits who had left their officer lying in his own blood on the courtroom floor. Another bloody bond, a covenant with Death himself. To be redeemed in full by the bearer, no doubt. A promise of further effusions and more bloody vengeance, an endless cycle to which the innocent seemed particularly heavily mortgaged. Telling must have noticed his gloomy expression. He doubled over beneath the opened windows and peered into the yard.

'They're up to something, they've had long enough, God knows!' Telling said, squinting down through the sullen snowfall. 'Besides, they'll be rock-bollocked with cold by now, they can't sit out there through the winter!'

BY

THE MERMAID,

PENMETHOCK

Penmethock was quiet now, lying beneath its fragile mantle of snow like a wounded animal, desperate to throw the pursuing pack from its trail. The fractured village had been broken in two, pulled out of its comfortable socket by the unwanted invasion. The rebels had driven the villagers, Trained Bandsmen, and displaced sailors from the lower end of the town, taking possession of the fabulously appointed warehouse, the soot-plastered, desiccated remains of the village inn, and the cluster of houses about the market cross. The Royalists left standing had found their way in small groups and bewildered twos and threes to the massive courthouse – standing dark and drab beside the windswept crossroads. They had taken advantage of the failing light and the cover provided by the tumbledown outhouses, working their way past drowsy enemy sharpshooters who were already half-blinded by the driving snow. Muffet had done his best, but his men were thin on the ground and running low on ammunition. The grey-haired veteran had listened to Sparrow's grim-faced report of the fight on the quay, shaken his head ruefully when the captain had reported the loss of the *Doubloon*.

'Well, what are we going to do now, then?' Nicodemus had squawked in alarm, his red-rimmed eyes blinking back tears of fright as he eavesdropped on their whispered conversation.

Sparrow had shrugged, gazing resignedly at the heavily reinforced assizes which dominated the high road and the bridge over the brook, blocking the rebels into the hard-won coomb like a cork in a bottle. He knew in his bones they had missed their opportunity. Their only real hope had been a sudden assault from the sea. Without the benefit of surprise any attack now would be met with the fiercest resistance. The men in the courthouse were fighting for their lives, after all, just as his own men would be if the tables were turned, he thought sourly.

The Roundheads had lost almost two dozen men killed and maimed, but the original expedition had been strongly reinforced by the prisoners from the quarry so their reunited party now held a considerable advantage in numbers. Unable to press home their advantage by subduing the stubborn Royalist garrison, they had drifted back into the chill town in search of shelter, leaving Muffet's long-suffering musketeers to keep an eye on the defiant pile.

'Fey'll think of something. I'm off down to see him now,' he said in a belated bid to cheer the miserable musketeers up a little. 'You know Gallen Fey. If there's a will there's a way,' he called cheerily. One of the strangers blew a sibilant raspberry behind his back.

Sparrow picked his way back down the hill past heaps of scorched rubble, the spluttering snowflakes sighing and hissing as they extinguished themselves in the residual heat of the burntout buildings. The ravaged main street was deserted now, the only sign of battle the occasional glimmer of a match fuming sullenly behind some splintered window as a musketeer kept his watch.

He passed a gang of shivering scarecrows from the quarry, muttering and cursing as they heaved a leaning dresser onto a fantastically overloaded wagon. They had backed the looted wain into an alley, an emaciated wretch in an elegantly frogged topcoat holding on to the horses while his colleagues hurried about their business. The boy looked up suspiciously as Sparrow crunched past, his half-starved features hidden behind drenching draughts of vapour from the steaming animals.

They had hauled the battered hearse all night, filling the wagon with anything which hadn't been nailed down from the ransacked hovels along the main street. Slim pickings from shabby houses maybe, but a sumptuous hoard to the dispossessed diehards from the quarry. They had kicked down every door, searched every room as they made their painstaking way back to the black quay. Candlesticks and coin, plate and ale, boots, clothing, weapons, and food all thrown into the back, half burying the poor maid all forlorn they had shot on the way down the hill. She was beyond caring now, and wasn't the only unburied body in Penmethock that eve, not by a long chalk.

Sparrow hadn't taken much notice of the bloody smears and ragged handprints over the oak beams, it was the toiling fugitives on the running-board who had caught his attention. 'I don't know how you reckon on getting that galleon out of here,' Sparrow called sourly. 'You men had best get back up to the cross.'

The removals platoon peered down at the inquisitive captain, unwilling to take orders from a total stranger when there were houses stuffed with loot to divert them.

'As soon as we'm done yere, sir,' one of the rogues called back cheekily.

'Mind you're quick. Sergeant Muffet needs hands up at the courthouse.'

They ignored him, backs bent to take the strain as they wrestled the heavy dresser over the back of the wagon.

Sparrow left them to their self-imposed assignment and strode on down the slope to the partially demolished inn beside the quay. He paused on the gutted threshold, threw his tired arms about his chilled frame, and tried to rub some warmth back into his bones. The suffocating heat of battle had evaporated from his bruised body just as the burning courtyard had cooled in the continued blizzard. He looked around, frowning at the charred bodies and scorched wreckage, the abandoned drums, splintered pikes, and stacks of muskets which had been carefully concealed by the relentless drifts. Stark silhouettes smothered under the feathery flakes, half a hundred atrocities hidden under a frigid blanket of snow lest they offend the furtively glimpsed moon.

The officers that were left had gathered in the burntout shell of the Mermaid. A blackened skull pulled from some plague pit, charred fissures for doors and smoky holes for windows. William looked over their anxious faces, stepped inside as the flurries chasing up and down the street tugged and slammed the drunkenly hanging shutters. The furious activity and sudden eerie calm had left him chronically tired and sick to his stomach. He wasn't sure whether his gut had been soured by the wickedly misdirected bloodletting or whether it was merely reminding him he hadn't eaten since the morning. His grubby hand strayed to his stomach once again, fingering the heavy padding beneath his reeking shirt as if it were some holy relic torn from a Crusader's tomb. He had wrapped the captured colour around his waist, partly to discourage idle pilfering, and partly to keep his kidneys warm. Woe betide him if they caught him with it and all, he thought gloomily. Damn it, if it came to the crunch he could escape by himself. A squad of trained sharpshooters could move more quickly than a noisy caravan of superannuated sailors. William pictured himself presenting the flag to McNabb, the instant fame and fortune the tattered rag would restore to his battle-shamed troop. He stood idly by, one ear on their gloomy council of war, wondering if he dared speak his mind.

Get out while the going was good would be his advice. They could climb the cliffs and lose themselves on the wild moors, hope to work their way back to their own lines avoiding the enemy outposts. Not even Prince Maurice's demon horsemen could keep watch on every back lane.

All he had to do was survive, to escape the bottleneck gorge they had mastered with such brutal conviction.

Gallen Fey's wretched description of the confrontation with the *Messalina's Purse* had sucked what little fire he had left from his belly, but at least it had taken his mind from the shambles in that damned hovel. The hewn bodies bleeding over their own hall. He shuddered with revulsion, closed his smoke-stung eyes.

'Is there any way we can repair her, make good?' he asked foolishly.

Fey, mortified to have had to make his report at all, let

alone repeat the principal points, scowled at the brooding captain.

'I thought I had made myself clear,' he rasped. 'She's had the best part of her bows shot away, sir, she'll not move another yard, save under,' he concluded, settling his bruised leather hat on the saturated strands of his hair.

Fey had taken his scorched sea-coat and log from the doomed *Doubloon*, but precious little else. A sack of coin and a pair of pistols had damn near dragged him down to the muddy bottom when he had finally been obliged to abandon the cruelly exposed deck and wade to the quay. A bare half a dozen of the ship's skeleton crew had escaped the slaughter – and all of them had been wounded to one degree or another. Their blood had bought a fragile freedom for Fey's long-suffering shipmates, rescued from Black Bob's quarry to face a future made more uncertain than ever.

'How are we going to get off, then?' the pock-marked lieutenant from the quarry asked, his sunken features waxy with alarm. 'We can't walk back to London! We'd have the devil's job getting into Plymouth with Prince Maurice's army sitting on the roads!'

Corporal Gillingfeather snorted into his beard, turned his bright brown eye on the reluctant stonemason. Forced out of the courtroom by Captain Cruickshank's unexpectedly severe onslaught, the hairy zealot was in a particularly filthy mood. Being beaten in a fair fight was bad enough, being bested by a godless whoreson like the pirate chief made the defeat twice as galling.

'We'll march, aye, or die where we stand,' he vowed with his usual relish. 'Lyme's not far, and we've friends there!'

Gillingfeather growled. 'Lyme? We might as well jump out of the frying pan and into the fire! The garrison won't last any longer than we will here, once Prince Maurice gets around to them!' Lieutenant Rhodes fretted. Fey scowled miserably at his rescued officer, wondering whether their bloody efforts had been worthwhile.

'Lyme's no good. We'll be marching straight towards the Prince if we go that way,' William pointed out, remembering the grubby charts he had studied back at the Rummer in Greenwich. 'These buggers are bound to have sent for help by now, and that's precisely the direction it'll be coming from.' He racked his tired brain. What was the other place Parliament still held along the coast? He clicked his fingers.

'Poole. We'll make for Poole!' he exclaimed. 'It's not that far, is it? We'd do best to split into small groups and find a way out over the hills. Stick to the moors, avoid the main roads.'

Gillingfeather shrugged, studied his filthy fingernails. Rhodes nodded cautiously.

'Gentlemen, there is only one realistic way out,' Captain Fey summarized, irritated by their haphazard suggestions. 'And that is of course by sea. The *Doubloon* and the *Purse* are holed and aground in the mud, so we must press their fishing fleet.'

The demoralized officers glanced at one another, wondering whether the iron-arsed captain, out of his mind with relief after delivering his captured crew, had finally lost his grip. 'Steal their fishing boats?'

'Five or six men in each, we'll link them with rope and I'll navigate us back to Plymouth, to London if necessary,' the wiry officer vowed. Gillingfeather, who admired Fey as a kindred spirit sharing his sacred cause, nodded his tangled head in agreement.

Grey, the no less righteous but rather more realistic man of the world, ran his tongue over his caked lips in hesitation. He knew the captain's scheme would buy them a one-way ticket to the bottom in anything but the calmest sea.

'That's all very grand for the likes of you and I, sir,' he said slowly, 'but these rascals, we've let 'em loot, and they'll not leave it behind now.'

Fey shrugged his narrow shoulders. 'My men don't need loot to guarantee their service, Mr Grey,' he said piously.

'Aye, sir, but they're not all our men, the others won't be as easily convinced.'

'Well, then, we'll leave them behind with their blasted loot. See what this Black Bob makes of their work when he realizes we've gone.'

'The godless scum, we don't need them,' Gillingfeather crowed. Sparrow glanced from his pop-eyed corporal to the equally deranged sea captain.

'What about the other men from the quarry?' Rhodes asked sourly. 'Are we to leave them behind as well?'

Fey sucked his cheeks in thoughtful deliberation, nodded at his rescued lieutenant. The scabby youngster had become the unofficial champion of the prisoners – seaman and stranger alike. The half-starved survivors were squatting anxiously over the watchfires they had started in the looted houses along the street, waiting for news of their half-cocked deliverance.

'I took account of every boat in the harbour. There's a place for every man, but no room for their damned loot.'

'Leave them, then,' Gillingfeather advised, eyes glittering.

'You can't run out on them,' Sparrow shouted, galled by the callous captain's glib self-assurance. It was Fey – bribing, cajoling, promising the earth – who had talked the volunteers aboard in the first place! 'Those men were promised the pick of the town,' he pointed out. 'Now they've got their fair shares you're suggesting we run out on them!'

'Indeed, sir, I am not. I am merely responding to changes in the tactical situation!' Fey rasped, equally angry. 'I had not intended to sacrifice the *Doubloon* to sink the *Messalina*!'

'Hadn't you?' Sparrow yelled back.

Gillingfeather showed his teeth. 'I would have sacrificed her and every man aboard, to square with that devil-spawned slut!' the agitator announced with a cock-eyed leer.

William felt his body flush with fury. Damn these fanatics! They would tear the world to pieces with their wars and vengeance! 'God's nails, man, you can't—'

'I can and will, sir! Is your way any better, scuttling away over the heath like quails before beaters? Hoping the way will be open for you?'

The wind howled, picking at their frail shelter. The squabbling officers looked up as Billy Butcher marched into the abandoned snug, heralded by another cold flurry of glistening flakes. The musketeer had wrapped himself in a smart if somewhat threadbare Dutch coat, the baggy sleeves hanging over his long musket. The cockney sharpshooter pushed his snow-capped hat back and grinned at the gathering, jerking his thumb over his powdered shoulders.

'Look what the cat's dragged in,' he invited them, stepping back as a squad of raiders pushed and prodded another gang of prisoners through the ruined doorway. Sparrow stood up with a wince, regarded the drooping fugitives as they came to a halt in the middle of the floor.

A gangly idiot in breeches and baggy shirt, wiping his snotty nose on his torn sleeve. A glowering clerk wearing a ridiculous tall hat, sober city-black suit powdered with snow. A bedraggled old devil wearing a miserably resigned expression on his heavily creased face, every wrinkle ploughed deep into the tired flesh about his cast down eyes. Beside him a frightened farmhand with slack mouth and twitching hands. A weeping woman with dishevelled hair hanging over her averted face, being escorted by her bustling red-faced father, stepping from one boot to the other as if he had an urgent appointment at the privy.

'Well, don't stand there gawping, my lad, get that fire banked up before we all curl up our toes!'

William's smoky features creased with bewilderment and then broke into a weary, disbelieving grin. No. It couldn't be. Not here, not now.

Sir Gilbert Morrison, turncoat and merchant, with his entire frosty household.

'We picked the boy there out from Mr Grey's prisoners,' the sardonic sharpshooter reported. 'Seems he got 'isself separated, bein' as the rest of 'im's been separated from 'is brain since Roundway. We caught old man Morrison creeping down the hillside, chased him into some crack in the rock. You could have hid a bleedin' army up there!'

'Morrison? The turncoat?' Fey enquired, turning his sea-mist stare on the bustling stranger.

'Morrison the merchant, by God's grace,' the gentleman replied, looking down his nose at the drab imp as if he had crawled from beneath a stagnant barrel.

William stared at the merchant's familiar features, his puffed cheeks as red as berries, his white hair a frosty riot on his livid head, standing out in hectic sympathy with the howling storm. His mobile mouth gleamed wetly, slick with secrets. He hadn't changed a scrap in the five months and more since William had last seen him.

'I'm glad we found you, Will my lad, your friends here wouldn't believe the trouble we've had down here.'

William glanced at Bella, his Bella – stung to his vitals she hadn't even recognized him. Had five months of war transformed him that much? Turned her sometime sweetheart into another bloody brute in a buff coat? She had looked up at last, her once bewitching features haggard with fright, saturated with sorrows. He stared in horrified fascination at the ugly crease above her eye, a hundred questions piling up in his throat. Her tears had cut jagged white trails through the sooty grime on her fine cheeks and her eyes resembled half-melted candle wax, glazed with unspeakable grief. She'd been in the wars and all, then, he thought, completely bewildered.

Sir Gilbert read William's glance in a moment, shook his head in shocked sympathy.

'I'm surprised at you, Will. Letting her lie in a cart like that,' he scolded gently.

The troubled captain raised his chin a notch. Wouldn't be the first time Bella had lain back in a wagon, he thought fleetingly.

'We've had to put up with a sight worse than a crook-wheeled cart,' he snapped, gnawed by insinuating memories, of half a hundred past slights he had received from the endlessly inventive merchant. Morrison frowned.

'Not my Bella, you fool. Anneliese. The poor splinter lying in the road there! Tossed in the back like trash, God knows how I'll break it to her mother.' Bella winced in mortification at the mention of her old friend's name.

Anneliese Ramsay? William wondered what the old fool was blabbering about. What on earth was Anneliese doing lying in the road in this weather? John Grey coughed, fracturing his puzzled train of thought.

'That was a mistake, I'll grant 'ee. One of those damn fools from the quarry, too eager to get even with a strange face. She died on the hill, trying to save your lad there, and we've had no time to make her decent.'

Bella sobbed wretchedly, a broken-hearted cry which tore through William's squirming innards like a cold dirk.

'It was your fault,' she croaked. William thought for one agonized moment she meant him, but the girl's trembling finger was pointing at her idiot brother. Poor Jamie, still as daft as a feather in a thunderstorm. He struggled to catch up with the withering twists in their shocked exchange. Anneliese shot down like a dog in the street? What harm had she ever done anyone? He glared at Grey, chewing his dirty paw in mortification.

'Don't blame the lad,' Sir Gilbert grumbled into his chest.

Fey sighed heavily, shook his narrow head. 'I am sure you are aware of the risks involved when one strays into the middle of a pitched battle. We regret the unnecessary death of the young woman, but in these circumstances due care and caution are luxuries which are sadly denied to us.'

Rhodes, who had been particularly horrified by the poor girl's agonized whimpers, her angelic suffering on the running-board, stared at the black wall as if it was covered in barely decipherable hieroglyphics, crucified by the knowledge his own colleagues had thumbed out the frail flame of her life. Sir Gilbert tilted his head as if in tacit acknowledgement of the captain's threadbare apology.

'Mr Rhodes, kindly ensure the young woman's body is recovered and given a decent burial.' Fey watched the pale lieutenant hurry out into the squalls to complete his assignment, then raised his chin to study the scowling merchant. 'Now perhaps you would like to tell us how it is you found yourself drawn to this viper's nest?'

Sir Gilbert stepped from one boot to the other, modifying his stance with the well-practised ease of an experienced trickster.

'Viper's nest? Never a truer word spoken. We are here, sir, because of false charges laid against my daughter here, by a certain bandit chieftain masquerading as a captain of His Majesty's dragoons. He kidnapped her and all her loving family besides from a church, sir, a *church*, if you'll credit it, to face the charge at the courthouse on the hill!'

'Where my people found you,' Fey suggested.

'Sneaking about,' Billy Butcher piped up.

Sir Gilbert flashed the cockney sharpshooter a look.

'Sneaking? Why, yes, I was sneaking. Sneaking up to try and see what was going on, sneaking about to try and find a way out of this damned hole! We were being held prisoners, sir, until your brave attempt somewhat disrupted that pitiful excuse for a trial!'

Fey stood up, walked over to the weeping girl standing distractedly by herself as her father babbled on regardless.

'On what charges were you being tried?' the captain asked, his icy demeanour somewhat thawed by the girl's evident distress. Bella noisily wiped her nose on her sleeve.

'Shooting his dragoons. It was all his fault, all of it!' she cried, nodding her dishevelled head at her brother, standing equally forlorn in the burnt-out inn. 'If he'd stayed put none of this would have happened and poor Annie would be back with us!'

'How so?'

'It was him as wandered into the village stark naked, had the dragoons on him for playing the fool. It was when Anneliese and I . . .' Bella broke down again, convulsed with sobs. Fey regarded her father, waiting expectantly at her side as if he was attending an audition for some mystery play. The merchant rearranged his features into a mask of concern, squeezing a tear from his heavily lidded eye.

'You mustn't blame the boy, sir, he knows not what he does, ever since Roundway. Tell him, Will, you were there with him!'

William nodded dumbly. Jamie had never been the same, since that hateful summer's day beneath the endless, senseless blue sky.

'The fact remains that the Parliament has issued a warrant for your arrest, Sir Gilbert,' Fey said quietly. 'You are a traitor and an enemy of the state.'

Sir Gilbert winced, his merry features paling visibly. Warrants? He'd had his fill of them.

'I have, on occasion, made mistakes,' he admitted.

'And by God I'll answer for 'em, aye, to men who can satisfy their Lord and Saviour they are blameless themselves,' he announced passionately, looking from Fey to Sparrow. 'Will here, he can vouch for me. He'll tell you what happened, how I came to stray from the path of righteousness. I wasn't the only man torn between serving his Parliament or his King. God knows I'm not proud of it, but it was honest bewilderment, sir, which led me to the King, not treachery, sir, never treachery.'

Sparrow remained stubbornly tight-lipped.

'And yet you eased your passage into the King's confidence with, how much was it, six hundred pound of Parliament's gold, intended for the pay and equipment of a regiment?'

Sir Gilbert brightened up at the mention of the money.

'Held in trust, sir, against a day such as this! That's what brought me back here, sir, to tell the truth, to see what the devils had done with my money!'

'It's here?'

'Aye, every penny and interest as well. I'll gladly deliver it back to the rightful owners, sir, just as soon as you get it back for me.'

'Get it back for you?' Fey cried. This merchant was an impudent wretch, with a serpent's tongue to match all twisted up inside his slippery mouth.

'Assuredly, sir. I saved some of it from the bandits, sir, hid it on my wagon, sir, in the courthouse yard. The rest . . . the rest they took aboard their damned ship, sir, the *Messalina's Purse.*'

'Their ship is sunk in the harbour.'

Sir Gilbert threw up his hands in horror. 'Sunk? What? Looted and sunk?'

'Sunk.'

The merchant wiped his mouth, his red brow furrowed in agitated concentration. 'But she's carrying gold, sir! Your gold and my gold and God knows who else's! They spoke of nothing else, sir, those long nights in the dungeons. A regular treasure house, sir, enough for everybody! A hoard to rival the busiest ships on the Spanish Main! My brother Maynard here, he saw it!'

The miller squinted at his blustering brother. He'd seen no such thing!

Fey bristled with anger, glared about the smashed inn at the suddenly attentive faces of the guards. 'There was no gold aboard her, sir! She was a cheap Channel privateer, not a galleon!' Fey cried, a little hysterically.

The merchant, glancing about the room to ensure the greedy dogs lurking in the shadows had heard him, feigned surprise. 'Ah, you've swallowed old Cruickshank's story too, eh? The truth is, sir, the *Purse* could barely float, she was carrying such a weight of—'

'Enough! Mr Grey, get these men back up to the courthouse at once! Double the guards, I do not intend to be taken by surprise this night!'

Gallen Fey had pursued the stragglers up the snow-laden street, harrying every gossiping, gold-hungry wretch from his crude shelter. He had broken up every mob he found, sent the tell-tales off to the furthest perimeter of his hard-won enclave, curses ringing in their frosty ears. But despite the captain's iron-jawed efforts, the news of the *Purse*'s reputed treasure hoard had spread like Greek fire in a powder mill, ensnaring even the dullest of minds, exciting every chilled heart. Fey could no more clamp down their grubby gossip than he could order a change in the weather. Within half an hour of the merchant's shrewd outburst, every man jack of them knew the *Purse* hadn't been able to escape because she had been loaded to the gunwales with a king's ransom. A fortune for every man, just lying on the softly oozing harbour mud. A fortune the strutting sea captain wanted to leave behind.

The captain had busied himself trying to quash the wildfire rumours, leaving the wretched prisoners in Will's bewildered care for a moment. Sir Gilbert lost no time in fastening himself on to the brooding youth, helping himself to the scrap of dried bread they had found in the smoke-clogged pantry. A few charred vittles and a couple of jugs of warm ale had kept the wolves of their hunger at bay for a moment, as they crouched and waited for the dawn in the stinking inn.

'Fancy folk you've taken up with, Will, all this shouting and bawling's fair turned my stomach.' The merchant patted his outsize belly in silent contemplation for a moment. 'But I know you of old, Will, a good, solid, plain-minded lad, if you don't mind me sayin'.'

William stared at the miserable remains of the fire they had banked up in the burnt-out grate, too tired to protest as the merchant poured honey into his sooty ear.

'I thought I'd best keep my mouth closed about the other business,' he said guardedly. William opened one eye, wondering what he was getting at now. 'Well, don't sit there grinning like a fish, boy, you know who I mean. Mary!'

'Mary? She's here too?' William asked hoarsely. He had barely come to terms with poor Annie's death without . . .

'I didn't like to mention it in front of that pale lickspit. You not being wed and all.' William sighed with relief as the merchant ruminated. 'She's away safe for now, back to the mill I shouldn't wonder. Too heavy to keep up, you see, when we went to the church.' He patted his belly in silent parody of Mary's rounded abdomen.

William ground his heavily stubbled jaw in frustration. He had heard all about the Morrisons' outrageous adventures, but hadn't suspected his own sweetheart might have been tied up with their nuptial arrangements. He dared not even contemplate bringing a child into the world now, not with the war ruining everything and everyone.

'I could take you back to her, if you can grab us a brace of good horses. You know I'm not exactly popular with the Parliament these days, to tell the truth, I've not exactly prospered with the King's men,' the merchant complained miserably.

William shook his head. 'You've cooked your damned stew, Sir Gilbert, it's up to you how you fork it out the pot.'

The merchant turned his eager amber eye on his former employee, too big for his boots with these damnable cut-throats he'd taken up with. Still, William had always been a kindly enough lad – and he'd always been partial to young Bella. He nodded shrewdly at the poor girl, squatting with her head between her knees on the far side of the lonely fireplace, tortured with guilt for her lost friend.

'I wouldn't ask for myself, of course. But Bella there, she's all I've got, the only scratch of summer I've left.'

William sighed. 'I thought you'd resigned yourself to losing her to that prickster Telling! I'd like to know where he's got to!' William observed, brightening up a little. How was it he could be transported hundreds of miles around the coast and still bump into the slender-buttocked stoat? Sir Gilbert chuckled to himself.

'Ah, he's more lives than a cat. And I had no choice when it came to him and my Bella. Good prospects don't grow from seed, young man, as I've often told you in the past. But the young whippersnapper's safely out of the way awhile. If you could only get us clear, I'm sure my Bella would be ever so grateful to you, forget all about the little shithouse.'

'Forget all about him? You've tried that one on me before!'

'Ah, William, I always preferred you to him, you know that well enough. Straightforward sort of a chap, down-to-earth. You and I now, we understand each other. That Telling's always up to some pie-eyed scheme, he's his head in the stars, that one.'

William thrust out his chin. 'I never knew you thought so much of me,' he sneered. 'All this time without a word.'

'Damn me, Will, but you've a short memory. Who was it gave you your commission in the first place? A start in the militia?'

'That scrap wasn't worth the paper it was written on and you know it,' William argued, losing his temper. 'When you buggered off you left me and Jamie to face it – good Christ, it's no wonder he's lost his mind, trying to keep tabs on your blasted wheeling and dealing!'

Sir Gilbert sat back with a distressed sigh, shaking his flushed head in disbelief. 'Trying to keep my head above water, that's all. Guilty of attempting to hold family and fortune together.' He dabbed a tear from his eye. William, vastly more experienced in all aspects of life after five months dragging around behind the colours, gave him a sour grin.

'You were banking on all this being over by now, the rebels packed off to the Tower or worse and all the King's loyal merchants busy helping clear up the mess. Nobody forced you to run out on us,' William accused.

'I didn't run out, lad, I merely realigned myself. By God, it looks as if you might have to think along the same lines, stuck in this damned hole. You're just as much a prisoner as I am!'

William recoiled, stung by the miserable truth of the merchant's outburst. With the *Doubloon* wrecked and the courthouse held against them, they would have to scatter like a flock of sand martins to stand any hope of escape. Chests of gold and jewels? They would be lucky to escape with their breeches!

'It won't be long before the devils get reinforcements. This is their county now, William. They'll be here in what, a day, two? And what then? You and your brave sailor friends, a few musketeers, and some half-starved magpies from the quarry. That'll be enough to stop Prince Maurice in his tracks, will it?'

William grasped his knees, seething with frustrated fury. The blasted turncoat was right, of course. Their only hope would be to take to the hills, sneak off by the back lanes and byways. Sleeping under hedges and stealing from isolated farms. How far was it to Poole? He cursed his inadequate geography.

'Think about it, William. You've no real ties to these people. They would leave you here to starve or slaughter without a thought, let me tell you. I know their sort, these mouthy buggers who get so hot under the collar it's a wonder they don't choke to death and do us all a favour. You get the horses, I'll show you the way out. That crack

411

young Butcher was spouting about, it takes you right up into the woods. We can be away to brother Maynard's mill, pick up Mary and be off. Bristol, Wales, the north.'

'What about my troops? Gillingfeather, Muffet, and the rest?'

Sir Gilbert shrugged. 'How many horses have you got?' he asked casually.

William snorted, stared back into the fire as if he could read his future in the glowing embers.

'Just you think about it, my lad,' Sir Gilbert suggested, edging away from the brooding captain and resuming his place beside his fitfully dozing brother.

William was still chewing over their demoralizing predicament half an hour later, when the muttering pack had finally worked up the will to challenge Fey's brittle plan of campaign. The furtive petitioners had slunk back down the street, holding impromptu conferences in every wrecked pantry. Three of them had been nominated as spokesmen for the gold-greedy mob, Bob Riley, a bow-legged country boy with a cast in his eye and a wet red tongue, John Ruell, his arms worked to sticks by two years' hard labour in the quarry, and Shem Bentham, a London sharper who had joined Fey's crew at Chatham. The latter, towering over the rest in his tall felt hat, brushed the worst of the snow from his rumpled coat, eyeing the startled captain cornered by the guttering fire.

'What is it? Have they made a sally?' William enquired, reaching for his sword. Bentham shook his head, glancing over his shoulder for support. Riley and Ruell were behind him, looted pistols in their fists. A crowd of anxious faces swarmed in the doorway, more of them peered in the smashed windows. William felt the hairs on his hot neck prickle with anticipation.

'Captain Sparrow, sir,' Bentham began, nodding his long, donkey's head in exaggerated servitude. 'You'll pardon us bargin' in, like, but we thought we might have a word.'

Sir Gilbert, rolled up beside the fire in a badly singed blanket, opened one eye, chuckling under his breath at his own audacity. It hadn't taken the dogs long to seize his bait.

William crammed his helmet on his head in an attempt to look as imposing as possible. Where in seven hells was Fey? Don't say they had already done him in!

'We've been wonderin', sir, that is, me and the men, like, about this gold we hear tell of.'

'You heard Captain Fey,' William growled. 'A silly story to impress some doxy,' he said casually. The grinning tribunal seemed to be staring straight through him, studying his pale reflection on the burnt bricks. They'd kill him without a thought, just like they had butchered the villagers.

'Aye, sir. We've all tried to pass it off and all, true we have,' Bentham said sadly. 'Only the trouble is, once your man there's planted the idea, it tends to stick in the old brain box, sir. And we was wonderin', sir, what 'arm there'd be, taking a sly glance down at her, sir. To make sure, sir.'

'In this weather? The tide's in – your blood would turn to lamp oil in a blink, man!'

'Well, that's true enough, sir, but with a hold full of gold aboard that wreck, sir, well, maybe it'd warm the water up for us, sir, beggin' your pardon, of course.'

CROSSBONE QUAY,

PENMETHOCK

The freshening wind worried the loose snow from the drunken tangle of masts and spars, blew the powdered flakes from the twisted superstructure of the partially submerged ships and into the faces of the silent crowd on the quay. The wrecks reminded William of beached whales on some Severn sandbank, their rotting hulks studded with broken timbers and shot-blasted ribs. Scraps of sail hung from their leprous masts. The tide had lifted their shattered bows and run the holed hulls against the harbour wall, the flooded holds awash with cargoes of scummy brine and inquisitive fish. The rushing water, dull grey in the first feeble glimmer of the dawn, looked lifeless, chill as a dead man's eyes.

William turned from the sullen harbour to the crowd of eager raiders, packed in behind him as if they were terrified they were going to miss something. As if the weary captain could summon their precious gold by power of thought alone. The wretched prisoner they had picked out from the dispirited crowd in the warehouse was gasping like a freshly landed pollack, convinced the Roundheads meant to throw him into the bobbing flotsam after their rightful prize. Sparrow wondered again where Fey had got to, what could have kept him at the other end of the village all this time. Surely they hadn't done him in already, trapped the surly sea captain in a snow-choked alley? Well, he knew one thing – he wasn't going to wind up lying in a dirty ditch with him. Fey could rant and rave all he cared – the stiff-necked fool would no more stop the men from seeking out their fortune than he could turn back the tide. Damn him and his damned pride.

The humble delegation which had assumed command of Fey's fighters was following his gaze, staring at the miserable wrecks like urchins weeping over lost toys. Sir Gilbert, who they had brought along as some kind of lucky mascot – a ruddy-faced diviner of hidden treasure – swallowed nervously, as if he was wondering how they would salvage as much as a brass penny from the sagging hulks. He had played a dangerous game, stringing them along with his fanciful tales, and would no doubt be the first to suffer if his dungeon gossip proved unfounded. William had spent an anxious half-hour eavesdropping on their cock-eyed plans, listening to the merchant outline some hare-brained scheme to the muttering cabal back at the inn. Whatever it was, the maybe mutineers had seemed reasonably pleased with Morrison's serpentine sorcery.

'This gold of yours – if it exists, mind you – could be anywhere,' William called, anxious to hang on to the little authority the merchant had left him. The *Purse* had settled on her side, pock-marked forecastle and leaning deck proud of the water. The partially demolished lower decks would be a nightmare of twisted wreckage and smashed guns, broken bodies bobbing in the drowned maze.

'We thought of that and all,' Shem Bentham snapped, irritated by the delay. He knew the tides as well as any, had he expected to stumble over a bursting chest, conveniently washed up on the mudflats? The Chatham dockhand scowled down at the water, knowing it was an hour and more off the ebb. The *Purse* would need to settle and drain before they could even think of venturing aboard, lifting the splintered hatches. He also knew he would lose his fragile influence over the mob, if he could not guarantee some kind of continued impetus. Bentham turned to their prisoner, a crooked wretch with a hastily combed-out pigtail. Bob Riley pushed the man forward, a dozen iron hands clamped about his narrow shoulders.

'Hold yer water, matey, we're not going to throw you in the oggin – not yet at any rate.'

The bloodily beaten seaman looked imploringly at William, as if the captain would leap to his rescue. The eager pack jostled and pushed, further alarming the sacrificial sailor.

'Now, lad, you're an old hand and it's no use denying it. You've heard the stories about Cruickshank's gold same as we have.'

The wild-eyed prisoner shook his head as if he wanted to part company with his shackled body. Admitting a career on one of the King's privateers would be as good as signing his own death warrant.

'I've ne'er heard no stories,' the man gasped in a thick northern accent. 'I've ne'er served aboard the *Purse*, sir, not me, ne'er!' he insisted, trembling like a feather in a gale. Bentham, giant with his own menace, picked up the man's hands and turned them over, inspected his callused palms.

'Nets, sir. I'm a netsman hereabouts.'

Bentham suddenly sidestepped his blubbering victim, tearing the ragged shirt from his back. He whistled in mock astonishment at the vivid scars, pink and white flesh knotted like knitting across his arched spine.

'You didn't get these in a mackerel boat,' he leered, grasping the man's tangled black hair and hurling him out over the sullen water – only dragging the screeching wretch back at the last moment. The prisoner writhed in pain, standing on tiptoes to retain his fragile contact with the quay.

'You're one of Cruickshank's crew, you beef-witted turd! Don't imagine you're saucing some prick-brained officer now, my lad!'

William ran his tongue over his teeth, paralysed with frustrated rage as the brute made sport with the prisoner.

'Now where does the old bastard keep his loose change, eh? Where's he hidden his baubles?'

'Baubles? I've ne'er seen no baubles, trust me, sir!'

Bentham lifted his dagger to the man's taut spine, tickled the skin with the wicked point. 'His trove, his gold, his jewels. He didn't work the sealanes for the benefit of his health,' Bentham threatened, working the blade between the squirming prisoner's vertebrae, releasing a starfish of bright blood. The prisoner howled with agony, throwing back his head like a wolf. William didn't recognize him. Perhaps it would have been easier to watch him suffering if he could have picked the man out as one of his tormentors. He imagined the memory of his own treatment aboard the wretched vessel would extinguish his natural sympathy – left him as stone-hearted as the greedy sailors. He could all too easily recall their laughing faces the day they were thrown overboard, the unquestioning obedience as they followed their mad dog of a captain's inhuman instructions.

'He kept a chest!' the man yelped, dancing on the digging blade.

'Where?'

'In his cabin, of course, hidden.'

'Where?'

'Don't kn–know.'

'Captain Sparrow!'

The expectant raiders pressed in around the vicious interrogation leapt about as Gallen Fey strode down the quay, a small squad of his trusted crew-members hurrying behind, muskets sloped and match fuming. He marched briskly across the snowy quay, pushing and shoving the belligerent raiders out of his path. William sighed with relief, his guts heaving under his prickly skin. He'd never had a taste for torture, even as a thoughtless child. Pulling the wings from birds or the legs from a slippery toad had never snared his imagination as it had some of his play-mates. Soldiering had opened up whole new vistas of pain and cruelty, but this helpless wretch's red-mouthed suffer-ings gave him no pleasure. He felt numbed, scoured by hurt he could not control. Fey burst through the leering tribunal, eyeing the bloody brutes with furious disbelief.

'Captain Sparrow,' he repeated, dry mouthed. 'I gave precise orders the prisoners were to be left in the ware-house. What is that tub of grease doing here?' He pointed his shaking finger at the canny merchant, who had taken up station behind the strapping deckhand. 'Get these men back to the works!'

William shrugged with helpless resignation.

'They wouldn't listen, once he'd started,' he reported, nodding at his erstwhile employer. 'They're after the gold.'

'There is no gold,' Fey shrieked. 'And even if there were it would stay precisely where it was!'

Sparrow closed his eyes, pummelled by the captain's ridiculous denials. He sensed the mood of the mob, the greedy faces darkening as they realized Fey meant to shoo them away from their fabulous hoard. The captain, used to the instant obedience of his crew, had failed to gauge their determination. It was a mistake which might cost them all their lives, God damn him. He peered up at John Grey, standing beside his master, weighing his sword, calculating the odds if push came to shove.

'I want you men back up at the courthouse. We attack in one hour!'

'You attack it, sir, we're staying here,' came a shout from the back.

'This man says there is gold aboard, sir,' Bentham reported, a model of ironic respect. 'Says he's seen it with his own eyes,' he elaborated for the sake of the waverers. 'Be a shame to leave it behind for the King's men, sir,' he said with cheery menace. 'Sir Gilbert thinks the tide will drop sufficiently for us to put a party of volunteers aboard.'

Fey closed his eyes as if pained by such a hideous suggestion, his spare features contorted by rage.

'Mr Grey, you will bind and gag that privy-sneaking merchant, and arrest Captain Sparrow here for inciting the men to mutiny. Mutiny, sir!' he exclaimed, turning his fanatical glare on the red-faced youth. 'I had my doubts about you in London, now I have had my worst suspicions confirmed!' The mob froze, holding their breath as if they might have fallen under his crazy spell. 'Well, sir?'

'I'm not inciting the men,' William protested, losing his temper at yet another unfounded allegation against him. 'I am merely pointing out—'

'You'll point nothing out to me, sir! Save your breath for your court martial!'

'There won't be a court martial,' Sparrow yelled, his temper snapping at last. 'You talked these men aboard for loot, nothing else! Now you must let them have their due! If there's any man here to be court-martialled it'll be you! This little jaunt is your own private crusade, it's nothing to do with the Parliament!'

Fey gasped at his impudence, glancing sideways at the burst of excited agreement behind his back, suddenly aware of the precariousness of his position. It was the second time in a matter of weeks he had stood at bay on that damned quay, surrounded by a sea of hostile faces.

'It would be better for all concerned,' William called over the tumult, 'if we searched the ship. If there is gold, we'll all get a share.'

'And how do you propose to move this gold?' Fey shouted in exasperation. 'You'll be lucky to get these men aboard the fishing boats, let alone their loot!'

'We'll carry it out, sir, don't you worry.'

'By road, you mean? Never! D'you think those dogs in the assizes mean to let us pass?'

'We'll worry about the courthouse afterward,' Bentham argued with dangerous patience, as if he was trying to convince an unruly schoolboy of the error of his ways. Fey turned from the leering sailor to the tormented captain.

'Traitor!' Fey snarled, shaking off the prying hands which had pressed in from all sides, pushing him forward, shoving him back in a deadly waltz. 'You put them up to this!'

'Put him down!' Sparrow ordered, shrewd enough to know the men would obey him now. Now he had given them his promise they would at least search the damned ship. The leering looters stood back from the apoplectic captain, who bristled and strutted and eyed Sparrow as if he had grown a set of horns and a forked tail.

'We'll need a couple of those fishing boats, and half a dozen strong swimmers. The rest of you will go back to the works with Captain Fey, Mr Grey, and Mr Bentham here.' The muttering mob didn't like the sound of allowing strangers to inspect the treasure-packed wreck.

'I'm staying,' Bentham growled.

'Then who will *escort* Captain Fey?'

'Escort, is it? You've a fine set of words to describe your treachery, I'll give you that.'

Sparrow ignored the captain's outburst. 'You will escort the captain to the assizes, keep an eye on the place till we get back one way or the other. You will not harm the captain nor any of his crew. Is that clear?'

The mutinous pack looked surly and uncertain.

'It'll be no use filling your pockets if the King's men come,' he warned. 'You'll need to buy us time to look over that damned ship!'

Fey shook his head in defiant contempt. 'And what if you do manage to fill their pockets with gold, Sparrow, have you thought of that? Do you think they'll stand and fight for you, do you imagine they'll march for you?'

Sparrow hadn't allowed himself to ponder the complexities of their escape. He had saved lives here, no matter what the short-arsed coxcomb claimed. Shem Bentham rolled his long head with serene indifference.

'I told you. We're not sailing out, sir. We're marching out.'

It was news to Sparrow. Damn that wily house snake Morrison! Marching out? Out where?

'Sir Gilbert has the details,' Bentham reported, nodding at the grinning merchant.

Sparrow felt a cold stone of doubt slide into his belly. He'd been embroiled in the merchant's schemes and ruses before now.

'Sir Gilbert knows a way out?'

'He's taken it himself. Nothing for you to bother yourself with now, sir.'

Fey bristled at the abrupt dismissal, realizing at last he had been effectively relieved, on pain of death, of his questionable command. 'I'm glad to see you've everything under control,' he sneered.

'As in control as you were, sir, bringing us in here in the first place,' Bentham replied with stinging contempt.

Sparrow waved his sword at the becalmed privateer. 'It'll do no harm searching her, sir. The decks won't take all of them at any rate. The rest will march back to the courthouse, tighten the cordon.'

Fey deliberately ignored the younger man's suggestion, folding his arms across his narrow chest. Grey, always a little more down to earth than his high-minded master, nodded soberly.

'Right you are. With your permission, Captain?'

Fey flicked his wrist like an insolent schoolboy. Sparrow sighed with relief. Fey could strut and pose all he wished. He was nothing but a damned martinet after all.

'Right, let's have the good swimmers to the front. Not you, Sir Gilbert.'

BY

SMAYLE TOWER,

OUTSIDE EXETER

They had been at it days now. Pick and shovel, sack and basket, repairing the defences Prince Maurice's army had rampaged through bare weeks before. Away across the frozen fields the toiling work parties could see the sun slanting from the tiles of the clustered homes, the warm winter billets they had confidently expected to be enjoying by now. By God, the Cornish infantry deserved a break, the toils and troubles they had endured that year on behalf of their distant sovereign. But instead of a well-deserved rest, the itchy-fingered rogues who made up Scipio Porthcurn's regiment of foot had been put to work out on the scant walls, making good the breaches they had torn in Exeter's overextended underbelly. The newly liberated city had been chosen as His Majesty's capital in the loyal west, and orders had been received to place the city in an adequate state of defence for the future. Porthcurn's men, wreckers and brawlers all, hadn't taken kindly to their unfamiliar role.

'Bliddy weeks gettin' in 'er, and no soon's taken they sez get 'er drawers back on,' a surly bricklayer in a soiled red suit complained, easing his muscular buttocks over a partly filled gabion. The cursing devils despised digging even more than they disliked drill. They were seamen, fishermen, farmers, not bloody miners.

Jethro Polruan lifted the tired red Montero from his head, wiped his wrist across his creased brow.

'God's bones, I'll swear they searched high and low for this ground and all. I never seen rocks like it.'

A clatter of hoofs away down towards the Water Gate drew their wandering attention for a moment before they resumed digging. *Rat a tat tap. Rat a tat tap.* The frosted soil clung to spade and mattock, the flinty trench which had been filled in for the assault resisting their best excavations. As fast as they scraped and hacked the trampled diggings were hidden by fresh flurries of snow.

'Mind you, boys, it could be worse. We might be off with the Princy feller to Plymouth, there'll be more dirty work there yet.'

'Plymouth? What's Plymouth got that Ex'ter hadden?'

Plymouth couldn't last long. Everybody said the same. Prince Maurice's veterans would swarm the breaches, force their way into the great port as easily as they had devoured Exeter. Gideon Wooly, the lanky pikeman in the badly dressed sheepskin, wasn't so sure.

'They said the same about Glo'ster and all, and look what happened there,' he observed smugly. 'Goin' on twenny thousand men, and we never set foot in the place at all.'

'That's cuz they left the job to them Oxford pricksters. If we'd been there we'd been in an' at 'em in a day or so,' Polruan boasted, knowing there wasn't a man in the company who would dare gainsay him. The red-coated veteran was a head and shoulders taller than any of the rest, and his frame bore more scars than a cannon barrel.

The regiment he championed had been assigned to guard the newly liberated rear areas, which had remained firmly in Parliamentarian hands up until that fateful summer. They had been left back at Exeter while the Prince continued his triumphant march. Maurice had assembled his most powerful army yet to complete the subjugation of the west, taking Exeter and Dartmouth in quick succession. But the veteran army had got bogged down outside Plymouth, and the sudden drop in temperature had not managed to blow the fever and pestilences from the frigid camp. Now if they weren't digging trenches they were scraping graves. It was said the Prince himself was at death's door, struck down with a sweating epidemic, and that the King had sent his magician of a surgeon, William Harvey, down from Oxford to nurse him. Whether their commander lived or no, his Cornish regiments had failed to force their way between Plymouth's defiant forts. Now the long summer of triumph and conquest looked like ending in a disappointing winter stand-off.

'Hello,' Simon Shevick called, lifting his hat to peer down the snow-capped hill towards the ragged clumps of tents and covered wagons which formed their nightly laager, 'here comes Scabby Poorcunt.'

Scipio Porthcurn's surly fighters peered out of their soil-heaped holes like red-coated moles, watched their scowling officer pick his way up between the blasted pits and ash-heaps which disfigured the frosty hillside. Behind him, a gaggle of eager young captains struggled to keep up with their hot-tempered chief. Scipio Porthcurn wasn't much more experienced himself: one of the youngest colonels in the army, a volatile disciplinarian with as filthy a tongue as his men. He had led them ever since Lansdown, when his unlucky predecessor had rushed too quickly towards a Roundhead trench and been beaten to death for his trouble. The rascals had tried to lead Porthcurn into similar scrapes, but the black-pated bastard generally managed to fight his way through anyway, and would then cheerfully berate his men for hanging back with the women and camp-followers. The burly Cornishman strode through the rubbish and refuse and crouched down amongst the diggers. Porthcurn caught his breath, frowning at the barely repaired defences. 'You idle tarts. I said six feet deep! You're not here to plant carrots, you scrofulous donkeys!'

The sweaty diggers bridled under the all too familiar outburst. Polruan, their champion and unofficial mouthpiece, settled his Montero on his frozen head, leering back at his tormentor.

'I was just saying, sir, this ground's like pig-iron. I'd sooner dig me mother's grave,' he observed with a wink at his cronies.

Porthcurn raised his black-bearded jaw. 'You never had a mother, Polruan, you were whelped by a poxy sea cow and got washed up on the last tide!' A few of them laughed.

'Ah, sir, we're not cut out for spadework and siegecraft and sichlike,' Simon Shevick complained. 'We're fighting men, not miners!'

'You needn't tell me,' Porthcurn replied, squinting over the deserted wastes toward the silent walls of the liberated city. 'I remember Bristol. Fill a wagon with faggots, boys, we'll bridge the bloody moat. Oh, no. Not you.' The colonel shook his head, slapped his hands on his thighs. 'Anyway. If it's a scrap you're after, we've got orders.'

The men crowded in, picks and spades clattering to

the hard ground as the soldiers pressed in about their bad-tempered chief.

'Seems the rebels have seized one of the supply ports. Penmethock.' There was a chorus of whistles and muttered comments. They had all heard of Penmethock, aye, and Black Bob. But wasn't Major Brinks supposed to be guarding the place? 'And there'll be scores to settle. They've done in half your comrades. Hung 'em up in the street like salt fish, so the survivors say.'

The muttered comments turned to shouts of outrage, as Porthcurn outlined the sketchy details he had beaten out of one of the miserable deserters who had stumbled into camp that dawn. A boatload of intruders, Vikings in red jackets crying King Jesus as they hacked and spitted the surprised defenders. Porthcurn had shaken his head too, when he had heard the news. Penmethock was supposed to be one of the most secure bases along the newly won coast, a veritable fortress. Sadly, it seemed the fortress had fallen like a ripe apple, and his bloody garrison with it. Somebody would be paying for that piece of insolence.

'They've turfed our boys out, it's up to us to get it back,' Porthcurn told them. 'After all, a few mad Roundheads aren't going to make me a laughing stock,' he vowed. Nobody on that frozen hillside doubted him.

PENMETHOCK ASSIZES,

DORSET

Black Bob had gotten away safely, that was one thing. But his younger son couldn't help wondering whether it would have been better for all concerned if he had been killed by a chance shot, cut down by a sharpshooter's bullet before he could put any of his increasingly unhinged stratagems into effect. His near demented insistence on the bloody persecution of the invaders would see chained men queuing under Black Bob's gallows, sow bitter seeds of vengeance in the hearts of their compatriots. The young lord had felt an immediate surge of shame for even thinking such a thing, but the insinuating doubts crept back into his consciousness, whispering heresies in his red-raw ear.

Black Bob wouldn't rest until he'd hung every man jack of the invaders from the Bloody Mare in the courtyard. He'd said so himself, storming about the upper floor of the besieged assizes while the snow squalled and the muskets popped into the never-ending night. Even the piratical Cruickshank had paled slightly as the old judge raved, the feeble spittle running down his chin as he berated the cowards and scoundrels who had dared set foot in his country.

'Ah, boy, I can see you've no stomach for strong medicine, never have had! But if you surrender yourself to mercy and meekness, this corruption, this canker of rebellion – ' he snarled the word as if it ran like bile over his tongue, 'it will spread like a pox, infect the entire state from top to bottom. Cut it out, I say. Out!'

The demoralized youngster had listened to his father rant, his slack-skinned hands clenched by his sides as he strode up and down the chill chamber. His father seemed to have sensed his reluctance to wash his hands in Roundhead blood.

'One breath of this foul rebellion and you are infected, undermined,' he warned. 'One spotted worm gnaws away at the roots, and eats the mighty oak out from beneath. Our duty is clear, at least to me. We must redouble our efforts, we must root out this pestilence, grind the grub beneath our boots!'

Clavincale's heart weighed ever more heavily in his chest, each sorry beat the hollow thump of a broken drum. His father would not rest until he had slaked his thirst, eaten his fill of vengeance. But the Roundheads who swung from their snowy gallows would surely multiply like Hydra's heads, a dozen fanatical warriors rising from each bloated corpse. Where would it ever end?

He looked up from his frozen post beside the window, watched Cruickshank make his way from man to man, murmuring a word of encouragement where it was needed, sharing a callous jest with his reunited crew-members. The lanky pirate grinned at Telling, waved him to one side as he studied the snow-clad village through Black Bob's perspective glass. The blackguard lowered the glass, frowned at the sleet blowing across the deserted courtyard.

The enemy had been tumbled out of the courthouse and then chased from the yard itself, terrorized by Cruickshank's blood-curdling yells and threats, piked and clubbed by the mad berserkers packed in behind him. Pale pillows of drifted snow marked the whereabouts of the unfortunates who hadn't managed to escape their swinging cutlasses. Their own men had reoccupied the outhouses, Clavincale could see the pale points of their match burning beside the pock-marked walls like tiny insect eyes.

Black Bob had been spirited away in the sinister lull after the fight, guided out of a gap in the wall by Abraham Bacon and a bodyguard of trusted musketeers, sworn to give their lives for that miserable, dried-up prune of a man.

Clavincale wondered where they had gone, guiltily aware they might have already been done in by the swarming invaders. Would they have set off towards the house? Surely they had seen the frightful pall of smoke over the hill the same as the rest of them. Taken cover in one of the hidden coombs which ran in all directions over the windswept slopes? The fact his own home might well have been reduced to ashes beneath that dreadful pyre hardly bothered him. It was nothing more than a web-shrouded belfry, a gutted tomb doomed to everlasting night. A place where laughter had been forgotten, driven out with Puritanical insistence by its ghastly master.

Perhaps the Roundhead raiders had lain in wait, enticed the fugitives into the house before setting the place on fire? His own father set atop the bonfire like a . . .

'They've been too quiet for my liking,' Cruickshank growled, startling him out of his disjointed reverie. The captain, who had been swaggering around Black Bob's courthouse like some eastern sultan following the judge's somewhat hasty departure, gnawed his knuckle in

430

momentary concern, nodding out of the window towards the distant sea.

'That was too easy, lad. A couple of hundred of the buggers and we only catch a dozen? Where's the rest, eh?'

Clavincale felt hideously exposed, his military short-comings all too obvious to the cunning devil in the wind-worn sea-coat. 'Driven off by the villagers?' he suggested, anxious not to look too foolish.

Cruickshank snorted, raised the spyglass, and swept it from right to left over the gloomy village. 'They're off long since, along with Brinks's pox-sorry specimens,' he growled to himself. 'What in God's bowels are they about, eh?'

Clavincale stared at the burnt-out husk of the village, wondering where the displaced citizens had hidden themselves from the foul weather. He wouldn't care to spend a night on the bare cliffs, not in these squalls, let alone the women and children who had fled their ransacked homes.

The weary captain rubbed his eye, grinned wearily at the young nobleman. 'Don't fret yourself, lad,' he encouraged, mistaking Clavincale's despondency for concern over his father. 'They weren't bothered with the judge.'

'You sound very sure of yourself, Captain,' Clavincale said shortly.

The buccaneer's hard life and long toils were engraved in the tiny wrinkles about his pale eyes.

'Aye well, they won't be bothering with Black ... your father, when they've trapped me. That hairy ape in charge of their musketeers, he was one of 'em. The old duffer and straw-head boy with him. And then that great Swede we saw hiding on the wagon. I knew 'em from somewhere.'

Clavincale frowned, trying not to look too bewildered. 'Deserters, I imagine?'

'Deserters? Probably. I took a passel of 'em aboard the *Purse* this summer for service in the Netherlands. Had a little trouble with a bull of a Roundhead in Lyme Bay, so I had to let 'em off.' Cruickshank's pumice-stone skin wrinkled as he shook his head, plagued by the memories of his own merciless exploits. Ah, it hadn't just been a few lousy Roundheads he'd thrown overboard, had it?

'You put them ashore, you mean?'

'Over the side,' Cruickshank corrected.

Clavincale stared at the seaman, mesmerized, opening and closing his mouth in mute incomprehension. This brute had thrown them overboard? And by some appalling chance they had come back, to Penmethock, to hunt him down? He wondered for a moment if the damned rogue was making a fool of him, sending him up in front of the men.

'I had no choice, see, if I was to save my ship,' he concluded heavily.

The puzzled lordling looked from the burnt-out town to the pewter-featured captain, standing forlorn beside him. 'You threw them overboard? And they've come ashore here, to exact their revenge on these people?' he demanded disbelievingly.

Cruickshank flicked his wrist in distraction. 'A coincidence. Nothing more. Tis of no matter now, with help on the way from Plymouth.'

The youngster would not be put off. He gripped Cruickshank's coat sleeve, pulled him around. 'Those men came here, to the heart of King Charles' loyal West Country, to square accounts with you! What other explanation is there?'

Cruickshank bristled, irritated by the young pup's ignorant accusation. 'They could have come for your father, he's not exactly popular with those candle-wasting pricksters in Whitehall!'

The shrewd lordling sensed the captain's peevish outburst had been intended to do no more than deflect him.

'My father's reputation might have preceded him to Plymouth, sir, but I do not imagine he is of serious concern to the Parliamentary High Command! If these men have come for you, then all this,' he waved his paw toward the smashed window, 'all this piggery is your fault!'

Cruickshank had never cared to be reminded of that black day aboard the *Purse*. He was a wild-hearted rover cursed with a fearsome, keelhauling temper. He'd regretted it since, God damn him if he hadn't. But he couldn't undo things now, couldn't bring poor Caleb back. He had ordered his own half-daft son to be thrown overboard with the prisoners, a merciless punishment for failing to spot the pursuing Roundhead man-of-war while he was on duty aloft. He had condemned his own flesh and blood for the simple-minded mistake, a mistake any man could have made, given the eye of the storm had been swirling about them. Not one of his horrified crew, not even his trusted mate Edward Callow, had ever dared remind him of his work that day. By Christ, they didn't need to. Cruickshank didn't care to be confronted by the restlessly rampaging ghosts of his past, still less by a snot-nosed boy.

'Not just for me lad, not just for me. This isn't my first trip to your precious pot, and I've had dealings with your family before now,' he said darkly.

'My family are not Tangier pirates, sir. My father has never condemned a man without a trial!' Clavincale exclaimed, misunderstanding the captain's point.

'A trial? Hah! Is that what it was? This honey blob merchant's girl of yours. Would she have got a fair trial if your old man had realized who she was? The girl was doomed the same as those bastards back there!'

Clavincale sucked in his cheeks, his blue eyes widening in anxious bewilderment. 'What do you mean, realized who she was?'

Telling, who had become increasingly alarmed by their acrimonious exchange, stepped away from his window, shadowing the argumentative pair.

'He didn't know maid's milk from vinegar! Your man Bacon had a notion, but I think he fancied his chances with her, same as me.'

Clavincale flushed with resentment. 'Knew what?'

'That she'd done in your lump of a brother,' Cruickshank snarled, as if he had been unable to keep a lid on the bubbling cauldron of his hatreds, as if he had told the boy in spite of himself. 'You must have heard the reports, same as I had. He'd taken up with some muck-raker of a merchant, fallen for his prick-teasing daughter. Merchant Morrison's daughter,' Cruickshank bellowed.

Telling blanched, wondering whether to run out on them or strike while the brute's back was turned.

Clavincale barely registered his existence. His world had collapsed about his burning ears. He felt the courthouse slide and pitch under his feet, as if he too had been roped with the sacrificial bundles aboard Cruickshank's foul ship. Bella Morrison, beautiful Bella, the cunning authoress of his own brother's murder? The bastard lied. His panic-stricken eyes flickered to the agonized Cavalier, as if he guessed the whole world knew his weakness for her.

Telling stalked up behind the captain, bristling with helpless agitation, dumbfounded by Cruickshank's breathless revelations.

'Ah, stare all you like, my little house dove. But I had it first-hand from an old matey of mine, a certain Colonel Nybb. D'you know him? He was there and saw it all. Done in by the harlot and her ballock-brained lover.'

Telling closed his eyes at the hideous description of himself, blushing like a pan full of cinders. Nybb had known his part in the affair and all, either this rogue was holding the information back for his own ends or he had forgotten the fact he was standing beside Clavincale's killer. Cruickshank glanced over his shoulder at the mortified youth, suddenly suspicious now the skinny wretch had crept up on him.

'And who's rattled your cage, my little storm petrel?'

Clavincale would not be shaken off. 'Bella Morrison, these men you threw overboard. All here.' He seemed to stagger at the vicious possibilities. Caught in a spider-web of conspiracy and cold-blooded murder. Bella!

Cruickshank, tickled by the obvious effect he was having on the gutless boys, seemed fit to burst with spite.

'And I'll tell you something else, laddie, before you go getting pious on me! Your brother's as much to blame for bringing them here! He talked me into taking the damned rebels aboard in the first place! Transport them to Antwerp, that was the deal, fifty–fifty on all proceeds.'

'Proceeds? You sold these men to slavery?'

'Into the Spanish army, sir! But the pay's about the same these days,' Cruickshank crowed. 'A fine company of men for the Archduke's Tercios. They'll not be the last, either, not by a long chalk!' He stuck out his weather-worn chin in defiance, daring the youngster to strike. Clavincale seethed with fury, his fists curling uselessly beside his breeches. Cruickshank grinned.

'Ah, you're a fine little turkeycock for strutting around beneath your father's wing, but you lose a little heat when he's not around to smother you all up, eh?' He peered over his shoulder at the Cavalier, stepping from one boot to the other in equal agitation. 'And you, get back to your post. I'm in command here, d'you hear?' Cruickshank stared around the room, jousted down every eye which dared hold his. The sullen defenders looked as if they had been turned to stone by their commander's tantrums. Humphrey Gale and his cronies, armed to the teeth and merry on Black Bob's brandy, grinned and winked, as full of themselves as ever. Cruickshank strutted over to them, instinctively recognizing the backbone of his support.

'Who's in command here?'

'You are, Captain!' the blackguards roared back. 'Huzzah for Crooksie!'

CROSSBONE QUAY,

PENMETHOCK

The brightly painted fishing boat stank like a whore's drawers, bobbing in the swell playing about the partially submerged wreck. Sparrow had squeezed in beside Sir Gilbert, who clutched the gunwale as if they were about to cross the Styx.

'I don't know what you told these buggers, but they'll be using your ballocks for shark bait if you've led them up the garden path,' William warned, watching Bentham steer the boat alongside the barnacled hull of the privateer.

'Damn me, William, if me own brother's lied to me. "A chest stuffed full of jewels and silver" were his words. He's fifty pound of mine aboard, at any rate.'

'Unless our friendly captain took it all ashore with him,' William said gruffly.

'Ashore? I wouldn't trust those bastards with a bent penny, I wouldn't. No, it's a fair bet he's left his hoard aboard, where he thought it was safe.'

'A fair bet? You've just said your brother saw it with his own eyes!'

'Well, not in so many words,' Sir Gilbert clarified, rolling his eyes at his jumped-up runner.

There was a muffled bump as the mutineers' mouthpiece stood up, tossed a grappling iron over the

Messalina's shattered belly, and made the boat fast. He grinned down at the scowling pair on the front thwart, winked at the others packed in behind. They had armed themselves with a variety of crowbars and hammers, coils of rope and tools looted from the gutted warehouse. Anything they could lay hands on which might be some use, ferreting out Mad Val's legendary nest egg. The wave-tossed volunteers reminded Sparrow of whalers coming up on their intended prey, harpoons at the ready. The boat lurched and leaped as Bentham tried the grappling iron, and then stepped gingerly onto the sea-smoothed planking, hauling himself up the taut rope like a monkey. He slipped and struck his knee, cursed and carried on, throwing his canvas-clad leg over the side and steadying himself aboard the leaning wreck. The deck fell away at an acute angle, slick with brine and tangled seaweeds. There was a clear tidemark around what was left of the gunwales, and trapped flotsam bobbed and washed this way and that within the flooded superstructure. Bentham waved the rest of them out of the boat and up the bloated belly, tugging Sparrow over by his coat. William held on tight, stepping along the angled deck to make room for the puffing merchant who followed – eager not to miss any of the fun. William slipped, made a despairing grab for the gunwale, and then lost his footing altogether. He slid down the deck with a furious squawk, splashing into the sullen water and kicking his legs against the bulging sack lodged against the shattered mast.

The sack turned belly-up with a revolting hiss of escaping gas, revealing the tallow features of Edward Callow, drowned mate of the *Messalina's Purse.* William squirmed away, teeth chattering as he thrashed through the shallow water running across the submerged deck. The bobbing body seemed drawn in his panic-stricken wake, following him like a bloated dog through the refuse washing through the flooded ship. Bentham grinned, watched his cursing progress toward the stern, the battered structure which housed Captain Cruickshank's gold-lousy quarters.

'Wait there, Captain,' he called. 'We're all in this together, you know,' he added warningly. Sparrow peered up at the scarecrow figure lurching along the gunwale, watched the dockhand haul himself hand over hand down the twisted rigging. Bentham let go, sliding down the deck on his canvas backside. He steadied himself, grunting as the cold water clamped his skinny legs, and waded over to the raised stern, pushing Callow's waterlogged carcass away from him. The companionway to the poop deck had been shot away, a splintered skeleton drowned by the grey water. The door beneath the jagged planking hung drunkenly on its torn hinges, the water washing in and out of the narrow gullet within. Sparrow peered down the submerged passage towards the great cabin, trying to reckon what little headroom the tide had left.

'We'll have to swim for it,' he told the suspicious mutineer peering over his shoulder. 'John, where's that rock-bollocked corsair of ours? Drag him on down!' Bentham gestured at the rest of the party, making their way along the dry deck with exaggerated caution, prodding their prisoner with them. The poor wretch was practically naked, his bunched shirt sagging over his torn breeches, hairy legs crooked with cold. John Ruell held on to the bunched clothing as the two of them skated down the deck, landing with a terrified splash in the lapping brine. The prisoner squinted down the drowned passage, his Adam's apple bobbing in his throat like the lost barrels banging against the hull.

The captain's cabin would be situated at the after end of the upper deck. Bentham stepped back, peered at the partially demolished housing trying to estimate the angle of water in the cabin. By his reckoning, a good half should be above the lapping waves. It might be enough for a thorough search, if they were quick. If not, they would have to swim back and wait for the damned tide to turn once more. And none of them could guess how long the enemy would allow them to continue their unauthorized salvage operations. He turned to Sparrow, nodded slyly. 'You go first, sir, we're right behind you.'

Sparrow frowned at the canny dockhand, a worn belaying-pin grasped in his scrawny fist. He turned back to the narrow passage, ducked his head under the torn doorway, and hauled himself along against the chilled current, the frigid water tugging at his striding legs. The cold gobbled his bones and froze his muscles, made every breath an agonized effort. He braced himself, his head jammed against the leaning ceiling. The ship must have settled on her stern, the water was deeper towards the back of the passage, sealing the captain's cabin from the grave-robbing intruders. He felt his belly turn over in anxiety, but the sour churning was lost in a rising tide of dry-mouthed excitement. What if the gold was there just as the merchant maintained? Just behind that flimsy little doorframe? He tried to batten down the hatches on his mercenary meditations, but could hardly help himself. The prospect of running his hands under a fountain of spluttering gold coins had taken a deep hold on his consciousness. God's wounds, he deserved something. He deserved something for his pains and labours, no matter what the ranters like Fey and Gillingfeather maintained.

Would they turn their backs on a potful of doubloons? He doubted it.

William made up his mind and breathed deeply, held his breath and ducked under the scummy wash. The water which had looked clear enough from the quay seemed to cloud up with every strangled step. He could hardly see a thing now, groping blindly against the heaving current. He tried hurrying on his lead-heavy legs along the gloomy passage, but the water seemed to be being sucked in and out of the ship's oak-panelled throat, drawn in and blown out by its barnacled lungs. The water bubbled and frothed about him, wrapping him, crushing him, tugging and probing at his eyes and mouth, dragging at his saturated clothing. William stumbled into the bulkhead, palms spread over the smooth wood. He squinted and blinked, cheeks bulging, fingers itching for a door handle. God's nails, where was it? He'd drown like the lousy looter he was. Food for the golden-scaled fishes, gaping mouths tugging at his crumbling, bloodless flesh.

His vision flared, and then his grasping thumb brushed against the submerged lock. His fingers fastened gratefully over the mechanism. He turned the handle and put his shoulder to the door which gave so slowly, slow torture in the drowned chamber. It felt as if he was pressing the narrow door into newly kneaded dough, a vast mattress stuffed with goose down. A cauldron of bubbles rushed past his bent body. He kicked for all he was worth, propelling himself into the captain's cabin.

He broke water with a racking cough, flapping his arms against the chill waters which would have trapped him. William heaved an agonized lungful of air, his throat raw with the effort. His vision stabilized slowly and he looked around the drowned cavern, taking in his new surroundings. The cabin had been completely submerged, and it would be again by high tide. Every shelf and rack had been scoured and emptied, charts and logs and letters and God knew what else besides draped over the upturned table and splintered chair, bobbing drunkenly against the rear wall. To his right, the captain's bunk and chest were submerged in six feet of water, soggy papers and items of clothing washing this way and that.

Bentham exploded out of the water beside him, clutching at Sparrow's arm as he hauled himself out of the flooded tunnel. The dockhand wiped his eyes with a furious splutter, blinking and gasping like a baited bear in a storm. He hauled himself up the leaning wall and began picking over the saturated shelving, a Thames mudlark all over again. William wiped the water out of his eyes, turning around slowly to make a cautious reconnaissance of the drowned cabin. The tangled boxes and rails under his feet snapped and grabbed at his chilled ankles, mantraps for unwary trespassers.

'What are we looking for?' he asked, eyeing the riddled timbers, the smashed windowframes which sagged between shot-twisted beams at the rear of the cabin. A few bits of pebble glass, not much thicker than the base of a beer jug, was all that remained of the elaborate decorations which had adorned the stern. He stumbled, steadied himself against the bobbing table, as Ruell propelled himself out of the pulsing vat of trapped water, hauling the spewing prisoner with him. The wretched man had swallowed at least a lungful of brine and was coughing raggedly over his captor's arm.

'Have you found it?'

'What does it look like,' Bentham growled, clambering

back down into the waterlogged hold. He waded through the water, grabbed the heaving prisoner around the neck, white fingers closing about the man's taut throat. He shook him like a dog, wrenching him through the cluttered swamp with a shriek of animal fury.

'Where's his chest? You've heard stories, you lousy bastard!' Bentham bawled, dragging his victim upright for a moment as if sheer terror alone could magic the treasure into existence.

'I've ne'er been in yere afore in me life, sir, on me word!'

Bentham snarled, pushed the terrified man face first into his own piss-green brine. The prisoner kicked and writhed, frothing spray splashing the grim-faced divers.

'To yer left! Under the bottles, that or his bunk!' the man shrieked, coughing and pointing at the wrecked furniture behind the mutineer's heaving shoulders. Bentham threw the half-strangled prisoner aside. Arms bound cruelly behind his back, he flopped into the floodwater, eyes bulging with horror as he kicked and struggled. William grabbed him by the arm and hauled his head out of the water, steadying the retching sailor as Bentham made a second forage up the wall, pulling and tugging the captain's wine bottles from their racks and lobbing them over his shoulder as he searched for the secret panel. He jabbed his sheath knife into the worn beading, prying for cracks. He worked his way along the leaning wall, tearing and tapping at the polished wood, grubby knuckles rapping out a fevered tattoo. Rat a tap tap. Rat a tat *tonk.*

Bentham froze, then redoubled his efforts, panting raggedly as a worn panel came away in his hand.

'I knew it! I knew it all the while!' he shrieked, tossing

the panel aside and bracing himself against the gloomy hidey-hole. Big enough for a man maybe, crouching like an owl in the bole of an oak. A sensible precaution for a sly buccaneer like Cruickshank. William watched the mutineer straighten up slowly, balancing himself on a submerged shelf as he cradled a small, tightly bound chest. His dark eyes glittered like the jewels he expected within, his scaly paw wrapped protectively over the inlaid lid.

'Got her! I knew it!' he cackled, jumping back down into the water.

'Watch it, you'll capsize us all,' Sparrow shouted, clinging on to the table as the ship stirred beneath them. Bentham tucked the chest under his arm, hanging on as Ruell clambered out of the water and ducked his head into the secret compartment, hidden from the inquisitive crew by the splintered panelling.

Not so secret after all, Sparrow thought, trying to settle the trembling prisoner on his feet. The terrified sailor was shaking so much he couldn't stand, slipping under the wavelets flexing his rope-bound fists. Bentham leaned over, grabbed the man's shackles, and thrust his bound arms up over his scarred back. The sailor flopped into the water with a bellow of agony, swallowing another lungful of brine. His frantic struggles knocked Sparrow backwards. He staggered into the drowned corner, splashing and kicking as he fought to find his feet. By the time he had straightened himself in the filthy hole, hauled himself up the woodwork, the prisoner had almost stopped kicking. His bound arms protruded from the bubbling cauldron at an impossible angle, rigid sticks in Bentham's pitiless fist. The white fingers pulsed and flickered, trembled and died. Bentham propelled the broken body into the flooded well of the cabin as if he was pushing a children's boat out over a pond. He staggered back with his prize, fingers busy about the lock. Ruell beamed down from the hidey hole, completely oblivious of their prisoner's squalid fate. He was holding up a handful of leather pouches by their saturated strings, the heavy bags ribbed and bulging with coin. Sparrow was panting like a broken-winded nag, glaring disbelievingly at the gloating mutineer.

'Ah, don't waste your breath on him, Captain,' Bentham advised evilly, his pale features almost transparent over his domed death's head, his wide mouth split over rows of bad teeth. 'He was dead the moment we clapped hands on him. We'll get no better, if they catch us down here, you know that same as I,' he explained with a peculiar, half-sad smile.

William was too exhausted to argue, too sick to his stomach to care. There was no point, no right, no reason in this drowned barrel, no sense nor pity in the dripping, weed-hung coffin. What difference would it make now, one more bobbing corpse? The sea would take all of them and more, aye, every man in England if necessary. He closed his eyes, his blood pumping listlessly around his chilled frame, slowing the sullen thoughts untangling themselves from the misty spheres of his reason.

He was no better than any of them, and probably never had been. The dormant seeds of everyday atrocity the men had carried from Chatham had flowered in his fists the same as they had in Bentham's. He was a willing co-conspirator, party to the squalid, pointless crimes being committed on those who had sinned against them. He shook his head, imagined for a moment he was sharing the dripping cavern with that precious barnacle-faced self-righteous Cromwell. What would the great man have made of this? How would he straighten this piggery with his all-powerful, all-forgiving God? Drowning men in their own piss-water, gutting women on long knives.

The tide crept higher, the rising water pulsing and thrumming around the battered hull, crushing the trembling plates of his throbbing skull so he had to hold on to a leaning shelf to prevent himself being sucked away altogether.

He was adrift with the rest of them, lost souls trying to soak up the anger and the agony of the bloody war just like the captain's saturated papers soaking up the sea around him. A carefully kept log detailing every death and danger, every bloody action the ship had seen during her brief and callous reign of terror, bobbing broken-backed in the bubbles past his bended knees. Smudged and faded, ink running like blood in the turbulent currents, the pages rifled and swollen, torn by the creeping fingers of the tide, chewed by ravenous wrasse. Her bloody deeds erased and her butcher's bill settled, squared by the all-conquering sea.

William stumbled and slipped back up the submerged passage, propelled by the *Messalina*'s lusty death rattle, carried like carrion on her bilge breath.

He was washed out onto the leaning deck, turning and tumbling on the current until he was hauled over the planking like a gasping tuna. Masts and barrels slid by his half-closed eyes, open mouths shouting gull-talk in his running ears.

The men were shrieking and yipping with excitement, Sir Gilbert leaning precariously over the frothing waist to peer down at their prizes. William braced himself against a ruptured crate, coughed a mouthful of bile-streaked brine down his trembling arm, staring at his wrinkled fingers as if he had strangled the drowned man himself.

It didn't matter who had held the prisoner under. They were all as guilty as the leering mutineer, standing like Neptune on the crippled privateer's blasted belly, chest under his arm as if he meant to hide it from the rest. Bentham was right. The nameless sailor had been doomed the moment they had picked him out from the rest. There had been no miraculous escape from the tossing waves for him, no steely hands to wrench him from the cold brink of oblivion. He imagined the body bobbing in the cabin, trapped in its tidal tomb. Perhaps one day the villagers would manage to salvage his fish-nibbled skeleton. Perhaps the sea would complete its work, carry the works and flood the defences, haul its bloodless prisoner down to the deep.

But at least *he* was alive, and if the damned war had taught him anything it was that staying alive was more important than anything else in creation. Never mind Fulke and Fey, Gillingfeather and the rest. He would rather be here on the deck, coughing his lungs up and fretting about the dead man than back in the cabin with him.

He felt a heavy hand on his shoulder, looked up to see the merchant, almost crying with relief at his expected salvation.

'God's bones, William, don't tell me you found my fifty!'

William blinked around at the bearded clown, wondering if he had the gall to pity the greedy huckster.

'Aye, we found your fifty. God be praised,' he said sourly. Sir Gilbert bristled.

'It's all right you getting all pious, laddie, they weren't about to string you up,' he snapped, making way as Bentham's triumphant searchers scrambled up the deck.

For those few all too brief moments on the quay they were transformed, their money-grubbing grimaces replaced by beaming smiles, capering about like mad things, their raucous high spirits bordering on the drunken. Bentham, their scowling champion, had fulfilled his promise and delivered their gold. All they wanted now was their fair share.

'Hang on, lads, it won't do to go sharing out this lot under the owner's nose! We'll make sure the stable door's bolted before we untie the horse, eh?'

Their grubby dreams were punctured in a blink. They frowned at one another, as if reluctant to undermine Bentham's fragile spell by protesting. Their apparent change of face had been misleading, their new-found enthusiasm only went so deep. Peering through their dull eyes William could almost picture their feverish calculations, their flexing brains pulsing with malicious inventions, throbbing with the primeval urge to run away and bury their ill-gotten fortunes. It was a miracle they had remained together this far, he thought glumly, trudging along behind them through the drifting snow which had obliterated the main street. Sir Gilbert was nodding and ducking like a prizefighter, as if he meant to dodge the snowflakes for fear of being scorched by God's crystalline creations.

'Damn them for a ragged-arsed rabble,' he complained. 'I thought you'd secured the place.'

William grunted, worked his frozen jaw before replying. 'You counted on them standing at their posts while their new-found friends searched the ship? I reckon you must be going soft in your dotage,' he snarled, sick, tired, and weary of the frosty wilderness they had inherited, the wretches he had been forced to count as his companions. He'd be glad to get back to the courthouse. An honest fight with sword in hand, let the best man win and stuff the rights and wherefores. Muffet and Butcher, daft Caleb and little Nicodemus in his outsize coat. He'd have that off his back and all, he thought vindictively. If he froze much longer he'd be as stiff as a board, cocooned for ever in his saturated rags. The merchant tugged his looted blanket tighter, rolled his eyes at his former runner.

'By Christ, lad, you've swallowed a little too much of your new master's sauce! You'll be crawling to me before we're out of this shit-pit, you mark my words!'

William raised his chin, glared defiantly at his wayward mentor. 'Oh, yes? Your little stratagem for getting us out of the gorge.' He had been wondering what the merchant had had in mind. Clearly it had been plausible enough to satisfy Bentham and his leering cronies. Sir Gilbert turned on his heel in a huff, bent his back against the blizzard playing down the deserted main street.

They lapsed into agitated silence, followed the filthy trails through the snow, and rejoined the battalion taking shelter around the village cross. The villagers' wagon barricade had been smothered, squashed in the middle of the street like a vast white loaf. Various settles and benches, tables and chests had been piled up behind it to form a rough stockade offering some protection from blizzard and bullet. William had expected to find the men busy dividing their spoils, shouting exchanges across the narrow street. But the wealthy mob seemed more downcast than ever, their spirits dashed by some new information from the long-neglected guards. William shook the snow from his soft hat, nodded at Long Col who had taken up station with his back to the market cross, his musket held loosely in the crook of his arm. The elder sergeant unpeeled the worn blanket he had thrown around his shoulders, wrapped the feverishly trembling captain in the warm rug.

'What is it? Reinforcements?' William asked dubiously, his teeth chattering. The veteran pulled his pipe from the corner of his mouth.

'They took the outhouses while you've been down there prospecting. We've pulled back to the village. That dew-cunt Cruickshank . . .' He shook his head in weary remorse. 'The buggers won't face him, you know.'

William peered up over the snow-clad wagon toward the menacing bulk of the courthouse. The ugly mausoleum was obscured by grey cloudbanks and slanting sleet. A formidable fortress blocking their exit from the gorge. It was either the road or the cliffs, or Fey's damned fishing boats. The buggers would slaughter them all before they would leave their loot behind. Drowning in the harbour with a coatful of coin, hah! He snorted in frustration, his weary frame weighed down with exhaustion, eyes stinging from the salt sea.

The last of their pitifully unreliable command were cowering or crouching where they could, miserably intent on staying within spitting distance of Bentham's fantastical chest.

'Where was Fey?' William snarled. 'He said he was going to organize an attack!'

Long Col laughed wearily. 'With this lot? They were

too busy craning their necks for news of your salvage job,' he said dejectedly. 'Buggered off at the first charge. Fey ducked into one of the houses there with Mr Grey and a few others and hasn't shown his nose since.' William grunted in disgust. 'Oh, aye, they've put his hooter out of joint, all right. The bloody fool would have got us all killed, facing up to 'em when they smelled shillings! It was the merchant's fault, of course. Damn this cold. Isn't there one place with a decent roof?'

Long Col sucked on his pipe, shook his grey head. Morrison's role in the sorry affair came as no surprise to him, at any rate. He'd had dealings with the slippery trader before, witnessed his astonishing double-dealing at first hand. He had also been at Roundway when the merchant's son Jamie – their acting company commander at the time – had been taken funny. The veteran had at least managed to take the daft youth under his wing, whistling him away with his reliable sharpshooters. Away from the clutches of his elastic-willed father and his weathercock cronies. You never knew when one of the trigger-happy bloats was going to let off next, or at what.

The cold had frosted Muffet's long moustaches, left glimmering snail trails of snot under his turned-up nose. 'They're a rotten crew, William. Mind yourself,' Muffet warned, nodding over Sparrow's shoulder at the approaching delegation.

'There you are, Captain!'

William looked up as the chief mutineer and his principal lieutenants pushed and barged their way through the muttering men, regarding the disgruntled officer as if they thought he was the author of all their misfortunes – but were too polite to say so.

'You've heard what's happened, I suppose. Cruick-shank sallied out and drove your boys from the stables! How d'you like that?' Bentham called.

Billy Butcher snorted with fury, wagged his finger at their half-frozen accuser.

'Leave us to do all the fightin' while you fuck off collecting seashells? We held 'em up all night and half the bleedin' morning! You've got a bleedin' nerve, matey!'

Bentham glared at the furious sharpshooter, modifying his expression as he turned back to his scowling commander.

'We was led to think Captain Fey was taking charge here. It was Captain Sparrow as suggested we salvage the *Purse*, he gave the order,' he argued slyly.

Sparrow yelped with laughter. 'You'd have searched that ship over our dead bodies and you know it,' he bellowed, every ragged-arsed musketeer and bewildered clubman straining his ears to eavesdrop on the acrimonious exchange. 'Now you've got your money, the sooner you divvy up the sooner we can get going,' he called. Bentham redoubled his hold on the chest in question, glanced at his doubting accomplices.

'You're in it as much as we,' he challenged.

Sparrow shrugged. 'We're all in it now. It's fifty miles to Poole, that's the nearest garrison. It'll take more than a pocketful of coin to lift you over Prince Maurice's horseboys,' he called. The famished attackers nodded miserably. Shem Bentham had found the gold, aye, but what good would it do 'em? The shifty-eyed dockhand fingered the precious chest.

'I reckon it's safer where we can keep an eye on it, go divvying up and we'll have half of 'em falling out, gambling their winnings away,' the Chatham philanthropist observed.

'I'm sure we're all touched by your concern,' Sparrow simpered, earning a ripple of ironic laughter from the tense fighters packed in around them.

'Well, you says it's that way and I say it's this,' Bentham snapped, hurrying on. 'What is it you're proposin', anyway?'

William glanced at Long Col, at the belligerent Butcher standing guard at the sergeant's shoulder. Sparrow frowned, thinking quickly. Whatever they did, they must finish it now and get out of it before they were surrounded and outnumbered. That at least seemed obvious enough. By God, they couldn't hold up in the village for the winter, slap bang in the middle of the Royalist west.

'We'll counter-attack right now, hit 'em while they're still congratulating themselves, force our way to the road, and get off,' he said. 'There's more of us than there is them. Did you keep your hands on those horses, Col?'

'We did, Captain,' Muffet nodded.

'Oh, aye! A dozen nags for a hundred of us! Who gets to walk, Captain Sparrow?'

'The wounded, for a start-off. We'll take turns. We can't stay here, man, you must see that! Force the road and we'll be off,' Sparrow insisted.

The rebels looked doubtful. 'They came out bold enough, Captain. Mad Val's a regular berserker when his blood's up!'

'There's no man here as can stand against him, not with a sword!'

'I wouldn't like to!'

Butcher glared at the sour-faced cowards, shaking his

tangled head in disgust. 'A ball'll stop him same as any other bugger,' he snarled.

'Many's the man who's tried!'

There was a chorus of discouraged agreement. Bentham waited for the hubbub to die down a little, sensing their fickle favour had swung back behind him. He beckoned the frozen merchant over to him. Sparrow eyed his former employer as he made his way through the crowd, lifting his boots daintily out of the slush and rubbish. He wondered what hare-brained scheme he had come up with, how he would spring this damned rabble from the trap.

'Sir Gilbert. You've got out of this damned coomb once. You tell 'em how it's done,' he called, unable to keep the note of triumph out of his voice.

The lousy wraiths listened to him as if he was delivering some fantastical sermon, granting divine blessings on the hopelessly forlorn flock. The merchant had begun quietly enough, feeling his way around the treacherous quicksands of their will, but had hardly been able to contain his familiar blustering enthusiasm. William wasn't sure whether the crafty huckster believed what he was telling the men, but he certainly appeared sincere enough to most of the twitching devils crouching in the churned snow at his feet.

'Well, as I said, the village militia wasn't my last military venture, as some of you might know already. I don't mind admitting I've made mistakes. I'm not perfect, and don't set myself up as such.'

'Get on with it, merchant,' Shem Bentham growled.

Sir Gilbert frowned, pulled at the straggly white whiskers.

'As I was saying. I've made mistakes, taken the wrong road same as some of you. Who here can claim solid service for the Parliament?' The cannon fodder staring up at him could not. They had fought in a dozen demolished regiments, fought various corners on various fields. But Colston Muffet and his sharpshooters, who had formed an unofficial elite platoon within the regiments they had served, had been Roundheads from the beginning.

And so had William.

They raised their hands, giving the merchant an ironic smile. Sir Gilbert gave them a sickly grin in return, hurried on with his flustered battle plan.

'Aye, well. I don't mind admitting it. It's a weight off my shoulders, now I've told you all.'

'Told us what?' John Ruell asked, wondering if he had missed something.

'Sir Gilbert here raised a regiment of foot for the King. That's what he's trying to tell us,' William called helpfully. His former master eyed the sardonically grinning youth. If looks were bullets Sparrow would have been shark bait.

'I was forced through various circumstances to prove my loyalty to the crown, after my long and loyal service to your . . . our cause,' he corrected himself quickly. 'But the whys and wherefores of the matter don't count for nothing. The thing is, I was given a commission, a commission to raise a regiment.' The doubtful mob of ill-armed, shivering scarecrows looked bewildered at one another, wondering what on earth this had to do with their escape. 'That commission,' Sir Gilbert went on, 'is still in my possession, well, as good as.'

'As good as?'

'It's tied up safe, with my personal belongings.'

'Where?'

'Under the wagon in the courthouse yard,' Sir Gilbert admitted through gritted teeth. William nodded slowly.

'Ah! So whatever happens, we'll have to force our way back into the court to get your precious papers?'

'Well, yes,' Sir Gilbert snapped. William blew a draught of air down his nose.

'This commission, then, how's it going to help us?' John Ruell wanted to know.

'It's a commission to raise men,' the merchant rasped, maddened by these ignorant wasps.

'So, so what?'

'So you men will become *my* regiment. A regiment of loyal Royalist troops hurrying to join General Hopton's forces presently assembling in Hampshire,' he concluded, raising his hands in a final flourish. The frost-bitten rogues frowned back at him.

'Change sides, you mean?'

Sir Gilbert sighed heavily. Shem Bentham shook his long worry-riddled head.

'Only as far as fooling 'em, you shambling prickster! We'll use Sir Gilbert's commission as our pass through the lines!'

The flimsy strands of their intention began to stick together, breeze-blown spider-webs in their numbed skulls. Sparrow folded his arms across his chest, blew out a dragon-breath of vapour.

'So we retrieve the papers from the wagon, hold this precious pass up, and walk straight past 'em, do we?' he called ironically. 'Dreadful sorry, there's been a terrible mistake, we thought we were burning London!'

Sir Gilbert wagged his finger at his surly critic.

'Don't be such a blasted fool, William! Of course we'll have to disengage ourselves from this place first!'

'Ah!' Sparrow called. 'So we're back to my plan, storm the damned courthouse and have done with it!'

'I'm with you that far, William,' Gillingfeather called. 'We came here to avenge ourselves on Cruickshank, and I mean to see we carry it through. Aye, all the way!'

Bentham showed his crooked teeth. 'Bugger your revenge. If you want to go tanglin' with Crooksie that's your lookout. The only reason we're going back up there is to get the bloody papers!' he yelled. 'Then Sir Gilbert here will lead us out, the way he went last time. The place your poacher boy there found him!' Bentham pointed at Butcher, the truculent sharpshooter, who glared back uncertainly. 'You tell 'em, they're your mates. This gully the merchant found leads right up into the woods. We'll get ourselves along the ridge awhiles, enough to throw the buggers off the scent, and then double back, go east by night marches. Once we're within spitting distance of London, we'll divvy up and go our separate ways. All of us, no questions asked.'

'I'll track every last man of you down, and watch him hang!'

The awestruck rabble turned their heads as one, stared at the captain who had strutted out of his burnt-out quarters to listen to the ill-natured debate. Rhodes, Grey, and a couple of nervously staring sailors stood at attention behind him, clearly intimidated by the far more numerous mob.

'I thought you'd taken yourself off somewhere,' Shem Bentham drawled menacingly. His cronies were springing to their feet all around the windswept cross and snow-banked wagon, clutching their weapons.

'I give you all fair warning. If you proceed with this outrageous course of action, I will be forced to desperate measures,' the bow-legged seaman called with all the menace he could muster.

'Aye, desperate would be about right,' Sir Gilbert called, stepping through the twitching mob to confront their superannuated commander. 'Do you think for one moment they are going to stop and listen to you now? We found the gold, just as I said. I've given them a way out, just as I said. What have you done for them, Captain, apart from shovel them into this shit-hole in the first place, eh?' The merchant, infuriated by the captain's dangerous interruptions, lost his temper at last, shouting and bawling and waving his arms before the insouciant seaman. 'I've heard all about it, the bribes and the promises. By God, you have the gall to set yourself up to judge me, me, an honest merchant trying to earn a few bob where I can. You persuaded these men to join your silly little mission, and then you start throwing your weight about expecting them to lie down and die for your damned cause?'

The unexpected outburst sparked the mob's fury. They packed in righteously about their bumbling champion, fingers flexing about their weapons. Fey stood like a statue before the hostile crowd, his grey face as inscrutable as stone.

'You treacherous snake, you wouldn't recognize any cause save your own! If you stray within five score miles of London you'll be caught and strung up for the dog you are!' Fey said with appalling certainty. 'You'll be the first on the gallows, ahead of these misguided fools, and I will be watching!'

William swallowed his anxiety, caught Mr Grey's equally uncertain stare. The old hand knew Fey was skating on thin ice just as he did. Encouraged by the mate's mute appeal, William stood forth once again. Why couldn't the murderous swines see reason?

'There will be no hangings, no beatings, and no bloodshed,' he said shakily. 'They'd be laughing at us now, up in that courthouse there, if they could see us falling out among ourselves. Whether we go my way, Fey's way, or the merchant's, we must stick together or we'll be slaughtered, sooner or later.'

Fey scowled, but Sparrow could sense the surge of support behind him.

'Don't presume to fight my battles, Sparrow,' Fey warned.

William, losing patience with his ridiculous obstinacy, decided to ignore him.

'These men have fulfilled the mission they were assembled for, and are no longer under Captain Fey's jurisdiction. The only matter to be decided is how we are to get them home.'

Home. It was a fragile talisman, but it could stop their hearts and fill their brains quicker even than the viciously contagious gold fever which had swallowed them up earlier. Home. Half of them couldn't lay claim to any such ideal. Most were drifters, vagabonds. Strangers everywhere they went. But the magical word worked as well on them as it did the older, settled sergeants.

'The captain's right. We have to stick together,' Goodrich warned.

Sparrow ignored the posturing captain, concentrated his attention on Mr Grey. If he wobbled, Fey's snake-charmer hold would be broken for good and they could get on their way out of there. Grey worked his mouth as if he were chewing a wasp.

'I reckon they're dead set on going, Captain,' he advised carefully.

Fey shivered at the unexpected treachery from his right hand man. *Et tu, Brute?* 'You are free to join them if you wish,' he said icily.

'I don't mean to go against you, Captain, sir, but I think the way's clear.'

'There will be no harm done to Captain Fey,' Sparrow called. 'He is free to go by any means he chooses, or with us if he wishes.'

Fey summoned up a withering smile. 'I am in your debt,' he said with heavy irony.

Sir Gilbert, at the end of his tether in the windy gully between the looted hovels, stamped his feet in frustration.

'Let the damned dwarf swim for it if he likes. The sooner we're gone the better! If I had my way—'

The sudden rattle of bullets and the hoarse yells of three dozen drunken throats bounded about the petrified village, bringing the acrimonious exchange to a paralysed full stop.

Long Col swung his musket to his shoulder, peered up the dark slope towards the monstrous assizes.

'Have a care! The enemy are upon us!'

THE VILLAGE CROSS,

PENMETHOCK

I t would have been difficult to determine which party was the more surprised, the mumbling invaders gathered beneath the snow-clad cross or the screaming scarecrows bounding down the street at them.

The mutineers stared up the howling white canyon, paralysed with fear as the yelling mob surged over the barricades and obstacles as if they were taking part in some hellish steeplechase. The Royalists, for their part, had been told the enemy had melted away towards the quay, hoping to regain their ships. Cruickshank had assured them they would be winkling out stragglers from the gutted hovels, not coming up against a whole pack of the frozen devils ready and waiting for them. Panic-stricken musketeers and half-hearted villagers clattered to a confused halt or threw themselves down behind the luxuriant snowdrifts, buried their rapidly cooling heads as if the kind-hearted inhabitants had hurled feather pillows out of their windows for them.

Cruickshank's banshee bodyguard ignored their doubtful allies and pressed on regardless, galloping up to the wrecked wagon and stamping the drifted snow to slush as they manhandled the heavy obstacle out of their path. Snow and sleet whistled down the street, pursued by angry meteors of red-hot lead as Muffet's veterans opened a sporadic fire. Bawling soldiers fell into the running gutters as Humphrey Gale's bandits tore at the frail defence, hurling planks and broken furniture at the milling Roundheads.

Muffet waved his men back into the gutted houses beside the cross, shoving and kicking the drop-jawed mutineers out of his way. In another blink the frightened parties had swallowed one another up, hopelessly entangled in the narrow street. William, bowled over by the furious impact of a dozen bewildered bodies, elbowed himself to his knees, clawing for his dropped sword. He looked up just in time to collect a vicious kick from a towering bandit in a pair of ridiculously baggy breeches, a leering Turk transported from the distant Orient. Gale towered above him, screaming challenges at the terrorized rebels and slashing at their hastily turned backs with his cutlass. William rolled over, grasping at the rogue's legs and dragging the roaring brute down with him. Gale cackled with anger at this outrage, brought the heavy pommel of his sword down on William's head. Sparrow ducked just in time, taking the bruising blow on his shoulder. He grunted with desperation, heaving the cursing Cornishman over and pinning him against the writhing wrestlers packed in around him. A mad stampede of boots and kicks, clattering weapons and belching pistols. The turnkey shoved Sparrow away, desperately trying to free his sword from beneath a pole-axed rebel. William threw himself at the outlandish corsair, pressing the bigger man back into the jabbering mob. Gale growled into his plaited beard, as if unaccustomed to such determined resistance from this puny vermin. He threw a punch, which missed, then kicked the shabby rebel in the kneecap. William gasped with agony, collapsing on one leg. The shoaling fighters twisted and heaved in the narrow street, each man waging some private battle in the frightening confusion of arms and legs, bruised heads and knifed bowels. William remembered the bilbo in his boot, tore the slim dagger from the rolled leather. He held it out in blind panic as the reeking beast dived on him once more. Sparrow's joints popped as the bandit impaled himself on the blade, thrashing and coughing on the cruel point. William dragged his bloody arm back, brought his own fist around into the wretch's filthy ear. Gale rolled aside, the dagger lodged in his ribs, blood blossoming over his shirt. William peered around him, desperately trying to pick familiar faces from the screaming mob. Another crowd of ragged fighters surged past, spinning him around in the slippery chaos.

Fey was standing at bay against a wall, defending himself with stony determination against a pair of terrified musketeers, who were jabbing and swinging their brass-bound butts at the captain. William tore a discarded musket from the trampled snow, brought the heavy stock down on a blue-coated back. The musketeer yelled, dropped to his knees, and curled up like a dried fish, his face twisted with agony. His companion took one swing at William, staggered back screaming as Fey lopped his right arm off beneath the elbow, sending a squall of bright blood over the snow. The twitching limb stained the slush, fingers clenched like a speared crab. Mr Grey had taken cover behind the wall, methodically hacking and jabbing at a stinking forest of arms grasping for him from the other side. A barefoot sailor hauled himself up onto the narrow ledge, threw out his arms, and dived down on the old mate, pinning his arms by his side. Fey turned on his heel and skewered the attacker on the point of his sword, tore it back with mechanical ruthlessness. Left, right, back, forward. Jab, parry, stroke. Fey had led a dozen boarding parties, and the riot in the street was meat and drink to him. William stepped into the breach behind him, tried to catch his breath for a moment as the rough and tumble rolled down the street.

He bellowed a hoarse warning as Humphrey Gale, pierced like a Spanish bull on William's dagger, lumbered forward with a broken pike couched under his enormous arm. Before any of them could react the bearded corsair had thrust the spear at the sea captain. The bloody point caught Fey beneath his armpit, the terrifying force enough to lift him from his feet and hurl him into the wall. William growled with rage, leapt forward, and crushed the monster's hate-twisted skull with his warped musket. Gale staggered back, blood running in a dozen rivulets around his broken nose. Grey snatched a discarded pistol from the snow, finished the brute with a ball in the eye. Gale kicked and writhed, dying as noisily as he had lived.

Fey collapsed into the snow beside him, grunting with pain as he lifted his arm to grasp the jagged pike point, bloody fingers flexing about the cold metal spike. His breath came in short sharp gasps, a series of agonized hiccups which stole the veteran sailor's breath. Mr Grey crouched down over the stricken captain, his loyal crew replacing the mate at the improvised barricade.

'Damn him, he's done for me, John,' Fey whispered through his gritted teeth.

'Ah, no, sir. Tis nowt but a scratch,' Grey warbled, his features mottled with grief as his clumsy fingers searched the spouting gash.

There was no time to reload, no time to prime muskets

or wind pistols. After the first furious fusillade the fighters had resorted to clubbing and cudgelling, knifing and gouging. A party of freed prisoners from the quarry, terrified by the desperate charge, broke and ran, galloping down the hill panicking the rebels further down the street into instant flight. Lieutenant Rhodes, reeling from a crushing blow to the side of his scabby head, staggered after them, bawling himself hoarse. Gillingfeather darted out of an alley, fired his musket from the hip at a screaming pirate in a looted coat who had locked his claws about the youngster's neck. The swarthy devil collapsed to his knees, dispatched by a stunning blow from the agitator. The energetic musketeer slipped a hairy hand beneath Rhodes' armpit and hauled him back down the alley.

Shem Bentham had drawn his sword and was hacking about him for all he was worth, desperate to defend his hard-won treasure. He strode backwards toward the sanctuary of the alley, searching for a friendly face in the muddy rush of friend and foe. Ruell fired a brace of pistols into a blue-coat's face obliterating the man's features, dropped the weapons, and doubled after his chief. A dozen of the hired hands saw the canny duo flee the fight, and struggled to follow them.

Sparrow watched them run, stepping over the groaning wounded and brutally hammered dead, tripping and sliding in their haste to escape. Damn them all to hell! Off after the loot leaving the few loyal men to act as a reluctant rearguard.

'Stand fast, you knaves!' he shrieked at their backs. He turned around in alarm as the enemy launched their final, murderous onslaught. A screaming sailor swung a musket butt at his head, missed his target, but sent the bawling lout flying. He was on him in a moment, reeking hands clenched about the startled Roundhead's neck.

Valentine Cruickshank strode into the deserted breach, a cutlass in either fist, bone-white teeth set in a demented grin. He had recognized the chest Bentham carried under his tattered arm, realized at once why the raiders hadn't pressed their attack, why there had been so few men left to hold the line about the courthouse. They had been too busy looting his ship, the dogs!

He stamped and kicked out at the helpless wounded, not caring for a moment whether they were his own men or rebels, leapt up on the base of the village cross to peer over the heads of the reckless fools who had remained to slash it out with their bitter rivals.

'Hold fast there! That's my chest!' he roared, silencing the squalling wind which drove the snow in their faces.

Cruickshank leapt down from his post and made toward the alley, pulling a pistol from his breeches.

Gillingfeather was feverishly reloading his musket, fingering powder into his pan and glancing up at the devil incarnate advancing on him, death writ large all over that never forgotten face. The pirate chief seemed to dwarf them all, towering above the grovelling scarecrows trying to pull their steaming entrails from beneath his pitiless boots. William forced his elbows between his stinking assailant's arms, pulled them apart with a hideous snap, and hurled the little wretch away. Before the ragged devil could prise himself to his feet, Mr Grey reached across his dying captain and thrust the bloody pike point into his neck. The man fell back, writhing in a shocking halo of blood, gargling on his own gore.

William rolled onto his knees, panting hard. He raised his ringing head and watched the fearsome combat on the other side of the street, mesmerized by the bloody confrontation. The pirate and the agitator, the bald-headed demon and the hairy angel locked in an eternal contest.

Gillingfeather was squatting on his haunches wrestling with his stubbornly locked musket mechanism, his tongue clamped between his teeth. He stumbled forward as another fighter emerged from the shadows, took his place at the gate.

A bulky, bareheaded lad in a padded coat, his cropped head stuck with tiny flakes of snow. Dull eyes fixed on the tyrant striding towards them, the coat-tails flapping about his long legs. The captain raised the pistol as his doomed adversary stepped over a huddled body and came to a halt in front of him, staring slack-mouthed at his tormentor.

William realized in a blink who it was.

Caleb.

Cruickshank's own son, the son he had hurled from his ship in a moment of blind rage as if he was nothing more than a bucket of slops.

The captain stared in astonishment, his mobile mouth working this way and that as he struggled to come to terms with the awesome vision. The snow howled, but the groaning wounded held their breath, electrified and appalled by the terrible reunion.

Cruickshank senior tilted his head, a nervous smile splitting his wind-worn features, transforming the fearsome mask which had sent half the enemy bolting away down towards the quay. His pale eyes seemed to widen as he examined the silently staring apparition, an innocent child gazing uncomprehendingly into a slaughterhouse. The bloody struggles behind him were forgotten, erased from his astonished consciousness. His treasure, his life's savings, away with a loose-limbed donkey in a badly fitting sea-coat. It was as if they had been cocooned from the rage and racket around them, brought together by some mischievous supernatural intervention. The bewildered captain loosened his tongue in his dry mouth.

'Caleb? Is it you, lad?'

The youth stood like a statue, staring straight through the transparent web and tissue of lies standing aghast before him.

Gillingfeather had no time for his ludicrously belated sentimentality. He remembered the day when poor Caleb had been roped and bundled with the rest of them, hurled over the groaning planking by his tyrannical sire. He gritted his teeth, raised his musket barrel level with the corsair's belly before the bewildered captain was aware he was there. The agitator turned his hairy head to one side and pulled the trigger with a grunt of disgust.

'God damn you, sir! God damn you to the hell you've cheated too long!'

The dead-eyed pirate staggered back in the choking smoke, his coat smouldering, dark blood running noisily down his back and splashing the trampled snow. The loose sword dangled precariously from his right hand, the heavily callused left dancing like some naked bird of prey in front of his ruined chest, bloodstained fingers dappling and dashing his well-cut coat as he pointed out his accusers in mute astonishment.

Caleb watched him caper backwards on his slippery heels, his pale, faraway eyes fixed unblinkingly on some infinite horizon. Cruickshank sat down heavily in the bloody shambles, his cutlass clenched in his fist. He stared at his prodigal son, his jaw clamped mechanically over a mouthful of bile.

In another moment the spell was broken. Staring soldiers became frightened fools. Fighters found their weapons weighing heavily in their fists. Leaders became cowards and the cowards searched for shadows and cracks where they could hide themselves from the horror.

'For God and Parliament!'

Muffet led the charge from the fortress hovel, tumbling the Royalist raiders back the way they had come. Muskets and swords clattered about the wrecked street as the anonymous mob stampeded back toward the courthouse like a flock of ineptly slaughtered sheep. William was caught up in the pursuit, delirious with his own survival, delighted by this easy, easy killing. He hacked at their backs, barged past bleeding bodies. Lifted his legs over the logjam of twisted limbs and broken weapons as if he would destroy them all, settle the score for ever. For Fulke and Fey, for the fear-frenzied man and wife lying frozen in their gutted home. Aye, and for his own slaughtered peace of mind too. He felt as if he could run for ever, pistol-proof like a dented back and breast. His seamless skin would turn blade and ball, as invulnerable as an ankle-booted Achilles. He roared encouragement to the terrified men swarming up behind him, the brittle air soothing honey in his battle-raw throat. The screaming fugitives ducked down alleys and hurled themselves over walls, the disintegrating mob shrinking with every agonized step.

William grabbed a running youngster by his flapping collar and swung the terrified boy into a wall. He stumbled over the youth's outstretched leg, just as a pistol shot knocked sparks from the brickwork above his head. The red-hot needles scorched the back of his neck as he ducked down instinctively over the groaning boy, instantly sobered by the close escape. William peered up the street, realized he had charged further than he had thought. The courthouse seemed to dominate the bruised sky, sullen flames illuminating the sheer parapet and massively fortified gate. What was left of the blizzard was blowing spitefully down the bare stone walls. A cursing officer struggled with his pistol, his bared shoulder swathed in sopping-wet bandages torn from his own shirt. He dropped the pistol with a stuttered curse, looked up as William launched himself to his feet and charged head down at the defiant gatekeeper. The officer turned to hobble into the yard, thought better of it, and held up his good hand in futile submission. William raised his sword, eyes jammed with crackling red mists, his face spotted by the loose gore from the dripping blade. Those tiny splashes seemed to cool the mad fires behind his eyes, to drench the glowing coals in his vitals. The miserable wretch was the same colour as the stone behind his head, convinced he would be slaughtered with the rest. His bristling moustaches were scabbed and clotted with dried blood and mucus. Weak from loss of blood, the King's man staggered back against the formidable pillar, his red tongue bobbing as he gabbled for quarter. William caught his breath, dimly aware of the musketeers and clubmen hurrying up past him and his prisoner. Muffet led them into the yard, a screaming mob of happy hunters, winkling the last of the fugitives from their holes. Sir Gilbert had appeared from somewhere, ventured out from whatever he had hidden himself now the fighting was done.

William recognized the merchant's florid features as he craned his head around the blockaded gate.

'Is it there? The wagon?' Sir Gilbert yelped anxiously.

William hissed with exasperation, felt the cold boulder of hatred he had bred for the battle slide and shift in his belly.

He realized the terrified officer was addressing him, nodding his pale head in earnest supplication. An officer and a gentleman, surrendering himself to him.

'Sir, the assizes are yours,' the wounded man gasped, looking up mournfully at his conqueror.

It was impossible to tell which side was getting the better of the furious struggle in the main street. Telling, Clavincale, and half a dozen others circled around the village, hoping to catch the rebels in ambush as they fled Cruickshank's main attack. It had been the captain's idea of course, as if the boastful madman had been bent on keeping all the glory for himself. Issuing his orders as if the assizes were his ship now, as if all of Devon was his private lagoon.

Hugo grunted with annoyance at the deadly challenge he hadn't dared answer, not with the blackguard's swivel-eyed crew packed in behind him, at any rate. The gloating captain had sent them both on their way, pointing his finger at the door as if they were naughty children caught scrumping in the local orchard. Poor Clavincale, barely able to comprehend the full extent of the disastrous conspiracies Cruickshank had revealed to him, had staggered out of the courthouse as if he was drunk, completely bemused by the perplexing twists he had barely been able to follow. Bella, the vision he had worshipped from his hole in the skirting board, the villainous whore who had enticed his own brother to his death. A pouting Jezebel, scissor-finger Delilah singing siren songs, luring his brother to his death on her rocky approaches. A brother who had traded in men's lives like some Arab trader patrolling the rich slave markets along the Gambia River.

Hugo glanced back over his shoulder, nodded encouragingly at the brooding youngster. By God, squatting in a ditch with his back to the boy – he could hardly give the bewildered lordling a better opportunity to avenge his elder brother's death. Thank the Lord, Clavincale didn't seem aware of the full details of that squalid murder in the woods, hadn't been informed of Hugo's disgraceful role in the affair.

Clavincale stared back, his eyes widening as the tumult from the other side of the mean hovels seemed to reach a nerve-shattering crescendo.

'We'll wait here while—'

Telling swirled around as the crouching figure rocketed out of the alley and crashed through a tangle of browned and bent beans, doubled across the unkempt vegetable garden toward the crumbling drystone wall which ran the length of the refuse-filled ditch. The ugly, donkey-headed wretch didn't seem to notice them, crouching among the stalks and turnip tops like hungry vagrants. The rebel looked this way and that, lifted his tattered legs through the clutter as if wading through a mangrove swamp, slashing at the coiling brambles cursing incoherently. He was followed by another reluctant warrior, a shifty-eyed scarecrow who spotted the intruders hiding in the ditch and let out a belated squawk of warning. Clavincale tensed behind him but didn't even raise his pistol. Telling growled with fury, shot out of the nettles brandishing his sword at the terrified pair. One of the blue-coats crouching in the ditch fired his musket, the dipping ball thudding into the second man's shoulder and spinning him around like a top. He let out a shrill scream and tumbled into the beanstalks, his collarbone smashed by the bruising impact which hadn't even broken his skin. He pawed and prodded his hot coat, eyes popping as he searched for a bloody wound, cursing and crying his foul luck. His colleague didn't waste time tending his fallen friend. He ducked down folding the precious box under his coat and shot off along the wall like a startled hare, Telling's musketeers opening fire from point-blank range. By some miracle of poor aim or misplaced pity, the firing squad managed to miss their braying target as he scuttled through the undergrowth. Their feverish musketry knocked sparks from the tottering wall and the shapeless felt hat from his head. The rebel bellowed with fright, lifting his great hairy legs over bramble branch and bean stem, eyes bulging from his misshapen skull. One of the musketeers, unable to control his bladder-busting tension, laughed like a drain at his antics, pointed his hairy finger.

'Shoot 'n down, boys!'

'Don't let him get away!' Telling yelled furiously, reaching down to snatch the pistol from Clavincale's limp fist. He raised the weapon and fired, squinting through the smoke as his comical target lurched into the wall, caught his breath for a moment, and then staggered on with jaw-breaking determination

'After me!' Hugo yelled, waving them on down the tangled ditch towards their intended ambuscade. They didn't move. Clavincale was staring after the wretch with the box, making his precarious way along the wall propping himself up on his shoulder, frightened to take his dirty paws from his treasure. A desperately dark stain was spreading rapidly over the back of his coat, as if his lifeblood was being squeezed out with every agonized step. The rest of them gaped in comic horror, as if unaware their smoking muskets had been capable of such cruel destruction.

Telling hurried on, leaving the gasping fugitive to the piss-poor patrol while he scouted toward the alley they had fled, trusting the rogues to obey his orders – at least while Clavincale was around to second his instructions with a bewildered nod of his head.

He picked his way carefully over the mossy stones, tilted his head to listen. The fighting seemed to have petered out, the brutal struggles hushed by the hissing winds. He stopped, alarmed by the sudden and deeply sinister silence. He could hear the pitiful moans of the wounded, the high-pitched shrieks of a dying man frightfully illuminated by his exploding bandoliers, blackened claws held to his scorched face.

And then a hoarse, inarticulate cheer, immediately taken up by a dozen throats.

'For God and Parliament!'

He imagined a frantic last stand, a handful of bloody rebels backed up defiantly in the shattered street. Telling slipped into the shadowed alley sword in hand, peered toward the eerily lit street. Men in an assortment of different coloured coats were hurrying by, lifting weapons from the trampled snow and joining the vicious pursuit.

But they were running the wrong way – back up the street towards the courthouse!

He had barely registered the stunning implications before a dim figure stepped into the narrow tunnel, peered back at him half paralysed with fright. Telling raised his sword and screamed a hair-raising challenge, sending the terrified youngster bolting out of the alley and back to his suddenly triumphant friends. Hugo didn't wait for them to collect their wits and come after him. He doubled back the way he had come, back to the feckless musketeers. They had caught up with their filthy quarry, surrounded the stricken fugitive crouched at bay under the leaning wall.

'What are ye staring at?' the wounded man rasped, his arms locked about the closely bound chest.

'What's he got there that's so precious?'

'What yer got, Roundhead?'

They closed in on him, brutally excited now, tearing his arms from the trove. The rebel looter winced in agony, doubled up in pain as he tried to resist. He flopped back exhausted, his blood sliding and dripping over the loosely packed stones. Telling sprinted back down the garden toward them, waving them away from the solidly bound box.

'Get back to the courthouse! It's a trap!' he bawled. They huddled together instinctively, jealous of their new prize, maddened by the posturing coxcomb giving the orders.

'Cruickshank's given up! Get back to the court,' the bedraggled Cavalier insisted, brandishing his sword at them as they examined their discovery, dirty features lit up with curiosity. They glanced up at one another, wondering what the damned house dove was mucking his breeches about. Clavincale stood a little way back, slumped and forlorn like some exquisitely turned out

475

village idiot who none of the other boys would play with. His cow-eyed bewilderment grated against Telling's woefully frayed nerves.

'RUN!' he bellowed, strings of spit catching in his ragged moustache.

A blue-coated soldier had leaned his musket beside the wall and was trying to prise the lid from the box with a rusty knife. He started walking, stumbling along the churned garden paying more attention to the heavily encrusted lock than the treacherous undergrowth. The rest of them seemed reluctant to leave him to it, clustering about him like wet hens as he sawed and prodded the clever mechanism.

'The enemy are upon you!' Telling cried wearily, his flagging spirits stretched beyond endurance by these knavish prospectors. He might as well plough with dogs as stand with this fornicating rabble!

He glanced over his shoulder, almost swooning with exasperation as a squad of Roundheads tumbled out of the damned alley as if on cue, raising their muskets to speed their departure with a stinging volley.

Hugo threw himself down as the sudden fusillade filled the overgrown yard with flying lead and chipped stones, the screaming musket balls cutting through coiling bindweeds and shattered beanpoles. A clubman in moleskin breeches spun around clutching his spurting elbow. Another, a seaman by the cut of his sailcloth trews, clamped his hands to his forehead and sank to his knees, blood bubbling between his clawed fingers. The blue-coated brute with his tongue between his teeth and the box tucked under his arm was hurled into the wall by a deflected shot, bringing the tottering structure sliding down around them. He groped wildly to hang on to his

slipping prize, but was immediately trampled by his petrified comrades who threw themselves over the crumbling
breach, the precious chest forgotten. They scrambled over
the loose scree and galloped off across the virgin snow-
fields beyond, shrieking like banshees unexpectedly
released from some hellish dungeon.

Telling leapt to his feet, his ears ringing at the rolling
retorts, and scurried down the ditch bawling warnings at
the miraculously unharmed lordling. The rebels rifled
their pockets for powder and ball to complete the delirious slaughter, shouting and hallooing to one another in
their excitement. A few moments before they had been
running like hares themselves, the difference between
victory and defeat balanced on a razor's edge of fate. Men
could stumble over their courage one moment and cower
like dogs the next, cursed to wander a wilderness of
quicksand indecision.

Clavincale was gaping at the chaotic steeplechase
beyond the broken-down wall as if he was wondering
which runner to place a wager on, stunned by the sweep-
ing avalanche of fortune. He bent down over the callously
trampled blue-coat, lifted the box from his crushed fingers, and straightened up uncertainly as Telling loped up,
features twisted with savage intensity. He held it out
awkwardly as if intent on making some kind of bargain
with the scowling Cavalier, as if he could buy the courage
he so sadly lacked with the contents of the cursed chest.
Maybe this money could make him a man, just as money
had unmade his elder brother?

Telling ignored the tightly bound present, grabbed the
youth with a startling lack of ceremony, and hauled him
by his coat sleeve out of the devil's playground. He gritted
his teeth, propelled the blubbering youth along the wall,

peering over his shoulder for the inevitable pursuit. He didn't know where he was going, what had happened to Cruickshank, what would happen to the Royalist survivors if they were caught in this butcher's pen. He could barely think straight, saving his evaporating energies for getting the pair of them out of the hideous bower. Clavincale tripped and fell but Hugo hung on, grimly determined to save the youngster and patch up what was left of his honour. He cursed and bawled at the crying youth, manhandled him out of the ditch and back along the smoke-ringed hovels toward the stark, brick-stacked sanctuary of the courthouse.

Suddenly a mob of men surged out of the alley to their left, clawing at one another as if they were fleeing a pack of wild beasts. Their terrified impact spun the lonely fugitives around, spurred them on the final dash to the courthouse gate. Telling bundled Clavincale through the massive structure, hauled him into the merrily lit interior of his father's stronghold.

Fallen stronghold.

Hugo groaned, unable to go a step further. The yard had been invaded and overturned by the triumphant rebels. Spartacus' slaves relishing their moment, capering in the ashes of a Roman governor's villa. The noisy rebels who had pursued them through the gardens clattered through the gate behind them, blocking their escape. They prodded the bewildered pair forward on their musket barrels with leers of mischievous delight.

'Off somewhere, me beaut?'

Hugo grimaced, peering around the ring of enemy fighters, glittering swords and smoking muskets clenched in their fists. Clavincale stumbled to his knees and vomited hotly, dropping the damned box, which clattered to a halt against a pair of filthy roll-top boots. He looked up slowly, blinking at the smoky-faced bandit holding court in his father's yard. The intruder's eyes glittered with exultation as he stared down at the fallen squire, his quick breath forming complex vapour clouds about his features. Clavincale shrunk back in fear as the well-built rebel bent down and locked his fingers about the unlucky chest, lifted his vomit-speckled prize with a grunt of satisfaction.

'Ah, Cruickshank's donation to Parliament's widows' and orphans' fund,' he said with a menacing chuckle.

Clavincale scrambled to his feet, dusting the wet snow from his breeches and wiping his wrist across his sour mouth. Hugo braced himself alongside him, panting like a broken-winded nag, studying the ring of anxious faces packed into the arena with helpless contempt. Further over the courtyard he could see Sir Gilbert, clambering over a wagon as if he would outrun the miserable mob which had so suddenly swallowed them up. Bella must be nearby, he thought fleetingly. But there was no sign of her. A handful of ragged blue-coats and bloody bandaged militiamen were shivering beneath Black Bob's cravenly struck colours. A few forlorn sailors, watching their captors with petrified wonder, tried not to look at Black Bob's gallows, silhouetted starkly against the far wall.

Hugo felt the familiar surge of sickened shame, a sour swelling in his abdomen, pressing his lungs and choking his throat. The brute with the box shoved Clavincale to one side and stood, legs spread like a tavern prizefighter, before the miserable Cavalier. Hugo blinked, rubbed his running eye, and squinted at the horribly familiar features.

And recognized his pestilential rival in love and war – that ghastly oaf Sparrow.

He closed his eyes, biting his lip bloody to fight back the tears of anguish.

Dear Lord above, what had he done to deserve such vicious humiliations? Sparrow, here? By God, he must have tracked him down from Newbury, followed him like some overweight bloodhound!

The burly Roundhead swaggered forward like the overbearing lout he was, the beginnings of a weary grin stretching his battle-stained features.

'Telling! You too?' he croaked, with barely the energy left to crow over his despised rival's downfall. Telling's lip curled back from his teeth in humiliated disgust. Let him do what he liked, he'd never duck beneath Sparrow's damn yoke.

'You've got what you came for, then,' he sneered, nodding at the luckless totem cradled in the big man's tattered arm. 'A handful of coin for you to share among your bandit friends!'

Sparrow looked down at the sealed chest as if he had forgotten it was there.

'This? Oh, well, it might go some way to covering our expenses.' He turned to his left, tossed the chest towards the grinning musketeer beside the gate.

Telling had a feeling he recognized the straw-headed tyke. A poacher or some such. The old fool with the grey hair, he'd seen him back at Kilmersden Hall and all. Rebel wretches, guttersnipes all too typical of Sparrow's blasted company.

'You know this man?' Clavincale asked dumbly.

Telling raised his chin a notch, nodded. 'We've met.'

'Aye, we've met. And to answer your question, you scrawny arsed shit-kicker, we came here for Cruickshank, not his damned savings!'

Hugo rolled his eyes in mock concern. 'I don't imagine a tub full of gold had anything to do with it.'

Sparrow's easy smile slipped. He thrust his dark features up against the pale Cavalier's nose, hissed through gritted teeth.

'The bastard threw me and my men overboard after we were captured on Roundway. Tossed us to the sharks along with his own bloody son, if you'll believe it!'

Sadly, Hugo could believe it all too easily. But he hadn't been able to choose his allies any more than Sparrow had!

William jammed his finger into Telling's shoulder, pressing the smaller man back. 'He left us to drown in our own piss, so don't talk to us about gold. We came here for his poxy pus-blood and by Christ we got it,' Sparrow bellowed, goaded by the Cavalier's supercilious expression. His filthy soldiers cheered and shook their weapons in raucous agreement, smeared natives gathered about their cannibal cooking-pot.

Clavincale warbled with fear; Telling thought for one moment he was going to fall down in a faint.

'You men were taken aboard the *Messalina*?' he asked hoarsely.

'That's enough,' Telling warned out of the side of his mouth. Sparrow's eyes flashed from his despised rival to the blubbering boy beside him.

'Aye, a company of us. Not much fun taking quarter, is it, you damned plover?'

Clavincale mastered his trembling lip, swallowed nervously. 'You misunderstand, sir. I owe you, all of you, a most sincere apology. My brother has brought dishonour upon the whole family.'

'Shut your trap, you blabbering fool,' Telling growled.

Sparrow frowned at the dishevelled youngster, trying to work out what the terrified clown was getting at. His brother? Owed him an apology? For this damned shambles? He masked his bewilderment behind an amiable grin.

'Apology, you say? What for?'

'He needs rest, he's been wounded,' Telling spluttered. Sparrow thrust him away, none too gently either.

'I have heard all about the shameful events on the *Messalina's Purse*, sir, from Captain Cruickshank. If you were one of the unfortunates . . .'

'Just a moment. Who are you?' Sparrow demanded, ignoring Telling's anxious yips and hisses.

'I am John Dyle, Lord Clavincale. My elder brother Anthony was—'

'Oh, I know who your brother was,' Sparrow simmered, snatching the boy up by his bunched coat. Sparrow stared into the poor boy's terrified face, tears pouring over his grubby cheeks and splashing his fists. 'He sold us like offal to the highest bidder!' Sparrow cried. The mob of soldiers tightened like a noose about the pitiful prisoners, muttering and pointing as they clenched their weapons.

'String him up with the rest of old Crooksie's crew!' Billy Butcher yelled from the gate.

'Shoot 'em all down, sir, exterminate the rogues!' Gillingfeather preached.

Sparrow listened to them shout and bawl, turned his attention back to the distraught youngster. God's blood, the boy had no more to do with the murderous piggeries on board the *Purse* than he had with the drawing up of the Grand Remonstrance! He set the boy down with a grunt of frustration.

'Cruickshank's paid for all,' he concluded. 'There'll be

no more bloodshed, not under my command!' Sparrow stalked along the anxious rebel ranks, staring at each man in turn. 'Or are you damned butchers forgetting we're forty miles from our lines? If we go slaughtering all of them, they'll put us through worse if they catch up with us!'

'They won't catch us!'

Sparrow swung around, knocked the defiant soldier's musket from his shivering fists. 'You can spy into the future, can you, warlock? You can see our way out of here!'

The musketeer looked away, his bloody jaw clenched. Sparrow turned to the rest of them, bellowed across the snowy courtyard.

'We'll collect the wounded and lock the prisoners in the courthouse,' he shouted. 'We march out, with Sir Gilbert's precious papers, at the crack of dawn. Is that clear?'

The sullen mob shifted their feet and scratched their behinds. 'But what about the gold?' a whining clubman called from the anonymity of the rear ranks. Sparrow closed his eyes in exasperation.

'We'll share it out equally,' he said wearily. 'Every man who marches with me will get his fair share when we get back to Poole. Then you'll be free to do what you like, run off over the hills for all I care. There, you have my word,' Sparrow called out.

The mutinous mob seemed satisfied for now. Clavincale was gaping at the heavy-set officer in something approaching awe, amazed at the unexpected leniency. His own father wouldn't have shown such mercy, he thought guiltily. The self-righteous chief justice had taught him the Roundheads were bloodsucking cannibals, sworn to wipe out every great house in the land. And yet this clumsy foul-mouthed ruffian had shown more common humanity than any of the back-stabbing weasels who had ruled Dorset in the name of the King. Telling wasn't so impressed by Sparrow's magnanimity, shaking his head in contempt as his despised rival stalked across the courtyard.

'Your word?' Telling crowed. 'I wouldn't trust you as far as I could spit!'

Sparrow came to a halt, fingers flexing. But he didn't look back. 'Get these prisoners into the dungeon, and send out parties for the wounded. Muffet?'

'Captain Sparrow, sir?' Long Col roared back.

'I want your men up on the high road as lookouts. They'll not leave us here longer than they have to.'

'Right you are, sir!'

Billy Butcher gave the elder sergeant a withering look. 'Lookats? In this wevah?' the sharpshooter protested. Muffet leaned over to whisper in his ear.

'Do as he says, you cross-eyed bleeder, or he'll lose the lot of 'em!'

Butcher caught on at last, threw his fowling-piece over his shoulder, and grinned at the ignorant apes beside the gate. 'Cor, he's as bad as old Crooksie, our Will!' he cackled, nodding encouragingly.

The motley assortment of fugitives and cowards, survivors and soldiers, the wounded, weary, and lame, shuffled off about their duties, nodding their heads in subdued agreement. Oh, he was a regular Caesar, their Will.

BRIDPORT,

DORSET

'The buggers'll be long gone by the time we get there,' Jethro Polruan rasped, tugging the flap of his Montero down over the raw scars where his ear used to be. The disgruntled musketeer had wrapped himself in a holed blanket liberated from some farmhouse along the way, like some wild, ragged-arsed kern off the boat from Ireland. His trudging companions had kitted themselves out as best they could against the ferocious weather blowing in relentlessly from the shiftless grey seas. Scipio Porthcurn had wrapped himself up on his Barbary horse like Ghenghis Khan himself, a bad-tempered mountain of Russian sable. He scowled and growled, ducking out of his saddle to peer at the snowy ruts, urging the trudging troops to make better time. Did they call this a road? The last decent bit of road in Dorset had been laid by the Romans!

Polruan peered between the frosted chink in his all-purpose blanket, watched their chief wave the shambling column on through the weather-ravaged landscape. An anonymous, petrified forest of stark trees and snow-laden hedgerows. Smudgy smokes hanging like silver ribbons on the frosted horizons.

'You reckon we were the only ones to sort 'em? We've

garrisons nearer than Exeter,' Simon Shevick moaned, trailing his pike through the trodden slush.

'Ah, we'll get all the dirty jobs, you'll see,' Polruan nodded, 'until ole Poorcunt gets his knighthood. Then he'll volunteer us for a barrowload more shite, until they make him a bliddy marquess!'

The colonel in question turned his horse through a particularly deep drift, cursing the prancing beast until it found its footing. The colonel had sent his small detachment of horse hurrying on ahead, but if it came to a fight he would be relying once again on these scoundrels. He watched the frozen sacks shuffle past, his waxy moustaches hanging over his rat trap of a mouth.

'Still moaning, Polruan, you beef-witted turd? You can bugger off to Plymouth and rot your arse off in a trench with the Prince, if you've a mind,' the scowling commander suggested with an evil leer. Polruan tugged his blanket tighter, trudged on muttering, staring at the hunched shoulders of the man in front. Another twenty mile should do it, and God help those rebels if they caught up with 'em!

William Sparrow watched his ragged Samaritans toiling through the snow, backs bent as they manhandled creaking stretchers through the slush, arms aching fit to burst as they helped some poor bastard back to the infirmary they had set up in Black Bob's courtroom. The snow had finally given in, but not before it had laid a smart new carpet over the ruined village. Dawn, and if you closed one eye and used your imagination, the place almost looked pretty. Well, not as bad as it had looked at midnight, Sparrow thought sourly. He stood back against a wall as a couple of swivel-eyed fisherfolk hauled a barrow through the gate, a bloody cargo of stiff limbs stuck up in frozen greeting. A handful of cussing civilians had been prodded out of their ransacked homes, smoked out of their shelters to look after the wounded and collect the dead. God knew there were enough of them.

Feverish villagers, burning up as their wounds pulsed with gangrenous humours. Dust-choked fugitives from the quarries, whose bloody exertions and hare-brained celebrations in Black Bob's wine cellar had finally overloaded their fragile constitutions. Dockhands and sailors, their hard-worked bodies bruised and buckled from the vicious street fights. Stomach wounds and pistol burns, sword cuts and smashed skulls. Blood and broken bones. Punctured and pulverized flesh, lacerated limbs and gouged eyeballs everywhere one cared to look.

Fey was still clinging to his arid life, his undernourished, agony-racked frame apparently shrinking away to nothing as he coughed and rattled in Mr Grey's arms. He had refused to acknowledge Sparrow when the captain had made a disheartening tour of the court that dawn, pointedly looking away as William enquired after his deadly wound.

'It's fatal, and that's all you need to know,' Fey had growled into John Grey's chest. 'But I've instructed Grey here to report your conduct in the proper quarters. You'll not get away with this,' he gasped. The burly mate had glanced up at Sparrow, his features twisted like molten iron, mouth slack with wretched grief.

A couple of dozen others, shot, clubbed, gouged, and hacked, would join the dead before the day was out. There was little point in making provision for them on the perilous journey they were about to undertake. It was a long way to Poole, and they wouldn't survive the first hours of their foolhardy flight through the snow.

William nodded at the strangers who shuffled by, averting their eyes as if in awe of his remarkable generalship, dumbly devoted to the man who had led them from the brink of disaster. Did they imagine he had planned their escape, calmly calculated Cruickshank's attack and laid his plans accordingly? As far as William could make out, they would have all been done to death if it hadn't been for poor Caleb. The dumb boy had stopped his father in his tracks, pulled the sky in on his bewildered head, torn victory from defeat without even raising his fist. He couldn't have made a better job of it if he had stripped the boy naked, festooned him with seaweed, and had him leap out of a whale's mouth bellowing curses.

William paused beside the heavy wagon, peered over the running-board at the pitiful wounded packed inside its bloody oak ribs. They were shivering and moaning, despite the blankets and coats they had stripped from the dead to keep the snows out. Algernon Starling was supervising the loading, casting his quick black eyes over the prospective passengers like some latter-day Noah inspecting the wounded two by two. One word from his errant master and Starling seemed to wag his black-clad behind, set about his master's dirty work with disturbing relish.

'D'you think he'll get far with his guts hanging out? Away to the court with him,' the waspish clerk growled, pointing his crooked finger at the evil-smelling infirmary. A morose musketeer helped his wounded comrade back over the courtyard as the more lightly injured men pressed forward to take his place. John Ruell grinned, hobbled up to the wheel with his arm in a sling. He winked at the stony-faced underling, expecting to nab the last place before they pulled out.

'And what's amiss with you?' Starling wondered, examining him disdainfully.

'Copped a ball right in me heart,' Ruell explained. 'It's a miracle I'm standing here at all!'

Starling gave him a sickly smile. 'Who am I to interfere with the Almighty? You'd best walk!'

'Walk? I'm black and blue! I can barely move me arm!'

'I'm not suggesting you turn handsprings,' Starling informed him curtly, 'but there's a fair walk left in you yet, my friend.' Ruell looked stunned, glanced around sheepishly at Sparrow as if he would overrule the insolent wretch. Sparrow folded his arms, daring the invalid to challenge him. Ruell snorted and stamped off over the snowy courtyard, an anonymous scarecrow all over again, now his friend Shem Bentham was lying naked in a broken-down dog cart with the rest of the smeared corpses.

Sparrow, who had known Morrison's formidable runt of a servant back in Bristol before the war, raised his chin in gloomy greeting. 'You'll not get many more in here,' he observed, tapping the oaken beams.

Starling shrugged, wringing his large hands together to keep warm. 'You ought to tell their foolish friends,' he suggested callously. 'It's no good taking places from them as might make it.'

Sparrow nodded, left him to his cruel assignment, and stalked off towards the courthouse. The blanket-swaddled guards saluted clumsily, raising their muskets as if he was the Earl of Essex himself. William was still chuckling at the astonishing alteration in his fortunes as he ducked under the doorway and took the short flight of steps to the hall. Nicodemus was crouching on the bullet-pocked landing, carefully binding their ragged colours about his waist. It wouldn't do to go marching out under Fulke's banner, would it? Not with half of Prince Maurice's army breathing down their necks.

'You'd best hang on to their damned rag,' Sparrow suggested, pulling up his reeking shirt and loosening the warm flag he had taken from Captain Took's demoralized company. The familiar colour might just get them past some frostbitten guard on their march back across the country. He meant to take Cruickshank's lousy banner with him and all, but the gaudy black ensign with its loathsome motif would hardly pass muster as an infantry company's colour.

He grinned sourly. The scraps of cloth would be his ticket back to service, bloody proof of his exertions confirming his long-awaited change of fortune. By God, he deserved something for six months of bloody misery! And if the captured colours weren't enough to buy his honour back, he could always console himself with his share of Cruickshank's gold, he remembered with a guilty twitch.

'We ought to bury Colonel Fulke, not leave him lying in that boat,' the boy croaked, interrupting William's mercenary reverie. Sparrow shrugged.

'He's better off where he is, lad. He went down with his ship, like those old Vikings. He wouldn't have wanted it any other way.'

He had made a brief reconnaissance of the quay, long enough to satisfy himself there was no use in trying to salvage either the vessels or anything of value from the stricken hulks. They had collected all the weapons and stores they could not carry and thrown them down into the gaily painted fishing boats before setting each merry vessel ablaze. The horrified fisherfolk hadn't dared intervene, with so many Roundheads strutting about their petrified town armed to the teeth.

'You think we'll fool 'em, then, Will, carrying their flags?' Nicodemus enquired with an enormous yawn, stretching his thin arms like a cat.

The captain raised his singed eyebrows.

'You've heard Sir Gilbert. He found his papers, aye, and all his cash, tucked in where he'd left it. He's blabbered his way out of worse than this,' he said encouragingly. 'And besides, Poole's not far,' he lied.

William left the boy folding his colours and followed his nose across the hall. He took one look into the stinking courtroom, the tiled floor swimming with blood, the haphazardly strewn benches draped with groaning wounded – and backed out in disgust. Christ Jesus, what a mess they'd made.

Bella Morrison followed him into the hall a moment later, wiping her arm across her mottled face and breathing deeply as if she had been swimming underwater. William had barely recognized her, a pale wraith sliding from one bloody bench to the other, ministering to the wounded like some shop-soiled angel, her apron sopping with blood and smeared excrement. Bella had been trusted to remain with the wounded while the survivors of the ferocious battle concocted their desperate escape plans. It hadn't occurred to them she would try and hide herself away – there was nowhere for her to run. She had accepted the duty as if it was some form of bloody penance, a suitable punishment for her role in the vicious affair.

By God, William thought, she'd changed from the feather-brained flutterby he'd known that summer. The carefree, careless girl he had worshipped with all his misplaced might reduced to this snivelling wretch, a ghost of a girl in a blood-smudged gown.

She looked up, smiled weakly, puckering the livid scar above her raw eye. William twitched with bewildered sympathy, shocked by her dreadful transformation. Six months of war had altered them both beyond recognition. It was as if they had all assumed completely different identities in order to survive their various adventures, to endure England's ghastly ordeal.

'William, I didn't see you there.'

She hadn't seen him in that damn shambles, that was for sure.

'I just wanted to say, about Anneliese. If there had been anything I could have done, you know,' he muttered awkwardly. He hadn't gotten used to the idea that the dark-haired girl wouldn't be coming skipping out to join them. She would have been in her element, tending the torn and bleeding men spreadeagled over the courtroom like Stone Age sacrifices on oak-panelled altars. Bella seemed to gather herself up as if she were defending her soul against reptilian invaders.

'You couldn't have helped it,' she said quietly. He hadn't been there, how could he have helped it? Will knew Bella was as much to blame as any of them for her friend's pointless death, filling her head with fanciful tales of glorious, exciting war. Glory? Excitement? She'd had her fill in the bloody infirmary, he thought sourly. He had heard the gist of their unlikely tale, the mad escapades back at Chipping Marleward and the furious flight south. Mary Keziah away again on some fool's errand to the north. Why hadn't the damned girl stayed in one place? Thank God she was safe, aye, and the baby she carried. He blinked guiltily as he remembered his own sweetheart's trials, the agony she would be enduring for him. He had forgotten all about Mary, worrying his head over Bella's fate. The tortured beauty hung her head as if she could read his wandering mind, absent-mindedly picked at her scar. 'And in any case,' Bella went on, 'I suppose we should be thanking you, for sparing Hugo and the rest of them,' she added darkly.

Sparrow grunted something into his constricted chest. He hadn't had much choice about the fate of the prisoners. Their continued survival might just save *his* neck, if the raiders were caught before they reached the safety of Poole. It would be no use pleading for quarter if he had ordered all his prisoners butchered in cold blood, would it? A red-cheeked Royalist lordling and a set of posturing officers? God knows, he might even be glad of Telling, to put in a word for him if the worst came to the worst. He frowned at the unsavoury prospect, grovelling on his knees beneath that little turkeycock. But who would be there to save Bella's neck, if the authorities caught up with her?

'You'd be safer with us, Bella,' he said thickly, set adrift all over again by the wayward girl. He'd never been master of his own mind where Bella was involved. 'Come away with your father and me.'

She shook her head, gave him a sickly, lopsided smile.

'I must go with Hugo. He has some connections, an understanding,' she said bashfully, 'with Prince Rupert.'

Rupert? Rupert was hundreds of miles away, what was he going to do, fly down to the south coast like the demon king he was? William knew Bella and Telling's flight across the war-torn countryside would be every inch as fraught as their own. The thought she would be eloping with her lover the moment his back was turned set his teeth on edge all over again. But what on earth was he to do? Call Telling out for some final showdown under the stars? The way he was feeling the damned rogue would in all probability slice him up for fish bait without drawing breath – Telling's luck was bound to change sooner or later.

Bella nodded her head, eyes brimming, porcelain features cracking over her skull as she contemplated their precarious existence. William felt his skin prickle at the thought of his former love cuddled up with that scrawny prickster.

'Well, then. Wish us luck.'

'Good luck,' she said blankly.

Was that it? Maybe she hadn't changed at all, William brooded, hurrying about his business away from the frightening reminder of his old self.

The prisoners were put to work digging a shallow pit beside the crossroads. It was the best they could do, in the circumstances, but Telling was not impressed. He, Clavincale, and the suddenly shorn Captain Took had formed a gloomy guard of honour for their fallen comrade. Sparrow watched them lower the major's naked body beside Anneliese's hastily nailed coffin and Fey's tightly wrapped corpse, shook his head in gloomy sympathy.

Telling insisted they bury Major Brinks' captured colour with its master, but Sparrow was having none of that.

'I lost my troop's colour on Roundway. We'll have no honour till I get these back,' he told the weary Cavaliers.

'You'll never share in any honour no matter how many flags you capture,' Telling snapped. 'But don't fret yourself. I'll see they are properly taken care of when you're gone,' he called across the steaming pit.

Sparrow held his defiant stare for a moment. 'Ah, I see your game. Keep us here beating you bastards into the ground to give your absent friends time to turn up. Hah! I'll see you in there with them before I spend any more time than I have to in this damned hole,' he vowed.

Telling tilted his head, as arrogant and irritating as ever. 'You'll never make it through our lines. If Prince Maurice doesn't catch up with you, Hopton will,' he called. 'You'll never get through to London!'

Who said they were for London? Still, it wouldn't do any harm letting the snot-nosed brat think they were set on walking the whole way. Poole was still held for the Parliament, they might be able to beg passage on a friendly ship and save their feet – as well as their necks. 'That's our lookout,' Sparrow muttered, tugging his gauntlets on with a final frown at the horrible pit.

Lieutenant Rhodes prodded the shabby honour guard away from the gravepit as another squad of villagers toiled up the track with a rickety cart piled high with stiffening bodies. Some of them had been found beneath the drifts, others scorched and blackened inside their gutted hovels. Sparrow clamped his hand over his nose at the stench.

'Was it worth it, Sparrow? Was it worth coming back for all this?' his relentless rival called, stumbling back down the rutted track encouraged by the scabby officer's jabbing blade. 'This is the King's country! Run wherever you may, but you won't leave this behind you! Do you hear me? You'll never walk away from this!'

They didn't walk away, they marched, temporarily invigorated by the blowing colours and tumbling drums. As cocksure of themselves as the blustering merchant, sitting astride one of Black Bob's captured horses with his handkerchief clamped to his nose.

'Good graves don't grow from seed, I know that, but you could have planted those fellows a bit deeper, William,' Sir Gilbert said nasally, nodding at the ragged mounds of earth alongside the crossroads. Sparrow was striding along beside him, one hand clutching the merchant's bridle in case he remembered he had appointments elsewhere.

William was hideously aware they would be relying on the merchant's glib tongue as well as his precious pass, if and when they ran into trouble. But if anybody could convince some suspicious provost he was a loyal Royalist squire hurrying east with this, his pitiful regiment, it was Sir Gilbert.

'Your friend Telling can see to them, once we're safely away,' William growled, glancing over his shoulder as the ragged column swung out onto the main road.

They had wondered about doubling back through Sir Gilbert's enchanted wood, but Sparrow had finally dismissed the idea when they realized they would have to leave the wagons behind. He wasn't about to abandon another score of wounded to those damned infidels – not to mention dumping their preciously piled loot. The badly mauled men he had been forced to leave behind hadn't stood much of a chance, and they would in all probability be dead by the time the Royalist relief force arrived. At least that turkeycock Telling would be there to see they were looked after as long as they lived, he thought ruefully. He grunted, racked by another chilling cramp. There was little point in worrying about the damn near dead, not with eighty-odd others to spirit away. The motley band seemed to be depending on him now, convinced of his martial prowess by his performance the previous evening. Cruickshank's conqueror was not a man to be trifled with, after all. Now they were as eager to please as a squad of fourteen-year-olds, striding out into the snowy wastes as if Poole was a brisk stroll over the next ridge rather than a fifty-mile nightmare of aching bones and nerve-stretching alerts.

William squinted into the thin early morning sunlight and made out the familiar figures of Long Col's sharpshooters hurrying down the lane to catch up with the nervous rearguard. Muffet doubled along the column, breathing hard and looking grim, tearing off his felt hat to make his report.

'Will. There's a troop of dragoons on the high road, three miles back.'

Sparrow swallowed, peered over the white wilderness toward the distant ridge in obvious alarm. Cavalry. Just what they needed, strung out on a lane like this. Their fragile plan shot to ribbons before they had gone a hundred yards.

'How long have we got?'

Muffet shrugged. 'We can hold 'em up awhiles,' he suggested.

William craned his neck, searching for gullies or cover they might take advantage of. There was nothing apart from the anonymously drifted snow, smothering every feature of the broad down. He turned, peered on up the invisible road toward the next ridge. It was a good mile away.

'Sir Gilbert Morrison's regiment, have a care!' he bawled, trapping their wandering attention. 'We'll have to double time to the top of the hill or they'll cut us off! Mr Rhodes, take a dozen men and help with the wagons!'

Scipio Porthcurn had left the moaning foot behind that morning, galloped on across the frosty fields following the tracks left by his advance guard of dragoons. They were new to the colours, recruited away in north Devon following the collapse of the Parliamentarian cause in the west, but they seemed to know their business well enough. Certainly they hadn't strayed too far from the coast road, and more importantly, hadn't been tempted to dawdle at every inn along the way. The colonel had whipped his horse into a lather despite the chill winds, pursued the pack down steep-sided dales and through immense banks of softly drifting snow. At times he had been obliged to dismount and literally stamp his way through the half-frozen obstacles.

He had ridden through the night, and spotted them on the next ridge that dawn, a dirty, slow-moving smudge over the perfect, shining snow. Porthcurn urged the stallion into a ragged canter and came up with his borrowed troops, who had dismounted to give their shaggy ponies a rest. Their captain, Theosophilus Curry, was a roly-poly butcher in a tightly bound buff, his fleshy features livid with the cold. He hurried over as the colonel pulled up in a flurry of snow, jumped down to listen to his eager report.

'Fires all night, sir. You can see the smoke from here!' the enthusiastic volunteer called, pointing a chubby fist on over the gently folded dales and snow-choked coombs. Porthcurn dragged out his perspective glass and studied the coast, the sea a smooth velvet blanket between the snow-capped outcrops. There was no mistaking the massive gull-crowned headland, the Hare Rock crouching comically above its squat cousins. A pall of dark smoke was drifting slowly over the racked cliffs, belched from the town hidden beneath its feet. Porthcurn grinned with delight. They were still at it, then, that was something. He waved them on again, the excited recruits grabbing their bridles and swinging themselves up on their tired beasts. Captain Curry spurred his cob as fast as he could, trying to keep up with the bandit colonel, clods of snow splattering against his richly seamed face. They thundered along the ridge, the snowy mantle no more than a frosting of flour over the grey shoulders and jagged outcrops. A long diversion inland saved them the effort of battling through the drifts in the dale, brought them up above the cross-roads. Porthcurn hauled the panting stallion to a halt, dragged out his glass and scanned the deserted down. A one-eyed frog could have followed their tracks across the snowy waste, muddy trails, and wheel ruts scarring the virgin snowfield toward the eastern downs. Porthcurn spotted the movement beside the crossroads, made out dim figures beavering away on their earthworks. A dozen, maybe more. He glanced around the eager-eyed troop, their faces flushed with cold and excitement. Curry was shielding his eyes to peer down the slope at the wretched fugitives.

'They've left a rearguard to hold us up, look, while the rest of them bugger off on the Dorchester road,' Porthcurn growled, making up his mind in a moment. 'Are your men on for the pursuit, Captain?'

'Rely on us, sir!' Curry cried. But not these horses, he thought sourly, feeling his grunting cob heave beneath his thighs.

PENMETHOCK ASSIZES,

DORSET

The moment he was freed from the reeking cell Telling shoved his way past his grim-faced saviours and dashed up the steps, fleeing the dungeons as if the whole sorry structure had been chalked for the plague. He sprinted down the hall peering into every room, screaming Bella's name into the bloody ruins. Please God she hadn't gone with her father after all. He pictured her crying and kicking, thrown across Sparrow's saddle bow like some pale-skinned slave girl. His furious flight up the staircase gave him a precious head start over that panting fool Clavincale. The bewildered boy had been quiet enough in their dripping cell, but he might have been silently plotting against Bella, relishing his chance to avenge his brother's squalid death outside Gloucester. He could no more stand by and watch Clavincale lay hands on his beloved than he could Sparrow, Sir Gilbert, or that murderous rogue Speedwell.

'Bella!' he bellowed. Where was she? Hugo ground his teeth in furious resentment, his fists clenched as his wasted frame was racked by new doubts. No, surely she hadn't left him now. She'd never run out with her miserable trickster of a father and that half-wit Roundhead, taken her chances on the snowy road to London?

He would sneak her off while he had the chance, hide

her away in the anonymous sanctuary of the camp. He'd whisk her away from Clavincale's vengeance and protect her from his mad father's gimlet-eyed officials. She'd be safe there, secured to his saddle if necessary. He'd never let the wretched girl out of his sight.

Hugo stood in the hallway, hanging on to a banister while he panted like a lame lurcher. And then he saw her, a hesitant figure in a grey cloak, stepping out from the infirmary obsessively wiping her sticky red hands on a torn shirt. He staggered down the hall after her as if they had been cast adrift on a bobbing boat, his snowy horizons tipping this way and that behind the bullet-scarred windows. He opened his arms with an inarticulate groan and locked his hands behind her arched back, holding her up as she leaned into him, pressing her weeping face into his chest. It was as if he was clasping a ghost, her frail spirit freezing his thumping heart.

'It's all right, I'm here for you now,' he said hoarsely, cramming his nose and mouth into her hair, her neck, her ear. 'We must away. Before it's too late,' he croaked.

'Ouch! Hugo, you're hurting,' she protested feebly, too drained to push the panting youth off. He leaned back, his weary eyes illuminated like stained-glass windows in an enchanted cathedral, delirious with relief and yet petrified with worry. He'd never let her out of his sight, he'd swear it on the Book! 'We'll ride back to Rupert and be married. I'll never let you go again, Bella, you believe me, don't you?' He shook her, as earnest as he had ever been in his short life. She nodded dumbly, her eyes fixed on her trembling fingers clamped in his coat. The furiously chewed nails were pared back to the quick, but still bore tiny crescents of waxy grime. She stared, eyebrows furrowed, as if she couldn't quite believe the filthy digits belonged to her.

'Fetch a cloak, something to keep you warm. We can't wait here,' he insisted, his nerves stretched taut as bowstrings by their vicious plight. He would have to find horses quick, or he'd watch her hang yet.

'The charges? They mean to try me all over again, is that it?'

Telling grimaced. 'You'll not get another trial, Bella, my love,' he said heavily.

The demoralized villagers saw the cavalry coming down the hill and didn't stop to enquire whose side they were on. They scrambled out of the gravepits and sprinted off toward the fuming courthouse, shrieking warnings to their neighbours, half-frozen scarecrows who had finally ventured down from the hills to poke about in the slush and ashes of their opened homes. Porthcurn saw them run, whooped to the rest of his men as they kicked up flurries of snow behind them, each dark rider surrounded in a halo of glittering crystal. By Heaven, no wonder the cavalry never had any trouble recruiting, Porthcurn thought, urging the tired beast on down the track.

'Sir!' Curry's bawled warning penetrated his chilled head despite the wind singing in his ears. The horseman glanced over his shoulder, saw the portly captain gesticulating to their left. He followed his pointing gauntlet, and saw a lone rider kick his ragged pony up the opposite slope. The rider seemed to pause on the summit, look behind him for a moment before disappearing over the reverse slope.

'Leave him!' Porthcurn yelled. His horse was on its last legs already, without chasing after every ragged-arsed waif who had managed to corner some stray to flee the scene of their insolent crime. Never mind stragglers, it was the main party he was after. 'Follow me!'

A hundred yards further on, and Porthcurn noticed his panting horse was following half a dozen spidery trails in the snow. He leaned over the beast's sweaty shoulders and squinted at the footprints. The blurred outlines were already being obscured by fresh flurries of snow, and it was impossible to tell how long ago the tracks had been made. He cursed under his breath, followed the snowy trail toward the muddy crossroads, where it was immediately lost in a morass of churned slush and wheel ruts. He looked up, his pistol free in his fist. Where had the dogs got to?

On the far side of the trampled roadbed, the careless villagers or unexpected invaders had thrown up a crude earthwork. His horse whinnied in terror, nostrils flaring in the chill air as it picked out the meaty odours mingling in the blizzard. Porthcurn stared, clinging on to his reins in revulsion as he realized the bloated bundles he had taken for sacks of meal were in fact carefully stacked bodies. Barrows and carts stood by the opened pits, creaking under the dead weight of firewood corpses – shovels and picks stuck into the clodded earth. They had been burying their friends, not building forts! Porthcurn dragged the stallion to a slow walk, picked his way through the carnage. Most of the bodies were stiff as planks, naked as babes. Earth and stones had been flung over staring faces. But some were still clothed, fresh blood splashed over the raked snow.

A couple were still moving, face down in the hastily scraped pits as if he had interrupted their imminent execution. Porthcurn growled with rage and leapt out of the saddle. He lifted the nearest prisoner, rolled him on his bloody back. The man's face had been obliterated by a musket butt, and his jaw hung brokenly from the bloody mash of his mouth. His breath bubbled in and out of the trampled red maw, tiny bloody bubbles exploding in a rain of ruby droplets. Porthcurn grimaced, lifted his pistol, and placed it at the man's temple. He looked away and pulled the trigger, mercifully releasing the doomed wretch. Captain Curry pulled up behind him, panting in his saddle as he gaped at the revolting butchery. 'They've killed their prisoners,' Porthcurn commented unnecessarily, his mouth slick with bile. Curry paled visibly, unable to believe anyone could practise his trade on fellow human beings.

'The Roundheads?' he asked.

'No. Worse luck. The villagers.' Damn them all to hell.

The suddenly subdued patrol walked their horses down the main street, staring about the devastated village as if they were following in the path of some biblical tornado. Every house seemed to have been burnt out, every tiled roof trampled by some malicious giant. The fearful inhabitants that were left peered out at the newcomers, loudly reassured by the shabby officers who had turned out to greet them.

'They're ours, you can come out now!' Captain Took, what was left of his scorched hair hidden beneath a looted helmet, waved up at the scowling colonel.

'Captain Took, is that you?' Porthcurn growled, his black horse pawing the trampled slush as if it would get to the bottom of the bloody conundrum.

'It is, sir. They caught us by surprise, the day before yesterday, I think,' he said, shaking his head in bewilderment. Porthcurn looked over the rest of his ragged command. A surly Cavalier in a tattered shirt streaked with blood, his sparse moustache scabbed above his mouth, hopping from one foot to the other as if the trampled snow concealed a pit of smouldering ashes. Behind them, an angry crowd of muttering villagers and unarmed soldiers.

'You spend your time butchering prisoners while the enemy get away, is that it?' Porthcurn demanded. Captain Took grinned feebly.

'You weren't here, sir. To see the . . .'

'Who gave the order to kill those prisoners?'

Took looked sheepish. 'Well, sir, it wasn't a matter of giving orders, sir, they rather took matters into their own hands, sir, goaded as they were by—'

'You stood by and let them beat wounded men to death, you prickless swine?'

Took swallowed, glanced about him nervously as his colonel raged.

'Where's Brinks?'

'He's dead. Along with most of your men, sir,' Telling reported. 'We tried to stop them, but there were too many of them.'

'Aye, and you wouldn't be so worried if they'd just sacked your town, mister!' an old crone yelled from one of the smoke-blackened windows. 'Butcher all of them, is what I say!'

'There'll be no more butchering down under my command! Took, are there any of the poor bastards left?'

Took shook his head mournfully. Porthcurn cursed under his breath, glared at Telling.

'And who might you be?'

'Captain Telling. Prince Rupert's lifeguard of horse.'

'Rupert's, here?' Porthcurn snorted, his dark head swivelling on his padded shoulders. 'Well, you ought to know better, sir! No prisoners to interrogate? No word as to where these dogs have gone?'

Telling winced, lies and deceits piling up in his throat. He'd been too busy thinking of ways to save his own skin to worry about the enemy wounded. By God, he'd been trying to get his Bella out of their bloody clutches when the alarm had gone up from the gravepits. No time to find a horse now.

As soon as Sparrow's ragged army had marched out of sight, the demented villagers released the Royalist prisoners from the dungeon, gleefully expecting them to join in the slaughter of the unfortunates the raiders had left behind. The badly wounded men Sparrow had been forced to abandon were dragged out of the courthouse and hauled up the street like stranded porpoises, beaten to death with whatever tools came to hand as the few remaining officers stood by in hopeless disgust. Telling glanced around the smoky, unfamiliar faces. Where had that puppy Clavincale got to? He of all people might have been expected to exercise some control over the snarling fiends.

'Ah, don't you scowl so, my lords! We're only doing your job for you!' one bloody oaf called from the back of the bad-tempered mob.

Telling shivered with self-loathing, tortured by his unholy predicament. If Hugo were to tell Colonel Porthcurn all that he knew about Sparrow's recent escape he might be jeopardizing Bella's life all over again. Her own father guiding the renegades out of the coomb, armed to the teeth with passes and commissions and God knew what else? Telling knew full well that if any man could pull off such a fantastical escape it would be Sir Gilbert. That wouldn't look good to Prince Maurice, would it? A battalion of murdering vagrants escorted to safety by his own father-in-law? There were plenty of witnesses in the mob behind him and all – Hugo dared not allow the furious villagers to make his sweetheart the scapegoat for their misfortunes. God alone knew what the rogues were capable of, where their seething venom would be directed next. Hugo was intending to follow the wretched fugitives himself, slip away inland with his bewildered lover as soon as possible. He had been looking for a horse when the villagers spotted the cavalry riding around the ridge of Cairns Hill and raised the alarm all over again. Hugo thought about escaping over the frozen fields with her, but two fugitives on foot wouldn't stand a chance against men on horseback. He had cursed with anxiety, left Bella in the hated courthouse while he joined the delegation on the steps to greet their long-expected relief.

Porthcurn pulled at his beard in agitation as he listened to their disjointed reports, his piercing eyes probing the crowding faces.

'Where is my lord Clavincale?' he asked.

Telling shrugged. Perhaps the boy had remained behind, moping down in the dungeon. Too shocked by the hateful events of the last few days to dare venturing out into the frozen world ever again. He bit his lip in agitation, wondering if the broken-spirited boy would point the finger at Bella, demand the girl face the charges which had been brought against her. He hadn't looked as if he was aware of anything, hounded into a shambling coma by the horrors of the siege.

The furious colonel studied the shivering delegation from beneath his bristling black brows. Telling noticed his snow-splattered charger was shivering with exhaustion, and clearly wouldn't carry him another foot, not this day at any rate.

'He was safe when I saw him last,' Telling mumbled.

Porthcurn wiped his forefinger over his greasy moustaches, unfamiliarly awkward. He lowered his voice so only Telling and Took could hear him.

'I am afraid I have some bad news for him. His father arrived back in Bridport last night with his clerk. They put him to bed and warmed him with coals, but the ordeal proved too much for him. He did not wake.'

Telling nodded dumbly, staring out over the demolished village as if he could see through the scorched bricks, the haphazardly stacked beams, and heat-splintered tiles to the open hills beyond. As if he could see his own future, winding like the bloodily trampled tracks away over Bay Hill, read the consequences in the smothered entrails of the sacrificed soldiers. Black Bob dead? Would his surviving son persecute his beloved Bella as he had done? To the grave, if necessary?

Captain Took shook his shoulders beside him as if trying to restore some heat to his bruised body.

'Please God the weather will claim the rest of them,' he said crisply. 'That is, the rest of the damned raiders, sir.'

Porthcurn's lip curled back from his strong teeth. 'The

enemy is long gone, sir, more's the pity. If your men had pursued them rather than wasted their time making sport with captives . . .' He flicked his wrist in disgust, tugged the tired horse's head up from the trampled snow. 'Have they left any decent horseflesh at all?' he asked gruffly.

'Driven off everything with legs, sir! Everything they hadn't butchered!'

'I saw one of them on the ridge, they can't be far,' Porthcurn growled, bitter and tired and frozen through.

'I saw 'is worship ride off not twenny minutes ago,' an old crone piped up, squinting up at the barbarian on the black charger.

Porthcurn glared at her. 'You saw my lord Clavincale?' he snapped.

The old woman, homeless now and with dead husband, brother, and children to bury, nodded her toothless head in agreement. 'Back off yonder.' She pointed her raw finger toward the snow-clad eastern slopes.

The east? Telling frowned, wondered at the alleged identity of the straggler. Clavincale? No wonder he'd not noticed him before now! The damned boy had deserted them! Baffled and confused by the piggeries in the village, appalled by Cruickshank's vicious confessions in the courthouse, the poor boy must have taken it into his head to join that blasted Sparrow! And all because his elder brother had sold the vile crew into slavery! The more he pondered, the more it made sense – as much as anything made sense in that frozen hell-hole. Perhaps Clavincale was intending to settle some debt of honour, make up for his own brother's repulsive trading activities, was that it? Hugo stood back with a sigh of frustration, hopelessly bewildered by these spider-web treacheries.

There was no honour here.

But then, he reflected sourly, he had lived without honour since those desperate days outside Gloucester, when he had murdered the boy's brother. How could he despise another man's conscience, when he had silenced his own for so long? So long as he had his precious Bella nothing else seemed to matter any more. Her frail presence drew him like a magnet, drew him down the bloody, bullet-clipped steps of the courthouse. He longed, he ached, to lock her in his arms, to steal her away from the trawling war and all the fishes tangled in its spread nets. Abstract concepts like duty and honour and pride – they were all very well and good locked away indoors, tucked up at home with the ladies and the lapdogs. Fine ideas to jabber on about beside a well-banked fire with a belly full of fine wine. Hugo thought fleetingly of his own pious father, the Reverend Telling, holding court at the end of the table, his bullying elder brothers bowing their heads murmuring agreement with everything he said.

Things were different out here in the howling cold, up to your balls in blood-splattered snow, listening to savages slaughter savages besides shallow-scraped gravepits. Bella would be his pride and honour now, Bella would be his cause. Nothing else mattered, not after the bloody battle in Penmethock.

They hurried on and paused, hurried on and paused, listening for the muffled clatter of the pursuing cavalry. Sparrow's ragged command reached the top of the ridge and looked back the way they had come, dismayed to see the dirty brown tracks they had left behind them, deeply scored into the snow. The snow clouds had piled up around the headland, enormously bruised and heavy with squalls and blizzards. William waved them on down the other side of the slope, let the straining horses have a rest as the heavy wagons freewheeled down the hill. The hurrying column passed over the narrow bridge, constricting like a well-fed snake as it negotiated the ancient arch and ploughed on through the snow past the deserted church. Sparrow held on to Sir Gilbert's bridle, standing beside the invisible track as his hunchbacked ghosts shuffled past, broken-down boots churning the firmly packed snow. Large flakes the size of musket balls began to drift down from the deep grey sky, spotting their bunched blankets. William peered back over the dale, watched as the stone bridge was swallowed up by the swirling outriders of the storm.

'Keep moving! We'll shake 'em for good if we get to the next ridge!' he bawled over the mournfully howling blizzard. 'We must get to the next ridge!'

And the next, and the next.

The snow seemed to blot the sky, filling the air with drifting shapes.

Sparrow's veterans trudged on, broken backed against the squalls. Going home.

ACKNOWLEDGEMENTS

The one thing my research has shown me in the three years I have been writing this series is that I could have based each book solely on real-life events. The Civil Wars abound with larger-than-life characters, and incidents like those described at the fictitious port of Penmethock occurred on an almost weekly basis up and down the coast. One look at H. P. Smith's *History of the Borough and County of the town of Poole* or C. W. Cullingford's *History of Poole* will convince readers I have not exaggerated the vicious firefight on the harbour. Thankfully, there are historians as keen on recording their inspiring details as I am in incorporating their brave deeds into my stories. My thanks must go as always to the Sealed Knot. Attending various musters up and down the country immediately rekindles my enthusiasm – there's nothing like a good pike push to sort you out after a hard week at the word processor!

Many members have carried out far more detailed research into aspects of the period than I have, but have always been glad to share the fruits of their research with me over a pint or three. They will hopefully forgive me distilling years of painstaking reading into soundbites for the more general reader.

Typical of these incredibly clued-up gentlemen is Stuart

Peachey of the Stuart Press, whose fine set of pamphlets is available at Sealed Knot musters or from 117 Farleigh Road, Backwell, Bristol BS19 3PG. Stuart also organizes genuine seventeenth-century banquets for Sealed Knot regiments, one of which I was lucky enough to attend (only in the interests of research!). For those wanting a more general view of the Civil Wars and a good idea of uniform, tactics, and weapons, look out for Philip Haythornthwaite's *English Civil War* (Blandford Press). For the military minded who want the details on the many skirmishes and battles of the three civil wars, then Brigadier Peter Young and Richard Holmes' *The English Civil War* is essential reading. Peter Young's *Civil War England* (Longman Travellers Series) provides a pungent guide to the best battlefields and castles to visit, as well as thumbnail sketches of some of the lesser known combatants. C. V. Wedgwood's *The King's War* (Penguin) provides the full political and strategic overview of the conflict, and further details of the bloody struggles on the Continent can be found in her excellent *Thirty Years War* (University Press). Details of the efforts made by the Royalists to organize themselves are reported in Ronald Hutton's *The Royalist War Effort* (Longman). The Osprey Elite series on infantry and cavalry of the civil wars provides good background on uniforms and organization, as well as including sets of excellent illustrations by Angus McBride.

While I have endeavoured to make 'The Shadow on the Crown' series as historically accurate as possible, there are inevitably occasions when a little journalistic licence is required. Please forgive any unintentional errors as to when and precisely where certain events took place.

Nicholas Carter, pikeman and pamphleteer.